OPERATION: Ωmega

A Political Novel by

R G Cruise

OPERATION: Ωmega

★★★★★ ★★★★★ ★★★★★ ★★★★★ ★★★★★

President Trump has declared the Liberal Democrats a clear and present danger to the health of the country and now they need to be addressed in the proper manner. At the suggestion of an ex-Navy SEAL, Theodore Justice Law, otherwise known as TJ Law, the Central Intelligence Agency starts a top secret pilot program known as the Omega Agency which conducts OPERATION: Omega.

Congressional Liberal Democrats are either disappearing or are found deceased and the Left are blaming the Russians since a Russian clue is being found near each cadaver. But some Liberal Republicans are being found dead as well.

The fake news, CNN & MSNBC, is having a field day reporting that the Russians are behind these nefarious acts. However, they must battle the truth telling, Conservative Fox News at every turn. The Left is blaming the Russians and the Russians are blaming the Cubans…or is it the Chinese? A seductive Chinese woman, who is employed by the CIA as an analyst, knows the truth behind every vicious act of death.

This book was written for Conservatives, Conspiracy Theorists, Military, the Left and the Right. However, if you are a true Conservative, you will more than likely appreciate this political novel the most as this book employs a providential ending…enjoy!

---R G Cruise

Author's Note

In the Holy Bible, King James Version, Revelations 1:8, 21:6 and then again 22:13, mentions the term *Alpha and Omega*, which Christians deemed to mean the beginning and the end as the Greek letter A is the beginning of the Greek alphabet and the Greek letter Ω means end as it is the last letter of the Greek alphabet.

A Word from R G Cruise

Dear Readers,

I'm delighted to welcome all Conservatives, Conspiracy Theorist, Military and Political Junkies…this book is for you!

There is a devastating storm approaching America and the United States is in the direct crosshairs of this Liberal turbulence with one man (or two) who can possibly save the country. He is ex-Navy SEAL, Theodore Justice Law---or better known as TJ Law---with a professional military resume of dealing out death and destruction. After spending ten years in the United States Navy, TJ retires from military service and finds himself working for a well-known defense contractor, mainly on the C-17 program in California.

Leading up to the 2016 Presidential Election, he took notice of how events involving the Liberal Obama Administration are reshaping the country for the worse. He thought about running for a Congressional seat but decided against that. With 535 members of Congress---mostly corrupt---one man would have a very difficult time in trying to make a difference in the "swamp" that is known as our capital city…Washington, D.C.

Instead of running for Congress, TJ writes a letter to President Trump suggesting a 'catch and kill' idea for ridding the country of an alarming number of degenerates that are preying on hard working Americans and that are deteriorating the American way of life and the pursuit of happiness. He wasn't sure if the President would even receive the letter let alone read it. Shortly after mailing his communiqué to the President however, he received a letter back from the CIA inviting him to Langley, Virginia to talk about his idea.

TJ was offered a position in the CIA under a new, top secret pilot program known simply as the Omega Agency---funded with CIA dollars---and he accepts.

A beautiful Chinese girl falls in love with TJ and seems to be involved in some nefarious and deadly actions against Republicans posing as Democrats and he has to sort out his own feelings for the country that he loves or the girl that he thinks that he might love. This may be his hardest mission yet, but TJ is up to the challenge.

Thank you for your purchase of this Political Novel!

Sincerely,

R G Cruise

*To Law Enforcement
and Military (past and present),
I thank you for your honorable service...*

Prologue
Ω

"Propaganda tends to distort people's perception on political issues…the wrong perception leads to Left, while the Right perception leads to Conservative!"

---Curt Bateman

The Liberal Obama Administration has deteriorated the leadership of the United States on the world stage through actions of 'leading from behind.' It has replaced common sense and logic in favor of diversity and stupidity and it is involved in the largest government corruption scandal ever witnessed in the United States!

Donald J. Trump, a successful billionaire businessman living in New York City, decides that he can no longer sit idly by and watch the country he loves flushed down the drain by corrupt Liberals or unqualified Republicans...or both. Two days after his 70th birthday, at Trump Tower on June 16, 2015, he announced to the world that he would run for the President of the United States…as a Republican!

Against all odds, Candidate Trump was able to beat all comers: Hilliary Clinton, Liberal Democrats, Republican Never Trumpers and the dishonest media, as well as, 16 other Republican Candidates running for the presidency, which was a tall order to be sure, but one that was delivered on time for the American people and for the benefit of the country!

Candidate Trump won the election of 2016 by an electoral landslide…232 to 306, which is what lawfully counts in U.S. elections.

President Trump now wants to share his success with all of America and that means making some basic decisions that are not popular to the far Left Liberals in Congress, but will benefit most Americans in the long run. He realizes early on that the needs of the many outweigh the needs of the few and calls on TJ Law's professional military abilities.

On November 9, 2016 at exactly 0300 EST, citizens of New York City and T.V. viewers all across the globe, witnessed the most outstanding display of fireworks ever seen in the history of the United States…all thanks to Hilliary Clinton and her $2 million dollars! In her narrow-minded view, she could not fathom Donald Trump winning and spent $2 million dollars for her victory celebration that instead turned into her most celebrated funeral! However, in her moment of grief and meltdown and depression and shock---much to the chagrin of her campaign headquarters---she forgot to cancel her fireworks display that she had scheduled which lit up the New York City skyline, just as if the founding of America had just occurred!

This became the starting point for Hilliary's Trump Derangement Syndrome otherwise known as TDS. A disease that can only be cured with Trump's removal from office and her becoming the president of the United States, especially since she had three million more votes; popular votes that is. However, her disease was not diagnosed in an expedient manner and she found herself growing more distressed every day which turned into some mental challenges for her. She launched herself into writing her second book as a means of calming the demons that she discovered to be residing in her mind. Daily, she would question when the government would come for her and escort her to The White House; her White House. That day finally comes…

Chapter 1

Ω

Theodore (Teddy) Justice Law snapped awake and reached for his pistol which was located in a drawer next to his chair. He listened intently as the sound outside grew louder in the night. He had been watching his favorite T.V. sitcom when he fell into a half-sleep with a red Solo cup clutched in his hand; a show about a dysfunctional family living in modern day Chicago. *What family would want to live that way?* Teddy had questioned before closing his eyes momentarily.

Using his remote, he muted the volume and crept towards the front door. Peeking outside through the window, he caught a glimpse of a dark figure making his way to his pickup.

"I'll be damned if they think they can steal my truck," Teddy thought out loud. He continued his surveillance and watched the figure trying to pick the lock with a Slim Jim. *Doesn't that jackass know I have an alarm system installed?*

Instead of waiting for the alarm to sound and wake up his neighbors, Teddy decided on a military tactic that he has used several times in the past. He would basically just utilize the laser on his 9mm Beretta. It seems that folks tended to chill with a laser dot on their forehead or body.

He opened the door without a sound and squeezed his laser button on the pistol's grip to emit the red light.

Looking around, the would-be-thief just happened to notice the red dot on his chest and dropped to the ground like a rock. He then rolled under the vehicle, jumped up and took off like a Delta rocket!

Teddy chuckled to himself as he closed the front door. *Well, I don't reckon he'll be back anytime soon. Why can't our government deal effectively with our growing number of degenerates in our country? Probably an illegal!*

Teddy lived in average neighborhood in Costa Mesa, California where he held a low view of dirt bags and losers. People that wanted to take away things from hard working Americans who earned them and these same people who added "no value" to society whatsoever. While serving in the U.S. Navy as a SEAL Team Leader for 8 years and another 2 years before that for training before retiring, he always believed that it is the government's responsibility to eliminate waste, fraud and abuse even if it is in our society. With more than 2 million people incarcerated in just the U.S. alone and probably another 2 million or more that needs to be in prison, something clearly needed to be done. He thought about the letter that he sent to President Trump on his thoughts about creating a secret agency of the federal government that could effectively handle people that offered absolutely no value to society or were degenerates and/or those that offer a clear and present danger to our nation and our way of life with their radical and crazy ideology or otherwise known as Liberals. He wrote the letter to the president out of frustration of what he saw happening to California and his country. Friends have told him that we are headed to becoming a third world country and he felt in his heart the truth of those words. *Didn't the empires of Japan and Rome fall? We can't stay on top forever,* he thought, *unless…we change our current course by making smarter decisions. There must be a continuous effort to ameliorate our nation. God blessed our country for a reason and we shouldn't take our standing in the world for granted.*

With so many convicts being let back loose into society to continue on with their unlawful ways; with illegal's entering our country every single day; with drug cartels stepping up production of illegal drugs and trafficking children and women; with terrorist on the loose wanting to crush our freedoms; with degenerates preying on the good and decent folks of society; with Liberal Democrats out to destroy the country for the sake of greed and power, it just doesn't make much sense to keep doing the same thing over and over. Teddy recalled the quote by Albert Einstein that stated that the definition of insanity is, 'doing the same thing over and over while expecting a different result.' Most people don't consider that since they are plain stupid.

Teddy wrote his letter to the President expressing his ideal about creating a low profile agency that could remove deserving individuals candidly and carefully from the ranks of society. He didn't really expect a response, but felt compelled to send the letter anyway.

He was working for the largest defense contractor in the world on the C-17 program in management. Several weeks went by before receiving a response from the government on his letter that he had sent to President Trump.

Arriving home after work one Friday afternoon, Teddy was going through his stack of mail; a bill from the electric company followed by another bill from the cable company and a postcard from a political hack running for re-election for his district. Thinking that he never receives any good mail or that is interesting, the next envelope caught his eye…a letter from Langley, Virginia with no return address. It was short and to the point, "Dear Mr. Law, thank you for writing to President Trump. In the interest of national security, we would like to invite you to the CIA building, 1000 Colonial Farm Road, Langley, Virginia 22101 on Tuesday the 31st at 1000 for intelligent and stimulating conversation. If needed, you may contact me at (505) 855-5811." It was signed by Director Lannister, Central Intelligence Agency.

That was next week! So Teddy expediently made reservations to fly into Reagan National Airport on Southwest Airlines on the Monday before his meeting. Additionally, he also made reservations for the Holiday Inn Express in McLean, VA. Being a Gold Elite member, he was assured of shuttle service from the airport to the hotel and then again to Langley the next day. *It pays to be a Gold Elite member,* he thought to himself. He really liked the hotel chain for their hospitality, clean rooms and their cinnamon rolls! He made his reservation for 3 nights, but that was flexible also due to his membership status.

Next, he needed to request time off from his work and made a call to his boss's cell phone.

"Hello," his boss answered.

"Ron, its Teddy and I need some time off due to an emergency."

"Hi Teddy, I'm fine and thank you for asking…how are you?"

"Sorry boss, I'm good but I need some time off."

"For what?" his boss inquired.

"I can't say right now, but trust me, it's important."

"Well, how much time do you need then?"

"I'm not at all sure but at least a week I guess. Why don't you put me down for 2 weeks to be safe? I actually have 58 days of leave on the books."

"Well, I guess we could manage that long without you. Are you staying in town or going someplace?"

"I'm flying into D.C. on Monday."

"Washington D.C.?" his boss echoed. "Should I ask whatever for?"

"Not really. How about I explain everything to you when I come back to work?"

"Are you coming back?"

"Of course, why wouldn't I?"

"Ok, but be careful, I hear that there is a lot of corruption in that region…you know, Congress and all."

"Don't worry about me boss, I was in the military, remember?"

"I know, I know, just making chit chat, but still be careful and call if I can help with anything."

"You got it and thanks for your understanding."

Teddy next packed his military bag and arranged for a ride to John Wayne Airport with a friend and thought about the adventure that he was about to embark on.

★ ★ ★ ★ ★

Monday came fast but Teddy was more than ready and excited about his trip. As he stepped outside to wait for his ride to the airport, he noticed that the birds were singing and that the sun was shining and all seemed good within the world. But he knew that this was very shallow thinking with all of the bad news stories on Fox News. Well unfortunately, or fortunately, he is not a politically correct person and believed in calling a spade, a spade. *Thank heaven that I voted Republican,* he mused. *The Democrats are so two-faced that it is quite unbelievable! If it weren't for a double standard, then the Democrats wouldn't have any standards!* Until this last election of 2016, he did not realize how fucked up these people really were. Trump winning the 2016 election revealed their true colors and they were not red, white and blue…they were corrupt, deceit and lies; in short, they are criminals! The only good thing about them that he could relate to is that they all pulled together as a cohesive team whether right or wrong, good or evil, corrupt or honest. Now, if only the Republicans can unify like that. From the military, it was hammered into his physic about the fundamentals of teamwork and the positive outcome that could be achieved. Apparently, the Democrats had discovered that secret where the Republicans had not. His ride to the airport was uneventful, other than the usual traffic issues. *This is what happens when you stick too many people in one place*, Teddy thought.

His direct flight to Reagan National was on time and only took 4 hours and 17 minutes. *Not too bad,* Teddy contemplated, *at least it's faster than driving.*

After securing his bag at Reagan National, he located the shuttle and was taken to his hotel. He approached the front desk with his Gold Elite card out and handed it to girl stationed at the front desk.

"Good evening Mr. Justice and I don't need your card. Our driver radioed in and announced your arrival. My name is Marie and I will be checking you in. I see that you have a regular reservation, but that will not work for us, so… we'll just have to bump you up to a suite at no extra charge of course. If you can sign here please and our porter will take your bags to your room. Your room number is 777. I hope that that's acceptable Mr. Justice?"

"Thanks Marie, that's perfect and maybe it'll bring me some luck. Also, can I get a wakeup call at 0800 please and I will need a ride to the CIA building in Langley."

"Of course Mr. Justice, the shuttle will be leaving here at 0900. Does that give you enough time to get ready?"

"That'll work Marie," Teddy stated.

As he followed the porter to his room, he thought about folks calling him mister all the time. *I'm not that old and that sounds awfully like they're addressing my father.* Teddy's father was also in the Navy and retired after 32 years of service as an Aviation Storekeeper Master Chief from the USS Ronald Reagan (CVN-76) in 2003. His father, Samuel Roosevelt Law, was the only reason that he joined the Navy in the first place. He was very proud of his father and wished that he was still alive so that he could tell him about his visit to the CIA. He always kept his father's discharge picture in uniform on his desk to remember him by and to add inspiration to his life.

Theodore Justice Law was born and raised in Dothan, Alabama. One day his father explained to him about how he came to be named. Theodore---was after his father's favorite president; Justice---was what he hoped his son would dispense one day, maybe as a judge; Law---was from his great grandfather who legally emigrated from England and had set up a law practice in Dothan. The very first legal act of his great grandfather was to change his last name from Halliwell to Law. He chose Law as a last name since that was going to be his field of study and practice. *What if I'm allowed to dispense some measure of justice with the CIA?* Teddy wondered. *This CIA business may be a godsend and an omen to my true destiny!*

The porter opened the door and allowed him to enter first. As he looked around the room, he noticed that it was perfect and in taste with his values. Teddy turned to tip the porter and noticed that he had silently slipped out. *Well, I better unpack and get some rest,* he thought. *Tomorrow's a big day for me. Almost like when I joined the Navy!*

The next day, Teddy awoke on time and prepared for his meeting. As he looked out his window, he realized that he had a great view of the area and that it was cloudy and was threatening to rain; the kind of weather that he liked most, next to snow. He made it out the door and downstairs in time for the shuttle.

On the way to his designation, he had time to reflect on his past and what this meeting would entail. When he watched Fox News this morning, there was more crap from the Left about Russian ties to President Trump. *Amazing*, he considered, *that so many people are duped by the dishonest media and the corrupt Democrats; it's actually hard to believe. President Trump is a successful businessman and doesn't need the Russian's help. Oh well, our country is changing and it doesn't seem to be for the best...other than Donald J. Trump becoming our president!* Teddy calculated silently. The Liberal Democrats and the dishonest media seemed to be taking their election loss hard. It's just like their still in shock! The sooner that they realize their loss, the sooner that they can make their peace.

The shuttle dropped him off near the front of the CIA building. Walking up to the front doors he had a sense of awe about this place. Teddy knew that much happens here that helps to shape our country and other countries around the world.

As he entered the CIA Headquarters, he noticed that the lobby area was very intricately done in marble and other materials commonly used in the day that it was built. What really caught his eye was the CIA logo on the floor that read "Central Intelligence Agency United States of America." Teddy couldn't help in feeling pride for his country. *So this is some of what people like me contributed to by serving in our Armed Forces,* he contemplated. Furthermore: *our country is the most powerful nation on Earth due to men and women sacrificing their life, liberty and health for all of the things that we currently have today. They should not be forgotten or taken advantage of. Freedom as we know it isn't free…someone always pays the price!*

Teddy walked up to the front desk area and told the woman that he was expected and gave his name. She asked him to have a seat and that she would announce him. Instead, he walked over to an acknowledgement wall with stars that claimed "In Honor of Those Members of the Central Intelligence Agency Who Gave Their Lives in the Service of Their Country." He thought that it was nice that we don't forget those who gave their lives for the freedoms that we enjoy every day. Then he noticed down a ways was a museum of some sort. He was still in awe about the interior of the building when someone approached him.

"Mr. Law, will you follow me please? I'm Intelligence Agent Jerney." They briefly shook hands and headed down the hallway, past a spiral staircase and the CIA museum to an elevator and went to the sixth floor. They entered an office that had on the door the words, 'Panama.' He wondered about the name.

Upon entering a man arose and stuck out his hand.

"Mr. Law, I'm Director Lannister and I want to welcome you to Langley and also thank you for coming on such short notice. I hope that everything has been agreeable with you up to this point as we have been anxiously waiting for your arrival."

Teddy shook hands and replied with, "No problems sir."

Another man approached and also extended his hand and introduced himself as Randy Morgan.

A splendid looking woman entered the office just then and asked about drinks and snacks for anyone. Teddy said he would have a chocolate donut if available and coffee with cream.

"Gentlemen please sit down. Mr. Law, I won't beat around the bush. You wrote a letter to the President about your idea for an agency to conduct, shall I say, covert operations and elimination of certain people who are detrimental to the United States. Well the President likes your idea. As you know from being in the military, the function of the CIA is covert activities and to collect intelligence for the United States and our allies. The difference is that we are primarily utilized for missions outside of the U.S. President Trump however, recognizes that we need the same for the interior of our country. Basically, we need to guard against clear and present dangers from within. What I'm about to disclose to you is of a highly secretive nature and I know that your security clearance is still effective, so I will proceed. The President has identified Liberals as a clear and present danger to our country. Liberals have infiltrated our government through the Democratic Party and is costing our country much, including, becoming a national security concern. Their ideology is a cancer on our country and the President believes, as I do, that if this is left unchecked, then it could lead to our country becoming a third world nation. If that were to happen, then either terrorist and/or political enemies of the United States would infiltrate our country and change our way of life as we know it today and we cannot allow that to happen. It's bad enough already without making it worse by allowing Liberals to continue to gain a much larger footprint in government. However, we can't just ask the Liberals to stop being Liberals as they don't display any common sense whatsoever and they only know corruption and power at any cost, even at the cost of our country's health. So, we need to eradicate this ideology by eliminating the Liberals that are infecting our Congress and our country. The President wants to bring the Democratic Party back to the middle of the road instead of being too far to the Left. This view is not political as the President wants to accomplish his goals to Make America Great Again. These Liberals stand in the way of not only common sense, but also from our country making progress in President Trump's vision for America. As you know Mr. Law, our country is greatly divided. The Democrats have lost seats in Congress, over 1,000 seats nationwide in state government and have now lost the White House to boot and have become unhinged because of it, especially since President Trump beat their flawed candidate, fair and square. Even when they corruptly stacked the deck in her favor, Hilliary still lost. It appears that the Democrats absolutely will not accept her loss with grace and dignity and have become unhinged because of it, so they look to place the blame on everything and anyone, including the Russians."

Teddy was taking all of this information quite seriously and couldn't really believe what he was hearing as he listened intently as Director Lannister continued.

"President Trump sees an opportunity with your idea to, shall we say, 'neutralize' some of these leading Liberals in the Democratic Party. If you are interested in helping your idea to become reality, then you will be our only agent for this pilot program known as the, Omega Agency. You will work under the guise of the CIA, with credentials of course. The President has given the CIA, and military, full autonomy to conduct ourselves in a manner that is beneficial to our country. So, we have identified certain people that need to, shall we say, disappear forever. But, we have to cover our tracks and that's where you come in, as your SEAL training allows you to do that so effectively. Being that the dishonest media and the Liberal Democrats all believe that Mr. Trump is involved with the Russians, we will make sure to leave a Russian clue behind so that the Russians will shoulder the blame. These factions that I previously mentioned, will believe that the Russians are involved, and in turn, will eat this shit up, because they believe in conspiracy theories. So, we'll give them the Russians while we continue to do our mission under the code name of, Operation: Omega.

"Mr. Law, please keep in mind while doing your job for your country, that there is a special place in Hell for these corrupt Liberal Democrats and we are counting on you to send them to their next designation…are there any questions?"

At this point, the woman returned with their snacks and refreshments and then left again.

"Actually, I have a lot of questions," Teddy admitted.

"Ask away Mr. Law. We knew you would have a few questions for us and about implementing your idea," Director Lannister stated.

"If I accept, where would I be working from, what's my salary and will I be instructed on how to eliminate someone, for starters?"

"Mr. Law, you will be hired as a Central Intelligence Officer and have an office here in this building on this floor in fact and Mr. Morgan will be your immediate boss. Due to the nature of the operation, your salary will be $200,000 a year to start, with benefits of course. You and Mr. Morgan will have the most input into the Omega Agency since it is a pilot program. The CIA has budgeted money for this agency that will be working incognito. If you are successful in your mission, then we will be able to continue to operate. If for some reason it has to end, you will be retained by the CIA for other projects. We will not tell you how to do your job. You will be instructed who the target is and at your discretion, will make that decision. But we will want the targets eliminated, for good, with a Russian clue left behind. Discretion is of the utmost importance when carrying out your mission. To sum up, we need to rid the swamp of swamp dwellers for the benefit of our country and we need you to start right away. Is there any problem with that Mr. Law?"

"I reckon not."

"Good, Randy will show you to your office," Director Lannister stated and stood and shook hands again with him and then remembered something important. "I forgot to ask you if you accept our proposal."

"I do," Teddy stated with finality.

So he walked down the hallway with Randy thinking of his new beginning in life. He was really blindsided with this turn of events. He felt deep in his heart about how his country was heading for disaster and that he would like to play at least a small part in reshaping America and regaining some semblance of a leadership role in the world while smashing corrupted Liberals. Under the last administration, the president believed in leading from behind and was proved to be a coward's, coward. What kind of crap was that? If the United States doesn't lead the way then some other country would, but it probably wouldn't be in the best interest of the U.S. That's why he believed that a president should have some military experience and/or some balls at least, because they would understand that philosophy. However, he had an undying faith in President Trump. This phenomenon with President Trump overcoming all the odds to become the 45th president was truly a remarkable godsend for the country!

They arrived at a door with a brass placard that read *'Parabellum'* and entered into an office that was neatly furnished. Teddy knew that *parabellum* was Latin for, "prepare for war" from his time in the military. A fitting name he realized that defined his mission quite well.

"This will be your office Teddy," Randy intoned. "Judy, our personal assistant, has an office through that door right there and my office is on the other side. Why don't you look things over and let Judy know if there is anything that you need, otherwise, I'll see you later for lunch in the cafeteria."

Teddy nodded to his boss in the affirmative as Randy took his leave. Teddy looked around at his office and noticed that it was equipped with a Philippine mahogany desk complete with a leather chair behind it and two leather chairs in front and one on the side; a couple of large filing cabinets; Panasonic Toughbook laptop computer and two Brother printers; flat screen television; a small refrigerator; phone; bulletin board; a couple of walnut bookcases along with a medium sized Winchester safe. Adorning the walls were some really nice paintings. There was George Washington, Abraham Lincoln, Teddy Roosevelt (his favorite president), John Kennedy and lastly…a picture of 'Old Rough and Ready' himself---Zachary Taylor. The brass plate attached to the picture read, "President Zachary Taylor, 12th President of the United States, March 4, 1849 – July 9, 1850." Teddy knew enough about history to know that President Taylor died while in office.

Speaking of history, government and history were his favorite subjects in high school and college and when he graduated from the university, it was with honors and he earned a Bachelor's of Science degree in Management. He was the only one in his family with a degree he knew and it was important for him to graduate at the top of his class. It took extra effort, but he figured it was worth it; he was right. Teddy also appreciated his time spent in the military…it gave him a sense of direction. He felt proud about his military service to his country. He recalled how his father was retired from the Navy after 32 years of faithful and honorable service as an Aviation Specialist Master Chief Petty Officer. His father served his country well, he reflected. *Now, I still have that opportunity to continue serving my country when it is really needed,* he thought critically.

He finished his daydreaming just as Judy entered his office. She spent some time going over his phone contact list, setting up his password on his computer and other odds and ends (such as the combination to his safe) that he needed to know.

Judy noticed the time was almost noon and escorted Teddy over to Randy's office. He noticed that his boss's office was furnished similarly with the exception of the pictures on the wall being different.

The two men chatted and walked to the elevator and they descended to the first floor. As they trekked through the halls of the CIA building, Randy took the time to point out some of the most important locations in the building such as the CIA library…and others.

"As you can see Teddy, we have a Burger King, Subway and a Famous Dave's, which is only open for lunch and dinner I might add. This here is our cafeteria which is open 24 hours a day and my personal favorite." From his research, Teddy knew that there were more than 21,000 employees in the CIA and understood why these restaurants were here. Not only were they here to help feed the hungry employees, but to help keep the morale up as well.

As they entered the cafeteria, Randy handed him a tray and Teddy grabbed some green beans and carrots---his favorite---along with meat loaf and some macaroni and cheese with some coffee while his boss took a Russian salad, strawberry yogurt and garlic toast with coffee as well. Randy showed his badge instead of paying for both of their meals and then further explained that their meals are included in their salaries for CIA officers.

The men took a table near a window where you could see an outdoor eating area and sat down to consume their food and to talk business.

"Teddy, after we finish with lunch, I want you to go get your credentials. We actually have a lot of work to do in getting you up to speed in a short amount of time. So, as they say, you'll be learning a lot of stuff on the fly. We'll head back to the office and get cleaned up a bit and then I'll have someone escort you to our biometrics office."

Teddy readily agreed as he was excited about receiving his credentials. That would help him in accepting this reality.

The men finished with their meal and departed for their respective offices.

Back at his office, Teddy learned from Judy that he had his own bathroom outfitted with his favorite toothpaste and mouthwash.

"Judy, is this just a coincidence that my favorite toothpaste and mouthwash is here?" he inquired.

"Now Mr. Law, what building are you in? Don't you know that 'big brother' knows all about you?" she stated and animated air quotes for big brother.

"What about these pictures on my wall?"

"We know where your tastes lie and outfitted your office accordingly."

"But how is that possible?"

"Mr. Law, you were previously employed in the military, were you not? You might have mentioned things like your favorite presidents, food preferences and colors for example. The government knows these things. But not for everyone though. Your career and accomplishments in the Navy caught you on our radar. I can tell you that before you wrote that letter to President Trump, you were already being considered for a similar position. Your letter probably helped to speed up the process."

Well, that's food for thought, Teddy reflected and asked: "Do you know what was in my letter Judy?"

"No I don't Mr. Law as I'm not privileged to classified information. However, I do know that your letter was sent here by the President and it became classified upon arrival," Judy replied and then turned and left Teddy to his own devices.

He went ahead and brushed his teeth and rinsed out his mouth. Teddy knew that dental hygiene was just as important as anything else concerning the body. As a Navy SEAL, he was not used to such luxuries due to the nature of his work. A lot of time he ended up brushing his teeth with saltwater!

As he sat down at his desk, Judy knocked on his door and entered along with Intelligence Agent Jerney.

"Mr. Law, Agent Jerney will now show you the way to our biometrics office for your credentials. Also, I have your cell phone here for you," and she handed him his phone. He noticed that it was a compact flip phone by Sprint similar to the one that he had for his own use and clipped it onto his belt. Later, he discovered that it was already programmed with contacts. Of course, most were unknown to him, but he was sure that they had a purpose for being listed on his phone.

As they left for the elevator, Teddy asked Agent Jerney where they were headed. "Down to the basement is where we keep our biometrics office…under heavy security of course," he added and the elevator doors closed and they proceeded downward.

On the way to the biometrics office, Teddy questioned Agent Jerney about what he liked to do for fun.

"Well, I play racquetball in the gym or tennis sometimes."

"You mean that we have a gym here?"

"Of course, what kind of CIA do you take us for? Our racquetball courts are all indoors and we have both, indoors and outdoors tennis courts so we can play all year around. Maybe we can play sometime?"

"Works for me, as I love playing racquetball and tennis when I get the chance," Teddy confessed.

The elevator stopped gradually and as the doors opened, they exited and walked across the hall where Agent Jerney inserted his ID badge that contained an embedded microchip. A beep and clicking was heard as the door unlocked and they were allowed entry. *This is all very surreal,* thought Teddy; *I'm in the CIA building becoming an intelligence officer…who would have dreamed it?!*

Teddy followed Agent Jerney through the bustle of activity where men and women were doing important work for the country…our country.

They went through another door that read "Biometrics" and approached a counter where Agent Jerney introduced Teddy to Nora.

"Nora is our biometrics manager here and she will take good care of you and get you started. However, if you need me brother, I'm listed as a contact on your phone, feel free to call me anytime, especially if you have a hankering to lose at racquetball!" he stated quite frankly while winking at Teddy and departed for parts unknown.

"Ok Mr. Law, if you will follow me please, I will take you to Dan who is one of our biometrics specialists and who will be working with you on your credentials," Nora requested and led the way not waiting for a response from him.

So Teddy followed Nora to another area in the same large room and approached a man seated at a desk who acknowledged their arrival by looking up from his work and standing.

"Ahhh Nora, I was expecting you and this must be Mr. Law? Pleased to meet you Mr. Law," he said as he pumped Teddy's hand.

"Thank you Nora for escorting Mr. Law here. Are we still on for dinner tonight at Famous Dave's?"

"Of course, like every Monday silly," she pivoted and left.

"Mr. Law, I need you to look over this security form and sign at the bottom please. You will be given a top secret security clearance for the time that you are employed by the CIA. Once your employment ends, your security clearance will terminate and your credentials along with any other CIA property must be returned."

"That's just common sense," TJ readily agreed and looked over the form and signed it.

"Ok Mr. Law, based on the information that we have in your file from your prior military service, we made your credentials already. Look them over carefully and please inform me if there are any errors."

Teddy scrutinized his credentials; a gleaming badge on one side with an identification card with an embedded microchip nestled inside a dark brown wallet on the opposite fold. There was also a separate Maryland driver's license. He noticed his picture as well as his name and address on his I.D. Card and driver's license and carefully crafted his next question.

"Dan, I notice here that you only used my initials, is this how it's always done?"

"Not all the time. Mr. Morgan requested that we officially change your name to simply TJ Law. Is that acceptable to you or I can place a call to Mr. Morgan with a concern…?"

"No that's fine, I was just curious is all."

"As you noticed, we have included a Maryland driver's license in your new name along with your badge and credentials. We used your Navy picture that we had on file for you since you haven't changed all that much."

Teddy, now officially 'TJ' noticed the address on his new driver's license as being, 382 Victoria Street, Liberty Park, Joint Base Andrews AFB 20762.

"What's this address on here?" TJ inquired.

"The government has provided a home for you on Joint Base Andrews where you will be close by and comfortable. Does that work for you TJ?"

"Ahhh, that's fine…of course. What about my home in California?"

"You can keep that one as a vacation home or you can have us sell it for you if you prefer. It's your decision."

"I guess I'll keep it for now. What about my things?" Teddy questioned.

"Let's not be hasty Mr. Law. Your home here is totally furnished and stocked with food that we know you like. The government will be providing you with a vehicle of your choice and of course, anything else that you might need."

"Well, that's good to know. So what's next?"

"I will now swear you in with the Oath of Office that we administer to all employees of the CIA. This will be similar to the one that you took upon entering your military service. If you will place your left hand on the Bible and raise your right hand and repeat after me please…"

TJ Law placed his left hand carefully and reverently on the Holy Bible and raised his right hand to receive the CIA's "Oath of Office" and repeated these words that were so dear and near to his heart: "I, TJ Law, do solemnly swear (or affirm) that I will support and defend the Constitution of the United States against all enemies, foreign and domestic; that I will bear true faith and allegiance to the same; that I take this obligation freely, without any mental reservation or purpose of evasion; and that I will well and faithfully discharge the duties of the office on which I am about to enter. So help me God."

Dan reached out and shook TJ's hand with pride knowing that the CIA had just hired them a real winner and saying: "Welcome to the CIA, TJ."

TJ knew enough about the role of federal employees: "To establish justice, insure domestic tranquility, provide for the common defense, promote the general welfare and secure the blessings of liberty." That's one reason that he accepted his current position…especially, insuring domestic tranquility and to defend the Constitution against all enemies, foreign *and* domestic!

"Thank you Dan…what's next?"

"I will now escort you over to our WAS department."

"WAS department?" TJ asked with one eye lifted.

"Sorry, I forgot that you haven't had any of our classes yet. WAS stands for Weapons & Ammunition Supply. They will issue you a weapon or weapons of your choice. So if you have no more questions…?"

After securing his credentials, TJ followed Dan to a most secured area in which was also in the basement and was introduced to Jim.

"Jim Thomas, this is TJ Law, one of our newest intelligence officers and a former Navy SEAL. TJ, this is Jim who is a retired Army Ranger."

As they shook hands, each man sized each other up. TJ felt a camaraderie with this man. Just something about him that seemed oddly familiar but comfortable.

"Well TJ, what did you have in mind for a handgun?"

"I'm partial to a Beretta 9mm."

TJ followed Jim into a huge weapons and ammunition locker and picked out a stainless steel Beretta 9mm. This gun was similar to his own with the exception of the engraving on the frame which read, *"Carpe Diem"* and "U.S. Gov't."

"This is a used gun of course, but our gunsmith goes over them with a fine tooth comb as they are turned in," Jim stated officially.

The gun came with a leather shoulder holster, a leather belt holster and 3 filled magazines and he was given a pair of handcuffs.

"Not looking for anything new, just functional, practical and familiar."

"Do you need a smaller caliper also?"

"Not at this time, but if I do, I suppose that I can get that from you at a later date?"

"That's right. My number's on your issued cell phone. If you have no more questions, I'll escort you to Mr. Morgan's office as he requested."

On the way back to his boss's office, the two chatted like old friends, everything from past military experiences to Jim being a huge supporter of President Trump.

Back at Randy's office and sitting in front of his boss's desk, Randy started the conversation.

"So how's it going so far TJ?"

"Busy, but its going."

"Great. I hoped that you didn't mind too much that we changed your name," Randy stated instead of questioning, TJ noticed.

"No, that's fine. In fact, I actually like it."

"Good, now we need to get you something to drive. I know you have a Toyota Tacoma in California. Would you like the same thing out here or something else?"

"No, a Tacoma is fine by me."

"Good, we just happen to have a 2015 in stock with a cap and we'll get it cleaned up and ready for you by tomorrow. Now, I think that we are done for today and will do it all over again tomorrow at 0900. Also, we should be able to get you settled in your new home tomorrow. I know you have a room at the Holiday Inn Express but we *do* have rooms here if you want to stay the night."

"No thanks Randy, I better go back to my hotel and that way I can cancel the rest of my reservation."

"Ok, I'll see you in my office at 0900 and we'll get started again."

Randy had the unmarked CIA shuttle take TJ back to his hotel. The driver agreed to pick him up at 0800 and dropped him off at the front door. As he walked in, Marie noticed him and greeted him warmly including a smile that was to die for. Back in his room, he lay down on the bed to just rest for a few minutes and dozed off to a dreamless sleep. When he awoke, he was hungry and went downstairs in search of a good meal if one was to be had. At the front desk, Marie had just finished with a guest.

"Mr. Law, it's so nice to see you again. Can I help you in anyway?"

"Hi Marie, I just wanted to let you know that I will be checking out tomorrow."

"Oh, I do hope everything is ok."

"Everything's fine Marie. I just found out that my job has a home for me to use since I will be living here now."

"You mean the CIA?"

"Now Marie, you know that's a secret. So…if I told you anything then I would have to kill you," he stated quite seriously.

"Oh Mr. Law, if only you knew how many times I have heard that one before...a lot!"

"I'm just kidding you Marie. It looks like I will be maintaining their computers."

"That's great Mr. Law."

"Thanks Marie. Also, I'll need a wakeup call for 0700."

"No problem Mr. Law, I'll do that right now," and she typed it into her computer. "Done…is there anything else that I can do for you?"

"Yes Marie, I need some palatable food if possible."

"Of course Mr. Law…there is a Golden Corral just two blocks down and a…"

"Golden Corral!" he interrupted her, "my favorite!"

"Do you need the shuttle sir?"

"Come on Marie, do I look that old to you?" TJ asked rhetorically. "I'll just walk, thank you so much though."

TJ walked the two blocks to the Golden Corral and had a good meal. However, after his meal, he discovered that a fight was going on outside and he heard the manager yell to one of his staff to call the police. TJ hurried out and grabbed both men by their necks and banged their heads together. That seemed to get their attention and then he had them sit down right in the parking lot. He could smell the alcohol on their breath and watched over them until the police arrived. In a few minutes, the police showed up and got their stories. TJ went ahead and proudly displayed his CIA badge for the first time. The officers thanked him for his assistance and both men were taken to jail to be booked. One was booked for assault and was an illegal alien while the other one had an outstanding warrant.

One of the officers confided with him that if Obama was still president, then they would have been pressured to release the illegal alien that was cited for assault. He conveyed to TJ that Obama seemed to be against law enforcement and that he was sure glad that Trump won the election. He added that morale was back up in their department.

Sounds good to me, TJ reflected. *President Trump seems to be gaining ground fast and Making America Great Again*! In fact, TJ had heard on Fox News that illegals coming across the border were down by 70% and arrests of illegals were up by 40%. What a difference a true leader can make! He felt proud that he would be working for President Trump…at least indirectly.

With all of the excitement happening lately, he almost forgot that he needed to call his *former* boss in California and terminate his employment; he made a mental note to do that.

Chapter 2
Ω

"The political divide in our country is not a black and white issue…its red and blue."

---Joy Ryan

Democratic Resistance Party Meeting

At Representative Stoner's office in the Rayburn House, several members of the Liberal infested Democratic Party (and one other) are meeting to discuss important matters affecting the party. In attendance were the following:

Representative An Gozol – (D-TX)
Representative Nadia Paloma – (D-CA)
Senator Cyrus Simpson – (D-NY)
Tim Payat – DNC Chairman
Representative Maybel Wileen – (D-CA)
Kadin Elkhart – DNC Deputy Chairman
Senator Maro Wesley – (D-VA)
Senator Esmeralda Willow – (D-MA)
Senator Burney Sherman – (I-VT)
Representative Abel Stoner – (D-CA) Resistance Party Chairman

And via conference call:
Senator Jace Melvin – (R-AZ)

"Ok, this unofficial meeting of the Resistance Party is called to order. All of us are present including

Senator Melvin who is on a conference call for obvious reasons. The purpose for this meeting tonight is to discuss Trump and what we can do to obstruct his success in office. Our real leader has called for us to create enough chaos and carnage so that by 2020 she will become our new president. Any ideas?" asked Abel Stoner.

"Impeach 45…impeach 45…impeach 45…" called out Representative Wileen.

"He called me Pocahontas that son of a bitch," yelled out Esmeralda Willow. "That means that I'm a savage!"

"Well he called me the Head Clown," stated Cyrus Simpson.

Not to be outdone, Burney Sherman put his two cents in as he stated in his raspy voice, "He called me Crazy Burney so I endorse Hilliary for president…she's an honest and hardworking person who believes in America and I believe in her by damn!"

"Hold on people. We are not here to relive the past or about name calling. Let's pull it together. At least the American people think that we have it together, so let's act like it. Now, the question is what will our first step be in sinking Trump?" Abel Stoner asked.

"How about we steal votes away from Trump in 2020?" Tim Payat asked.

"How do you propose that we do that?" asked Chairman Stoner.

"Easy. We act all concern for illegal aliens and their children and make Trump out to be the boogey man. As you know, with several states allowing illegals the right to have a driver's license or I.D. card, they can unofficially, officially vote…now," Tim added as an afterthought and winked at Stoner. "Let's act outraged and demand open borders for our Hispanic friends and to end these illegal detention centers. We can even act like we care about the so called 'Dreamers' and the 'DACA kids.' That should win us some sympathy votes as well from the American people."

"Have you forgotten that some time ago we were against illegals entering our country?" Representative Stoner questioned.

"I have a great idea; let's go with the Russian-Trump connection. The American people are so stupid that they will eat this crap up," Senator Sherman responded.

"I say we file Articles of Impeachment," Representative Gozol stated.

"Impeach 45…impeach 45…impeach 45," screamed Representative Wileen again.

"What if we released that it was discovered that millions of illegals voted for him and the true election belongs to Hilliary?" questioned Maro Wesley.

"No. That's kind of stupid since they voted for us and we know it. Better leave that one alone," Kadin Elkhart flatly stated.

"Who are you calling stupid you piece of shit?" screamed Maro Wesley. "I'm on the intelligence committee you dumbass. Only smart people get on that committee."

"Can I say something," asked Jace Melvin over the speaker.

"Go ahead Senator Melvin," replied Abel Stoner.

"Thank you Abel. I'm just glad that I'm a Republican. You dumb asses couldn't find your own snake if it wasn't attached."

"What snake is he talking about," Nadia Paloma inquired seriously. "I haven't seen one in years around here."

"I believe that," someone replied.

"Don't worry, you don't have one," stated An Gozol.

"People, people…can't we just get along?" asked Abel Stoner. "The American people believe that we agree on everything. If they could hear us now with all this bickering, they would think that we're all Republicans."

"Amen," whispered Jace Melvin.

"What was that?" Abel asked.

No one replied. All of a sudden the room grew quiet as well as the phone speaker as everyone collected their own thoughts. Then, broken only by the silence came…

"Impeach 45…impeach 45…impeach 45…" called out Maybel Wileen once again.

Cyrus Simpson was the first to reply. "Will you shut up you old bitch? Impeach him on what you fool?"

"I tell you again folks," the square-chinned Republican chimed in over the speaker, "thank Heaven I'm a Republican."

"Then what are you doing colluding with us?" asked Esmeralda Willow.

"I'm with you folks because I can't stand that idiot."

"Who are you calling an idiot?" queried Cyrus Simpson.

"I'm talking about Trump you clown!" stated Jace Melvin.

"How in the hell can we win in 2020 with all this bickering?" Abel Stoner asked. "Now, I say that we all go along with the Russian-Trump connection for now until we think of something better. Also, let's try and get people to protest whenever they see members of the Trump Administration out in public; that should drive some of them to resign. Other than that, we can try other ideas later. Let's take a vote and conclude this meeting."

It was unanimous that the obstruction would start with connecting Trump to the Russians. Once a solid connection was established, then articles of impeachment could be filed. Even though the cold war was over, they all knew in their heart of hearts that the American people still held animosity towards the Russians. The Russians were an easy target due to the fact that they continually aligned themselves with opposite views of the United States. For example, Russia was friends with Iran, Syria and even North Korea. The Resistance Party felt that by getting the American people onboard with this theory, that it would strengthen their cause. They knew that for years they had duped the American people and they knew that they would be able to continue that strategy. The Resistance Party, being made up of Liberals, had the dishonest media in their back pocket due to the fact that Liberals had infiltrated the mainstream media. So now, the dishonest media and others knew that if Hilliary could win in 2020, then favors would once again be flowing freely for those friends that had made donations to the Clinton Foundation.

So, the group then used their media connections to plant the evil seed about the Trump-Russian connection.

On the news, the American people heard the deranged Maybel Wileen cry out to "Impeach 45" and Representative Gozol screamed out that his office was going to file Articles of Impeachment. Senator Melvin called for an investigation of the Trump-Russian connection in order to put the whole issue to bed. Abel Stoner condemned the Trump Administration for covering up the Trump-Russian connection and he stated that there would be a Congressional investigation. The other Resistance Party members did likewise with the dishonest media. Fox News did report about the bias of the partisan and dishonest media as well as the murder of Saul Rafe, a Democratic National Committee employee who had been murdered in 2016. The Right-Wing theory was that he was killed for leaking information to WikiLeaks of the DNC's emails. Soon after his death, WikiLeaks offered a $20,000 reward for information about Rafe's murder leading to a conviction. Now why would they do that? Any normal person could connect the dots and would come to the same conclusion as the Right did. The dishonest media downplayed all of this and valiantly offered that Rafe was killed in a robbery attempt…even though nothing was removed from his body. However, you don't have to be a rocket scientist to see what appears to be the 'real' truth.

These and other similar events were happening to reform the country. People naturally took sides, Democratic or Republican, wrong or right. President Trump would say repeatedly: America was truly divided. It did not appear that this divisiveness was going to end anytime soon even as President Trump called for unity.

While TJ attended classes at the CIA, the Republicans were hard at work also trying desperately to calm and defunct the stories and innuendos as the Liberal Democrats were colluding with the dishonest media. So half of the country (through the mainstream news media), saw Trump colluding with the Russians as the other half saw the Liberal Democrats colluding with the dishonest media, each with their own agenda in mind.

In order to counterattack the Left's propaganda, the Republicans created a group inside their own party referred to as the Support Party.

Republican Support Party Meeting

"Ok, this meeting will come to order," Representative Curt Click announced in his office, located in the Longworth House Office Building, "time for roll call master-at-arms."

As the master-at-arms took roll call, the following were all present and accounted for:

Representative Curt Click – (R-NY) Support Party Chair

Representative Dwight Home – (R-CA) Master-at-Arms

Representative Lay Beebee – (R-PA)
Representative Tamar Meal – (R-PA)
Representative Kane Bundy – (R-TX)
Representative Mona Bu – (R-TN)
Representative Ken Charge – (R-ND)
Senator Care – (R-AR)
Senator Tut Smith – (R-SC)

And via conference call:

OPERATION: Ωmega

Senator Jed Med – (D-WV)

Once everyone was seated, the Chairman banged his gavel in order to get everyone's attention. As quiet replaced the voices that had been talking, Representative Click addressed his group of Trump supporters.

"I want to thank everyone for your time tonight as it is greatly appreciated and needed in support of our President. I want everyone to know that the situation is quite severe. The Liberal Democrats have simply come unglued with Trump winning and Hilliary losing. They just can't believe what happened to them in the 2016 Election and what that will mean with their way of life; simply put, that their corruption will be exposed and hopefully at least some of their number will be heading for prison. This will look bad for the Democrats if some of their members do go to prison and they stand a good chance at losing voters in favor of Trump. It is now clear that had Hilliary won, the Democrats would be destroying the evidence that would show the American people their true nature."

After a brief pause to allow his statement to sink in, Representative Click continued.

"We have all gathered here today to not only express our support for President Trump, but also ways that we can combat the Resistance Party. As you all know, President Trump is in favor of the American people winning, especially the silent majority. Well, with President Trump and our Support Party, they won't have to be silent anymore as we will be their voice," Representative Click stated positively; "anymore thoughts people?"

Senator Smith cleared his throat before speaking, "I just want to point out an obvious fact. I remember when the Liberal war cry was that Candidate Trump is unfit for office. But if you look at the other side, they are coming unhinged. We very much have a divided country and the main reason that it is divided is because we have good and evil, Right and Left views and Conservatives versus Liberals…in other words, right and wrong. I don't see this changing any time soon. But for the time being, we must be the champions for the American people and do all that we can to support our President and suppress the Leftist ideology."

"Thank you for that summation Senator Smith. I believe that you have summed it up very nicely. But the question still stands, what is the best way to support our President?" asked Representative Click.

Representative Home raised his hand and was called on to speak. "To counter those damn Liberals, we need to do the opposite of whatever they are currently doing."

Then from the conference call speaker came the voice of Senator Med. "I know that I'm just a Democrat, but I want everyone to know that I'm not a Liberal and that's why I am here with you all today. We need to stop this infiltration of Liberals into politics. Otherwise, they are going to cost us the country as we used to know it. They have woven their lies and deceit and corruption into the very fabric that is our country as well as eroding our basic traditions that our country was proudly founded on."

"I know what we must do," offered Representative Beebee. "We have to beat them at their own game. Right now, they are in full force with the dishonest media with their ranting and raving about President Trump and their lies and trying to brainwash the American people. Well folks, we have a powerful weapon as well. We have the number one news media in America today…Fox News!"

Cheers went up followed by clapping at that suggestion and ended when Representative Bu spoke, "I have a contact at Fox News and none other than Judge Jeanine Pirro! I'll see if I can get on her show. With Judge Jeanine, there is no reason why we can't beat them at their own game. Like us, she can't stand those damn liars, leakers and Liberals."

"Hey, Sean Hannity is a close friend of mine and we even golf together. I can get on his show for sure," declared Representative Charge. "In fact, the last time that I was on his show was last year when President Trump was running for president. Consider it done."

"Does anyone else have any other friends in the honest media?" Representative Click asked.

"Well, I played basketball with Tucker Carlson one time for charity. Let me see what I can do. Maybe he'll remember me. The charity was called 'Balls for Boys.' We were trying to collect basketballs for our inner city youth. You know, if more of our kids were to get interested in sports, chances are they'll stay out of trouble," Senator Care informed the group.

"Well that's great!" Representative Click said with passion. "Remember people, President Trump is working hard for all of us and the least that we can do for him is no less. I'm meeting with him tomorrow and I will ensure him that we have his back…anyone else?"

When no one else spoke up, the meeting was adjourned for the night with all of the participants willing to assist the President and the country.

CIA Headquarters

After several weeks of CIA training, the department felt that TJ was ready for his first assignment. During TJ's training period, President Trump's nomination of Judge Neil Gorsuch was confirmed by the Senate on April 7, 2017 and at 49, he became the youngest sitting Supreme Court Justice since Clarence Thomas. The mainstream Americans cheered robustly and celebrated this second Republican victory. However, this was President Trump's first big win. But with the Democrats not playing fairly, the CIA believed that it was time to start leveling the playing field and TJ was called into Director Lannister's office along with his direct boss, Randy Morgan.

"Gentlemen, won't you have a seat please?" Director Lannister asked and waved to the leather bound chairs that were in front of his desk and the men seated themselves.

"I called you both in for a couple of reasons. First, it has come to my attention that TJ has finished his training and very superbly I might add; congratulations are in order Mr. Law. Secondly, I believe that we are ready to put TJ's training to good use. What do you think Mr. Morgan?"

"He's ready," Randy simply stated.

"TJ?" the CIA Director asked.

"I'm ready," TJ answered positively so as to instill confidence in his abilities.

"Good, that's what I was hoping to hear," Director Lannister conveyed. "Now, I have asked and received intelligence on what Liberal is the most damaging to our country right now and that means to our President and the American people as well. Gentlemen, the name that I received was none other than…Representative An Gozol. TJ, you have received some of the best training that the department has to offer besides your Naval SEAL training. You have been briefed on your possible missions under the Omega Agency and you have our assurances that we are behind you fully. I'm having Judy pull the CIA file on Gozol. I expect you to look through that and come up with an acceptable plan based on the guidelines of the Omega Agency in order to carry out your mission successfully. We do not need to know how your mission was carried out, only that is was successful and that a Russian clue was left behind. In other words, you'll fill out a report with that information. Any questions Mr. Law?"

TJ glanced at his boss while shaking his head in the negative and answered "No sir."

"Mr. Morgan?" the CIA head asked of Randy.

"No sir," Randy answered.

"Good. Ok gentlemen, let's get to it. TJ, any questions or assistance that you need, you will find that my door and that of Mr. Morgan's is always open. We need everything to run smoothly so that the Omega Agency will be successful and will carry on for many years to come, if necessary, to protect our country's vital interests and our way of life. Thank you gentlemen and I wish you both the best of luck in this endeavor," Director Lannister stated.

Randy and TJ walked back to their respective offices. TJ noticed that Judy had left a file on his desk containing information on Representative An Gozol.

Since the file was quite thick and would require some extensive reading, TJ asked Judy to bring him a cup of coffee with cream. In fact, he figured that he would need several more before he came up with a fool proof idea of how to accomplish his first important mission!

★ ★ ★ ★ ★

After several hours of meticulous reading, he thought that he had an idea of how to complete his mission. It seemed that Gozol was an avid fisherman and owned a small yacht in Houston---*which probably the American people paid for,* TJ thought. Anyway, it appears that whenever there was a congressional break, Gozol would fly back home to Houston and spend some time on his boat. TJ asked Judy to check on Gozol's schedule. Judy informed him that Gozol would be leaving Washington that night to go back home for two weeks. TJ then asked Judy for a military flight schedule for Joint Base Andrews going to Ellington Field. Ellington Field was a Air National Guard base as well as a Coast Guard Air Station just outside of Houston.

Scanning the military flight schedule that Judy brought him---that only listed flights for the next 72 hours due to security reasons---TJ noticed that there were no flights listed for Ellington Field and called Judy into his office. He knew that the department wanted to keep costs down as much as possible and frowned on utilizing commercial flights. Plus, commercial flights added another degree of difficulty being that he was armed. Not that he couldn't fly commercial with his weapon and credentials, he just felt more comfortable on military flights.

"Judy, I don't see any flights on here for Ellington Field and I need to get to Houston."

"What about taking Air Force One Mr. Law?" Judy asked seriously.

"I know that I have a lot of pull Judy, but I doubt that I have that much," TJ chuckled.

"I can schedule you on Air Force One Mr. Law. You see, President Trump is flying there tomorrow due to the past hurricane and we are allowed to fly on his plane…when needed," she added quickly.

"Unbelievable!" TJ exclaimed. "This job just gets better and better."

So Judy arranged for TJ to have a seat on Air Force One and instructed him on all the details.

The next morning at his home on Joint Base Andrews, TJ was already to go when a knock on his door confirmed to him that this was really happening and that the day held a promise of some excitement. The night before, he made sure that he had everything that he would need laid out and organized. He answered the door.

"Mr. Law, I'm Major Nelson assigned to Air Force One here at JBA and I'm here to escort you to the plane sir."

"Thank you Major. Please call me TJ."

"Very well…TJ."

As he climbed into the government vehicle, he noticed quickly how windy it was and saw and heard an American flag popping in the wind. *Would Air Force One be able to take off? We'll just have to wait and see,* he mused. *If the pilot had balls like President Trump, then he knew that they would soon be in the air!*

Major Nelson dropped off TJ and then drove away in the standard government issued black SUV.

TJ checked in with the Air Force One Liaison Officer. He wondered if they would make him hand over his gun but he was cleared to fly as is. He was escorted onboard and was seated by himself next to a window in a corridor. He thought they really did know his taste! So he pulled out a

Western paperback book from his cargo pants and started to read. He was told earlier that when everyone was onboard and seated, then the President would board. That occurred about 15 minutes later when Marine One arrived and within 10 minutes they were airborne. Apparently, President Trump didn't believe in letting grass grow under his feet!

After Air Force One was well on its way and as TJ was really getting into his book, a young woman approached him and informed him that the President would like to visit with him. So he followed her forward on the plane to the President's office. She knocked on the door and was invited in. She opened the door and without going in, holding it open for him, she announced TJ and left.

"Mr. Law, come in and have a seat. I have wanted to meet you ever since I was given your letter. Please have a seat. This is a real honor," President Trump declared as he waved to an available chair for TJ.

"No Mr. President, the honor is all mine sir," TJ asserted.

The two men visited for about a half hour then TJ returned to his seat carrying a gift from the President. What did they talk about you wonder? Not in this book will we reveal that as it is classified and private and will remain so. In fact, my publisher requested that the above be redacted which I readily agreed to. I can only disclose that to someone with a Top Secret security clearance *and* a justifiable "need-to-know" request and of course, with the President's permission. Otherwise, I would have to kill everyone who reads this book! But TJ did contemplate on something that the President did say which was that it seems that those who contribute the least are usually the ones who consume the most. He couldn't agree more with the President while thinking of certain Liberal Democrats.

He returned to his seat and continued reading his book when the plane landed safely.

Since there was no lodging on base, Judy had made a reservation for him at a nearby Holiday Inn Express. TJ took the base shuttle there and checked in.

He flew back commercially to Langley two days later since Air Force One had left on the previous day…without him!

Chapter 3
Ω

"What separates the winners from the losers is how a person reacts to each new twist of fate."

---President Donald Trump

On May 9, 2017, President Trump fired the Director of the FBI, Jaron Cowan, basically because public trust and confidence had been eroded, most notably in dealing with the Hilliary Clinton scandal---or inaction thereof. Mr. Cowan decided that the best course of action for him would be to write a book and get his story out in the public quickly to all who wanted to read about it; at least, his version of the past events!

TJ was in his office working late familiarizing himself with some top secret CIA business and currently reading the CIA's *Sentinel Times* news publication. *At least with this paper, I don't have to worry about "fake news,"* he observed. The CIA paper was only distributed inside of the agency and was all fact and no hyperbole. This was because the CIA wanted their employees to know the truth. However, the paper was not allowed to be removed from the building, otherwise, the penalties were quite severe.

Concerning Jaron Cowan, TJ thought that the former FBI Director was a piece of shit and good riddance. Cowan got too political and fucked up several issues like properly dealing with another piece of shit...Hilliary (TJ believed in calling things as he sees them and NOT being politically correct). With all the possible charges against her and the Clinton Foundation, she should have been imprisoned long ago with Bill and some of their other cronies...including Obama. He thought that it was crucial and justified when he learned that President Trump fired the FBI Director... "Drain the Swamp!" *That's a start*, thought TJ, but he knew it was a big swamp with many swamp dwellers including Obama. He knew the former President was in the thick of all of this corruption.

TJ turned on the Fox News channel as Hannity was about to start. Hannity was really someone that he could relate to as Sean had a tendency to speak his mind truthfully. *I'll have to find some justification to go visit him sometime*, he considered. *Maybe I'll write a book and receive an invitation to come on his show*! Sean has said several times on his show how someone should write a book about all that is happening since its quite unbelievable...really unbelievable!

"Welcome to Fox News and I'm Sean Hannity with a Fox News Alert. President Trump has just fired the FBI Director, Jaron Cowan. We will have a full report later and we will tell you what you will not see in the mainstream media. But first, another Fox News Alert involving Representative An Gozol. Representative Gozol, a Congressional Liberal Democrat from Texas is missing. His yacht was discovered earlier today off the coast of Houston floating aimlessly and was reported to officials by local fishermen. We currently don't have all the details but we can tell you that a miniature cocktail toothpick with a Russian flag was recovered on deck. Representative Gozol if you remember had threatened to file Articles of Impeachment against President Trump. Unless he is found, I guess he will not be filing them now. Our friends from the Clinton News Network, you know who I'm referring to, the dishonest media, is reporting that Congressman Gozol was kidnapped by Russian agents on a request made by President Trump...unbelievable! You can't make this stuff up. Someone, please write a book and I'll buy a copy of it. Anyway, here at Fox News, we will not report on anything like that unless we can verify it first. We know that's why our viewers turn in everyday for balanced and honest reporting.

"Now let's turn our attention to Jaron Cowan. He was finally fired by President Trump and it's about time. Personally, I thought that he should have been fired on day one when President Trump took office…"

TJ muted the television as Judy entered his office and informed him that the director would like to see him and Mr. Morgan right away. He stopped by Randy's office and together they walked the short distance to Director Lannister's office. After they closed the door and seated themselves, Director Lannister began speaking. "Gentlemen, I take it that you have heard the latest news concerning Representative Gozol?"

Both Randy and TJ confirmed this.

"Well congratulations are in order as long as he is gone for good," he stated as he directed his look at TJ.

"He won't be coming back…sir," TJ confirmed.

"Good. I was just watching CNN and they are reporting that the Russians are clearly behind his disappearance and that they have in fact, kidnapped Congressman Gozol and are holding him for ransom, on a request by President Trump…unbelievable! However, they are clearly the epitome of fake news. Well, that should give the President some relief though and predictably, they are doing exactly what we want. I just bet those Liberals are madder than a slapped hornet!

"With that being said, I have our next target for TJ," Director Lannister stated matter-of-factly and handed a file marked Top Secret to TJ. As he was casually viewing the prospective file, the Director continued.

"Representative Nadia Paloma of California is our next target gentlemen. View the file carefully and don't be in a hurry TJ. It is imperative that we get this right and not fast. Her file is Top Secret due to her previous committee assignment on the Intelligence Committee before becoming the Minority Leader…any questions gentlemen?" Director Lannister asked.

"What's with Cowan getting fired sir?" asked Randy.

"I told that asshole to knock this crap off that is bringing a lot of unwanted attention to him. But Jaron is very self-centered and apparently loves the lime light. He also was clearly a puppet of the Clintons. Too much was happening too fast and he made mistakes. If only he thought about putting America first, he would still be here today. Our intelligence has uncovered that Cowan was an operative of the DNC even though he was registered as a Republican. It is clear to us now that that was a tactic to throw off the American people as well as certain Republicans on certain committees. So we always want to make sure that we are putting America first ahead of our own needs gentlemen."

The meeting concluded and TJ decided to head home with the agreement to meet with his boss tomorrow afternoon to discuss how best to pull off the next mission successfully. In the morning, TJ had agreed to play Intelligence Agent Jerney in racquetball at 0800.

That night at home, as TJ tried to sleep, he kept thinking about his next target…a woman. Well, she shouldn't be caught up in all this political crap. He knew from news reports that she really was a piece of work. She thought she was holier than thou and was a clear and present danger to the country.

Democratic Resistance Party Meeting #2

Meanwhile that same evening, the Resistant Party conducted another meeting with the usual suspects…I mean the usual Democrats and one Republican minus one Democrat at Representative Paloma's office in the Cannon House Office Building.

"Ok people, we are all here with the exception of Representative Gozol. Does anyone have any information on Gozol?" Representative Stoner questioned.

"It's the Russians. I bet they kidnapped him for a ransom. Are we going to pay if they ask for money?" Kadin Elkhart asked seriously.

"Impeach 45…impeach 45…impeach 45…" Congresswoman Whitney chanted.

"Knock it off Maybel, this isn't the time or the place right now for that crap," Stoner commented. "We have to figure out what the hell is going on. This is serious people. Also, that line about the Russians is what *we* told CNN to release. I suppose it could be them but…well I don't know for sure. Why would the Russians so boldly announce that they were present? Can anybody else come up with any other ideas?"

"It could actually be that he fell overboard and was lost at sea," Tim Payat remarked.

"What about the Russian toothpick flag that was found onboard?" Stoner asked.

"Maybe it was in his martini and fell out…as he fell overboard," interjected Senator Simpson. "Who knows?"

Then coming from the speaker the voice of Senator Melvin sounded. "Maybe it could have been a gift you dicks! Who gives a shit?"

"Maybe he had some Russian in his bloodline?" Representative Paloma queried. "It's a possibility."

"He was black and from the south you dimwit," Senator Wesley shouted. "I suppose you think that he flies a rebel flag at home too!"

"Who are you calling a dimwit you colossal…idiot!" raged Paloma.

"Colossal idiot you say, really…me? Why don't you up and die you old bitch since you won't retire?" Wesley suggested.

"People, people, can't we all just get along, without the name calling please?" Stoner pleaded. "We better damn well care about what's going on. This stuff doesn't fit our current plans. I wonder what the boss will say about all of this stuff when she hears." It grew quiet, almost somber. "Now then, everyone, think about this and let the Resistance Party know if you think of anything. Meeting adjourned."

★ ★ ★ ★ ★

The next day found TJ at the CIA gym ready to play racquetball with Intelligence Agent Jerney. About 15 minutes late, Jerney walked up followed by two others.

"Sorry I'm late TJ…traffic, you know. I want to introduce you to two of my friends who also play racquetball. This is Intelligence Agent Ray who retired from the Navy as a Chief Petty Officer and this is Stefan. Stefan is an analyst."

TJ shook each hand in turn and greeted with a, "nice to meet you."

The teams were TJ and Jerney against Stefan and Ray. After two hours of play, TJ and Jerney won 6 out of 8 games. Showers happened next and then TJ headed for his office a little tired but none the worse for wear. He actually felt pretty good today.

While viewing a stack of paperwork and a file---that of Nadia Paloma's---that Judy had left for him that morning, she entered with a cup of coffee and two cinnamon twirls which she knew was a favorite of TJ's.

With his coffee and rolls in hand, TJ felt ready to get down to brass tacks and attack the mountain of stuff that required his attention. Then after lunch he went to see his boss.

"TJ, have a seat. Have you had a chance to look at the Paloma file?"

"I did. I noticed that she has a home in Wheaton. I think that will give me my best opportunity. I think I will stop by maybe for a cup of coffee…?" TJ left this last sentence hanging.

TJ did not reveal to his boss his plan for his next target. Not because he didn't trust his boss, but because he wasn't sure himself. He thought that once he got into the home that he would play it by ear.

He finished up his work and headed for the CIA swimming area, located down under, where a hot tub was residing for him. Of course, he brought a Western with him to read while soaking. After an hour or so he headed for home. He decided that tomorrow he would case out Paloma's neighborhood. He wasn't in a hurry and in fact, he couldn't afford to be in a hurry and make a mistake.

The next day, but not too early so as to give Paloma the chance to get to work, he drove through the neighborhood of Gold Springs in which Paloma was residing these days when she was not in California. After several hours, including checking the home carefully, he had the intelligence that he felt he needed for a successful conclusion and headed back to the office. He had no illusions about this mission compared to the last one…this was going to require more patience. At least he was on his own time schedule.

Back at his office, TJ took the time to analyze all the information that he had collected. Wheaton was 27 miles from TJ's home on Joint Base Andrews. It would only take about a half hour then to get there. The top secret file that he reviewed from the CIA had Paloma arriving home between 2000 and 2200 about 90% of the time. That means by 0300 she should be well asleep. After much thought and planning he felt that he was now mentally and physically prepared for his next mission. While as a Navy SEAL, the military taught him that metal preparation was just as important as physical preparation. Without the proper amount of either preparation, mistakes could happen. Since the Omega Agency was critical to the country's health, he knew that he couldn't afford any slip ups. He even studied Paloma's home from CIA aerial views and felt that he was as ready as he would ever be. So to help him relax a little, he decided to try out a movie at the CIA's movie theater. He asked Judy about movies and times that were playing for today.

"Mr. Law, we have Baywatch playing in an hour if you are interested in that," Judy stated. "We have it before it's released to the public and its 2 hours long."

"That's fine Judy. I'll be there for the movie and then I'll go home to get some rest as well. Also Judy, you may call me TJ since others do."

"Sorry Mr. Law, but that's not protocol for our agency. Others may do so due to their position in the agency, but personal assistants are not allowed to be so formal. Actually, that policy was put into place right after President Clinton was impeached due to sexual scandals with some women that were around him."

"Ok, thanks Judy, I did not know that."

TJ thought back to that point in time and remembered the story well. Being well versed in history he knew that sometime in December 1998, the House of Representatives initiated the impeachment process of Bill Clinton on two charges, one of perjury and one of obstruction of justice. "Obstruction of justice…?" TJ thought out loud. "That doesn't sound like a Democrat!" Of course he was being facetious. These charges he knew stemmed out of a lawsuit brought on by Paula Jones against Clinton. However, President Clinton was acquitted of these two charges by the Senate in February 1999 for cooperating with the investigation. *Oh well, what the hell…*

TJ enjoyed the movie favorably enough, especially with The Rock starring in it. He recalled the first time that he saw Dwayne Johnson in a movie called Walking Tall. It was one of his favorite movies because The Rock was not politically correct…imagine that…he must be a Republican!

TJ then headed for home with a quick visit at Wingstop on base for some wings. While he waited for his order, an American soldier entered and placed his order for

20 classic wings and cheese fries. TJ liked the drums plain and then used Famous Dave's BBQ sauce on them.

After his dinner at home, he turned in early for his mission the next day.

★ ★ ★ ★ ★

TJ showed up the next day for work a little later than normal. He stopped by his bosses' office first to let Randy know that his mission was accomplished. Randy told him that he would inform Director Lannister and reminded TJ to type up his 203 report. Back at his office he found a stack of paperwork that needed his attention again. *That Judy,* he thought, *is a very industrious person*! He went ahead and typed up his report and tackled the other paperwork that Judy had left with him. He skipped lunch this day but attended to his food needs for dinner at the cafeteria and wondered if Director Lannister was going to call him to his office; probably not since the director was busy with other issues.

After dinner, he challenged Ray to some tennis since Ray informed him that besides racquetball he liked to play tennis as well. They played in the environmentally controlled basement of headquarters at the very well maintained tennis courts and Ray won two out of three sets. With that done, TJ went home and was back at his office early the next morning. He even had breakfast in the cafeteria since he really didn't like to cook. Plus, the food was included as part of his employment…so why not?

TJ spent the day doing various tasks and when he turned on his TV to Fox News, Tucker Carlson was on with another Fox News Alert. This was his second favorite show on Fox News next to Hannity.

"I'm Tucker Carlson and we have a Fox News Alert. It was just released that law enforcement officials have discovered the body of Nadia Paloma at her Wheaton home, in her foyer dead from hanging. At this time, it's not clear if she hung herself or had some assistance. However, police did discover a gold Russian Imperial Eagle pin near the body and have called in the Feds, meaning I guess the FBI. We will update you as we get more details."

Meanwhile, CNN reported the following contrasting report: "Officials in the City of Wheaton have just discovered the body of Democratic Minority Representative Nadia Paloma in her home in Wheaton dead from strangulation. The FBI was called in and found a Russian Gold Crested Pin that would indicate the Russian government had some involvement in this dastardly deed. In fact, it is our belief that since the ransom wasn't paid by the federal government for the release of Representative Gozol, the Russians took this opportunity and hung Representative Paloma in her home. CNN is calling on Congress to place greater sanctions on Russia and for the FBI to quickly reveal what Russian operatives was involved in this death of a beloved stateswoman and bring them to justice…"

Meanwhile, back on Fox's Tucker Carlson show, Attorney General Jeff Sessions was speaking on this matter: "It is true that the body of Representative Paloma has been discovered as she was hanged in her foyer. It is also true that a Russian Federation lapel pin was discovered near the body of Representative Paloma. It is also true that we do not have concrete evidence at this time contrary to a possible suicide by Representative Paloma. However, I want to caution the American people on jumping to conclusions about the Russian involvement in this case. Our investigation into this matter is still too early to come to a successful conclusion. So let's have a little patience before jumping to conclusions involving our Russian friends as I am confident that our FBI will indeed discover what exactly happened here today. Thank you."

Back in TJ's office, Judy entered and told him that Director Lannister wanted Randy and him to come to his office.

TJ met his boss Randy at Director Lannister's office.

"Gentlemen, sit down please," Director Lannister said. "Congratulations are in order again as the dishonest media is having a field day with this latest event. I can't express how impressed I am of your skills and ingenuity TJ."

Randy decided to put in his two-cents as well with: "I am also really impressed with TJ's abilities. He is meeting his goals and commitments and I have received some feedback from others in the department on how well he is liked by our teammates, including me. But I don't need to report his discipline, attention to detail or determination as we knew well in advance what we would be getting. So my hearty thanks for TJ in being what our country needs so badly at this time and thanks to you Director Lannister for your follow-through on his idea in assisting with our country's needs even though a lot of people may not understand what is happening to our country right now. But it is quite clear to me that our nation was in trouble before President Trump came into office. Our country is better off for these two individuals working to Make America Great Again. I enjoy working with him very much and look forward to several more years of our teamwork in the Omega Agency, if needed."

"Thank you for your vote of confidence Mr. Morgan. My sentiments exactly as I too look forward to our team working together for years to come. Anything you would like to add Mr. Law?" Director Lannister asked.

"Who's my next target?"

Chapter 4
Ω

"I'm a Christian, a Conservative and a Republican in that order."

---Vice President Mike Pence

"Love lifted me. Love lifted me. When nothing else could help, love lifted me. Love lifted me. Love lifted me. When nothing else could help, love lifted me…" the congregation sang on.

TJ, being a Born-Again Christian, would attend a small church named Grace Assembly on Sundays when he was growing up as a kid in the South. However, this was a similar but somewhat larger church located in Arlington, Virginia called, Assembly of God that was close to the cemetery. Stefan and his wife invited TJ to attend with them this Sunday and he decided to take them up on their invite. He was also filled with the Holy Spirit and missed going to his own church in Anaheim, California. He accepted Jesus as his Savior back when he was seven and was baptized at a young age as well. His family was a God-fearing close knit family. His parents taught him values such as doing unto others as they would do unto you and so forth. But as he grew older and with a stint in the Navy, he became cynical and viewed most people as dishonest until they proved themselves otherwise.

After the singing of two more hymns, the pastor spoke to his flock which included Vice President Mike Pence and his wife who was in attendance this Sunday.

"For those of you that are new here, I am Pastor Young and for those of you who are our regulars know me as Brother Young. That is because we are all brothers and sisters in the Lord's eyes as He is our Father. God loves each and every one of you. God has plans for all of us. Always remember that no one person is perfect in God's eyes but His Son Jesus died on the cross for our sins. He gave His life up freely so that we may have eternal life; eternal life by accepting Jesus Christ as our Savior. Friends, I ask you, who here would like eternal life? We all should desire eternal life. God forgives us for our sins if we just accept Jesus into our hearts and only then will we receive the blessing of everlasting life. In your Holy Bible, please turn to John 3:16 and follow along with me. 'For God so loved the world that he gave His only begotten Son, that whosoever believeth in Him should not perish, but have everlasting life.' There it is friends. The road to salvation is through Jesus Christ. Are you depressed? Are you lonely? Are you lost? Through our Lord these things can be resolved. It's just that simple. We all have sinned," shouted Pastor Young with passion at the assembled, "but we are all forgiven through acceptance of Jesus Christ into our hearts and His love cloaks us all."

As Pastor Young viewed his congregation, he continued on, "Who has sinned? Romans 3:10 says 'For all have sinned and come short of the glory of God.'

"Romans 6:23 says, 'For the wages of sin is death; but the gift of God is eternal life through Jesus Christ our Lord.'

"But God commendeth His love toward us, in that, while we were yet sinners, Christ died for us.' Romans 5:8.

"Romans 10:13 says 'For whosoever shall call upon the name of the Lord shall be saved.' Finding everlasting life is as easy as A B C folks. A is for accepting Jesus Christ into your heart as your savior. B is believing in Him and last, but surely not least is C, which means confessing to others of your acceptance of Jesus Christ as your savior…"

As the service continued on, TJ reflected on his mission and his religious beliefs. He was sure that God forgave him and understood his mission to stamp out evil in his country. His conscious was clear and he felt at peace with his God. In order to win over evil, there were some that needed to be sent to Hell. God had blessed America more so than any other country in the world because the United States was a compassionate country as a whole and tried to do the right thing. Unfortunately, there were those that had no conscious and did not believe in God's love or the golden rule for that matter. Greed, corruption and power coupled with people who did not believe in ethics or the fear of God and was without conscious thought, made for a bad combination, commonly referred to as Liberals.

Pastor Young was now having alter call with church members filing up to the front to be prayed for. TJ noticed that Brother Young was anointing them with what was most likely olive oil since that was what his pastor would do in tradition to the Bible.

Soon, some of the members that were up front being prayed for started talking in tongues. TJ was well aware of this process since he went through it once as a kid in his own church. He was told by his pastor that when you talk in tongues that you are really talking to God directly and only He knows what you are conversing about. When TJ did talk in tongues on that hot Wednesday night in June, it was after 2230 when he was shaken out of his conversation with God by his pastor who remarked, "You sure must have a lot to talk about son." It was a very surreal experience, and frankly, a little scary to him as well until he went through the process. Now it doesn't bother him anymore because he understood and felt that he received the gift of the Holy Spirit and at the same time was given a guardian angel to watch over him; it was a pleasant thought.

After the service and on the way out, TJ was able to shake Vice President Pence's hand and as they hugged, Pence whispered into his ear: "Go with God my son and know what you are doing is just in His eyes." TJ made eye contact briefly with the Vice President and nodded and then moved on down the outside stairs and looked back. He didn't see Vice President Pence, but he did notice that beneath the steeple, all the people were filing out and shaking hands with the man who gripped the gospel gun…Brother Young. He was reminded of when he was a kid growing up in Alabama and that it felt just like another Sunday in the South.

Does Vice President Pence know what I do? Or maybe, he knows that I work for the CIA? Oh well, it sounded supportive in any case!

TJ liked Pence since he was a Christian and a good man.

Some on the Left might say that TJ was a hypocrite being a Christian and doing the job that he is being paid to do---if they knew, that is---but he knew in his heart that God understood him and forgives him for doing what he believes is right for the country, and, it was also his government work. The Left seemed to think and wanted others to believe that if you are not politically correct then you are simply a bad person. TJ knew that the United States is the most generous country in the world and with that said, the country received God's blessings the same as Israel did. He also knew that his country harbored a lot of bad actors as well and he didn't believe that God wanted or expected others to stand around and do nothing. So in his mind and as a balance in life, he served God and his country at the same time and was at peace with himself.

Kremlin Meeting

President Vladimir Putin was meeting with Prime Minister Dmitry Medvedev. Putin was seated behind his desk while Dmitry was seated in front.

"Yes your Excellency, I would have to agree with you that those Americans are so stupid. They knee jerk at everything before having their facts straight. With they're

Liberals involved in politics and the media, it makes our job easier. They seem to think that we are kidnapping or killing off their members of Congress…what a hoot, as the Americans would say!"

"I wonder *who* is killing them off Dmitry? I would really like to know and see what manipulations we could utilize in our goals of conquering a super power. I would love to help the United States of America with their downfall. Ask our operatives working in the U.S. to see what they can uncover. It feels like the work of the CIA with one exception…the CIA has never been known to kill Americans though. Find out what you can and get back to me Dmitry."

Dmitry nodded while taking notes in a notebook.

"Also Dmitry, send a thank you note to the United States for the 20% of their uranium that they basically gave us."

Dmitry was writing this down when Putin interjected, "Never mind, I was just joking. Who would we send the letter to…Hilliary? That's funny. Just think Dmitry, by just planting a seed, these Americans are so ready to believe that we influenced their election. It's so easy to manipulate them…just like taking candy away from a baby. Why would we influence an election to benefit those Republicans? The Republicans are mostly trying to do the right thing. On the other hand, the Democrats can be bought and bamboozled. Just think Dmitry, we captured 20% of their uranium for a measly $140 million dollar donation to a non-profit that fronts for America's most corrupt administration since…since I don't know when. And Dmitry, do you know what else?" Putin asked as Dmitry shook his head in the negative. "We can write it all off on our taxes!"

As both men shook with laughter, they hardly paid any attention to spilling some of their black Russian drinks.

"You know Dmitry, if I was going to help any certain political party in the United States, I would have helped those Liberal Democrats. Do you know why

Dmitry?" When Dmitry shook his head in the negative Putin continued, "Because I want another 20% of their uranium!"

Once again the men laughed so hard spilling their drinks. After a minute of laughter, Putin shared his thoughts about Trump.

"The bad news Dmitry is this Trump…I don't think that he can be bought. I don't know yet what to do about him. However, he does have his hands full in dealing with us, Iran, China and North Korea and those awesome Liberals! I think we shall be able to find some more opportunities to fuck with America though. Yes I think that that will be true. Right now in America they have their hands full with investigation after investigation; everything from this Uranium One deal to impeach 45! Just think Dmitry, here in our motherland, we cannot afford all of these kinds of investigations and that's one reason that we don't have them, and also, because I don't like to be investigated!" Putin shouted and banged his fist on the desk.

With tears filling his eyes from laughing so hard, Dmitry was still able to refill their glasses yet again.

"Yes your Excellency, these Americans are so stupid…"

"Wait Dmitry, not stupid really, just naïve like children; but what the hell, same thing as being stupid!"

With his suit moist with vodka and coffee, Dmitry moved and sat on a couch nearby and continued: "In any case Vladamir…"

"Hey," Putin interrupted, "What happened to your Excellency?"

"I guess I'm too drunk and my sides are hurting too much from laughing so hard."

"That's ok my friend…go on with what you are saying."

"The uranium that we got from them Clintons is being put to good use. It is going into our newest submarine class right now…starting with the Obama!"

"Dmitry, you are too much. But why name a class of subs Obama?"

"Because, it was Obama who allowed the Clintons to help us and prosper from all of this corruption, and of course, because our subs are black!" he stated amusingly.

Both men laughed heartily again. Dmitry could clearly see that Putin was pleased with his antics. He knew this was good because, no matter how long they have been friends, other friends of Putin's have been known to disappear…mysteriously and for good! But no one seriously dared to question Putin about that at all.

"Mr. Putin, do you know what else is funny?"

"Now it's Mr. Putin is it? Go on and tell me comrade."

"Well, I was just thinking how we did not need an import license to get hold of the uranium," Dmitry forced out between tears of happiness.

"An import license?" shouted Putin. "Mother Russia doesn't need a stinkin' import license!"

After several more rounds of laughter, Putin continued on in a serious tone: "You know Dmitry, it is good to name our newest class of submarines the Obama class. He and his administration has been very helpful not only to our country, but to our friends in Iran as well. What idiot would give a country like that over a $150 billion U.S. dollars? You know Dmitry, if I were the American people I would be asking what team is Obama on. America, what a great country! A great country for the rest of us that is, my comrade!"

Now the men shared a subdued laugh.

"Dmitry, let's have a toast to our friend Obama. He is the worst president for the United States but the very best President for mother Russia!"

The men cheered Obama and clicked their glasses together. Then Dmitry just happened to have an idea to share with his friend.

"Vladimir, I have an idea."

"What is this idea that you are having my friend?"

"Since Obama is a great speaker, even better than Bill, I think that we should invite him here to give a speech and pay him one million dollars."

Putin gave Dmitry a stone cold hard look with that suggestion and Dmitry felt compelled to apologize.

"Sorry my leader for my bad suggestion as that would probably put him into more hot water with the American people."

But then slowly a smile came across Putin's face and he replied, "What the hell? Make the invitation for next month. That's when we will be christening our newest submarine, the RTUS Obama."

"What does RTUS mean?" Dmitry cautiously asked.

"Russia Thanks United States…Obama," Putin answered.

Yes, another round of laughter could be heard from the hallway if you were near Putin's office.

"That is great my Excellency. What if we name our second Obama class sub after Hilliary?" Dmitry asked seriously.

"Are you nuts Dmitry? That would be bad luck and she would probably sink as fast as her namesake!"

★ ★ ★ ★ ★

A couple of weeks went by and TJ decided to visit Senator Simpson's rented home in Seat Pleasant which was a small community located in Maryland. From the files on Senator Simpson, TJ noticed that he only went home when Congress was not in session and preferred a large home in this small community when Congress was in session.

The town was situated close by so TJ did not feel a need to hurry anything. He parked across the street from Senator Simpson's home and broke out his binoculars to surveil the surrounding area as well as the home. Nothing special caught his attention and it should be a relatively easy mission. But he also knew not to take anything for granted and spent more time surveilling the home. After a couple of hours, he headed back to the CIA Headquarters where he was going to meet Intelligence Agent Jerney for dinner at Famous Dave's.

TJ waited patiently while Jerney was exactly 23 minutes late and then they ordered the "Feast for Two" to share with drinks consisting of ice tea and lemonade.

After some small talk, TJ asked Jerney why he joined the CIA.

"Actually, I had thought about it for a while but finally pulled the trigger when Trump won. I can't stand these Liberals and wanted to do something great for my country and work under President Trump. What about you?"

"Hold on a second now. Why didn't you like…join the military?"

"I don't like to get up early."

"How's that working out for you?"

"It's not…seems like almost everyone has to get up early for work."

Intelligence Agent Jerney was a young 23 year old with big ideas. He confided in TJ that after President Trump finishes his two terms, then he was going to be a day trader the rest of his life and make easy money that way. *Ok*, thought TJ, *we'll just see how that pans out for you.* After dinner, TJ headed back to his home on base. He rose early around 0300 to take care of his next mission and then he returned back home upon the completion of said mission.

TJ was back in his office by 0900 and had breakfast in the cafeteria consisting of a ham and cheese omelet---with cheese sauce, bacon and extra crispy hash browns with coffee and milk. Sitting at his desk, Judy entered and presented him with more coffee and a chocolate donut. *Good thing that I didn't fill up at breakfast,* he reflected.

His first order of business was to inform his boss that the mission was accomplished. However, Judy informed him that Mr. Morgan was coming in late today. So he kept himself busy with other tasks until 1600 when he turned on Hannity.

"Welcome to Hannity and I'm Sean Hannity. This is a Fox News Alert. We have a major breaking story right now. Democratic Senator Simpson was just discovered dead at his home in Seat Pleasant, Maryland a few hours ago. This is what we know so far. A neighbor reported seeing a body in the senator's driveway and called police. Upon arriving, the police discovered that the body was that of the senator's. It appears that the senator was struck by a vehicle and was dead by the time that the police arrived. Now get this. A known prostitute was found in the home and police have taken her downtown to police headquarters for questioning," Sean stated and continued after a brief pause:

"I just received word that the police chief of Seat Pleasant is having a news conference…let's go there now to our Fox affiliate."

"Thank you Sean. I'm Hogan Roberts here in Seat Pleasant, Maryland at the rented home of Senator Simpson where he was found deceased from being run over by some type of vehicle. Ok, it looks like the police chief is about to speak so let's tune in."

The camera then swung over to cover the man at the microphone dressed in a dark blue shirt with a shiny badge that identified him as the police chief. The police chief raised his hands for quiet before speaking.

"I'm Police Chief Aguilar for the City of Seat Pleasant. I will tell you what we know so far. Senator Simpson was discovered in his driveway deceased today. A neighbor discovered the body and called 911 to report the finding. We have taken a young woman who was living with the senator in for questioning and at this time she is not a suspect. She admits that she is the senator's mistress and has been living with him here for the last 4 years. She does have a police record for prostitution and she was charged with that crime previously 3 times. At the time that the senator was discovered by police, he was found with a red foam clown's nose attached to his own nose. Forensics tells us that the senator was first backed over by a vehicle and then run over again as the vehicle pulled forward and then backed over once more as it left the scene. Near the body, detectives discovered a Russian playing card. It has not been determined yet if the playing card is somehow connected to this possible crime. That's all we know so far and we will keep all of you posted as other details emerge; thank you for coming today."

The police chief was then escorted through the throng of reporters to his car by other officers while reporters continued screaming questions at him. Once in his vehicle, the police car spun off.

Clinton Home in Chappaqua, NY (built in 1889)

The Clinton home in upstate New York was filled by heated discussion about President Trump this night in the Clintons study.

"I tell you Bill, that buffoon Trump is keeping his promises to the American people and do I need to remind you that that isn't good…for us?" Hilliary questioned.

"No, of course not my dear," Bill replied.

"Don't call me *dear* you asshole," shouted Hilliary. "Save that shit for the cameras. If only you didn't play around and screw with those other women. Especially when you have me at home! I told you that you can take me any time you want, but that wasn't good enough for you."

"But honestly Hilliary, I used to like climbing the 'Hill,' but you don't excite me anymore. I don't mean to be the way that I am and that's the truth." After a brief pause, "Life is too short and I'm attracted to other women…what can I say?"

"Do you have any idea how your actions have hurt and embarrassed me? It cost me the presidency…thanks Bill. I could have been a president also. It fact, I really am the president you know with three million more votes than that New York shyster."

"You can't blame me for that. You knew my past when *you* married me. I'm a horn-dog."

"You're an animal alright…a jackass!"

"Listen, we have stayed together because we wield more power and authority that way. Just look at all the money that we have stashed in Switzerland. We don't have a care in the world."

"You mean other than going to prison?"

"They wouldn't dare put a Clinton or Obama in jail." Then Bill pointed to a life size teddy bear in the study and said: "That bear there has a better chance of going to jail than we do. Let's just work together like we have for more than 30 years now. Barack and I are former presidents and they don't put former presidents in jail."

"Yeah…but what about me, dipshit?" asked Hilliary.

"Don't worry Hilliary, Barack and I will take care of you. You know that."

"No, I don't know that."

"Listen, we need each other like a candle needs a flame for our own benefit. I don't love you anymore and I know you don't love me either. But that doesn't mean that we can't be civil with each other. Maybe you'll run for president again in 2020," Bill reminded Hilliary.

"I am running for president again you dumbshit and the Democrats know that and are behind me 100 percent in that decision and I'll smash that dumb fuck next time."

Bill started laughing then.

"What's so funny asshole?" Hilliary questioned.

"I was just thinking about the fireworks that you bought for 2 million dollars that you forgot to cancel and that fired off in New York City, Trump's home city no less," chuckled Bill.

"Yeah, what's so funny about that?"

"Well, it appears to the American people that you are celebrating Trump's win and that's funny."

"You're an asshole and a pig."

"Ok sorry, I deserve that probably. But on a more serious note, just think, you were able to transfer $6 billion dollars of America's money while in the State Department to our overseas account and nobody the wiser. These Americans are so stupid it's unbelievable! I tell you, we don't have anything to worry about Hill."

Bill walked over to the liquor cabinet next to the television and poured himself a drink. As Hilliary sat down on the leather bound sofa, she spoke demandingly to her husband that she didn't love anymore.

"Turn on Fox News while you're standing there."

"Why not CNN?" questioned Bill. "You know…Clinton News Network."

"I don't want to hear from the dishonest media right now, I need the truth damn it!"

Bill turned on the television to the Fox News channel and Hannity was still on with a different story that was of interest to Hilliary…

"Joining us now is former Republican, New York City Mayor, Rudy Giuliana. Welcome to the show Mr. Mayor and how are you these days?"

"Just great Sean, I really do feel great these days. That's probably in large part to our new president that I'm so proud of."

"Mr. Mayor, I would like to play a segment to our viewers that we aired last year with you and then we can discuss it some. Can we get that up?" Sean asked of his producers.

From a previously aired episode of Hannity last year…

"So let's start with Jaron Cowan mayor. We were discussing something back stage. Would you like to expand on that?"

"I would and will. I was stating to you earlier on how Cowan is using a play on words to benefit Hilliary Clinton. I'm sure you noticed that instead of using the words that she was 'gross negligent' he used the words 'extremely careless' Sean."

"So what is that telling us Mr. Mayor?"

"Well, under federal law, 'gross negligent' is a crime compared to 'extremely careless' which is not."

"What about lying to Congress?"

"That's a crime as well. In fact, being a former United States Attorney, I have identified 15 items that need to be investigated."

"Let me put your chart up so the people at home can follow along because this is extremely important."

Using a split screen, Hannity viewers---including Bill and Hilliary---were then able to view a list of crimes that Mayor Giuliani identified to have been committed by the Clintons alone.

"What a crock of shit," Hilliary stated venomously as she viewed the chart. "They have no proof of anything. You know, if Fox News had been around when you ran for president, we probably wouldn't have won."

"Hold on a second, I want to hear the rest of this," Bill stated firmly as the following chart appeared on the screen...

1. **18 USC** § 201---Bribery
2. **18 USC** § 208---Acts Affecting a Personal Financial Interest
3. **18 USC** § 371---Conspiracy
4. **18 USC** § 1001---False Statements
5. **18 USC** § 1341---Fraud and Swindles
6. **18 USC** § 1343---Fraud by Wire
7. **18 USC** § 1349---Attempt and Conspiracy
8. **18 USC** § 1505---Obstruction of Juctice
9. **18 USC** § 1519---Destruction of Records in Federal Investigations or/and Bankruptcy
10. **18 USC** § 1621---Perjury
11. **18 USC** § 1905---Disclosure of Confidential Information

12. **18 USC** § 1924---Unauthorized Removal and Retention of Classified Documents or Material
13. **18 USC** § 2071---Concealment of Government Records
14. **18 USC** § 7201---Attempt to Evade or Defeat a Tax
15. **18 USC** § 7212---Attempts to Interfere With Administration of Internal Revenue Laws

"These are very specific things that you said should be investigated, and are real felonies and real crimes. People have gone to jail for these?" Sean questioned.

"That's right Sean, even just for one thing. That's what Martha Stewart went to jail for, only one of these."

"Wow. This has to be exposed and investigated thoroughly as the American people have a right to know. We have only 30 seconds left Mr. Mayor…last word."

"I'll tell you this Sean, it's so unbelievable that this can happen in our country at this day of age, just the monstrosity of all this corruption and with our national security being compromised and exposed as well…unbelievable. You think that Watergate was corruption? Take that corruption and multiply it by at least…I say twenty fold and that's what we have here today. The reality is that the American people have been repeatedly raped, not only by the Clintons, but by the entire Obama Administration as well, and, I'll tell you right now on your show for your viewers, that if we don't take back custody of our government and take corrective and future preventive action, we are well on our way to becoming a banana republic and I'm afraid that we will lose our country and our way of life…maybe forever. In other words Sean, we will become a politically unstable nation and be open for a hostile takeover by an aggressive country and the President doesn't want to see that happen. As a successful businessman, President Trump has great clarity in this possible scenario occurring and that's why he ran for the presidency in 2016 as he felt that he couldn't stay on the sidelines any longer and watch this happen to our country that he loves with all of his heart and soul," Mayor Giuliani stated with passion.

"Like what hostile country per se?" Sean questioned.

"China for example; they hold 20 percent of our debt, they have been stealing our intellectual property for years, they have been building up their military for some time now, and, they have announced to the world their desire for global dominance. We better wake up and smell the roses or prepare for the worse…war with China, which would most likely draw in Russia, Iran and North Korea. That's all that I can say about that Sean…World War 3."

"Ok, absolutely last thought Mayor."

"Corruption in our government needs to be thoroughly investigated, people prosecuted and held accountable and many need to go to prison. If we don't 'Drain the Swamp' and squash all of this corruption while we have the opportunity, our country will self-destruct as we know it…mark my words Sean. People need to go to prison with this out of control corruption and massive abuse of power. When people go to prison and are held accountable, that acts as a deterrent for possible future political corruption. When no one goes to prison and no accountability occurs, that acts as an accelerant."

"We may need more prison space then…a lot more I would imagine. Let's go to a break and when we come back, we will ask the Mayor Giuliani about Hilliary's mutilation of 13 cell phones…with a hammer."

"If I may say so quickly, that's destruction of federal records in a federal investigation Sean. If you have nothing to hide, then why would you destroy all these cell phones with a hammer no less that were under subpoena?"

"What about bleach bit and wiping the servers clean? I tell you Mr. Mayor, you can't make this stuff up…unbelievable. Unfortunately, this all makes for a good book that I am hoping someone will write and I'll buy a copy or five, if they'll autograph it for me that is. This will even make a better movie I bet. Alright, we'll be right back."

Bill turned off the television as a commercial came on for Snuggle Soft Toilet Paper.

"That crap again," Hilliary raged. "Why can't they just let it go? Son of a bitches…all of them! Especially that Hannity! I think that we need to find some way of shutting Mr. Hannity down…and soon! I'm the only real president of the people…I had three million more votes than that stupid fuck! That should count for something!"

CNN
Augaytus Corbett 69°

"I'm Augaytus Corbett and I want to welcome former presidential candidate Hilliary Clinton to our show. Welcome Mrs. Clinton to 69 degrees."

"Thanks Augaytus. I have to tell you that I love watching your show. You make good sense with your political calculations."

"Well thank you Mrs. Clinton, I appreciate that."

"Please, I think that we know each other well enough that you can skip the formalities. Just call me Hilliary."

"That's fine. I want to let our viewers know that last week we asked Mrs. Clinton…excuse me, I mean Hilliary, to come on today so that we can explore what went so wrong with the 2016 election and how a fascist, homophobic, Islamphobic, misogynist, racist, sexist and xenophobe become president, she agreed and is here now to help our viewers gain a fundamental understanding of what went wrong. What went wrong Hilliary?"

"I won the places in our country that are diverse, optimistic, looking forward and the people that voted for him are looking backwards. They are all backwards, uneducated hicks and basically a basket full of deplorables. From the outcome of the election, it seems that unfortunately, the fabric of our country is impregnated with deplorables. What I mean is that the majority of our country is made up of these types of people. They are not educated whatsoever and that's why Senator Sherman and I wanted to offer a free college education. Just look at what our country has become with so many uneducated people in our society. Why do you think Walmart's profits are going through the roof? I tell you Augaytus, people without an education are lost souls and do not understand how to vote properly."

"I would suspect that there must be other reasons as well."

"You are right. Blacks and Mexicans were told by the Trump campaign that I don't care about them…and that's not true. I do care about *all* people whether they vote for me or not. I was told that polls have uncovered that boyfriends and husbands told their girlfriends or wives to vote for Trump. It's ashamed that these same females don't have an independent thought in their head or enough of a brain to vote for me."

"Are you planning on running again in 2020 Hilliary?"

"Yes I am Augaytus. My advisors are advising me to run again after Mr. Trump finally screws up the country. After four years of Trump, even the deplorables will feel the need to vote for me since they will be too afraid to vote for another chuckleheaded Republican and I have the full support of the Democrats."

"I see. Do you have a different strategy prepared for the 2020 election?"

"Yes I do. I was just told recently by a friend of mine that when you are at a Walmart, you can smell the Trump supporters, so we'll be visiting several Walmarts across the nation and we'll be bringing our message of hope for the country to these deplorables."

"What exactly will be your message to the country?"

"I'm glad that you asked that question Augaytus. We will raise your taxes; have open borders; abolish ICE, especially since they are racist and are not adding value to our country; free college for those that want to escape the deplorable title; reparations for Hispanics that have been separated from their children on the border; *real* gun control, as it's about time that we start confiscating guns in order to make our citizens and non-citizens safe, and I might add, shutting down these stupid, criminal investigations that are costing tax payers millions."

"Why raise taxes? Isn't that a bad thing?"

"The reason that we'll raise taxes is to pay for all of the social programs that the American people want and expect from their government. Like free education for all that want it, free medical for our Hispanic friends that are either living here or visiting for an extended amount of time, in fact, free medical for all and a pay raise for our folks on unemployment. Under Trump, the cost of living is going up and so should people's social benefits."

"Ok, let me ask you about open borders then…what's the advantage of that for the United States? In fact, is there an advantage?"

"Of course, there is an advantage I think. With President Trump creating more jobs in America, that is driving the need for more workers to fill those positions. It is just common sense Augaytus…just common sense," Hilliary stated while shaking her head and smiling like everyone should be able to understand and relate to this rationale. "More jobs for more workers."

"I am being told that we have a commercial break coming up and when we come back with Hilliary, we'll ask her for some more information on these social programs for those that need or want them…"

CIA Headquarters

TJ was just told by Judy that Randy and the Director would like to see him in Randy's office. So he trudged over to his boss's office via Judy's reception area. Randy greeted him warmly and asked him to sit down. He informed TJ that Judy taped CNN and that he wanted to play it back to see what they were reporting about Senator Simpson. Judy brought coffee in for the men as they made themselves comfortable in their seats and Judy started the recording of CNN...

"We now have the details involving the death of New York Senator Simpson, at his home in Seat Pleasant, Maryland. His body was discovered by a pedestrian passing by who phoned in the call to the police. Upon arriving at the scene of the crime, police discovered Senator Simpson already dead. While investigating the crime scene, police discovered a Russian playing card. The police are now speculating that a Russian operative must have followed the senator home and ran him over with some type of motor vehicle. The senator's housekeeper, who was at home at the time of the crime, has been taken to police headquarters for more extensive questioning..."

Randy hit the mute button on the remote when TJ was about to reply.

"Wow, that's a little different than what Fox News reported and what I know to have happened. Fox News is much closer to the truth. It seems that CNN just flat out lies," TJ commented.

Randy cleared his throat and replied to TJ's comment: "This is what is happening to our country now politically with mainstream news organizations outright lying about stuff that don't favor the Liberals and hence you have the dishonest media; fake news. At least, Fox News does try to get it right and are by far the most honest."

Director Lannister took a sip of his coffee and nodded his agreement and turned to TJ to ask the question that was on his and Randy's mind.

"What really happened, TJ?"

"I didn't find the senator at home early morning, so I decided to come back at another time," TJ explained. "As I was backing out from his driveway, I hit something. I was backing up a little too fast maybe, and at first, I thought I hit a dog so I pulled forward. I got out with my flashlight to check the spot behind my truck and immediately discovered that it was our target and that he was deceased. I suppose that he died from head trauma. I surveilled the area carefully and realized that no one was the wiser for the incident and quickly left."

"Well everything worked out fine but we have to be careful you know…good job under the circumstances," Director Lannister complemented. "However, I think that it's time we send you to camp."

Director Lannister looked over to Randy for a confirmation nod while TJ looked askance of his boss since he had no idea what the director was talking about. Randy did give his nod of approval and noticed the questioning look on TJ's face.

"What he's talking about is an assignment to Camp Mayberry," interjected Randy. "Camp Mayberry is an area of the Marine Corps Base in Quantico, Virginia that has allocated a parcel of land designated as Camp Mayberry. It opened in 2012 as a retreat for CIA, DEA and FBI agents to relax and unwind. They have a golf course, tennis courts, gym and free-standing apartments and of course, you are able to utilize all the comforts of the base as well. It's the best of both worlds…CIA and Military."

"We'll let things cool down for a while and then we'll have you come back to work when we feel that it's ok to do so. Think of this as a well-earned, paid vacation that you deserve," asserted Director Lannister. "Don't look into this as anything other than a break. We will inform you when to return. When you come back, we will have your next target identified for you. Just relax and enjoy yourself. That's the purpose of going away to camp."

The Director then handed TJ his orders for Camp Mayberry and went on to say that he will check in with the site manager there. So TJ set up a final racquetball meet with

Jerney, Ray and Stefan. Afterwards, Jerney and he went out to eat at the nearby Golden Corral.

★ ★ ★ ★ ★

While at Golden Corral, TJ explained to Jerney about being assigned to Camp Mayberry for a while.

"That's great TJ! From what I hear from other agents that have been assigned there, you'll absolutely love it there buddy as it is a really nice place. They have these small, but quaint, free-standing apartments with maid service included, horseback riding and even canoeing on the Potomac River! I wish I could go there with you instead of where I am going."

"Where are you going then?" TJ asked with concern in his voice.

"I'm being transferred to PI…the Philippine Islands for intelligence work there."

"What part of the Philippines?"

"My orders say Lumbia Air Base which is in Mindanao."

"It won't be that bad. I went there a few times when I was in the Navy. When do you leave?"

"I leave tomorrow morning…and you?"

"I leave tomorrow as well."

The two friends finished up eating and then went their separate ways as the next day would be a new and exciting adventure for both men

.

Chapter 5
Ω

"The most terrifying words in the English language are: I'm from the government and I'm here to help."

---President Ronald Reagan

TJ arrived at the Quantico base the next day with his military bag in tow. He displayed his badge and the guard at the gate told him where to go. As he was driving to the next gate for Camp Mayberry, TJ notice what a nice day it was. It was sunny with some fluffy clouds, no wind and a mild temperature. He also noticed that the base was bustling with activity. He knew from research that this base was established in 1917. *A lot is actually happening on this base,* he considered. *The FBI, CIA and the DEA were all here for some significant purpose.*

The FBI Academy was located here as well as the DEA Training Academy…and of course, Camp Mayberry, which was utilized only by the CIA, DEA and the FBI.

As TJ approached the next gate, he had his badge out to show the guard. However, this was not the correct protocol and the guard informed him quickly.

"Sorry sir, I will need to see some official orders please," the guard ostensibly requested.

"Sorry, I'm bad…my first time here."

So TJ dug out his orders and showed the guard who then waved him on after giving him directions to the site manager's office where he would need to check in. After parking in front of the office, he walked in with his orders in hand, just in case they were needed again.

"Checking in?" the woman behind the counter questioned.

"Yes ma'am. TJ Law…CIA."

"Yes, I have you right here Mr. Law. My name is Jean and I'm the site manager here at Camp Mayberry and it's nice to meet you. TJ Law…I like that name," she told him as they shook hands.

"Let me tell you a little bit about us here. We have 196 free standing apartment homes all with basements. In the basement is a workout area and upstairs is a bedroom, kitchenette, laundry room, bathroom and a front room. We have maid service every day; if it is not needed, just hang the sign out on the door knob. Maid service is between 1000 and 1200…if needed. There are two televisions, one upstairs and one downstairs, with plenty of channels to watch, including, Fox News, the Military Channel and of course, The Andy Griffith Show. Camp Mayberry was so named in honor of Andy Griffith and the other stars in the show. Actually, Ron Howard, the only living star from the show I might add, visited us here last year! He was a guest of the base commander and was informed about the camp and he just had to come by to see Camp Mayberry for himself. A very nice man I must say. Andy would be sooo proud of him."

TJ was just nodding his head while listening as Jean rambled on, but it was kind of interesting, he allowed, especially since he loved the show and all of its characters.

"Ok Mr. Law, I am giving you apartment home number 109. Here's a map of Camp Mayberry and I highlighted how to get to your apartment home already. I was so looking forward to meeting you…love that name. Also, here is a map of the base. Here, take my business card in case you need anything. My phone number and pager are listed there if you need anything; any questions?"

"Thanks Jean. What about activities?"

"Good question…glad you asked," Jean responded as she reach under the counter and pulled out another piece of paper and laid it on top for TJ to view.

"This is an exhaustive list of activities on base and in the camp. The ones that are highlighted require an appointment and you can do that through me. Otherwise, just relax and enjoy yourself. We all know that you people work hard in keeping our country safe and sound and we really appreciate it so much. Is there anything else that I can do for you?" she asked.

As Jean handed TJ his key, he questioned her how big the camp was and she told him that it was around five-thousand acres.

He took his key and climbed into his Tacoma and headed to find his new home for…who knew how long?

TJ found the home alright and was pleased that it even had an awning for his truck. He unlocked the door and was really impressed with how clean it was with that pine scent in the air; as if they had just mopped it. He checked out the home before unpacking his bag and then settled in with…Fox News of course!

Democratic Resistance Party Meeting #3

The Resistance Party was meeting again this time with now three of their members 'missing in action.' However, two new Republican members have joined…by conference calls along with another Democrat.

In attendance were the following:

Tim Payat – DNC Chairman
Representative Maybel Wileen – (D-CA)
Kadin Elkhart – DNC Deputy Chairman
Senator Maro Wesley – (D-VA)
Senator Esmeralda Willow – (D-MA)
Senator Burney Sherman – (I-VT)
Representative Abel Stoner – (D-CA) Resistance Party Chair
Representative Jarl Lidio – (D-GA)

And via conference call:

Senator Jace Melvin – (R-AZ) Line 1
Senator Bow Cutler – (R-TN) Line 2
Senator Jory Flann – (R-AZ) Line 3

"Ok, this meeting will now come to order," Representative Stoner sounded. "I want to inform everyone about our three newest members…on conference calls we have on line two Senator Bow Cutler and on line three is Senator Jory Flann and everyone I believe is already familiar with Senator Jace Melvin who is on line one. Also, Representative Jarl Lidio is joining us as well."

For some that may not know him, Representative Lidio stood up and took a bow upon his introduction.

The others shook their heads in acknowledgement. Tonight's meeting was taking place at the Hart Senate Office Building on the 3rd floor at Senator Maro Wesley's office in his conference room. Looking around the chamber, one would notice pictures of well-known Liberals such as Barack Obama, Bill and Hilliary Clinton and even Esmeralda Willow!

"Can I have everyone's attention please?" requested Representative Stoner. "We have a lot to focus on tonight people. We have now lost three of our dearest members to…what? We don't really know what is going on. It appears to be the work of the Russians, but who knows? Great work with the media as well everyone. Let's keep it up."

"Impeach 45…impeach 45…impeach 45," chanted Representative Whitney.

Over the speaker from line 1 the voice of Senator Melvin rang out with, "Will someone shut that stupid bitch up please?"

"Maybel, let's save that chant for the media please," Abel stated. "Now then, we need another plan for Trump.

We can still work with our first plan, but now we need to move on to step two…any ideas?"

"I know what we can do," answered Senator Wadd. "We can hire someone to take him out. You know, like we did with another someone who was leaking private email information to Wikileaks."

"Well, since he is the President, that would be a tall order, don't you think?" asked Senator Flann from line 3. "Let's get real folks. I'm not here for dumb shit."

"Then why are you here Flann?" questioned Senator Cutler from line 2.

"I'm totally here to get rid of that pervert," announced Senator Flann.

Senator Sherman, who had about nodded off, stirred when he heard the word 'pervert' and asked, "Who me?"

"No not you, you stupid fuck," retorted Senator Flann. "I'm talking about Trump. He called me a flake. Can you believe that?"

"Don't feel too bad, he called me Pocahontas!" stated Senator Wadd.

"We are getting away from our mission folks," Senator Crenshaw reminded everyone from line 2. "I simply don't like the ass and that's why I'm here. I want him out of the office one way or another. Can we get down to brass tacks now?"

"It's a sad day for our country when we can't seem to get rid of a president who is unhinged and shouldn't be in office anyway," reflected Tim Payat. "Let's get this moron out of office."

Once again, Senator Sherman stirred awake with, "My constituents want free and unfettered education and medical for all, including our undocumented friends from the South!"

Everyone was looking at Senator Sherman when Senator Wesley announced, "I say we allow Senator Sherman to lie down in my utility room since he seems to be low energy today, and every day in fact, and I do have a nice cot in there."

"I don't need to lie down scumbag. I just need to get free education and medical for my peoples. That's what we all need for our constituents I might add," Senator Sherman replied passionately.

"Do you even know what meeting you are at old man?" asked Kadin Elkhart.

"Of course I know what our agenda is…you punk. We are here to secure free education and medical for our constituents as per our leader's request," responded Senator Sherman.

Sighs went up from the group just then.

"What?" Senator Sherman questioned looking confused.

Representative Stoner took control of the meeting again and explained to Senator Sherman the purpose of their meeting this night.

"We are here to identify another cause of action to take down the President. Anyway, I do have a special guest that I would like to introduce now."

Stoner walked over to a door that led to another room and opened it and invited someone to enter the room. A tall man nicely dressed followed Stoner into the conference room.

"Does anyone know who this gentleman is?" questioned Stoner.

When no one confirmed knowing the gentleman in question, Representative Stoner then continued with the forthcoming introduction.

"This is Piran Styles or otherwise simply known as 'PS.' He works in the FBI and he's helping our cause. He is anti-Trump and has been working for the same conclusion as the rest of us…impeachment of Trump. Also, he is working to help our true leader to rise up and take her seat as the head of our country. Does anyone have any questions for our *special guest*?" asked Representative Stoner.

Senator Wesley spoke first with two questions, "What are you planning to do for us Piran and what have you already done to help the cause?"

"First off, let's get my name straight…shall we? You people are allowed to call me only by my working name which is PS…not BS and not Piran. What are my qualifications you ask? Well…let's see. Does helping the Clintons earn money from the Uranium One deal to the Clinton Foundation count? What about keeping our leader Hilliary from being interviewed under oath by the FBI? How about keeping Clinton's emails from being discovered? Or, digging up dirt on the Trump campaign that is now in an investigation by the deep state? What about arranging Bill to meet with the Attorney General on the tarmac? What about changing the wording from 'gross negligence' to 'extremely careless' for Hilliary? There's a lot more that I have done for our leader and our American Liberal friends that I won't mention. So now, what more can I do? I will keep the pot a stewing and continue working behind the scenes and you people do what you can in the media, even if it is trumped up stories on that dumbass President that we now have to contend with. I'll tell you all this, so pay close attention. You are probably wondering what went wrong and I can clear that up as well. We took it for granted that Hilliary would win. However, we discounted the Electoral College. But, you will be the first to know that we are working on getting rid of that system. I won't say how so don't ask. Also, there are others just like me in the FBI working towards a common goal for all Liberals. That damn Fox News refers to us as the *deep state*…to be sure. We are a deep state and we will continue to make progress toward our goal. Do I need to mention what that is again? Good, I was hoping not. You Congressional people don't seem to live in the real world…but I do; bottom line is we will stop Trump at any cost!"

Piran Styles, otherwise known as PS, took a deep breath and continued.

"In future meetings, I will update everyone on the good works that we loyal Liberals are making in the FBI. Are there any questions now?"

No one made a move to speak as if all was in awe of this hardened and clearly dedicated and loyal FBI man to the cause. The meeting adjourned shortly later and all the participants went their separate ways.

★ ★ ★ ★ ★

TJ was having a very relaxing vacation at Camp Mayberry, when he had an epiphany. He was amazed that he was getting paid for doing something that he loved…what a great life he thought! He worked out at the gym, played tennis and even went horseback riding! But one thing that he really liked was The Massage Hut. This was where agents could go and receive massages for free! What a country…what a CIA! However, only one one-hour massage was allowed per day. When he went there for the first time, he was assigned to Lisa who was a nice Japanese girl that knew how to make him feel better. So every appointment that he made was made with massage therapist Lisa. She was truly beautiful and had a touch that would make a man sit up and beg for buttermilk! She seemed to like him as well.

He had been stationed there for several weeks already and made two close friends and allies; one was from the CIA and the other from the FBI. These were both men that he had a lot in common with such as serving in the Navy, Trump supporters and respecting the rule of law no matter the politics involved.

FBI Special Agent Bob Mingo was a no non-sense kind of person who believed in standing up for his beliefs no matter what…right or wrong, and you were not going to sway his thinking. But TJ found him to be an honorable man with his strict beliefs against illegal drug use.

CIA Intelligence Agent Conrad Lonzo was also a very credible fellow with strong beliefs about how our country was headed in the wrong direction. He was a little less serious than Bob, but could become earnest in a moment's notice. He was a direct shooter and generally fun to be around. He liked hearing John Denver songs, especially the song called, Country Roads.

All three men felt a bond and agreed to keep in touch. Even though none of them could speak about cases that they were assigned to, they all agreed to cooperate with each other as needed. TJ felt that this was beneficial for him as he now had an FBI contact.

On this day, Bob needed to go into town for a bank transaction and all three men agreed to go together. They jumped into TJ's double cab Tacoma and with Bob in the back they were off for Dale City. After a fifteen minute drive, they pulled up to the Dale City Heritage Bank.

"We'll just wait here Bob and you go in and take care of your business," TJ suggested.

"Ok, I'll be right back, shouldn't take me too long though…unless there is a bank robbery in progress," Bob replied in jest.

However, a few minutes later, TJ and Conrad became suspicious of three men wearing long coats that were seen going into the bank; it wasn't cold out. The federal men felt compelled to enter the building and to take up positions to cover their friend as well as the other bank customers…just in case.

Upon observation, TJ noticed that Bob was talking to a well-dressed individual in the corner. One of the suspicious men was in line as the other two were in position on either side of the lobby. Conrad and TJ took similar positions as no communication was needed.

As the line started to shorten, the suspicious man in the black trench coat moved up to the window and handed the teller a note. The teller read the note carefully and then was frantically scrambling to present stacks of bills on the counter. Conrad and TJ calmly walked up to both of the other men with guns drawn and positioned them behind their heads.

The dirtbag that TJ walked up to heard him whisper, "Don't move lowlife or I'll kill you."

Conrad must have told the other scumbag something similar because he didn't move either. The third loser, probably feeling that something was wrong, turned and looked behind him for his support. Seeing both men incapacitated, he started to raise his pistol when TJ shot him in the head…instantly quelling any possible action that maybe he was precipitating.

As Conrad and TJ were putting the other two in handcuffs, Bob was showing his credentials to the gentleman that he had been speaking with…the bank's president, who then instructed a bank employee to call the police and alert them that the attempted robbery was stopped in progress by three government agents.

After the police arrived on the scene and took statements from everyone, the three federal men were allowed to leave. As they were leaving the area, TJ noticed that one of the losers arrested gave him the finger. *Must be telling me that I'm number one,* he concluded. Back to Camp Mayberry the three men returned where they checked in with Jean for messages. Both Conrad and TJ had orders to return to CIA Headquarters the next day. What choice did they have? So Conrad and TJ immediately scheduled another massage…of course.

The Obama Mansion in the Kalorama Neighborhood in D.C.

Michelle had just helped her mother to bed for a daytime nap in her mother's own suite upstairs, of their rented 8,200 square foot home and then continued on downstairs to the white painted kitchen, where she knew Barack was waiting patiently to talk to her about something important. As she took a seat, Barack continued to stand and started the conversation.

"Michelle, I've been thinking. The Democrats look to me as their leader for the party still even though I'm not officially in politics anymore."

"I thought their leader was Hilliary," Michelle stated.

"I thought so too. But I was talking to Representative Jarl Lidio and he as much said that some of the other members want to oust Hilliary and have me back coordinating things."

"But you can't run again honey."

"I know that dear. They just want me for my organizational skills and speaking abilities. Jarl also asked me to pick someone competent to run against Trump in 2020."

"Do you have someone in mind Barack?"

"Well, what I was thinking about is President Michelle Obama; your thoughts dear?"

"We've talked about this before and I don't really want to get involved in politics. You know that Barack."

"I know that Michelle. But your country needs you."

"What do you mean by that?"

"I mean that for the good of the country Michelle, we need you to be president. It's like this. You are the only Democrat that is popular enough to beat Trump in 2020. Also, we need to stop these damn investigations that are going on right now. I know that they don't put former presidents in jail, especially when they are popular like Bill and me, but I would feel much better having you in office. If we can get The White House and that other House back, then I'm sure that we can hold on to power for generations to come; especially with more and more illegals voting now. That damn idiot Trump took us all by surprise when he won, but I should have figured out that Hilliary was a flawed candidate and the Democrats should have offered someone else instead."

"Barack, you knew that the Democratic Party was having money issues and that Hilliary was able to substantially add funds to their coffer needs from that $6 billion that she took from the State Department that is now in her and Bill's overseas USB Switzerland account. Plus, we didn't really know how all of this was going to play out dear. Don't beat yourself up for it."

Barack just shook his head as he was in deep thought.

"Barack, what about Hilliary? You ought to know that she is expecting the Democratic Party to endorse her in 2020 for president…again"

"Michelle, the reality is that she's a loser. Right now she's a two time loser. Can the Democratic Party really afford a three time loser? I ask you to think on that for a moment."

The couple paused in their thinking about future options for the Democratic Party, which were few in number, when Michelle spoke again.

"Ok Barack, I'll run if they want me to, but what about Hilliary? Won't she take this hard?"

"I don't care dear, the greater good is at stake here."

"Who is going to tell her Barack…you?"

"No Michelle, Jarl said that he would join the Resistance Party and gradually work you into the mix. You know that he pulls some weight with that bunch of idiots. It shouldn't be a problem. Hilliary is old and old news. On the other hand, you are young, beautiful, graceful and intelligent."

"Thank you Barack. Sometimes you say the sweetest things. No wonder the American people are in awe of your speaking ability," and they both laughed.

"Don't worry Michelle, she'll get over it. Bill and her can live a nice, quiet life with all that money that I allowed them to, well, let's just say, borrow. Plus, Bill promised to pay it back someday," Barack chuckled at this as if he really thought that the Clintons would really pay back that money that technically belonged to the American people; no chance of that happening.

The Obamas, like the Clintons, felt absolutely no guilt over what they were doing to the American people and to the country. They considered the American people to be inferior to that of the ruling class. Barack thought that if the American people are so stupid, why not fleece 'these sheep' for all that they are worth? The ruling class is superior anyway. *What was that cliché,* thought Barack, *from Darwin? Oh yeah, 'the survival of the fittest.' That's us,* mused Barack. *You only live once so why not make the most of it?* He then thought back to the day when they invited the Trumps to The White House. *What an idiot Trump was. He told me, on camera no less, that I was a great man. At least he called that one right!*

Michelle jarred Barack out of his thoughts.

"Barack, I forgot to mention that we received a message from Vladimir yesterday."

"What does that old reprobate want now? We gave him twenty percent of our uranium already."

"Barack, he wants you to speak the first Friday of next month at a christening of a new Russian submarine class."

"Have Joni (Barack's personal assistant) tell them I'm busy with a horseshoe convention raising money for our intercity youths and can't make it. Besides, I remember how much they paid Bill."

"They are willing to pay you $1 million for your speech and they are naming their newest submarine class after you honey."

"Well, that's different now. Since Vladimir pays more than them damn horseshoe players, have Joni write me a great speech for Putin and tell her to cancel my horseshoe convention!"

★ ★ ★ ★ ★

The next day, Conrad and TJ returned to the CIA campus and to their respective work areas. TJ learned that Conrad's work area was located on a different floor than his. He also learned from Judy that the director had a meeting scheduled for 1300 that afternoon for all CIA personnel and that Director Lannister wanted to see him at 1000. *He probably wants to give me my next case,* he convinced himself.

Being well disciplined from the military, TJ was on time for his meeting with the director. As he entered the director's office, he noticed right away that his boss was there as well as a young woman all prim and proper sitting there.

As he entered the office, the director stood and came around his desk to greet TJ with a firm handshake.

"TJ, it's good to see you again. How was your *time off*," Director Lannister asked sincerely.

"Actually it was…pretty great. I made friends with a couple of other agents while I was there."

Director Lannister waved TJ to an empty seat.

"Good, I'm glad you had some quality time off, but now it's back to work. Let me introduce you to Jessy."

Jessy and TJ shook hands with a, "Nice to meet you," greeting.

"Jessy is an analyst for us and will be providing you with any files you need from now on. She's assigned to you but has other duties as well. But I want her to give you priority when needed."

The director and Jessy locked eyes as Jessy was nodding in the affirmative. She understood the communication that came from the director's eyes.

"No problem Director Lannister. I'll do all I can to assist TJ."

"Good then." Director Lannister commented. "Also, don't forget about our important required meeting at 1300. I want everybody there and on time in our auditorium."

The director then dismissed Jessy so he could talk to Randy and TJ in private. The director gave Randy a confirmation nod and Randy started the conversation.

"Your next target will be Senator Esmeralda Willow," Randy stated. "You'll get her file from Jessy and I want you to study it carefully. Her department is on the first floor, north side. Just follow the signs that say 'Analysis Department.' Jessy's in cube 312 by the way; you can't miss it."

TJ returned to his office and figured that he would pick up the file after the important meeting. He wondered what the director was going to talk about that was so important. Anyway, his next stop was the cafeteria for lunch.

Just as he was about to leave, Conrad phoned.

"Yeah?" TJ answered his phone. He knew that it was Conrad calling since they had caller ID.

"It's Conrad."

"Yeah, I know. Caller ID…did you forget?"

"Your right, I'm bad."

"I'm just giving you a hard time. Want to join me for lunch in the cafeteria? I'm buying."

"I was just calling you for the same thing and I'm buying!" Conrad stated.

"Ok, you win Conrad…you can buy this time."

Both men had a good laugh at this and thus agreed to meet in the cafeteria.

Out in the hallway TJ bumped into Jim the CIA Weapon's Specialist.

"TJ, how are things with you?"

"I'm fine Jim, and yourself?"

"Mother-in-law died."

"I'm sorry to hear that Jim."

"Why, I'm not. But thanks just the same. She was really a pain in my ass if you know what I mean; a real PIMA."

"I'm single and don't want any wife or a mother-in-law for that matter," TJ asserted.

"Good for you and don't get married. That's my advice for you and at no charge."

"Well, thanks for the free advice. Heading anywhere special?"

"Down to get something to eat…why do you ask?"

"Conrad and I are eating lunch in the cafeteria…want to join us?"

"I can do that since I haven't seen Conrad for a while."

So the men headed down the hallway for the elevator.

"What's this meeting about that we're going to…you know anything about that Jim?"

"The scuttlebutt from my sources is, that it's an 'all hands on deck' and a 'come to Jesus' meeting about the corruption plaguing the FBI and that's tells us that it's a very serious meeting. We'll find out soon enough anyway."

TJ thought immediately about his new found friend Bob and hoped that he wasn't involved in anything nefarious at the FBI. However, he knew about some of the corruption that was being discovered since the firing of Jaron Cowan. He decided to ask Bob about Cowan the next time that he saw him.

The men finished their lunch and headed for the auditorium and arrived on time with a few minutes to spare. All three of them grabbed seats in the back and made themselves comfortable as possible. Looking around, TJ noticed the architecture and figured it for art deco. He knew that art deco was a popular design from the 20's and 30's. The auditorium was huge and he didn't know how many people it could hold, but he did notice that most of the seats had asses in them.

At exactly at 1300, Randy walked out onto the stage that was displayed with both American and CIA flags and made an impressive introduction for the director. Director Lannister then walked out on cue and shook Randy's hand

and thanked him for such a fine introduction. As the clapping tapered off, the director started to speak:

"I want to thank you all for coming today. I feel it's extremely important to keep everyone in the loop and articulate what is happening with our sister department…the FBI. President Trump has been voicing his concerns about the corruption inside the bureau and about the national security of our country. Since Director Cowan was fired, many more items have come to light. I want to make sure that we don't parallel what is negatively affecting the FBI. I don't care what your politics are, but we will be non-partisan when it comes to our jobs. Mr. Trump is now our President, duly elected by the people and for the people and he is our leader now and we will respect him as such. For those of you with a heartburn and can't adjust to the now present situation, I encourage you to see me in my office after this meeting and I will help you out with your issue…literally."

TJ looked around to discover any disconcerting body language but detected none. In fact, he noticed how quiet it got and figured that you could have heard a pin drop.

After a minor pause to let everything sink in, the director then continued.

"What I'm speaking of is very serious people and the law of unintended consequences will apply…if necessary, and I don't mean good either. If we have any deep state crap going on in our agency, it better depart our midst and I mean damn fast. We work for the President and the American people and we don't need 'political hacks' inside the CIA. If you want to be a political hack, I would advise you to run for a Congressional office. If you have any hard feelings about Mr. Trump being our President, get over them or get the hell out. It's just that simple folks."

Another pause and then the director resumed speaking.

"I have met with President Trump personally and sincerely believe that his love for our country is foremost in his mind. I see what a difference he is making as well…a great difference I might add and I for one want to support that. I don't need to remind you that we are considered a world class intelligence agency and I don't want to see that tarnished in any way. We are the envy of the world and it's because of our finest traditions, dedication to our job and our love of country. All of us in some way contribute to the success, or the failure, of our agency and we need to stay the course for success. I do not foresee any issues in our agency at this time, but I wanted to be proactive and make sure that we are all on the same page. We are a team of professionals for the American people and our primary mission is to collect, analyze, evaluate and disseminate intelligence to assist the President in making informed decisions relating to national security.

"So I urge you, let's just do our job to the best of our abilities, support our President which is what's best for the American people and our country. Our nation unfortunately is greatly divided, but in the CIA we don't have to be. We all have an honorable mission, a nice place to work and a great salary with benefits, and more importantly…great teammates to work with!"

That seem to break the tension in the room somewhat and a few laughs could be heard.

"Also, on a lighter note" the Director continued, "some of you may already know that we do have a new FBI director and his name is Christopher A. Cray. Director Cray was sworn in on August 2nd after being confirmed by the U.S. Senate. I don't envy the mess that Director Cray is facing in the bureau and I have offered my support for his success in cleaning up that disorder that he's facing. I know Mr. Cray from past experiences and I can tell you that when he is done, the FBI will be an agency that all of us can be proud of, compared to the tatters that it's in now."

A brief pause…

"Ok, that's all I have for now. Thank you all for coming."

As everyone filed out of the auditorium, TJ bumped into Jessy who offered to escort him to her department for the file that he needed to pick up. On the way, the two of them discussed how they came to be working for the CIA. TJ mentioned his military background was similar to the CIA's mission. With Jessy, she had been working at her mother's fruit stand in California when she applied for her current position on the CIA's website---www.cia.gov/careers---and had to jump through the usual hoops for her employment.

"I'm currently a contract employee," Jesse stated, "with hopes of becoming a career employee sometime in the near future."

Once they arrived at cube 312, TJ told her what file he needed and she asked him to have a seat and that she would return with his file, which was located in the "file vault." He took a seat and noticed a picture of a nice looking woman on Jessy's desk. *Probably her mother* he realized and thought that she seemed to be in pretty good shape. *She must work out at the gym* he concluded. In the picture, she was holding a watermelon at what looked like a fruit stand in the background.

Jessy returned shortly with the file on Senator Esmeralda Willow. She knew better than to ask why he needed the file because that was not allowed or appropriate, even though she had a Top Secret clearance. She had to constantly keep in mind that while working here in the real world of the CIA, it was *CYA*...Cover Your Ass or else it was HTGT...Here Today Gone Tomorrow!

So without comment or question, she handed the file to TJ who thanked her and headed back to his office eager to start on his next mission.

Chapter 6
Ω

"The modern definition of 'racist' is someone who's winning an argument with a Liberal."

---Peter Brimelow

Trump Rally in Huntsville, Alabama 2017

As the estimated massive crowd of 12,000 waited impatiently for President Trump to make his appearance on stage, the noise level truly rose when he started to walk out wearing his signature red hat that read: "Make America Great Again." It was clear that these people loved their President!

Behind the podium that the President would speak from, was a large American flag. The crowd was waving Trump/Pence signs all the time while yelling at the top of their lungs. If you had been there, you could have felt the electric buzz in the air. Yes, the atmosphere was definitively charged this night!

President Trump allowed the crowd to unwind as he waved to his American political base---and to the cameras---while many in attendance waved the now famous rally signs of: "Make America Great Again," "Veterans for Trump" and of course, "Blacks for Trump."

Finally, President Trump stepped up to the microphone and as the crowd quieted down he started to speak.

"Isn't this a great crowd folks?"

A cheer went up.

"Do we love our military or what?"

A much bigger cheer could be heard clearly by those at home who couldn't attend the live event. President Trump raised his hands to calm the crowd before starting to speak again.

"Do we love our country or what?"

More cheering and flag waving occurred.

"Make America Great Again. Don't worry, she will be. We are working on it with Attorney General, Jeff Sessions."

The crowd started booing Jeff Sessions's name. But the President was able to capture control again and added: "We love Jeff Sessions, he's doing a good job for us and trust me…you will all be pleased with his work."

The gathering seemed to take this at face value and President Trump continued:

"Luther Strange will be taking over for Jeff as a U. S. Senator for the great state of Alabama and he will be good for our country. Jeff is doing a good job at protecting our borders. I just recently returned from a meeting at the United Nations General Assembly…"

Then as the cheers and clapping intensified, President Trump pulled away from the microphone and was clapping as well. Then the chant…USA…USA…USA… President Trump raised his fist in the air and shook it. As the noise finally died down, the President continued with his speech.

"We have some mighty bad people in this country, but we will take care of them. I'm working with our partners in this endeavor and I promise you, we will fix our country…one way or another. Keep your faith in God, in our country and in me and in that order. One of the greatest honors of my life is to represent the American people."

Then from someone in the assembled crowd came a shout: "We love you President Trump!"

"Thank you, I love you people too as well as our whole country," Trump responded. "The world is finally starting to respect us again for the first time in a long time. As you know, and I know you do, Obama was leading from behind with examples of sending more than $150 billion dollars to the number one state of terrorism and, apologizing to Iran for being in *their* international waters when they captured some of our sailors and, reducing our military drastically. And I do mean drastically folks; quite frankly, to very dangerous levels for our country and for our national security. When he sent some of those $150 billion dollars to Iran, it was on a private plane, with no markings on it and in the dead of the night. Isn't that what drug dealers do? People that exhibit that type of behavior have something to hide. Who in their right mind would do that? When I heard about it, I turned to Melania and asked her, 'What side is Obama on.' She just shook her head. This type of stupid behavior is hurting our country with national security and dumb ass decisions…unbelievable. Obama is a coward and I'm not afraid to speak the truth here and tell you that he has greatly damaged our country and he will be held accountable for his actions…I can tell you that. He and others I assure you will be held accountable. He doubled our National Debt in just eight years; put our National Security at risk, like no other time in history I might add, and, has allowed corruption to flourish within his administration to greater levels than that of Watergate by far. This is the man that the Democrats are so proud of? It took over 200 years for our country to acquire a National Debt of $10 trillion dollars, and with Obama, only eight years to double that figure…incredible! Obama, Bill and Crooked Hilliary and other political hacks will be dealt with to the full extent of the law…I can promise you that."

The Trump supporters sounded off when the President announced that last statement and started chanting: "Drain the Swamp…Drain the Swamp…Drain the Swamp." President Trump assured the audience that the "swamp" will be drained, if we have strong, tenacious Republican leaders in Congress. He communicated to the crowd that the country needed more Republicans elected to help his mission of making America great again since the Democrats are obstructionists.

Then the President went on with:

"We want peace with every nation, but we don't support a nut who wants to launch rockets all over the place."

President Trump pointed to the audience and said, "You know who I'm talking about…that's right, little Rocket Man!"

The noise level rose once again as President Trump backed away from the microphone and turned and captured a look at the American flag that was draped down behind him while clapping with his many supporters. After a short time, when the noise level dropped, the President walked back up to the microphone and continued:

"North Korea should have been handled a long time ago folks, with Clinton, Obama and I won't mention the Republicans. I believe that Obama was afraid of little Rocket Man. But don't worry. Our people and our allies are safe as we have their backs. We will take care of little Rocket Man. His days are numbered…if he doesn't change his ways and fast. I can tell you that. But don't worry, we are going to handle it because we have to. Obama…he left all of us with a hell of a mess, but working together with the American people, we will clean it up. I can tell you this…little Rocket Man is watching us right now, I can guarantee that. He's watching us like never before."

Then the President mentioned some other items as well, including Senator Jace Melvin not supporting the, "Repeal and Replace" of Obamacare. The crowd then went from cheering to booing…and quite loudly.

President Trump then mentioned that if Crooked Hilliary had won the election, and became the next president, then Alabama and the rest of the country would be required to turn their guns in. As the President paused for the moment, the crowd then started that familiar chanting: "Lock her up...Lock her up...Lock her up."

Finally, after more than an hour and a half, the President wound up his speech with pointing out the dishonest media and how Americans need to take back their country. He also included his favorite line... "We Will Make America Strong Again...We Will Make America Wealthy Again...We Will Make America Proud Again...We Will Make America Safe Again...and...We Will Make America Great Again!

"Thank you Alabama...I love you all! Thank you Alabama and God bless the USA!"

President Trump departed the stage with God Bless the USA playing and the audience was cheering like nothing before. As the sun was setting in Alabama, President Trump was back onboard Air Force One and heading to Joint Base Andrews and then on to The White House where plenty of work was waiting for his attention.

CIA Headquarters

TJ studied Senator Wadd's file carefully and took note of the fact that the President referred to her as "Pocahontas." Thinking back on the reason for this, he remembered that the President coined the name to her because she had lied about her ancestry claiming being a partially, "Native American" in order to advance her career in the nineties with Harvard Law School. *What a piece of shit!*

The senator's home was located in Cambridge, Massachusetts. *Interesting,* thought TJ. While in session, she shared a home with another senator in Falls Church, Virginia.

He continued reading her file. The next section that he looked at was her medical record. He noticed right away that she had degenerative neck disc disease...*a pain in the neck, huh? But she's a pain in the ass for the President*! In another section of her file, he noticed something very disturbing…

His phone rang and when he answered it he discovered that it was Intelligence Agent Ray asking about racquetball. TJ locked up Senator Wadd's file and headed for the gym. He figured that he could finish his research the next day. Since Intelligence Agent Jerney was on a mission in the Philippines, it was just three of them now with Analyst Stefan for "cutthroat."

★ ★ ★ ★ ★

Back in his office the next day, after breakfast in the cafeteria---and a cinnamon roll that Judy brought to him along with his coffee---TJ was studiously reading Senator Wadd's file. When he had read enough, the next step was to find out when she would be going home again. He discovered that she was due to go home in three days. He was going to ask Judy for the flight schedule going to Hanscom Air Force Base when, he remembered that Judy showed him how to do it on the CIA's secured web link. Pulling up the flight schedule from Andrews to Hanscom, he noticed that there was at least one flight every day. He then scheduled a flight for himself for later that day along with a reservation for Air Force Lodging for the next three nights. He also contacted the car rental company on base and reserved a SUV for his use. He called his personal assistant Judy to find out if his boss was in. Good…she relayed that he was in.

TJ then made his way over to Randy's office to inform him of his upcoming mission. His boss was very supportive of his work and had no issues with his trip and wished him good luck. He also reminded TJ to not forget to take a Russian clue with him to leave behind. TJ already had an idea of what to take with him and proceeded to the CIA's "Russian Items Locker."

The CIA, as well as other federal agencies, managed storage of items gathered from other countries that could be used in investigations or other matters. TJ retrieved something from the Russian Items Locker for an "other matter." The items stored in these lockers came from many sources, including: investigations, raids and stuff that had been abandoned or discarded.

Later that day, TJ caught his flight to Hanscom Air Force Base from Joint Base Andrews without incident. While on the C-17---this was his first flight on one even though he worked on them previously with his former employer---he started thinking about the political system in the United States. Too many political hacks were involved with the governing of the country. *Why did this seem to be a growing problem in Congress,* he wondered? Garbage in and garbage out was his private, personal opinion.

He then remembered what Candidate Trump said to former President Obama when he visited The White House and the cameras were rolling: "He's a great man." Obviously Trump was being facetious but Obama probably really took it as a compliment. What a dumbass! President Trump is doing circles around the Dems and the dishonest media. Concerning President Trump being in office to this point, TJ was reminded of a Latin phase, *"multum in parvo."* The Democrats only mission right now is to feather their own nests, which is actually second only to taking down President Trump by using any and all means necessary and at any cost, of which both is bad for the country; they retained no authentic desire whatsoever to ameliorate for the American people.

The C-17 landed smoothly at Hanscom Field and was guided up to the terminal by the pilot. Since Air Force Lodging was nearby, TJ just walked there and checked in. After an hour's rest, he then left to pick up his rental SUV. The car rental place had a 2017 4x4 Jeep Renegade available that he liked, so he took it and went to find something to eat.

Right outside the base was a Golden Corral so this was where he decided to eat…but it wasn't a hard decision for him.

Finished with his supper, TJ walked out to the parking lot and as he closed in on his vehicle, something caught his attention and he remarked out loud: "How about that? Someone stuck a note on the bumper of my SUV." He removed it and read the contents: "If you are really a Christian, then don't park so close to my vehicle next time," and it was unsigned. Obviously a deranged person; must be a Democrat!

Oh well, tomorrow was another day to get stuff done.

CNN

"This is CNN and I'm Augaytus Corbett live with a special guest tonight. With us we have Representative Maybel Wileen. Welcome to the show tonight Congresswoman Wileen. We wanted to talk to you because we had heard that you have some special and exciting news for our viewers…what have you got for us Representative Wileen?"

"Impeach 45…impeach 45…impeach 45…" she started her chant again.

"Ok Representative Wileen," Augaytus cut her off. "How are the Democrats planning on doing that?"

"Oh, we have a plan Augaytus…we just don't know what is it yet."

"Uh, my producer says that you have some exciting news for our viewers about how the Democrats are planning to impeach President Trump…"

"We do Augaytus, they just haven't told me yet."

"What do you mean exactly…that they haven't told you, yet?"

"Because silly, I don't know and they don't know yet either."

As Augaytus cleared his throat and repositioned himself in his chair, he looked very uncomfortable with the situation that he found himself in.

"I see. Do you have anything for our viewers Representative Wileen?"

"Impeach 45…impeach 45…impeach 45…"

"My producer is telling me that we have a commercial message coming up now. We'll be right back, (hopefully with some answers for our 600,000 plus viewers!) stay tuned."

CNN then went to a commercial and Augaytus was heard saying, "Get that deranged bitch out of here."

Democratic Resistance Party Meeting #4

The next night, the Resistance Party called for another meeting. All were present again with the following, including one new member:

Senator Cole Burris – (D-NJ)
Representative Jarl Lidio – (D-GA)
Tim Payat – DNC Chairman
Representative Maybel Wileen – (D-CA)
Kadin Elkhart – DNC Deputy Chairman
Senator Maro Wesley – (D-VA)
Senator Esmeralda Willow – (D-MA)
Senator Burney Sherman – (I-VT)
Representative Abel Stoner – (D-CA) Resistance Party Chair

And via conference call:

Senator Jace Melvin – (R-AZ) Line 1
Senator Bow Crenshaw – (R-TN) Line 2
Senator Jory Flann – (R-AZ) Line 3

Representative Abel Stoner called for the meeting to come to order as there was a lot of chatter happening.

"Ok people, this meeting will now come to order. Kane, will you have a seat please?" Stoner questioned and then continued on. "I want to welcome our newest member to our group, Senator Cole Burris. Senator Burris, if you would like to stand up and let us know why you decided to join our Resistance Party please."

"Thank you Chairman Stoner. From the news that I have been listening to, I could tell that the Resistance Party needs some help with their mission. I'm already tired of Trump acting like his crap doesn't stink and at all costs, we need to preserve the Democratic Party. We must come together for the good of the party. The power that we could wield with control of the House, Senate and The White House is needed for the future success and longevity of our party. I believe that once we are back, we will be in control for a long time to come my friends. I want to see Trump in Hell. I mean, not literally. We can do more if we pull together and now is the time to act."

"Ok Senator Burris, thank you for those fine comments," Representative Stoner stated. "Now let's hear…"

"Wait a minute, I'm not finished yet," defied Burris. "I want to announce, right here and right now that I'll be running for the presidency in 2020 because I am Spartacus!"

Quiet settled over the room as this statement sank in to the members. The statement had the right effect that Senator Burris wanted. He believed that Hilliary was "old news" while he was a much younger choice and he could relate and communicate with the younger Liberals better and that he would be able to represent this faction of the Democratic Party much better.

After a moment or two, the buzz of conversation started with the members.

"People, can I have your attention please?" Stoner asked. Then from out of the chaos came that familiar chant that the members were clearly getting tired of: "Impeach 45…impeach 45…impeach 45…"

"Shut up Maybel and sit down everyone," yelled Representative Stoner. Once quiet settled in, he resumed speaking.

"I appreciate your enthusiasm and desire to run for president Senator Burris. However, the Resistance Party was started with supporters of Hilliary. So maybe you need to…"

"I mean to say that in case Hilliary doesn't run, then I will be and I hope to have all of your support. I'm loyal to our leader as well as you fine people."

"That's fine," Representative Stoner stated. "Everyone heard what Senator Burris said so let's move along with our meeting. At the last…"

"I just wanted to say that I think Trump is a piece of shit and I want a hand in taking him down. Also, I was watching CNN when that crazy, old woman there was on and I can tell you from that alone, that we definitely need more help...that's all that I have to add," Representative Lidio stated and sat down as all eyes went to Representative Wileen, who remained quiet.

"Ok people, what do we have to report?" Representative Stoner asked.

From line 1 the voice of Senator Melvin sounded with his report.

"I've been working close with the President letting him think that we're friends. I think that he's starting to relax around me now and when his guard is down…wham, I'll let him have it."

"I'm going home tomorrow for a few days and you can believe that I will have a brilliant idea when I come back," Senator Willow insisted. "In fact, I'm meeting with someone that I knew from Harvard Law and we will have a plan formulated…I promise. Also, I have something at my home that will help us…but I won't tell you what yet."

The meeting continued for another half hour, but was unsubstantial in its outcome. After the meeting,

Representative Stoner and Representative Lidio stayed behind to chat about the future of the Democratic Party.

"Did you have an opportunity to talk to Barack?" Representative Stoner questioned.

"I did," confirmed Representative Lidio. "He said he would try and talk to Michelle again. Hopefully we will have good news for our group."

"I'm thinking that even if she agrees to run, it may be too soon to bring that announcement forward. But, when I talked to the some of the other members---some of which are not among the living anymore---they seemed to like the idea of switching our loyalty to Michelle. We'll wait until the time is right, then I'll make the announcement and we'll take a vote."

Representative Stoner thought that his private meeting with Representative Lidio was the most productive part of their overall meeting this night.

Justice with Judge Jeanine

"I'm Judge Jeanine Pirro and you're watching Justice with Judge Jeanine. But first, my opening statement: I'm so tired of hearing from Trump hating, self-righteous, Socialist, condescending, Hollywood elites, that think they are so much better than the rest of us. We finally have a President that truly loves his country and the American people and they want him in office, regardless of you so called elitists, the American people who gave Donald Trump the green light to become our 45th President of the United States. I'm so sick and tired from hearing from these Left-wing Snowflakes, how the world is going to end because we finally have a President with some balls and who will stand up to the rest of the world and who's first priority, is the safety and national security of this country that we all love so much. Why do those losers on the Left want to oust Trump? I'll tell you why. They can't stand to see a successful businessman succeed where they are failing;

someone who can stop the Liberal advancement of their misguided, ill thought of ideologies in their tracks. The Liberals don't care about the American people, or about having a strong military or about national security. No. All they can think about is advancing their own sick ideology on the rest of us, even if it means costing us the country that we love and cherish so much and taking down our President---that you the American people duly elected---at any cost. And I'll tell you another thing I'm sick of is when we give more credence to illegals that are here illegally over American citizens. Yes, it turns my stomach sick when I hear cities declare themselves as 'sanctuary cities' and now that dumbass in California, Jason Brent, has declared California as a 'sanctuary state' it makes me want to puke. These people that cross our borders illegally are no better than 'common criminals.' Yes I said it and I'll say it again, 'common criminals.' There Mr. Jason 'Sunstruck' Brent, did you just hear what I said? The hardworking people of California deserve someone better than you as Governor. So, at the cost of the majority of Americans living in California who are not Liberals, you'll keep on advancing your Liberal friends agenda until the State of California fails. You make me sick Governor Brent. You're a liar and a fraud to the people you serve and the oath you took to protect them. What does illegal mean to you Governor Jason 'Sunstruck' Brent? Doesn't it mean when people from another country comes over our border without proper documentation that they are illegal? That the first thing they did in entering our country is breaking the law? And then you dumbasses in the state government give them driver licenses? What other country would hand out driver licenses to illegals? Just name me one Governor Brent. And then these illegals who are carrying valid driver's licenses can now vote. Something is strangely wrong and dark and sinister about that thinking. The Liberal Democrats thirst for greed and power has led them to massive corruption and mental instability; becoming unhinged, the same thing that they accused our President of.

These sick and demented Liberal Democrats are jackasses; why do you think the mascot symbol for the party is the donkey, or jackass? They even accept it with honor! And that's my opening statement."

The judge was seen by the viewer's shuffling some papers before continuing with the program.

"Today, we have a special guest on the show from the Republican Party. She is part of the newly created Support Party for President Trump. Welcome to the show Representative Mona Bu. How are things in the Republican Party these days?"

"Thank you Judge. First, I want to tell you that I love your opening statement. Talk about hitting the nail on the head. You are very obtuse and direct in your statements Judge and that's what I love about you. Things in the Republican Party are moving right along. As you know, due to the Democrats establishing a Resistance Party we had to counteract that by establishing our own Support Party for our President who is doing wonders for this country, I might add."

"Great, I'm glad to hear it. How many members do you have so far?" Judge Jeanine asked.

"Currently your Honor, we have ten members."

"All Republicans I suppose?"

"We actually have one Democrat Judge, believe it or not."

"Who's the one Democrat I wonder?"

"Well Judge, I don't want to say as that's for that person to come forward if they choose to."

"Why wouldn't they want their name known as a person who supports our President?" Judge Jeanine asked innocently.

"It's not that they are not proud of supporting our President, it's just that as the Democratic Party is starting to come unhinged, they are still affiliated with their party and as you know Judge, there is a lot of partisan politics involved here."

"Boy do I know it. Ever since Donald Trump beat their unbeatable, unstable, disgusting, corrupt, lying, denying, demonizing, deflecting and flawed candidate, the Left has really lost their direction and message and has become unhinged. Currently, they have no coherent or intelligent message for the American people to follow. Why would anybody vote for them these days I wonder?"

"That's the Left's agenda is to feed their Liberal friends while making the rest of us out to be racist. Think about it Judge for a moment. In order to gain power, the Democratic Party has sunk to a new low. Their political platform these days is illegals, felons and freaks. They feel if they can win over these groups of people then they can win not only The White House, but other Democratic Party races as well."

"But I thought that illegals can't vote…hence the name illegals?" Judge Jeanine queried.

"You are right Judge. However, their home base in the State of California, the most idiosyncrasy, perturbable and jingoism, gives them driver's licenses, free education and medical care and even now, a secure place to live, all paid with California tax payer dollars! In order to vote, all you need to register with is a driver's license."

"But I had heard that California has a statement on their license's that says if I remember right, 'Federal Limits Apply.' That way they can't register to vote?" Judge Jeanine asked.

"You are correct Judge. But with that statement in fine print, the reality is who will see it. For example, if you are a Liberal working at the Voter Registration Department, it would be so easy to 'overlook' that tiny statement. And, as California has proclaimed them as a sanctuary state, then who will punish their employees for these so called 'minor' mistakes?"

"Well certainly not Jason Brent. I don't even want to call him the governor anymore he's so disgusting. Ok, what about felons then?"

"Judge, these Liberal states are backing laws to allow felons to vote ever since the corruption came out with the Obama Administration and the Clintons in the election of 2016. Now we are even seeing the corruption spilling out from our top law enforcement agency…the FBI."

As Judge Jeanine just shook her head in shock and wonder, Representative Bu moved on with: "It was quite clear in the election who stood for law and order and that was Candidate Donald Trump. It's like this Judge. If you are a crook yourself, and, you see the corruption surrounding the Democrats, and, you see the Democrats not supporting our law enforcement, and, the FBI is consumed with corruption, and, is covering up for the Obama Administration and the Clintons, and, that President Donald Trump is for law and order, who would you vote for?"

"I see where you are going with this Representative Bu," Judge Jeanine shook her head sadly.

"The Liberals have this all figured out. Now, we need to get the Republicans to open their eyes and take this Liberal movement seriously, before it's too late. They are a scourge on our country and need to be stopped. Right now, Republicans have control of The White House, the House of Representatives and the Senate. We need to pull together as a Party and pass President Trump's common sense legislation. I can testify that President Trump is a very intelligent person Judge."

"You're preaching to the choir, boy do I know it. Just look at his accomplishments. Illegals crossing the border are down by 70%, GDP is up as well as the stock market, and unemployment is down. These are things that Obama couldn't figure out or didn't want to figure out how to accomplish. So what's the deal with all of these freaks now?"

"They are just freaks Judge. Most are on drugs and many don't believe in the rule of law. We have found out through studies that drug use makes you more susceptible to believing in the propaganda coming from the Left; true story Judge."

"I believe you. So what's next for the Support Party?"

"We are going to continue to work on getting the President's message out to the working class Americans and hopefully get more Democrats and Republicans to join in our Support Party movement, and I might add Judge, Make America Great Again!"

"That's great Representative Bu. Keep up the great work that you guys are doing as our country needs more people like you; in other words, more Republicans." Judge Jeanine stated and shook hands with Representative Bu.

"When we return, Street Justice will be the order and I'm going to ask New Yorker's on how they feel about how our President is doing, stay tuned, you won't want to miss this."

Chapter 7
Ω

"You don't have to taste the fish to smell the Liberal stink."

---Brad Roberts

TJ had already cased the home before Senator Willow arrived from Washington. From the inside of her home, he saw things that married up with her intelligence file. He had word that she would arrive later this day. Now it was just a waiting game…waiting for her to come back home. So he was spending his time on base keeping his mind occupied by being constructive and sitting in a hot tub reading his current Western book. He would return later that night and hopefully would find his next target at home…alone.

Hannity

"I'm Sean Hannity and we have an action packed show for you tonight. First, let's start off with the murder of Kuma Shirley. The illegal involved in her shooting will go free. We just received word that the jury found her murderer, not guilty. Unbelievable and beyond belief! But we should have expected no less from Liberal California, the home of hypocrisy and double standards, the home of the Snowflake Liberals, the home of insanity and those that are coming unhinged. These are the people that were on the jury, a jury of the killer's peers; really? These Trump hating Liberals that oppose the rule of law and believe in sanctuary for illegals…on this jury. I don't get it. The jury found the defendant not guilty of First Degree or Second Degree Murder. Not even guilty of Manslaughter…really?

"Manslaughter is defined as 'the unlawful killing of a human being without express or implied malice.' Ok, let's say that this *was* an accidental shooting, it would still be manslaughter. I know if that was me that I would be going to jail and so would you. This is a travesty of justice because this is no justice for anyone, including the family of Kuma Shirley. I would like to ensure our viewers that things can't get much worse than this, but from all the sources, it can. Thank God we have Donald J. Trump as our President and not that other psycho.

"One of our special guests tonight is Laura Ingraham. Laura, welcome to Hannity," Sean expressed with genuine affection as he reached over to shake her hand.

"Thank you Sean, it's great to be here tonight."

"Laura, I just want to ask you about the murder of Kuma Shirley. I personally think that they are all nuts out there in California with their Liberal ideas of what really took place and their own form of twisted justice; your thoughts Laura."

"I agree with you Sean. But I came up with an idea how President Trump can honor Kuma Shirley and embarrass San Francisco at the same time."

"Ok, let's hear it. I'm open for new ideas and I can tell by the way that you are smiling that it has to be good. Am I right?"

"You are correct my friend. Here is what I would do if I was President Trump. I would take the San Francisco Maritime National Historical Park and change its name to the Kuma Shirley Memorial Park. The President can do this with a simple proclamation. This would really throw the Left into a spiral freefall."

"You know Laura you are bad. That is actually a really great idea though and I hope President Trump is watching our show now. Let me just share this website with our viewers. If you go to www.whitehouse.gov/contact, you can contact the President and make that suggestion. I would highly encourage all of our Fox News viewers to do just that.

"Now, stay right where you are my loyal viewers because we have former Ambassador John Bolton coming up next and thank you Laura for coming on with that really great tip…I love it. We'll be right back."

★ ★ ★ ★ ★

As TJ sat in his rented Jeep casing the home of Senator Willow, he noticed a lot of women showing up this night and one man, all around midnight. *So she wasn't going to be alone for a while*, he pondered.

Parking in the long driveway was becoming congested with a variety of automobiles. When it looked like no one else was showing up, he left the security of his vehicle and crept up to the fence bordering the backyard, since he noticed that a light was on in the back.

In position where he could view the scene, the women formed a circle around the one man. TJ focused his compact binoculars on the man and discovered it was none other than the billionaire, Mike Craig, who didn't care for, or respect the President. Then he counted the number of women in the circle. Including the senator, there were thirteen women, none of which he recognized other than that of the senator and all chanting, "Satan take Trump." He knew that thirteen witches formed a coven.

He further knew that they were conducting a Sabbat, which he remembered from reading about, that it was a midnight assembly of diabolists (13 witches and 1 warlock). This was to renew allegiance to the devil through mystic rites and orgies. Also, probably a way to curse the President since they were chanting, "Satan take Trump." It sounded like one of the President's campaign rallies when Trump supporters yelled out, "Lock her up." They are taking a page right out of the President's playbook he realized and using it against him. Further scrutiny revealed to TJ that all of the trees had been stripped of their leaves and at least three cats were present.

This gathering reminded TJ of a freak and drug fest that occurs every year in the desert outside of Reno, Nevada at a place called Black Rock. He would never understand why the federal government would allow this type of event to take place. More than 60,000 druggies and freaks show up every year to attend this event. Sounds like a golden opportunity for Naval Air Station Fallon to "accidentally" drop a couple of bombs in practice!

After several minutes of this chanting, the witches sat in chairs that formed a *Magic Circle* around the warlock, Mike Craig, who started to speak next.

"We are all gathered here tonight to give thanks to our ultimate higher being…Lucifer. He has helped our leader Hilliary, but his power was not enough for her to take her proper place as our president. So, we are gathered here tonight, at the request of Senator Willow, to extend a request to Lucifer, to invite Trump to Hell!" Craig yelled out.

More wailing sounded as the witches started dancing around the lone warlock with music that was playing in the background, but not loudly. The warlock raised a pitch fork up in the air toward the light of a full moon, which was shining down on a cloudless night, as he made his request over and over again.

TJ had seen enough and returned to his vehicle to await an opportunity to finish his mission. He thought that this will be one mission that he will definitely enjoy, since it involved an increased level of pure evil. He was reminded of a quote from the First Daughter, Ivanka… "There's a special place in Hell for these people," for Satanist…and Liberals!

At 0213 exactly, the group of evil worshipers started to exit the front door of the home. The backyard light was then turned off, probably by the senator.

He allowed an half an hour to pass before leaving his post…hopefully for the last time tonight. He couldn't wait to get back home and file his report the next day as the CIA will want to know about this latest event involving Mike Craig.

Rybachiy **Nuclear Submarine Base**
(Russian Naval Base)

"President Putin, Prime Minister Dmitry, comrades and friends. I have been asked to join you this historic day in this christening of a new Russian nuclear power submarine that carries my name…the RTUS (Russia Thanks United States) Obama, SBN (Submersible, Ballistic, Nuclear) 911." (the Russian Navy plans on building another seven of the Obama Class subs, with such names of Biden, Paloma and of course… Simpson!)

The crowd of almost one thousand people roaringly applauded. The multitude was small in comparison to a Trump rally for one simple reason…the highly classified nature of the base. Only government, military and dock workers were allowed to attend. One man who was waving a Trump flag was *accidentally* shot and killed by a Russian military officer. If there were any more Trump flags out there, then they were not displayed after the so called *accident*!

As the noise somewhat subsided, Obama continued, "This is a great day for your country as everything is good. If you look up into the sky, the sun is shining, the birds are flying and the country is finally getting a brand new nuclear ballistic submarine."

The noise level increased again as Obama proudly waved and smiled to those in attendance. Once again as the noise level tapered off, he resumed speaking.

"The reason for your submarine becoming a reality today is due to the United States donating twenty percent of our uranium to our friends here in mother Russia. I have often told the American people that we need to do more for our comrades to the north of us. Actually, northwest of us.

Russia is a great country, and, can and will go a long way in helping the United States to rein in terror threats all across the globe as well as stabilizing the world for peace and brotherhood. I do believe in President Reagan's and Trump's slogan: 'peace through strength.' By allowing the Uranium One deal to go through, Russia has acquired more strength to assist the United States in keeping the peace. All Americans may not feel as strongly as Bill and Hilliary and I do about this deal, because others don't have a degree from Harvard Law School I might add, but clearly this is a great deal for your country…I mean for both of our countries."

The people clapped loudly at this last statement. Some whistled and waved Russian flags proudly. Obama gasped, as some of the people shoved to get closer to the roped off area where he was speaking, but the Russian military as well as Obama's assigned Secret Service Agent kept the gathering at bay.

Hurriedly, Obama began speaking again: "Because of this Uranium One deal that President Putin and I worked out, we have now formed a more perfect union between our two countries. As you all know, I was hoping for Secretary Clinton to win the election and become the 45th President of the United States, so we could give your country another twenty percent of our uranium."

Obama paused as the Russian people cheered and shouted at the top of their lungs. Passively, Obama waved to the cheering crowd. He continued as the noise lessened.

"However, that didn't happen."

Now the gathered Russians started booing at the top of their lungs. After a short while, Obama was able to continue his speech.

"The good news is that we will have another Democrat in office in January 2020. Another Democrat who supports the Russian people, another Democrat who will not let the Russian people down, or for that matter, another Democrat with another twenty percent of our uranium to share with our Russian friends," shouted Obama over the crowd noise.

When the crowd calmed down once again, Obama raised high and shook the bottle of Russian Vodka that President Putin handed him for the christening. He then moved closer to the submarine's conning tower and slammed the bottle against the sub. The bottle was smashed into pieces and the liquid was splashed back onto Obama and soaked his soft, Italian tan suit. Just as Obama thought it couldn't get any worse, a seagull that was flying overhead dropped his duty right smack on the front of his expensive, American paid for, Italian tan suit. Then he realized just how wrong he was…it could and did get worse!

Republican Support Party Meeting #2

Later that night, after Obama gave his Russian speech that was carried on national television, including Fox News, the master-at-arms took roll call and the following were all present and accounted for:

Representative Curt Click – (R-NY)
Support Party Chair
Representative Dwight Home – (R-CA)
Master-at-Arms
Representative Lay Beebee – (R-PA)
Representative Tamar Meal – (R-PA)
Representative Kane Bundy – (R-TX)
Representative Mona Bu – (R-TN)
Representative Ken Charge – (R-ND)
Senator Thornton Care – (R-AR)
Senator Tut Smith – (R-SC)

And via conference call:

Senator Jed Med – (D-WV)

"Our meeting will now come to order," Representative Curt Click announced as the group quieted down in anticipation of Click's forthcoming question. "Did anyone else see Fox News earlier?"

Everyone started laughing about what an ass Obama made of himself. He probably didn't even realize what a legitimate jackass he is and that he truly belonged to the party *of* the asses, Representative Click considered as he brought the meeting back to order.

"I'm sure happy that Obama isn't our President anymore, I'll tell you that! How about that bird dropping some shit on him?" Representative Click asked. "That sure was fun!"

Laughing resumed once again when Representative Meal spoke next, "And I heard that they paid him a million dollars for that speech. Boy o' boy, did Russia get screwed on that deal; serves them right since we lost 20% of our uranium to them Russkies!"

More laughter sounded again as the quiet reined over the gathering with Representative Click motioning for calm before speaking.

"I want to thank Representative Bu for the great job that she did on the Justice With Judge Jeanine Show."

Everyone clapped and there was some congratulatory remarks being directed to Representative Bu who was pleased for the recognition.

"Ok everyone, I believe that that was a blow for the Dems as well as that Obama speech in Russia. But we have to keep the ball rolling. Does anyone have anything else to add…anyone?" Representative Click asked while scanning the room.

"I'm scheduled to be on Hannity tomorrow night," Representative Charge stated. "I can tell you this that Sean is fired up, especially with all the corruption that is coming to light, so it should be a good show."

"I have talked to Tucker Carlson and he said that he will schedule me for his show, but I haven't heard back from him yet," Representative Care informed the group.

"If that is everything, then this meeting is adjourned," Representative Click stated and brought his gavel down with a firm bang.

★ ★ ★ ★ ★

TJ was exhausted as he returned to his room on base and lay down to get some shut-eye. While his mind went to parade rest, his subconscious remained at attention as he drifted off into the peaceful abyss known as dreamland…

He found himself on some military base along with his boss and Director Lannister who were yelling out instructions to servicemen and women that were working around a C-17 cargo plane.

"TJ, let's get these people on the plane and quit fooling around," his boss directed him.

As he looked around, he realized that there seemed to be dozens of people with their hands cuffed behind their backs all wearing pink t-shirts with the words, "I hate Iranians." Everyone was wearing a parachute. Continued scrutiny revealed some of the people that he knew, if not personally, then from watching the news. There was Bill and Hilliary, Obama, Mike Craig, Representative Whitney, Representative Wileen, Kadin Elkhart, Senator Wesley, Representative Stoner, FBI Director Jaron Cowan, FBI Special Agent Piran Styles, Senator Burris, Representative Lidio, Senator Sherman, Journalist Augaytus Corbett, CNN 's Political Anchor Will Boutros, MSNBC's Host Evening Poe and many others.

Obviously, this was going to be a plane load of bad people that he was assigned to load on the aircraft he realized, but he still didn't move as if he was in shock, until his boss, Randy approached him and asked him:

"What's wrong TJ? We have to get this shit load of bad people loaded so we can drop them off over Iran." His boss noticed the look on TJ's face and added: "Hey, what better way of getting rid of crap and corruption than transferring them to a very deserving Iran?" Randy questioned.

Through a very surreal sensation, TJ started ushering these corrupt and evil people on the plane with a sense of satisfaction knowing that he was helping to clean up America and Draining the Swamp. Hilliary feinted and had to be carried on. Too bad he thought, you should have been a good person.

Senator Sherman stumbled on the lowered ramp and was helped up as he trudged on. There were no seats on the plane, so people started to sit on the deck near the front. TJ knew that there would be no bathroom breaks on this flight and that it would get messy due to the length of the trip. Oh well, as long as he didn't have to clean up the mess. Air Force personnel would be assigned to do that.

As everyone was loaded on the plane and the ramp was raised, Director Lannister walked up to him and asked him, "So you didn't think that I still do grunt work huh? Wrong. I still get into the thick of things every once in a while. Check on that other plane and make sure that it gets loaded and come back here as we'll be waiting for you."

TJ walked over to the other C-17 being loaded with cages of cats. He walked up to the Loadmaster and asked, "What's going on here Staff Sergeant?"

The Staff Sergeant looked up from his clipboard and asked, "Who are you?"

TJ pulled out a black, leather, bi-fold wallet with his badge and ID and presented it and replied, "Omega Agency."

"That says CIA."

"Ok, I'm CIA. Now what's going on here?"

"We are loading these cages of cats that have been collected all across the U.S. from animal shelters to drop

over North Korea. The President knows that the people there are starving and we have too many cats here already. There's a parachute on every cage, so they won't be harmed upon landing and the cages will automatically open to let them out. Additionally, this will also be a distraction for the North Korean military as they try to round up, or shoot, these cats to keep their people from eating."

"What's the distraction for?"

"President Trump is planning an attack on North Korea, same as Iran with the people being dropped there, acting as a distraction as well. We will be dropping some well-known convicted Liberals for our first mission such as, crooked politicians and some dishonest media folks."

"I saw the billionaire, Mike Craig onboard. What's the story with him?"

"He was just in the wrong place at the wrong time sir…bad luck I guess."

TJ looked up as he heard the engines for the first C-17 being started and the Staff Sergeant continued, "Our intelligence tells us that the Iranians will capture these people and either use them as slaves or torture them slowly. However, that attack isn't planned to happen for approximately three months after the North Korean attack. Don't they tell you CIA boys anything? We are dropping them at night so they won't be shot, at least right away. If the Iranians were to see all of these parachutes coming down in daylight, they would think that the Americans are invading them. Well actually, the Americans will be invading them, just not our military though."

TJ watched in silence as all of the cages were loaded with thousands of cats, all of which seemed to be meowing, thinking about what another mess it's going to be like in this plane as well!

After the plane was loaded, he headed back to the first C-17 and boarded up front with his boss and Director Lannister. He took a seat in an area that was sectioned off for the Cargo and Load Masters and of course, the three CIA men.

Once the plane was in the air, the Cargo Master approached and handed each of them a Popeyes Chicken Box. Popeyes were one of TJ's favorites. As he looked inside his box, he noticed that there were three pieces of chicken, green beans and a biscuit.

A military serviceman approached him and asked what he wanted to drink and TJ answered with, "The good stuff" and was handed an ice tea!

The mood with the prisoners seemed festive, especially when some of them started singing Jingle Bells with a twist... "Jingle Bells, Jingle Bells, Jingle all the way, oh what fun it is to ride in a four engine cargo plane, hey..."

He thought that at least they are taking their situation well. He wondered if they knew what is in store for them.

As his eyes grew heavy, he started to see black spots and closed his eyes for a brief moment. When he opened his eyes a few seconds later, he was at home in front of the television watching Hannity.

The voice of Sean Hannity came from the television, "This is Hannity and this is a Fox News alert. Due to overcrowding in some of our federal prisons, President Trump has ordered the release of several, well known Liberals. Yes Fox viewers, you heard right. Do not adjust your dial. However, they are being released over Iran in the dead of night. I remember when Obama sent billions to Iran in the dead of night, of your money, in an unmarked plane; almost the same thing here, except, your money is safe here in our country and President Trump is keeping his promises with draining the swamp. I was invited to The White House and talked to the President on this breaking news and this is what he had to say; can we play that clip please?" Sean asked of his producer.

As the clip played, you could hear the satisfaction of his decision clearly vocalized in the President's voice.

"Thank you Mr. President for allowing us this exclusive interview, we really appreciate it. I know that this is only for our Fox viewers as CNN, MSNBC and other dishonest media is not getting this rare opportunity."

"Well, it looks like the dishonest media is not going to stop their Left-wing, ideological propaganda and lies and I'm tired of it. I will say this though, Fox News has really treated me fairly and I really don't mind giving your company this opportunity, and quite frankly, other opportunities in future interviews."

"Thank you Mr. President, as I know that I am speaking for our viewers as well."

After a moment of pause, Sean continued:

"Now why did you make this decision about 'releasing' some of our high profile prisoners like Bill and Hilliary, Obama and Jaron Cowan to the Iranians?"

"You know, I'm a straight shooter Sean and I will tell you honestly, these are very bad people who do not want to conform to the 'good side' of society and are pure evil. So why should the American people pay to house this vermin when we can unload them on one of our enemies? Let the Iranians deal with them. I am not going to ask Congress for more money to build more federal prisons when Iran is available for a nominal cost. These are all convicted Liberal felons who offer no value to society and who prey upon the American people. They are predators Sean and America is better off without them. Also, this sets a new standard that showcases our resolve to bring honesty and integrity in government service back to the American people. We will have future flights as well and, we'll be saving our country billions. However, these flights are not exclusive to corrupted Liberal politicians. States that are overflowing with felons will be able to transfer some of their population to the federal system. This process will save millions of dollars for states and require no new state prisons to be built and they don't have to release criminals back into society to create more space for other criminals; that's insanity. That's

just like the "catch and release' program for illegals; judges have been known to go 'easy' on certain felons knowing the true cost of housing prisoners and the overcrowding conditions. My first priority is for the safety and security of the American people and I take my responsibilities seriously and don't want a 'revolving door' for criminals to continue their egregious behavior...not on my watch. Once we start making an example of people and hold them accountable for their sins, I think that you will see a 'real' reduction of repeat offenders; especially if they are no longer in our country!" President Trump laughed. "Maybe something like three strikes and you are automatically transferred to a federal penitentiary who will hand out your punishment. Bad decisions should have negative consequences Sean."

"What about the plane load of cats that you had dropped in North Korea sir?"

"As you know Sean, Kim Jong Un was starving his people and we had an abundance of cats in our country and needed to free up space at our animal prisons as well; it's a solution. Also, we created some chaos in their country and while their military is chasing cats, it gave us the distraction needed to take out their nuclear missile sites. Now because of our effulgent actions, South Korea will now be able to unite the Korean Peninsula once and for all, and the suffering of the North Korean people at the hands of an evil dictator is over and the North Korean people are now free to experience, life, liberty and the pursuit of happiness."

"I think you are on to something great Mr. President and all of us at Fox News and our viewers wish you all the success you deserve for your tenacity and intelligence that you bring to our country. We finally have a President that leads from the front and not from behind and that we can be proud of and who puts the American people first."

"And don't forget Sean, working together, we can all 'Make America Great Again' and take back our country."

As Sean was shaking hands with the President...

TJ woke from his dream suddenly. *Wow...what a vision!* He didn't think that President Trump would go to those extremes, but some of his dream had an underlying current of intelligence and merit.

TJ understood just how critical in time it was for the country. If the government were to allow Liberals the opportunity to take over our nation, we wouldn't have a United States of America anymore; at least not the America that he grew up with. However, the Democrats were smart enough to know that they are in trouble after losing the election to an outsider and a champion of the people. Additionally, he knew that the Democrats did not care a whit about the American people, they just wanted the greed and power of The White House and by targeting felons, freaks and illegals, they hoped to recruit more votes for their party and sick agenda; a cesspool of corruption already existing in DC exacerbated by the Liberal Democrats.

He also understood just how sick the country was and the need to treat the disease with something other than what has been attempted in the past. *For the greater good,* he thought. *For example, why should taxpayers pay for illegals to be in our country? Why don't illegals apply and come to our country legally...like other people? Shouldn't we pick who comes to our country? Shouldn't it be based on merit? Shouldn't it be those who love our country and embrace our way of life? Shouldn't it be for those who can offer some measure of value to our country and not just come here for work in order to send money to their country of origin? Shouldn't common sense be common anymore? All good questions to be considered intelligently...*

The bottom line was that the American people want legal immigrants that love and respect our country and that can, and will, add value to our society...it's just that simple.

Chapter 8
Ω

"Courage doesn't come by doing what everybody else says."

---Nikki Haley, U.S. Ambassador to the United Nations

Kremlin

The next day after Obama made his "famous speech," President Putin and Prime Minister Dmitry were meeting again at the Kremlin, located in the heart of Moscow, overlooking the *Moskva* River to the South.

"Tell me my friend, what did you think of Obama's speech?" Putin asked of Dmitry.

"To be honest…I don't think that it was worth one million dollars your Excellency."

"Don't forget Dmitry, it was *your* idea. Now, I will ask again, what did you think of Obama's speech?"

"Come to think of it, it was worth every penny…sir!"

"Since we are friends my comrade, feel free to call me Vladimir…if you want. I didn't think it was that great. Maybe he's slipping. But it was quite funny when that seagull shit on him…what an ass!"

Both men were laughing now as Dmitry poured drinks for both.

"I suppose we could cancel that check that we gave him…Vlaimir."

"No, let him keep it, we have plenty to spare. Especially since the Chinese are paying us protection money."

"I don't understand why they are doing that. They have the largest military in the world…so why my friend?"

"Dmitry, your mind is soft sometimes. Even though they have the largest military in the world, they don't have the extensive ordinance that we have to match the United States. As you are aware, China is sponsoring North Korea and is facilitating the overthrow of the South Korean government. South Korea is a rich country and North Korea is a poor country. If North Korea attacks South Korea, the U.S. will attack North Korea. If the U.S. attacks North Korea, then we will attack the U.S. China wants to stay out of any fighting with the U.S. so as not to interrupt the massive trade imbalance that they have going with the U.S. You know, the U.S. buying all this 'cheap junk' from China changed them from a third world country into the powerhouse that they are today. So, China pays us millions every year for our support. Once the U.S. is defeated, then the China-Russian partnership will be the undisputable superpower of the world. Then my friend, we will take Ukraine and other countries as well."

"But, if we defeat the U.S. on China's behalf, wouldn't that interrupt all of the trade with China?"

"Not necessarily my friend. China is planning to establish a massive military base on the East Coast and we will establish another base on the West Coast and together with China, the U.S. will then be shared by our two countries. We will utilize the resources of the U.S. to our own advantage. That's why I won't cancel that check that we gave to Obama…we may need him later."

"But when we defeat the U.S. and share the country with China, should we change the name of the country?"

"You are correct again my young friend. Obviously, I have spoken to President Xi about this and we came up with a new name for our shared, new, country."

"What is it to be Vladimir?"

"Tell me Dmitry, what do you think of the United Federation of Russina?" Putin asked; "otherwise known as UFR."

"I like it. But I think that we need things to speed up faster so that we can defeat the U.S. sooner than later."

"Be patient my friend. There is a time and place for everything. Someone once told me, 'give a president enough rope and they will hang themselves,' and that is what is happening now. Drug use is rampart in the United States and causing great harm to their nation, countries are starting to hate the U. S. and, their overwhelming Liberal corruption in Washington far surpasses anything that we could do ourselves. Yes Dmitry, for all practical purposes, it's only a matter of time. We'll let them defeat themselves and then move in for the kill. What could be better I ask you?"

"Is that all there is to it my comrade?" Dmitry asked as he settled into his seat and took another sip of his drink.

"Not quite. You see, we do have another ace in the hole, and that is that the United States is over confident and overzealous. Over confident that nothing can happen to them and overzealous in that they want to solve all the problems of the world; like our famous scientist, Alexander Gruber, once said to me, 'you don't have to be a rocket scientist to see where the U. S. is heading.' "

"What about our friends in Iran? They have been very helpful to our cause."

"Dmitry, I have gotten assurances from China, and I concur, that Iran is welcome to have Alaska. They deserve that little gem that we sold to the United States years ago, for the work that they are doing, running drugs into the U. S. through that terrorist organization, Hezbollah. We are grateful once again for Obama blocking their intelligence agencies from taking direct action against them, as that would have thrown a monkey wrench into our plans."

"That's a good idea. What about Hawaii? Who would get that?"

"That will be your new home my friend."

As Dmitry was left speechless, Putin walked over to the window facing the river and looked out.

"Dmitry, come here and look out the window."

Dmitry did as Putin requested and looked out the window next to Putin.

"Now what do you see?" Putin asked.

"Well, I see the *Moskva* River and parts of Moscow."

"You are correct. But I also see old. Do you see the old my friend?"

Dmitry nodded in the affirmative and Putin continued with his thoughts.

"Wouldn't it be nice to have a new place to work from…maybe from Hawaii? Nice weather, beautiful women and plenty of Kona coffee; I know how much you love Kona coffee."

A wide smile spread across Dmitry's face as he imagined a nice office, some beautiful women working for him and, Kona coffee…with vodka!

"I can see that the cat has got your tongue. That's kind of our plan if we can work everything out. Our biggest asset that I'm betting on is the United States. However, President Trump is a very smart man and should be taken seriously, unlike the stupid Americans that think that he's a nut; that honor would go to Obama and the Liberal Democrats, and a few others I might add. We will have a much harder time with Trump in office than say with Hilliary, if she would have won. But, I'm betting on these Liberal Democrats to take the country down for us. They don't realize that they are the ignorant ones."

President Putin sat down at his desk and Dmitry took a seat in front of him.

"Vladimir, what does China get out of all this? Surely they wouldn't have agreed to all of this without some compensation."

"Their compensation is the new country that we will share with them…and the Philippines! I have promised them that much as well. This way it's cheaper for them than building military islands in the South China Sea. They will confiscate all of the Philippine bases for their own use…and ours too. Don't you agree comrade with that idea?"

"I agree and it makes sense. Only if the United States knew what we were planning."

"Even if they knew my friend, they wouldn't believe it and the Liberal Democrats would have their Congress wrapped up in red tape. Here's to red tape and the stupid Liberal Democrats," Putin raised his glass in a toast.

The two men toasted each other and Putin became serious again.

"What have we heard from our operatives in the United States about members of their Congress being killed off?"

"They figure that it's the Cubans."

"The Cubans!" shouted Putin. "How did they come by that theory, or, do they have proof?"

It's a theory, and this was predicated on the events leading up to…" Dmitry started checking his notes and then resumed when he found the name that he was looking for. "Here it is…when their Representative Gozol came up missing."

"Don't make me ask twice Dmitry, get to the point. What are these events on which you speak about?"

"Yes my Excellency. This is the theory. When Obama resumed relations with Cuba, they were apparently pretty happy about that, and we were not, so we cut off their aid to them and they got mad at us. Then, Trump comes along and tightens things up a bit and it affected their economy. So, instead of coming back to us and ask for more aid again, they made the decision to handle things on their own, starting with the USW's that we gave them."

"Refresh my memory on what the hell you are talking about Dmitry."

"Several years ago, you authorized the Russian Federation of Technology to equip the Cubans with

Ultrasonic Weapons that they just recently used on the American Embassy. They worked and some of the American workers were harmed. So President Trump ordered all of the embassy workers back to Washington. When the American doctors examined them, they found inner ear damage."

"Good thing that they didn't turn them USW's up a bit more…huh Dmitry?" Putin asked coyly. "Otherwise a higher frequency would have caused their eyeballs to vibrate, bleed and blindness would have occurred. Go on my friend."

"Thank you Vladimir. As I was saying, the Cubans are now mad at us and the United States as well. Everything that I have told you so far is a fact and here is where the theory comes in. It is believed that they have an operative, or operatives, working inside the U.S. taking out members of Congress that are opponents to the President, which just happens to be Liberal Democrats. Now, because they leave some Russian clue behind, we are being scrutinized by their media and possibly by their intelligence agencies."

As Putin was shaking his head, it was clear that he was deep in thought. After a few minutes while Dmitry was refilling his glass, he continued on.

"Mostly it's the dishonest media and the Liberal Democrats that are most destructive to our image."

Another pause and Putin seemed in shock as he continued thinking about the Cubans. Just like children he reminded himself. What to do about unruly children?

Dmitry knew to stop talking at this time, for his own peace of mind, and sipped his Black Russian quietly.

When he was ready to speak, Putin cleared his throat and said to the Prime Minister, "Get with the KGB and find out what our options are for fucking with the Cubans. If they want to be like unruly children, then they must be treated like unruly children."

★ ★ ★ ★ ★

TJ slept in late and flew back to Joint Base Andrews, this time on a KC-10. From working at Boeing, which used to be McDonnell Douglas, he knew that the refueling tanker was designed on the same body as that of a DC-10. It was a very high quality aircraft, just like the McDonnell Douglas designed C-17.

He was not able to fly back until the evening, and when he did land at 1947, he immediately headed for Golden Corral, due to hunger pains, and he made it there in the nick of time before they started to lock the doors. This was the same Golden Corral that he ate at when he first arrived here and had to break up a fight. Hopefully, no altercations this time!

As he filled up two plates with green beans and steak, he noticed that there were not too many customers inside. As he sat down at his booth, a well-dressed man approached him. *Now what could this be about,* he wondered?

The man greeted him warmly with his hand extended, "Hi, I'm Dave the manager and owner here. Are you the FBI Agent that broke up that fight in my parking lot a while back?"

TJ shook hands with the man but didn't feel like correcting Dave on the incorrect agency, since most people felt that they were the same anyway. He nodded in the affirmative with a mouthful of green beans and signaled for Dave to have a seat.

"I just wanted to shake your hand and say thank you so much."

"Your quite welcome Dave and it was not a problem," TJ said and then quickly added, "just doing my job you know."

"Well, in any case, it's still appreciated. I can't stand unruly behavior anywhere, especially at my business." Dave noticed that TJ seemed to enjoy, not only the green beans but the steak as well and pointed this out.

"I see that you enjoy our steak and green beans. So I'll tell you what…next time you come in, just ask for me as it's on the house," Dave beamed.

"Yeah, you don't have to do that Dave, but it's really appreciated though. I'm paid well enough so it's no problem."

"Is there anything I can get for you?"

"Well actually, how about some more seasoning for the green beans?" TJ asked. Seasoning was what Golden Corral called the bits of ham and steamed pieces of onions that made up their famous green beans and he always seemed to need more. At some of the Golden Corrals that he ate at, they would provide him with extra when requested and Dave was no different, as he was only too happy to assist.

"Not a problem, I'll be back with some."

Dave returned with a plate of green beans and on top spread evenly was plenty of the seasoning that TJ loved so much that gave the green beans their distinctive flavor.

Dave and TJ seemed to hit it off well enough and spent the time talking about how Dave was able to procure a franchise license from Golden Corral. He told TJ that one of Golden Corral's franchise requirements was, that he needed to have access to two million dollars, this was to pay for the building and equipment and still leave him enough for at least three month's operating expenses and to ensure that he would be successful. Even though Dave didn't have a lot of money, he was able to secure a VA Business Loan due to his time in the Air Force. He retired after twenty years at the rank of E-9, a Chief Master Sergeant, with a nice pension. Dave's last mission was at Travis Air Force Base and he was assigned to overseeing the base's swimming center; an easy assignment for him considering Dave's stellar career in aircraft maintenance and his planned desire to retire after this last PDS (Permanent Duty Station). Dave confided in TJ that when he left the military, that he should've been a cowboy. Then his next thought about what he should do was to become a master plumber with his uncle in Yazoo City, Mississippi. Instead, circumstances led him to owning a Golden Corral in McLean, Virginia which TJ was thankful for.

Dave explained how a friend of his that was high up the corporate ladder in Golden Corral, encouraged him to open a restaurant in McLean. It seems that the company wanted to target business in that area, chiefly due to the CIA and nearby military bases. Since Dave was a veteran, it seemed like a match made in Heaven for both sides. So Dave applied for a VA loan and was approved.

TJ then shared some of his Navy experience with Dave and even telling him how his father retired after 32 years as an E-9 as well as a Master Chief.

By the time that he left the restaurant, TJ felt that he had made a true friend in Dave, and vowed that he would now return more often. This seemed to please Dave immensely.

The White House

President Trump was in the Oval Office hard at work when an aide entered and told the President about Obama being on the news and that he might want to watch. The President agreed and lifted the remote and turned on the television to Fox News…of course!

He watched as Obama christened a submarine named after him and saw the vodka splash and the bird incident: *What a dumbass…he's an imbecile*! After he finished watching Obama make an ass out of himself, President Trump returned to his paperwork. He was pouring through a proposed tax bill that the Republicans wanted to introduce into the House and Senate that would give most Americans a much needed break on their taxes, as well as to spur the economy. The Democrats did not want to be a part of this tax break because it was a Republican led bill, and besides, they hated Trump. In order to take down the

President, they were willing to sweep Americans aside for their own sick, Liberal agenda. President Trump figured that once Americans could see the tax cuts working, then the Democrats would regret not getting onboard with this tax bill.

Thinking of the Democrats, he figured that they are really going to have problems going forward into the New Year. Corruption, bad decisions, obstruction, sex scandals and more. However, he was hoping that by 2020, a lot more Democrats would be willing to vote for him.

With his *almost* first year in office completed, he learned that politics was harder than he had imagined and that the Democrats hate for him was greater than any other concern that they might have had for the country and he truly felt that the American people really appreciated his substantial efforts.

He thought about what an abuse of power that Obama did to the country and about the erosion of a fiduciary relationship that existed between the ex-president and the American people.

Breaking into his thoughts, an aide entered the Oval Office and announced that Sean Hannity was there for his appointment with the President. President Trump instructed the aide to usher him right in as he was always happy to see the top star at Fox News as the President truly loved winners…and Sean was clearly a winner to be admired, hence his large salary at Fox!

Sean entered with a smile on his face and walked directly to President Trump with his hand out. Both men shook heartily with the President's other hand laid fondly on Sean's shoulder as if they were family. Once both men were seated and agreed on what drinks they wanted, an aide left to fulfill their order, President Trump started the conversation.

"Sean it's good to see you again," the President beamed as he said this.

"Mr. President, the honor is all mine," Sean stated truthfully.

"It's really mine as well. You have the number one rated show on Fox and bring pleasure and truth to the American people and I appreciate that."

"You also Mr. President...you are very successful with our viewers and our country overall."

"Well, your success has led you to a nice salary of $29 million a year, and you deserve every penny of it I can tell you that."

"Don't forget your salary as well Mr. President."

"How can I forget...I get .25 cents every quarter, and after taxes, it's even less!" President Trump declared. "But I don't mind Sean, you know that. I'm here for the American people and of course, I don't need that salary anyway."

Both men had a nice laugh at this as President Trump waived the usual presidential salary of $400 thousand for a measly $1 dollar a year, that by law, he had to accept.

"The reason that I invited you here today is to thank you in person for all of your hard work that you do for our country along with almost everyone else at Fox with the exception of one person that I won't name. I truly feel that you, Tucker and the Judge is a real asset to our country and I hope that you will keep up the great work. Is there anything that I can do for you Sean?"

"There is one thing Mr. President that comes to mind."

President Trump nodded his head and smiled almost knowingly and waited for Sean to continue.

"Laura Ingraham came up with a really great idea of how to honor Kuma Shirley by changing the name of the San Francisco Maritime National Historical Park to the Kuma Shirley Memorial Park. We have had great support from our television viewers---and your base I might add---on this terrific idea and I would like to ask for your assistance on making this into a reality for the family of Kuma Shirley, as well as on the behalf of the American people Mr. President."

Once Sean started speaking about the subject, he knew what was coming and was already prepared to answer with a response.

"Tell Laura for me, that next month, she will be invited to The White House as my special guest and that I will be signing a Kuma Shirley Proclamation just for that purpose."

"Thank you Mr. President, I will tell her. However, you do know that by doing so will send the California Liberals into a frenzy?" Sean asked seriously.

"You should know me by now Sean that I live for that. It's actually a lot more fun fighting the Liberal Democrats than when I was filming The Apprentice. Don't worry, they'll get over it or they can go to Hell as far as I'm concerned."

Both men had a good laugh and Sean agreed with the President. Just then, an aide brought both men their drink order…unsweetened ice tea for both!

As the President and Sean sipped their drinks, they covered everything from the Russians to the massive corruption that had taken place under the Obama Administration. After a short time, and when their glasses were empty, President Trump had a question for Sean.

"Do you have enough time to have lunch with me today Sean?"

"Of course Mr. President…how can I say no? Will this be in the White House's Dining Room?" Sean asked hopefully.

"No, I had something else in mind and we'll take my ride."

"That's great Mr. President."

"Under one condition Sean," as President Trump pulled out a bright red hat that read, 'Make America Great Again,' his signature hat with his autograph on the bill, and handed it to Sean, "you have to where this."

"I would be proud to Mr. President," as Sean sized it and placed it on his head immediately.

While the President was admiring it on Sean's noggin, the First Lady entered and graciously presented Sean with The White House's official Christmas card and gave Sean a kiss on the cheek, wished him a Merry Christmas and then excused herself and left the Oval Office to parts unknown.

Sean thanked her and noticed that on the front of the card was a picture of President Trump beside the First Lady, Melania, with a decorated and snow covered (fake snow) Christmas tree; a flag was displayed noticeably in the background and the picture was obviously taken somewhere inside The White House. Opening the card was the words, "Merry Christmas and a Happy New Year to the Hannity Family," and was signed by the President and the First Lady, including, Barron Trump, the First Son.

Hannity looked up at the President with moist eyes and thanked him sincerely. He radiated with happiness as he quickly reflected on how lucky he was with his life and he realized that he had more than most, and a friendship with the President that he cherished was something special. President Trump excused himself in order to attend business in the First Bathroom.

Viewing the Christmas card some more, Sean thought back through the last eight years when Obama gave out official White House cards at Christmas time, none of which included the words, "Merry Christmas." They either read, "Happy Holidays" or, "Seasons Greetings." It was refreshing to have a President that appreciated the words, "Merry Christmas" and supported that same sentiment with most of the American people.

Sean looked around the Oval Office and noticed a picture of President Jackson and recalled the similarities between the two Presidents. He thought that President Trump was in good company with President Jackson. *Thank Heaven that he has nothing in common with Clinton, Obama or Nixon,* Sean reflected.

After several minutes, President Trump returned to the Oval Office and addressed Sean.

"Sean, if you will follow me please and we'll go get a bite to eat," President Trump stated incontrovertibly.

"May I ask where we are heading sir?"

"No, just follow me."

Sean followed President Trump through the halls of The White House and out onto the South Lawn where Marine One stood waiting to whisk the President and himself away to someplace unknown. But what the heck he thought, this is going to be so cool…going to lunch in Marine One!

Once they were airborne, the President still refused to tell him where they were going and accepted a phone call from Barron. After finishing his phone call with the First Son, the two men talked little as the flight wasn't a long one and landed at Joint Base Andrews. Once on the ground, the President's car, often referred to as "The Beast" (code name Stagecoach), was prepared to zip them away to some eating place on base…Sean figured.

The armored limo sped through the base with military precision utilizing a Military Police escort in front and Secret Service following. As this was Sean's first time on Joint Base Andrews, he scanned the area longingly until they pulled up at his favorite restaurant, Bob Evans. What a wonder he thought, to have a nice eating place on base besides the well-known "chow hall" for our men and women in uniform. He was a big supporter of the military, past and present, and respected the lifestyle the men and women was subjected to; not an easy way of life he thought.

He was about to open his door to exit from the car when the President checked him and explained that the proper protocol was that the Air Force personnel was tasked with opening the doors. *I have a lot to learn*, Sean thought, *if I want to be an American President someday!*

Two airmen arrived and opened the doors for the two men and they quickly exited the car and entered the establishment. It was quite obvious that they were expected by the staff that ushered them to a comfortable booth as all eyes were on them.

Even though dinner was not served at lunch time, when you were with the President, it was served anytime! President Trump ordered the Slow Roasted Pot Roast with fresh baked bread while Sean ordered the Slow Roasted Chicken Pot Pie with freshly baked bread.

As the two men heartily ate their satisfying meal and while talking of various subjects, he thought to himself, I'll never forget this day as long as I live…thank God I work for Fox instead of the fake news!

★ ★ ★ ★ ★

TJ was eating on base at Bob Evans for lunch on this same day, when he looked up from his Slow Roasted Turkey & Dressing meal, with green beans, and noticed President Trump with Sean Hannity closely following the President coming towards him. When President Trump was close enough to his table, they made eye contact, but the President did not acknowledge him in any other fashion. *Probably due to the nature of my work,* he thought.

This was the first time that he viewed Hannity in person. He was a big fan of the show because Sean was a very direct person and wasn't afraid to say what's on his mind. Love him or hate him, Hannity was direct…especially when it came to the crooked and very much, Liberal Dumbocrats. In his mind, TJ transposed Democrats to Dumbocrats as it seemed to fit their party quite well!

He was also a big fan of Tucker Carlson and Judge Jeanine as well; they were also straight shooters.

He finished his lunch and was going into work late today. He had nothing pressing that he knew of and just needed to unwind a little. His boss understood this and was very supportive due to the stressful nature of his work.

Because of traffic, he arrived at the CIA Building in about an hour. As he entered his office, Judy entered from the other door with his coffee and informed him that Randy needed to talk to him, when he had some time; she indicated that he did not need to hurry.

While enjoying his coffee, he typed up his very unique report. He finished his drink at about the same time that he finished his report. He then printed it out and took it with him to Randy's office, via Judy's area. He could have emailed the report, but since he had to go there anyway…

He knocked on Randy's door and was given permission to enter and did so. He sat across the desk and gave his boss a full report of everything, including, the devil worship ceremony that he had witnessed and the drugs that he had found in the home as well as seeing the President at Bob Evans.

"You didn't have to bring me a hard copy of your report," Randy stated.

"I know it, but I was coming here anyway and I knew that you will have to print it out and give it to Judy for filing. Plus, I wanted to enjoy my coffee and needed something to do to unwind."

"Well thank you then. This last mission turned out to be quite something. Our ICA's (Intelligence Collection Analysts) will appreciate some of this new information that you are introducing and will update the pertinent files that are affected; great job by the way. Anything else that's strange about this mission that I should know?"

"Oh, I almost forgot to mention this, but it is in the report. At the Sabbat, I spied Mike Craig attending the ceremony."

"The billionaire?" Randy questioned incredulously.

"The one and the same," TJ admitted.

"What was he doing there?"

"Believe it or not, he was the warlock for the coven, and you think you know some people…huh?" TJ asked.

"Wow…just wait until our intel folks gets a hold of this information! At least it won't be exposed to the media as they would have a field day with this kind of stuff."

"Maybe they *should* get a hold of it, but the dishonest media would probably just spin it into something else," TJ quickly added.

His boss readily agreed with his assessment.

TJ was about to rise and head back to his own office when his boss stopped him.

"Wait a minute TJ. I have your next target for you."

"Well that's fast."

"That's because you have been on an extended vacation…remember Sunshine?" his boss teased him.

"You're right…I'm bad. Go ahead and tell me who our next target is."

"No, you're good and that's why we hired you to get our country back on track."

TJ shook his head in acknowledgement as Randy paused to let this statement sink in. He really wanted TJ to understand just how valuable and needed he really was, not only to the CIA but more importantly…to the country and the President.

"Our next volunteer," Randy paused for effect, "is Representative Jarl Lidio. He's a newer member to the Resistance Party and we feel that we need to make an example out of him in order to deter new members from possibly signing on. However, these Liberals just might be dumb enough to keep on joining as their membership in the Resistance Party keeps declining. I guess time will tell."

This time he rose without being halted and trekked through Judy's area back to his own office. He grabbed Senator Willow's file from his desk to return to Jessy and headed for the analyst department. Once there, he sat down across from Jessy's desk as she was on the phone.

Jessy finished her call and gave all of her attention to her number one priority which was Central Intelligence Agency Officer…TJ Law.

"Hey TJ, I bet you need another file?" she questioned.

"Yes…and to return Senator Willow's file to you."

"Thanks…who do you need this time?"

"I need the file on Representative Jarl Lidio please."

"Ok, give me a few minutes. Grab that magazine right there and enjoy it until I get back. I just brought that in today," Jessy stated as she walked away to the file vault.

He took a seat and picked up the magazine that she referenced that was lying on top of her desk and noticed that it was Farmer's Magazine. As he was flipping through the pages casually, he sensed someone beside him and looked up to see a beautiful Oriental woman with dark, almond shaped eyes wearing professional business attire.

"Hi, are you waiting for Jessy?" she asked shyly.

"Uh…yeah," TJ stuttered and then swallowed. "She went to the file vault for me."

"Oh, that's nice. I'm Ching Ching. I am other analyst right next to Jessy; me from Beijing, China. How are you Agent…?" she asked while looking at him obliquely.

"I'm TJ."

"Are you new here TJ? I don't recall seeing you here before?"

"Not that new, but Jessy was just recently assigned to me."

"So what are you working on TJ?"

The look on TJ's face must have revealed his surprise at the question because she quickly added, "I'm sorry, I forgot that I'm not supposed to ask that question. I'm from China so I'm a very direct person. Are you married Agent TJ? That question *is* ok to ask."

She really is direct he thought, but before he had a chance to answer, Jessy showed up with his file and addressed Ching Ching.

"What can I do for you Ching Ching?" Jessy asked sternly with her arms crossed across her chest.

"Nothing, I was just introducing myself to our newest agent, TJ."

"Fine, now if you don't mind, we have work to do."

Ching Ching's facial expression did not change when Jessy as much kicked her out of her cube. She turned on her heel and left.

Jessy then confided to TJ, "I don't like her or trust her. There's something about her that I can't put my finger on."

"Just her personality maybe," TJ suggested.

"Maybe," Jessy replied as she wrinkled her nose. "Here's your file and that's all that I found. Just feel free to inform me if you need anything else TJ."

He thanked her and ensured her that she would indeed be the first person that he would call upon if he needed anything else from her department and headed back to his office.

Chapter 9
Ω

"A person's character is not defined so much by what they say…but what they do."

---Alex Morgan

Democratic Resistance Party Meeting #5

The following were all present at this highly anticipated meeting with the exception of Senator Willow and the addition of one new member:

Senator Cole Burris – (D-NJ)
Representative Jarl Lidio – (D-GA)
Tim Payat – DNC Chairman
Representative Maybel Wileen – (D-CA)
Kadin Elkhart – DNC Deputy Chairman
Senator Maro Wesley – (D-VA)
Senator Burney Sherman – (I-VT)
Senator Evan Sinclair – (D-CA)
Representative Abel Stoner – (D-CA) Resistance Party Chair

And via conference call:

Senator Jace Melvin – (R-AZ) Line 1
Senator Bow Crenshaw – (R-TN) Line 2
Senator Jory Flann – (R-AZ) Line 3

"Where is Senator Willow?" Representative Stoner asked. "Has anyone seen her lately?"

The attendees looked at each other but none answered. They wondered if this situation was somehow connected to past events, resulting in either disappearance or death.

No one answered.

"Senator Sherman, I believe that you two are somewhat friends, tomorrow can you check on her for the group please?" Representative Stoner questioned.

"I can and I will," Senator Sherman replied and then added, "what about free education for our young people?"

"Screw the young people you stupid bastard, we have a more important concern at the moment," Senator Crenshaw hotly stated. "And this is a resistance meeting anyhow you fucking old fool."

Is someone calling me an old fool?" asked Senator Melvin from line one.

"No one is talking to you dumbass. Put your hearing aid in if you are going to attend these meetings!" yelled out Senator Wesley.

Through the chaos, of course, came the high pitched voice of Representative Wileen as she stood up and chanted with: "Impeach 45…impeach 45…impeach 45…"

"Shut up you insane bitch," from Senator Flann on line three and some unknown party threw a pencil at Representative Wileen and she quickly sat back down and was quiet again as Representative Stoner tried to restore some semblance of order by using his gavel and shouting over the contentious political body.

"That's enough! Stop it now…stop it and sit down, everyone!" he banged his gavel furiously. "This crap is serious people. Let's not come unhinged like Trump has." These words caught everyone's attention and order was soon restored.

"That's better. Like I said before, Sherman you check on Willow," Representative Stoner stated clearly dropping their surnames now. "Now let's move on to the next order of business. Wait a minute, I almost forgot to announce our newest member to the Resistance Party...Senator Evan Sinclair."

Senator Sinclair raised his right hand in acknowledgement as some people voiced their welcome to the newest member from California.

"Now then, I believe that Wileen has an announcement, and if you mention the word impeach, then I'm going to impeach your black ass right out of here," Representative Stoner stated firmly.

This was the first time that everyone had ever seen Representative Stoner this upset and Representative Wileen took it to heart and meekly spoke her declaration.

"I just wanted to deliver some, 'Season Greetings' cards for everyone to pass out to family, friends and their constituents," she informed her fellow members of Congress and Democratic National Committee members as she bent down for some of the small boxes to hand out. They were passed around the table with everyone keeping a box.

Kadin Elkhart was the first to read the card and he read it out loud for the group, "On the front here we have a wreath with a blue ribbon tied in a bow and two pine cones on either side of the bow and the words inside the wreath says 'All I want this year is,'" as he then opened the card and continued reading, "'Trump impeached!' And below that is, 'Keep hope alive.' Great...I like it," he exclaimed. "I might need another box or two!"

Two more boxes were passed down to Elkhart as Representative Wileen smiled thinking she finally hit a homerun this time!

"Good job with the cards Representative Wileen. I take it that you have plenty of these in stock in case we need more?" Representative Stoner questioned.

Representative Wileen just continued to smile and nodded her head at the Chairman.

"Good. So if anyone needs more of these anti-Trump cards, feel free to contact Representative Wileen. Great work!" Representative Stoner praised and asked: "Any other pressing business?"

Representative Wileen stood proudly holding one of her cards close to her chest, "I'm going to be on CNN with Will Boutros tomorrow. I told them about these cards and they want me on. So, people that donate to the Democratic Party will receive a box of cards. A minimum donation of $20 dollars is required, per box, so that we can help to refill our Democratic coffers. Currently, the DNC has around $4 million, and in comparison, the RNC has $45 million. These cards are manufactured in China for pennies on the dollar, so we'll be able to bring in some dough and we have exactly, 100,000 cases to sell."

"Unbelievably great work Representative Wileen and I applaud you!" Tim Payat sounded off.

Representative Stoner glanced around at his small group and could now see everything finally coming together. He thought that this should definitively help to get the American people fired up and to pound that final nail into Trump's coffin…once and for all!

Clinton Home

It was just another day in paradise in the Clinton Home. Hilliary was in her office working on another book with a nice, warm, fire burning up some of the Cherry wood that she had Bill and Oscar (Hilliary's secret service agent) cut up. On the shelves in her office, she had probably a hundred of her published book proudly displayed. She figured that you couldn't have too many on hand in case visitors stopped by wanting one; she would autograph one for them every so often. I'm a superstar she thought to herself. Also, I'm really the President of the United States. I got three million more votes…how can that dumbass take away what is rightfully mine?! My second book will be to

144

tell the American people that they need to rise up and help me to reclaim my seat of power, and, I'll tell them how to do it by damn!

She picked up a hardcopy of her published book, *"What Happened"* and looked at the cover. She couldn't understand why it wasn't selling as well as she thought it would. Barnes & Nobel was currently selling it for only $12.94. *No wonder I'm not making much off this, they are not asking enough money for it. The American people are so stupid. If Barnes & Nobel asked for twice that amount I'm sure more would sell. Oh well, it's not that important since I have all that money in my overseas account. At least Chelsea and her family will be taken care of, for generations to come,* she reflected. *Donald Dumbass doesn't know that I'm a billionaire like him. To get his billions he had to really work...I just had to work the American people is all!*

Then she thought of Bill...*I'd ditched that piece of shit if he wasn't a former President. I probably could have done better if I would have taken up with that other boy...what was his name? Oh yeah, Burney, now a successful senator for Vermont. At least he doesn't chase women; probably can't anymore. But I'm not sorry that I had to knock the tar out of him last year in the primary. He was old and weak and I was younger and more beautiful. Also, I had the DNC on my side and in my hip pocket. He actually thought that he could run against me and win? He's a wannabe Democrat but an Independent in reality. Although, he has done pretty well for himself; have to give him credit for that though. He really suckered those poor bastards in Vermont, making them think that he really cares about them...that's a crock. That is a weakness of the American people...they are so stupid and are sheep ready for the plucking by those of us who are they're superiors, or the ruling class as some would say on Fox. Here the American people have given me a great life. I'm a billionaire with my own security detail---Secret Service Agents Carl and Oscar--- that the American sheep pay for. Who could ask for more? And Trump wants to make America great again...I thought it was already pretty great and I told him so! If the American people ever got a brain and a backbone,* she thought...shaking her head.

Oh well, it is what it is thank goodness; now what about my next book? I should quit lollygagging and figure out a great name for it. I know I'll name it..."I Won!" Perfect, and then I'll tell my many, many followers how to take back their country and get me into office. As long as I get in before I turn 80 that should work. Once I'm the president of the United States---officially that is---then I can kick Bill to the curb, because I will be the most powerful woman in the world! Then I wouldn't need that stupid, horny ass anymore. I wonder why he's not horny around me anymore though and have to look to other women for love? I used to give him an afternoon delight every so often and now he doesn't even ask anymore. Could it be that I'm too dominant? No, that's not it. I'm still beautiful and witty. However, I'm still glad that he has his own bedroom though.

Damn it, I should have won the election, wait...I did win that fucking election!

Bill then entered and broke into her antiquated thoughts about what should have happened in the Presidential Election of 2016.

"Do you have enough wood honeybunch for your fire?" he asked her.

"Knock that 'honey' crap off. I'll let you or Oscar know when I need some more wood. Now get the hell out of here and leave me alone as I'm working on my next book jackass," Hilliary lambasted.

Bill turned around and departed feeling a little dejected. He knew that she was this way due to his *own* fault. *Bad decisions have bad consequences, he thought. He remembered when she used to love him and he blew it. Well, at least I might not have a wife anymore, but I still have a companion...somewhat; just a bitter, grouchy one now.*

Just then, the phone rang and he answered it in the kitchen. It was Carl letting him know that he's needed in the front. Probably another fan looking for my autograph he imagined. I guess I can give one or two since I'm not busy right now.

As he was walking to the entryway and passed by Hilliary's office, she asked him to see who is at the front door. He opened the door and was surprised to find a Congressional Master-at-Arms badge staring at him in his face; a man with an official looking document in his hand. He turned around and lamented for his wife, "It's for you Hilliary!"

★ ★ ★ ★ ★

The next day, Senator Sherman decided to call Senator Willow but to no avail; she did not answer her phone. So he decided to just fly there, rent a car and check on her physically at home, especially since she hasn't been seen around the halls of Congress lately.

Senator Sherman arrived at her Victorian mansion in the morning. He noted that she lived in a *very* desirable neighborhood with no close neighbors. He has known the senator for years and understood her passion to accomplish her goals. He did recall that she had some pretty lofty goals and chuckled at the thought.

He noticed right away that her trash container was still by the curb while no one else's trash container was visible on the street; strange.

He approached the double French front doors cautiously and rang the doorbell. After a minute with no sounds coming from inside the home, he decided to call her home number and heard the phone ringing inside and after three rings it was answered…by her answering machine and he heard her voice in greeting, "You have reached Senator

Willow, of the Cherokee Willows, please leave me a message after the beep…beep."

Senator Sherman decided against leaving a message and hung up and instead tried the door and found it unlocked. As he entered, he called out her name but received no answer. As he thoroughly searched her home, he was disturbed by some of the things that he was a witness to. He finally located Senator Willow; she was in her bedroom laid out on the bed with her arms folded across her chest. On her head was a headband with a single feather. *She looked somewhat regal*, he thought…*almost like an Indian princess. Maybe she really was an Indian.* For all practical purposes, she was deceased.

Better let the proper authorities handle this one, he decided as he dialed 911.

Tucker Carlson

"Good evening and welcome to Tucker Carlson. Tonight, we have a very special guest, Senator Thornton Care. Welcome to the show Senator Care."

"Thank you Tucker, it's good to be here."

"If I remember correctly, we worked together on a charity for our inner city youths."

"That's correct Tucker…Balls for Boys."

"That's right; we were rounding up some basketballs I believe. Alright, you are here to update us on what's going on in the Support Party for the Republicans. So how are things going?"

"Just great Tucker and President Trump *is* keeping his promises to the American people…Left and Right."

"So help me to understand, why does the President need a Support Party to assist him?" Tucker asked most solemnly.

"Tucker, we love and believe in our President like never before in my lifetime and the Liberal Democrats and the dishonest Liberal media don't play fair. As you know, the Democrats even have a Liberal Resistance Party working on trying to find ways to disrupt President Trump's successes. So we need to level the playing field a bit for our beloved President," Senator Care explained passionately.

"I see. Tell me---but I have heard through the grapevine if you will---that there are some Republican 'Never Trumpers' in the Resistance Party. How true do you think that is?"

"That's what we have wind of as well. These 'Never Trumpers' are Republicans meeting with the Resistance Party, who either don't like our President or the President lambasted them in the Primary, or both, and this is their way for revenge. They are acting like Democrats and should be treated as such."

"I see. Wouldn't they have been found out by now if they are meeting with Democrats?"

"Good question Tucker. I imagine that they are meeting by conference calls. Don't know for sure, but that would be my guess. If they are found out meeting physically with the Liberal Democrats, then their careers would be over with their supporters and they would lose friends in the Republican Party."

"Ok Senator Care, I want to also ask you about…hold on a minute. I have just been informed that we have a Fox News Alert. Ok, we are going to Cambridge, Massachusetts where a news conference is being held by Police Chief Martin and the FBI. My producer is telling me that Senator Willow was discovered dead in her home by Senator Sherman"

The news conference appeared on the screen for Fox viewers to witness…

"I'm Police Chief Martin and today the body of Senator Esmeralda Willow was discovered by Senator Burney Sherman at her home here in Cambridge and she was pronounced dead at the scene. We have found some disturbing evidence today, so I would suggest that if your viewers have young children, to have them leave the room."

The police chief waited for a minute or two for parents to hustle their children out of the room. Viewers watching noticed from the lights outside at Senator Willow's home, that it was lightly raining. If paying close attention, they also would have noticed dead body after dead body being removed from the home by wheeled ambulance stretchers, covered by white sheets.

"Senator Willow was discovered dead in her bedroom from a broken neck, with her arms crossed over her chest, wearing a headband with a single feather in her hair. Forensics has determined that the feather is that from a Russian Eagle, which are not native to the U.S. From the overwhelming evidence that we have uncovered, Senator Willow was a confirmed witch and an unconfirmed Indian. Her backyard showed signs where an earlier Sabbat had been held. All of her trees in her backyard had their branches stripped of leaves, there was a circle of chairs along with candles, and, I might add, three cats were found as well. Inside the home, drugs were discovered. That's what we know so far. If there are any questions, I'll be happy to answer them one at a time please. Also, please state what news organization you are with."

As Police Chief Martin looked around at all the media that were present, with their camera lights brightly lit, he knew instinctively that this was one big story. He almost couldn't believe it himself. In fact, he was in shock as he had met Senator Willow before and was not prepared for all of the mounting evidence swirling around this case. Some people you thought you knew, he mused. He didn't know the senator well, but he sure never would have guessed any of this. He thought to himself that he didn't think anyone could have imagined anything like this happening in his city, or to write about in a best-selling book, about a sitting senator who clearly was a witch and …unbelievable! He brought his attention back to the crowd as the questions started flying at him. He called on his first reporter by pointing a finger at him and said, "Go ahead sir."

"Yes, Fox News for Hannity. Chief Martin, can you tell us about all of the dead bodies being removed from the home? Are these members of the Sabbat earlier today?"

"We don't believe so. It appears that the senator had a crypt in her basement. Ten bodies were discovered there with marks on their necks. We do not know how long the bodies have been stationed there. Next question please; you there in the red coat," Police Chief Martin pointed.

"CNN for Augaytus Corbett; do you believe that we should curtail the guns that our citizens are allowed to have in our country?"

"No guns were discovered in the home at this time. Next question…go ahead ma'am."

"Fox News for Justice with Judge Jeanine; can you please tell us what drugs were discovered Chief?"

"We discovered cocaine, nightshade and marijuana. And before you ask, nightshade is a deadly poison derived from plants and known to be used by witches. We do not know if any of the deceased were killed using this drug. Next question, yes you sir."

"CNN for Will Boutros…can you tell us if any ammunition was found in the home Chief?"

"No, no ammunition was found in the home. Why would there be if no guns were discovered in the home? Next question…yeah, go ahead, you there."

"Fox News for Tucker Carlson Chief; how about the neck marks that were found on the dead bodies that you mentioned?"

"We believe at this time, that blood was withdrawn from the bodies through their necks." The Police Chief pointed at another reporter indicating that he was next.

"Yes, I'm with MSNBC for Evening Poe. Do we know yet if any of the dead bodies had hand guns on them?"

People that can read body language could clearly see that Police Chief Martin's facial expression held disgust with the Liberal media as he questioned loudly, "What's wrong with you people? I made it pretty clear that there were *no* hand guns in the home at all. Sounds like only two news media showed up here today; the Left one and the *Right* one. We're done here…thank you all for coming."

Back in the studio with Tucker and on cue from his director, camera one started streaming live and captured the moment as he continued with his show:

"Well, needless to say, that was quite disturbing; discovering a sitting senator who's a witch with three cats and dressed like an Indian and it's not even Halloween yet! What do you make of that Senator Care?"

"I agree with you Tucker…and she's a witch? I never knew. I knew her but obviously *not* that well."

"When you bumped into her in the halls of Congress, did she give you any outward appearance that there was something wrong with her?"

"Other than being a Democrat you mean? No way Tucker, no way. I'm just as shocked by all of this as you are."

"Ok, well thank you for coming on the show Senator Care and I wish you and your Support Party the best of luck. Keep up the great work if you will please and we would like to have you back on the show in the future for an update."

"Thank you Tucker for your support as well and thank you for reporting the news fairly."

"That's what we are all about here at Fox News," Tucker stated seriously and continued with: "when we come back, we'll talk to one man who plans to celebrate Donald Trump's Presidential Anniversary next month in a very cathartic way. Stay tuned and we'll be right back."

CIA

TJ was surfing through television channels trying to find something interesting on when he came across CNN with news about Senator Willow and decided to watch. He didn't need to hear the truth this time since he already knew what happened.

"This is Augaytus Corbett 69 and I'm Augaytus Corbett. We have some late breaking news for you tonight. Shockingly, the body of Senator Esmeralda Willow was discovered today by long term friend and colleague, Senator Burney Sherman. Reportedly, Senator Sherman journeyed to Senator Willow's home to wish her Happy Holidays and was most likely going to take her out to dinner, when he discovered her body on the floor with her medication in her hand. As Senator Willow was known to have high blood pressure, it appears as if she didn't take her medicine on time and died. We want her family to know that our thoughts go out to them in their time of need. Senator Willow will be missed by this station…"

TJ switched the television off and reflected on what he had just heard. First, CNN did not report the complete story. Second, CNN did not report truthfully on what they did report. Third, FAKE NEWS! If only the American people could see and hear what he was seeing and hearing. Clearly, some people did not want to know the truth no matter what. They lived in their simple, little bubble that was to them, a perfect world; a utopian society. Who wants to hear bad news…right? This was the same message that Obama preached so as to keep Americans thinking that they had no worries, and that this ideology somehow would make the country a better place. But did it really work in reality? He thought not. He figured that the only way to solve a problem was to first identify it and then figure the best solution based on facts. That's why I'm a Republican!

Republican Support Party Meeting #3

The following were in attendance, including two new members:

Representative Curt Click – (R-NY) Support Party Chair

Representative Dwight Home – (R-CA) Master-at-Arms

Representative Lay Beebee – (R-PA)
Representative Tamar Meal – (R-PA)
Representative Kane Bundy – (R-TX)
Representative Mona Bu – (R-TN)
Representative Ken Charge – (R-ND)
Senator Thornton Care – (R-AR)
Senator Tut Smith – (R-SC)
Representative Larry Gabriel – (R-TX)
Representative Jem Jerald – (R-OH)

And via conference call:

Senator Jed Med – (D-WV)

"I would like to take this time and welcome two new members to our Support Party," Representative Click announced. "Let's give a warm welcome to Representative Gabriel and Representative Jerald."

The group clapped their hands together and made the two newest members feel right at home. Once things died down, Representative Click continued on with the meeting.

"Let's see here. Representative Charge, do you have a date for appearing on Hannity yet?"

"I do. We will be taping the show next week. Sean told me that we had to push it back due to show requirements."

"Representative Care, have you heard anything from Tucker yet?" Representative Click asked.

"We are on for tomorrow night," answered Representative Care.

"Good enough," Representative Click stated and continued on with the meeting agenda.

One item that came up and was of a real concern with the members, was how the Department of Justice was turning a blind eye to rogue states that are legalizing marijuana for the benefit of raising revenue for their states. Under federal law, marijuana is a schedule 1 drug, the same as LSD and heroine. If the states would properly manage taxpayer's money in the first place, then they wouldn't have to look at other streams of revenue. So if the states mismanage the revenue from pot sales, then do they legalize LSD next for more revenue?

The following states have legalized marijuana in opposition to federal law:

1. Alaska – 2015
2. California – 2018
3. Colorado – 2012
4. Massachusetts – 2018
5. Nevada – 2017
6. Oregon – 2015
7. Washington – 2012
8. DC – 2015

But there was a darker side to this issue with the rogue states. Liberals want free love, drugs and free education. Actually, they wanted everything for free. Because the Democrats want their votes, they jumped onboard with their cause. The Democrats, without regard to public safety or national security, have adopted illegals, felons and druggies as their voting base; all for a vote in order to regain control of the government. They seem to be betting on the stupidity of the American people...so they might succeed! Due to the unbelievable stupidity that Californians are showing, everyone agreed that California is the "Land of the Condemned" including Representative Home who is from California.

Then the members of the Support Party brought up the question...is there anyone at home in the Department of Justice...at all? Apparently not, and then they decided that they need to bring forth a better candidate for Attorney

General than Jeff Sessions. What a big disappointment he turned out to be for President Trump and the country. Someone brought up the fact that their enemies are watching this closely. Given time, the "Dumbing down of America" will soon start showing negative results as outlined by the "Law of Unintended Consequences."

Chapter 10
Ω

"Liberals are almost always inherently tied to corruption…it's in their DNA!"

---Carlene Sullivan

Last month the Democrats in resistance to President Trump refused to sign on with a tax bill that would offer relief to most Americans as well as American companies. Now this month in the New Year, brought more of the same. The Democrats do not want to fund the government and a shutdown looms over the Nation because the Liberals want something in the funding that will create a path to citizenship for about a million illegals plus. Their game is clear as day. Fight for illegals. The Republicans will cave in and the Democrats will have another one million new voters plus and more that will arrive legally through "chain migration."

Currently there are 12 states and DC that allow illegals to obtain driver's licenses without substantiating legal status. These states only require a "proof of residency" from applicants in order to be issued a driver's license; legal status is not verified. The following states passed legislation to allow illegals this benefit that up to 1993 was reserved exclusively for American citizens:

OPERATION: Ωmega

States That Allow Illegals to Obtain State Driver's Licenses

1. Washington   July 25, 1993
2. New Mexico   March 18, 2003
3. Utah   March 8, 2005
4. Illinois   November 28, 2013
5. Vermont   January 1, 2014
6. Nevada January 1, 2014
7. Maryland   January 1, 2014
8. DC   May 1, 2014
9. Colorado   August 1, 2014
10. Connecticut   January 1, 2015
11. California   January 1, 2015
12. Delaware   December 27, 2015
13. Hawaii   January 1, 2016

Illegals now have the ability to vote in these states, even though it's against federal law to do so unless you are a citizen. Republicans need to be proactive and take action against this dishonest sleight of hand from the Democrats playbook---as they are trolling for new voters---or they might find themselves as the minority party and not in control anymore, which means, common sense will be missing in the halls of Congress as well as Republicans! It's much better to be "proactive" than "reactive."

If illegal aliens are not opposed to breaking our federal law of crossing the border illegally, then why would it matter if they vote illegally as well…or break any other laws? Illegals understand that they have nothing to lose from breaking our laws and everything to gain. When illegal aliens have nothing to fear or lose, they will be more than willing to take risks.

Another major issue is those people that come to the United States legally with an approved visa and then overstay their permitted time limit and become illegal. They are then forced to "hiding out" from the feds while simultaneously searching for employment with sympathetic companies---or legal residents---that are seeking cheap labor. Simply put, illegals don't respect and value our rule of law and companies with a desire to improve their bottom line will exceedingly, exploit illegal aliens for their own preferential gain. Illegals understand that the penalty for breaking our laws is generally deportation back to their home country of record, free of charge!

California---the land of the condemned---now is trying to pass a law that would allow illegals the right to *register* to vote. Isn't that contrary to federal law? It appears that California desires to leave the union and become their own country and there are those that would say "Goodbye and good riddance and don't let the door hit you in the ass on your way out!"

California also wants to pass a law that if a server at a restaurant gives a customer a plastic straw without requesting it, then the server would be fined and could possibly go to jail for six months. Really…how dumb can a state get?

The land of the condemned however does get an award…an award for having the highest poverty rate in the whole country…imagine that!

Then there is Carmela Montana who used to be Private Brenton Montana of the United States Army. He goes in as a male, gives away secrets, goes to prison for seven years, has a sex change---at taxpayer's expense--- and receives a pardon from Obama and is released as a woman and now announces that *she* is running for the senate in Maryland as a Democrat! Only in America…with the freaks coming out to vote for *her*! Obviously, there are some mental issues concerning her *and* her supporters.

Then through the Inspector General, it was revealed that the DOJ and the FBI had a "Secret Society" which certain members of the two agencies met and discussed how to keep Candidate Trump from becoming the President and when that effort didn't succeed, then the Liberal Left germinated a plan on how to impeach President Trump…amazing!

TJ sincerely hoped and prayed that his new friend, Special Agent Mingo, was not involved in this crap. He didn't believe so though.

These were just some of the thoughts that ran through TJ's mind as he studied the file on Representative Jarl Lidio. It was hard to concentrate on your work when your country seems to be going to hell. Just then, his boss Randy entered his office via Judy's reception area and seated himself.

"How are things TJ," he asked.

"Ok, just thinking about the hell that our country is currently experiencing while studying Congressman Lidio's file."

"Yeah, about that; we need you to put that one aside for now and look into Senator Cole Burris. You have the green light to take him out next."

TJ shrugged, "You're the boss and it's not a problem. I'll go down and see Jessy for the file. Can I ask why we are switching though?"

"This turd is using the senate floor and is grand standing dishonestly against the President. So, the powers to be---director Lannister and me---have decided that it's time for him to just leave; one way or another. Just store Representative Lidio's file in your safe for now and if nothing new comes up then he will be next in line."

TJ cleared his throat while picking up Representative Lidio's file from his desk and said, "Ok, I'm on it."

After Randy departed his office, TJ went to his safe and opened it and stuck in Representative Lidio's file. He then closed the door and stood up thinking that this might be a good time for lunch in the cafeteria. He popped in to Judy's area and advised her that he was going to lunch and then to the file vault to see Jessy. Judy nodded and said that she would hold his calls till his return; if there were any.

Today in the cafeteria, TJ asked Chef Tony for a steak done medium and some French toast with extra cinnamon. Chef Tony was a real asset to the CIA he concluded. He was always ready to assist TJ with his "food fetish," all the while keeping a smile on his face at all times. TJ then grabbed up some green beans with hickory smoked bacon along with a small glass of milk and a cup of coffee and added these items to his tray and approached the cashier who he knew, but could never remember her name.

"Hi Mr. Law, how are you today?"

He then took note of her name tag which read "Coco."

"Hi Coco, I'm ok and you?"

"Oh Mr. Law, of course I'm ok when you are here…you know that," she responded and smiled from ear to ear.

"I know that Coco and that's one of the reasons that I come here, just to see you smile."

He knew that she lived for compliments and he didn't disappoint her this time as her smile was infectious. He handed over his badge and it was swiped and he was given a receipt. He didn't understand why the cafeteria handed out receipts, but he displayed it on his table anyway which was actually a small booth. He bowed his head and silently said a quick but meaningful prayer. Just as he was opening his eyes, a voice broke into his thoughts.

"Hi TJ," greeted Ching Ching. "May I sit with you kind sir?"

Well, she was beautiful and an employee…sooo, why not? Plus, maybe he could learn something from her.

"Sure Ching Ching; have a seat," TJ indicated the opposite side of the table with a gesture of his hand.

"Thank you Mr. Law. I see that you seem to like the green beans here?"

"Actually, I love them and Tony grills an awesome steak by the way."

"Ching Ching is not into steak, but chicken ok."

TJ noticed that Ching Ching had some grilled chicken, rice and noodle soup on her tray.

"I like their chicken as well---especially their rotisserie chicken---but just decided on the steak today."

"You man and it's good for man to eat steak. But in my country, only the rich people in my village can afford steak. My father could afford to pay but no exercise and he died…bad heart."

Both were eating their lunch while chatting.

"I'm sorry to hear that Ching Ching," TJ commented honestly.

"Don't be, I didn't like him anyway. But he was my father so I do have some respect for him. What about you?"

He didn't exactly know what she was asking but he responded with, "I was raised to respect my elders also."

"No silly, what movie do you like?"

How did the word "movie" show up now he wondered? He was having a little difficulty in understanding her but continued on anyway.

"I don't really like movies too much as my work keeps me quite busy," he replied confidentially.

"I like cowboy movies sometimes. I know we can see beautiful American movie together. At the IMAX Theater nearby, they have nice movie called 'The Secret.' I know you like so what do you say?"

"Are you asking me out Ching Ching?" TJ asked amazed at her directness.

"No I don't. Ching Ching just helps to guide you into asking her and I accept."

"I don't know if I have time right now. How about a rain check later this week?" he asked.

"But the Weather Channel says no rain this week."

"No Ching Ching, that is just an expression. It means, I'll let you know when I have time and then we can go if you're free."

"No, Ching Ching is not free. I have to pay like you too."

How in the hell did she get a job with the CIA? It seems that we have a little bit of a disconnect going on, he thought; *communication gap!*

"I mean if you are available sometime in the future this week that maybe we can go together to see a movie," TJ reiterated.

"I see, but no funny stuff cowboy."

Apparently, she really did watch "cowboy" movies he admitted.

He assured her that "no funny stuff" was planned on his part and that he would contact her later in the week. When finished with their conversation and food, they parted company. Ching Ching said that she needed to use the restroom before returning to work and TJ stated that he was going to see Jessy.

When he arrived at Jessy's cube, she was not there, but a note stated that she would return in five minutes. So he had a seat and picked up her red ball cap that was sitting on her desk. As he turned it in his hands, on the front he noticed the words right away that declared: "Make America Great Again." Well, at least she has good taste he thought.

While at work, TJ was always on his toes and probing for any "deep staters" that might exist in the organization. He didn't want to see the CIA that he loved and respected so much turned into the same mess as the FBI. As a true Patriot, he was always looking out for his country's best interests; which included the CIA.

Jessy's return broke into his thoughts of love of country.

"Hey TJ, I didn't know you were coming by, or I would have been here for you."

"No biggie. Sorry for not giving you heads up, but I need another file. I still have the file on Representative Lidio though."

"We have to keep that file secured if you are not using it you know."

"It's in my safe," TJ replied. "My boss noted that to me already."

"Well, he did right the right thing. We don't want to have the same issues as the FBI or the damage that Hilliary caused to our country with unsecured files, email and servers."

"You got that right. She should be in prison already, just for the lack of protecting our country's secrets not to mention all of the other crap that they have on her."

"Do you think that she will ever go to prison?" Jessy asked seriously.

"I don't know, but I wouldn't be surprised. Right now, some members of Congress are fighting to uncover all of the corruption surrounding her, Bill and their foundation as well as the DOJ and the FBI. I just heard on Fox News the other day that email and text messages that they finally captured, showed that some of the upper management folks in those agencies were worried that if they came down too hard on Hilliary, and if she became president, that she would remember those that were against her before she won the election. Then of course, the shit would really hit the fan…pardon my French," TJ added quickly.

"Don't worry about my virgin ears. I work around a lot of men in this agency and I hear much worse all the time."

"I thought you would be ok with my language, but because of my passion and love of country, I just have to let things out some times."

"Yeah, I know that feeling. Been there, done that."

"Anyhow, I need another file if you please." When she didn't respond, he continued, "I need the file on Senator Cole Burris."

"No problem," Jessy replied as she began tying into her computer. "I just need to look up the location here. You wouldn't believe how many files we have in storage…millions."

"Well, you'll have to show me the file vault some time," he suggested.

"No can do bro. The file vault is a highly controlled area. I wouldn't be able to get you in even if I really wanted to…sorry."

TJ realized that she didn't know his true security level and it wasn't important for him to emphasize that. Maybe one day when he wasn't so busy, he would check out the file vault on his own. But right now, he needed to jump on this mission due to its urgent nature *and* a request from his boss.

"Got it," Jessy wrote the location down and reached into a drawer and pulled out a magazine and handed it to TJ. "Look at this will you and I'll be right back," she insisted.

He took the magazine and noticed that it was a copy of "Police Times." *Wow, I guess that she's really is into her job*, he thought. As he flipped through the pages, the hairs on the back of his neck pricked warningly and he looked around hastily. Ching Ching was just around the corner kneeling as if listening to his and Jessy's conversation. He felt an icy stab in his stomach that he couldn't explain. Standing up, he addressed her…

"Ching Ching, what's happening?" he asked her without acerbity.

"I'm returning from bathroom break and dropped my pen. Why you ask agent man?"

"You just startled me."

"Oh, so sorry to do that; I try and not drop pen anymore, agent Law," she stated quite formally and entered her cube.

TJ had an uneasy feeling about her but set it aside and went back to his magazine. Then, he realized that he didn't notice a pen in Ching Ching's hand. Maybe he just couldn't see it. But he filed that bit of information into his subconscious. After a few minutes, Jessy returned with his file.

"Here you go TJ," as she handed him the bulky file. "I noticed that in the front is some newly entered information. That means that this is an active file and has caught the attention of someone else in the agency."

He thanked her and headed back to his office. He dived right into his work and studied the file carefully and taking notes on anything that might be of interest in accomplishing his mission. Judy came in only once and brought him some coffee, just the way he liked it and some honey roasted peanuts. *How did she know that I like them?* he wondered. *Oh well, maybe she was a secret agent in disguise!* But he put the thought aside and continued reading while snacking on his nuts.

The senator he noticed was from New Jersey and was a previous mayor. He is considered a junior senator since he was still relatively new to Congress. Now the senator was already on his radar; what a shame.

As he continued reading the file, he noticed some petty crimes that he was involved with in his younger life, with some exceptions. There was one case of grand theft auto that caught his attention when the senator was 17. He was not sentenced to jail that time as the jury was deadlock on a decision and the judge in the case dismissed it since he was underage. There were other issues involving drug use with marijuana and heroin. He noticed that by attending some court ordered classes and community service in the Newark's South Ward, Burris successfully avoided jail time...once again. *Yeah, just what we need, more people in Congress with a criminal record,* he concluded sarcastically.

Additionally, the file revealed that the senator was involved in some protests. Most notably and recently in 2012, while as mayor, the protest involved a demand that the federal government was to give away free education to everyone who wanted it, including illegals. *Yeah, this is a deserving and legitimate dirt bag,* he mused.

From the background that he was reading about Burris, proved that this was your typical, Washington lowlife who was out to make a name for himself while using his Congressional position to feather his own nest at the expense of the American people. This was definitely one of the many "swamp dwellers" who President Trump often referred to at his rallies that should be *drained*. "Well, we'll just have to *drain* him then," TJ thought out loud.

Glancing back at the file showed him that this asshole is a confirmed Liberal. Ok, a Liberal, a lowlife and a dirt bag! The more he read the more concerned he became and understood the urgency in his boss's request. Obviously, the initial request would have come from the CIA's director based on intelligence. Seeing the latest entries in the file substantiated why he made Director Lannister's radar.

The file clearly showed that the company that the senator kept was with other political dirt bags and hacks, which didn't come as a complete surprise. TJ was then reminded of a proverb from the 16th century that fit this narrative well: "Birds of a feather flock together."

As TJ continued reading, he learned that the senator was not married, which was a definite plus. His file even hinted to the ideal that the senator may be gay, but nothing was substantiated as of yet.

Then, something special caught TJ's eye…the word "swim." It seems that the senator from New Jersey liked to go swimming at a place called the, "Brothers Swimming Center" located in DC. The file mentioned that he generally goes there in the evening, after work and would be there for as long as a couple of hours. This was a significant piece of information as TJ was at home in the water from his SEAL training while serving in the United States Navy.

So he figured to case the place that night and maybe with happenstance, the good Senator Burris would show up for one final swim. If not tonight, then perhaps another night; at least he would have an idea of the layout in any event. He had better bring along a Russian clue just in case an opportunity presented itself, and he knew exactly what to bring…something that he remembered seeing in the Russian

Items Locker previously. After securing his article of choice from the items locker, he left the CIA building and trekked to the nation's capital; a city named after our first President…Washington, who was considered to be the father of our country. He decided to leave a bit early in order to avoid the traffic rush…somewhat.

Republican Support Party Meeting #4

The following members were in attendance at this meeting which took place in a congressional conference room at the Longworth House Office Building:

Representative Curt Click – (R-NY) Support Party Chair

Representative Dwight Home – (R-CA) Master-at-Arms

Representative Lay Beebee – (R-PA)
Representative Tamar Meal – (R-PA)
Representative Kane Bundy – (R-TX)
Representative Mona Bu – (R-TN)
Representative Ken Charge – (R-ND)
Senator Thornton Care – (R-AR)
Senator Tut Smith – (R-SC)
Representative Larry Gabriel – (R-TX)
Representative Jem Jerald – (R-OH)

"This meeting will now come to order as the Master-at-Arms has completed his roll call with all present and accounted for…and that's more than we can say about those who are attending---or not attending---the Resistance Party Meeting," Representative Click announced which brought a chuckle from those in the room.

"How was that episode with Tucker Carlson, Senator Care?" Representative Click asked rhetorically and then stated, "That was awesome. Did everyone get to see the show? So now we have another *issue* with a Democrat showing up and she turned out to be a real bitch…I mean, a real witch! Who knew?"

Everyone was having a good laugh at the expense of Senator Willow. This was due to the fact that she was not one of them and that they felt that she got what she richly deserved. Representative Click allowed his Support Party members some time to savor this moment and then he continued on:

"I want to also give Senator Care two thumbs up for his part in the show."

Representative Click paused to allow everyone to show their appreciation by clapping and after a few seconds, everyone stood while continuing to clap---a sincere standing ovation for a good man. Representative Jerald gave Senator Care two thumbs up. Senator Care was beaming with pride knowing that he played a vital role for the good of the country.

Another thirty minutes later and the meeting completed with everyone dispersing the building for their respective homes and families.

Brothers Swimming Center

It was around 2100 when TJ finally noticed that the car of Senator Burris had finally arrived in the parking lot of the Brothers Swimming Center. He knew this information from the intelligence that he read on Burris back at the CIA. As the senator was exiting his 2016 Jaguar, with New Jersey plates that read: "BADASS," someone from the center approached him and some words were exchanged and then came a big brotherly hug that lasted at least fifteen seconds! After the two separated, Senator Burris started walking towards the front of the building while the other fellow climbed into his car and drove away.

Approximately a half hour later, TJ carefully approached the front double doors after verifying through a window that the senator was indeed swimming by himself.

One door was cracked open from a door stop that was wedged enough so that the door wouldn't be able to close and lock. *My advantage,* he thought. Otherwise, he would have to pick the lock or find some other means in. But this was definitely more convenient. *So Burris likes the water does he? So do I ...so do I!* TJ admitted to himself.

★ ★ ★ ★ ★

TJ's mission was another success and he was now on his way home. Maybe he would sleep in tomorrow a little he thought. Traffic on I-95 was light at this time of night. When he arrived at the gate, the guard checked his I.D. and waved him on. He pulled up into his driveway with the thought that it was good to be home again.

Once inside, he turned on Fox News to hear if there was anything new happening. On the show, they were talking with regard to a book of lies about President Trump. The name of the book was "Flame and Chill." That's all we need is another book on the market that is all lies against the President.

He poured a bowl of Raisin Bran and added some half and half and sat down in his reclining chair to relax. After finishing his cereal, he fell asleep and sometime before morning, he was in a REM state…

TJ found himself in a heat-searing desert. As he looked down, he noticed Senator Burris staked out naked close to a red ant hill. His bald head was gleaming in the bright sunlight and sweat popped out on his forehead in beads. He struggled weakly at his bonds that held him securely to the ground. TJ then realized that he was holding his Buck Navy SEAL knife with its 7 ½" blade.

"Why are you doing this to me?" Senator Burris asked extremely concerned.

"Because you're a lowlife loser and a corrupt political hack," TJ responded.

"Anything else you want to mention to me while I'm helplessly tied down?"

"Yeah, you're a dirt bag as well. You Liberal pigs are only exploiting the American people for your own greedy means and I take exception to that. You have been involved in crime or corruption your whole life and now you think that by cleaning up your act a bit and acquiring a slick tongue like your mentor, Obama, you somehow conceive this idea that that makes it all right...wrong! You corrupt Liberal dipshits have created a country of dichotomy and need to be held accountable. You created your own situation Burris, so now accept it like the political hack that you are and move on...oh, I almost forgot, you won't be moving anywhere, unless it's to Hell...enjoy!"

TJ wanted to scalp him but quickly realized that that was nearly impossible since the senator was already bald. The Indians back in the 1800's would not have like this guy a bit and probably would have hung him upside down over an open fire to roast his brains---which he obviously is lacking.

As TJ scanned the vast area that made up the desert, he noticed for the first time that there were other Liberal Democrats staked out as well with other Navy SEALs watching over them. They were yelling at their staked victims and some even landed blows to their heads. He recognized some of the corrupt liars and this brought a tight smile to his face. Then the senator brought him out of his thoughts with a question.

"What did you do with our party leader you bastard?" Senator Burris asked.

"Who is your 'supposed' party leader?" TJ questioned.

"You know who it is...Senator Simpson."

"Oh, you mean the head clown? Let's just say that he got in the way of something."

"What about our other leader...Representative Paloma?"

"Let's just say that she's hanging around...somewhere."

"What about Senator Willow?"

"Let's just say that she's resting peacefully in her home. Now shut up before I shut you up," then as an afterthought, TJ asked, *"are you ready to meet your maker?"*

Senator Burris all of a sudden started yelling and TJ glanced down again. As he was carefully watching, the senator started to squirm for some reason, then he noticed the fire ants making their way to his eyes and up into his nose, probably searching for moisture or shade and some was already marching across his balls and on his flagpole, only at present, there was no wind blowing...

TJ woke with a start and realized that he just had a bad dream, or a good dream depending how you wanted to look at it. He wondered what this dream was supposed to mean. He believed that God allowed everyone to have certain dreams for a reason. He would often study on a dream and try to figure out the meaning, but most of the time to no avail.

He turned off the television and headed for his bedroom and hopefully back to sleep with no more dreams for tonight. He contemplated about Senator Burris in his new predicament in the desert and smiled. *At least he didn't drown this time...just the opposite!*

The next morning, he awoke with a slow start as he realized that someone was ringing his doorbell and knocking on his front door. *What the hell?* He climbed out of bed wearing only his Navy sweats and a t-shirt and answered the door to find Special Agent Bob Mingo standing there with a smile on his face.

"What the hell do you want?" TJ unceremoniously questioned.

"I want to take you to breakfast...my treat." After some scrutiny of TJ's face, then he added, "You look like hell. What happened, bad night?"

"Thanks. I had a rough night alright and then a good dream…I mean a bad dream."

"Well get dressed and we'll go to Bob Evans for breakfast and you can tell me all about it."

TJ turned on the T.V. for his friend to watch while he took his shower and hurriedly dressed. Once he got some coffee and food in him, he figured that he would feel better. They both drove to the Bob Evans on base and ordered their food.

"So how did you know where I lived," TJ questioned Bob.

Bob pulled out his FBI badge and displayed it to his friend.

"That's right, I forgot," TJ admitted. "But I have a question for you."

"Ask away my friend."

"Are you involved in any of this corruption going on in the FBI?" TJ asked directly.

"No I'm not and I'm surprised that you have to ask. First, I'm an honest person. Second, I'm a Trump supporter because he stands for law and order. Third…ok, I don't have a third."

"I just wanted to see what you would say. So what do you know about all of this corruption that's going on? Give me the inside scoop if you will."

"I'll tell you what I know, but this is just between us…right?"

"Right," TJ affirmed.

"Where to start is the question." After taking a deep breath, Bob continued. "In case you didn't know, Bill and Hilliary are massively corrupt beyond belief. We---the rank and file---men and women at the FBI have known this for some time. The Clintons are part of a 'Secret Society' of greed and power that everybody seems to be afraid of, so that's why nothing is being done about it. The people of this Secret Society are made up of Obama, Biden, Bill and Hilliary Clinton, Cowan, McCabe and many others. This

Secret Society is comparative to the KKK…on steroids! Nobody wants to feel the wrath of this Secret Society. From news reports, you know some of this…Hilliary wanted the power of the presidency badly and Obama is complicit in all of this as well and is supporting her corrupt desire to grab the most powerful position in the world so that the Dems could stay in power. Obama has his fingers in a lot of this corruption, but is being protected by the members of this Secret Society. But the truth is, he is as dirty as a twenty dollar whore, I can assure you. The plan was that if Hilliary won, all of this corruption would continue and be kept *secret* and they figured that the Republicans would never be in power again; Hilliary was their ace-in-the-hole. But if Trump was to win, then they were to cover their tracks while dumping on Trump; impeachment. But I can tell you this much from others that I've talked with, that the Secret Society went completely insane when Trump won. They couldn't accept the election results and lurched into shock and disbelief, and I was told that milk and cookies had to be passed out as comfort food. On Election Day, these people were all together watching the results at a secret location. They thought that it was in the bag for Hilliary and came up disturbingly wrong."

As their server brought their food, Bob paused in his story and took a drink of his water. Once the server left, he continued:

"Now one or two or three members of the Resistance Party are part of this Secret Society of corruption. I can't tell you any of that though. But, this has been going on for years and expanded rapidly once Obama got into office. Basically, he put the word out that The White House was open for business…dirty laundry business that is!"

TJ just continued to look at his friend while scraping some grape jelly on his toast; his friend continued:

"You have no idea how big this is. A cesspool of corruption and it makes Watergate looks like child's play. I don't even know if all of this can be cleaned up it's so massive."

TJ finished his toast and then asked: "What about all of these Liberal Democrats that are missing or dying? Does the FBI know anything about that?"

"No we don't. If it's the Russians doing it, then they are very bad about their work with always leaving a clue behind that implicates them. But I don't think that the Russians are that sloppy. I think the Russians are being framed. Word has it in the department that it's probably the Chinese behind all of this. But that's only a hypothesis though."

TJ and Bob were both disciples of law and order. Besides being Trump supporters and Navy veterans, this was just another thing that they had in common and why they were good friends. Otherwise, Bob would not have shared this confidential information with him.

TJ thanked Bob for breakfast and vowed that they would do lunch or dinner sometime; his treat. TJ left the tip and both men departed for their respective agencies. TJ had a report to type up.

CIA

Back in his office, Judy brought him a cup of coffee and a cinnamon twirl.

"Morning Mr. Law, here's your morning coffee and favorite roll, in case you haven't had your breakfast yet."

"Thanks Judy. I did have breakfast but I still can handle the coffee and roll."

Judy smiled with pride. She really liked working for Randy and TJ. She was pleased that the CIA hired TJ as he was a valuable asset for the agency…even though she wasn't exactly sure what he did, being that his missions were kept a secret. She thought that she might have an idea from watching Fox News regularly, but it would have been inappropriate and unprofessional to say something and she could even lose her job if she wasn't smart enough to keep her mouth shut.

"Just let me know if you need anything else Mr. Law."

"Thanks Judy." As Judy turned to leave, TJ rapidly added, "I really appreciate how well you take care of me."

"It's no problem and it's my job and I sincerely enjoy it anyway," she replied and meant every word and returned to her own work area.

He turned to his computer and with a few clicks of his mouse, was able to access a blank 203 form and started typing…

Chapter 11
Ω

"Liberal change is good…so let's get rid of all of them!"

---Rod Reese

The Republicans, with the President's blessing, was able to release a FISA Memo for all America to see. Of course, the Democrats did not want that to happen and are working to release their own memo. President Trump has their memo at The White House and has five days to review it. Another government shutdown is looming…again. The Democrats refuse to take any responsibility for their actions that work against what's good for the country. Is their hate for President Trump greater than love of country? TJ clearly knew the answer to that question; their hate for the President *was* greater than love of country.

With these thoughts in his mind, he was studying the file once again on Representative Lidio and realized that it was time for Fox's Tucker Carlson. He turned on his T.V. just as the show was starting.

On a split screen, Tucker on the left while Representative Sinclair appeared on the right with the captioned underneath reading, "Liberal Media & Democrats Meltdown…What Was in The Memo That Americans Shouldn't See?"

"Good evening and welcome to Tucker Carlson. I just want to wish my grandpa who just turned 80 today, a happy birthday.

"The Democrats are making condescending remarks about our President including Representative Evan Sinclair and he joins us now. So congressman, many Democratic leaders including Representative Stoner, said that with the release of the FISA Memo that was put together by the Republicans, it would create a national crisis by revealing sources and methods. That turned out to be a lie of course. There was nothing in the memo that was classified and there was no reason for it to be classified in the first place. So why would they tell us that when they knew it wasn't true?"

With a half-smile on his face that probably indicated that Representative Sinclair was most likely thinking that he was in for a rough ride with Tucker, but also thinking that he was Democrat enough to take it and still come out on top…but sadly, he would discover just how wrong he was.

"Good evening Tucker and you should be concerned about this too. It does reveal sources and methods and you should read it…"

Tucker nodded once and cut in with, "I did."

Representative Sinclair then continued…"Just because you knew the sources ahead of time since it was released to Fox News before the other media, doesn't mean that you read it…"

"So please be precise on how it jeopardizes our national security if you will, because I never want to play a role in that…"

"Well you are playing a role in that right now."

"Tell me how."

"You're playing a role in it right now with bringing this subject up on your show, because, we don't reveal sources…"

"What source exactly are you talking about and how does that imperil our country?"

"Well the Memo goes into Papadopoulos and Page and others that you only knew about because it was reported on…"

"Wait, hold up here. You just accused me of being a traitor to my country and I want you to be very precise on how you are coming to that conclusion."

TJ paused the show on his DVR player as Judy entered his office with some coffee and asked if he would like anything else before she left. He knew that she needed to leave a little early today to check on her ailing mother at the nursing home.

"Well, maybe some fresh popped microwave popcorn…please? I'm watching a really great show on Fox with Tucker Carlson."

"I can do that, just give me three minutes."

Judy disappeared through her office door to get TJ his popcorn. He would wait until her return before continuing on with Tucker.

Judy returned in a jiffy with his popcorn and after she departed, he started the show again.

"I knew about it because Papadopoulos was indicted. The memo came out and we, the American people have now seen what was in it, so explain to me how I'm being a traitor and please be precise. I think it's only fair to ask you how I'm doing this."

"The larger danger…" Representative Sinclair started.

"No," Tucker interrupted the congressman, "I'm not going to let this slide. You have two choices here. You can apologize now and take back what you said previously or you can explain yourself," Tucker informed Sinclair.

"We don't reveal sources Tucker and…"

"I read the memo congressman and it doesn't reveal any methods or sources. If that is all you Democrats have; pretty weak if you ask me."

Clearly, the viewers could tell that Representative Sinclair was quite agitated as he raised his voice at Tucker while his face showed consternation.

"Tucker, why don't you join the rest of us and become an American and be a part of the American dream? Your show is so full of propaganda for the Right."

"First off, let's lower the tone congressman and I don't appreciate that first you call me a traitor on my own show and now you say that I'm not an American? I was born here in this country and unlike Obama, my birth certificate wasn't manufactured in Photoshop like I believe his was. Also, what do you think CNN is doing with the Left? It's strictly propaganda and brain washing."

"Tucker, shut your mouth about President Obama and CNN," stated Congressman Sinclair with his voice at a higher octave than before. "I knew that man personally and he was more American than you and I put together. And as for CNN, it's a great media outlet that your station will never be!"

"Let's lower you voice Sinclair and answer this one simple question. Why did President Obama give Iran over a $150 billion dollars? Why did the Russians acquire twenty percent of our uranium that we know is a valuable asset? In fact, I'm told with all the things that uranium is used for, that we don't have enough as it is. Then the Clinton Foundation is given $140 million dollars as a donation from the Russians? Frankly Sinclair, I don't see the Russians as being a very charitable people. Furthermore, why did Obama allow this country to double the national debt in just eight years? I believe, as an American, that these are all good questions and that the American people deserve an explanation. What say you congressman?"

"I say that I'm out of here and that this is the last time that you will ever see me on your damn Right-wing, propaganda show…that's what I say and your show sucks!"

With a mixed look of relief and surprise on his face, Tucker recovered quickly as he watched Representative Sinclair take off his microphone and throw it on the ground as he stormed off.

"Well, not like it hasn't happen before on this show, because it has, but this will be the last time that I'll have Representative Sinclair back on the show I assure you and I want to apologize to our viewers for his outburst as it is not very professional, especially coming from a sitting congressman.

"Coming up next, a man who is trying to make a difference in the world of disabled veterans, wait…my producer is telling me that we have a Fox News Alert."

Regular viewers of Fox News are more than used to the Fox News Alerts by now as it indicates that something of importance is coming up next.

"We have just received word that Senator Burris has been found deceased at the Brothers Swimming Center in D.C. and now I'm being informed that the police chief there is giving a press conference. We'll take you there now live…"

Fox viewers were then transported to the Brothers Swimming Center at night for the press briefing being held by the police chief of D.C. The press briefing was outside of the swimming center as the inside was still being investigated. Reporters had their lights shining on the microphone that the police chief would be speaking into. A minute later, a big black man emerged from the swimming center and approached reporters with what looked to be a file in his hand.

"I'm Police Chief George Thomas Madison Jr. the Third of the D.C. Metropolitan Police Department. I will start by telling you what we know so far and then I will be available for questions. Senator Burris was found dead earlier today by the manager who was opening for business. The manager reported that the senator was found in the pool where he liked to swim, floating face down. An initial finding from the coroner indicates that Senator Burris drowned. The cause of the drowning is still being investigated. We don't know at this time if the drowning was nefarious or not. The junior senator from New Jersey was known in D.C. as being a somewhat controversial person with some of his radical ideas, so our investigation continues. As a side note, we did discover a Russian Federation towel in the senator's gym bag. We do not know at this time if that is a clue or not, or if the senator was given the towel from a Russian friend or if he possibly purchased it off of the internet or at a local store, but as an African-American myself, I am here to assure the American people that we will not leave any rock unturned in our investigation. Now then, with that being said, I will open this press briefing to questions and I urge you to please be brief though. Also, we will use Thomas's Rules of Etiquette. For some of you junior reporters that may be in attendance tonight, this is where you will state your name and what news organization that you are with and then you may proceed with your question. I expect that when I call on someone, the rest of the media will have the courtesy to lower your voices so we can all hear the question that is being asked…ok, let's start."

Most of the reporters started yelling and waving their arms frantically trying to grabbed the police chief's attention to be the first to ask their question. Chief Madison first called upon a young lady that was not drawing a lot of attention to her. Everyone did quiet down and allowed the young woman to ask her question.

"Thank you Chief Madison. My name is Betty and I'm an intern reporter for Tucker Carlson at Fox News. I was just wondering how experienced of a swimmer was Senator Burris, sir?"

"Good question Betty. From what we have learned from the manager here at the swimming center, Senator Burris would usually swim around 50 laps or even more at times. So he was considered a very good swimmer. However, history dictates that even experience swimmers can have a problem or two. Once we conduct an autopsy, we should be able to learn if the senator had a leg cramp or something else. Good question though…"

The Police Chief then called on someone from CNN.

"Chief, do we know how many Russians were involved in this incident?"

The police chief only shook his head in disbelief while thinking: *Where do these dumbasses come from?*

"I'll take the next question," Police Chief Madison firmly stated.

But the CNN reporter refused to be ignored and yelled out again.

"Why not answer the question Chief? Is it a cover up for the Russians that is taking place here?"

"No it isn't, but to speak plainly…you're an asshole. I told everyone to state their name and affiliation and you couldn't follow simple instructions, so now you will be removed…sergeant."

A police sergeant moved forward and reached out to grab the obnoxious reporter who was able to slip away only to run smack into another police officer who was able to hold him. Together, while both officers were escorting the CNN reporter away from the press briefing, suddenly, without any indication of what he was planning, the reporter kicked the sergeant in the shin. Now, due to the assault on a police officer, they escorted him to a nearby police unit where he was handcuffed, searched and whisked away to be booked at the local precinct.

A couple of the local news stations had angled their cameras just right and had all of this on tape for their viewers to see.

After the incident had passed, the police chief moved forward to the microphone once again and called on another reporter for their question. This reporter did not make the same mistake as the last guy and stated his name clearly and it just happened to be a Fox News reporter for Hannity!

After a short press conference, viewers of Fox News were transported back to the comfort of the studio with Tucker Carlson.

"Well, tell me that wasn't disturbing and hard to watch…at first. Coming up next, we have a man who says that he can…wait a minute. I've just been told that we have another Fox News Alert. The body of Carmela Montana was discovered in American Park in D.C. early this morning. It appears that *she* was fatally shot sometime around 3:00 a.m. and seems to have been a robbery attempt. D.C.

Metropolitan Police Department is investigating and we will keep you posted on what they discover as it is released to us. We'll be right back…"

TJ muted the television and picked up the file on Representative Jarl Lidio thinking that he had better get back to work now, especially since he had finished his popcorn. As he was studying the file, Randy popped into his office and sat down in front of TJ in one of the high quality leather bound chairs in front of TJ's desk.

"I just watched CNN about Senator Burris and great job by the way," Randy stated.

"What did they say exactly?" TJ inquired.

"They reported that Russian operatives broke into the Brothers Swim Center nefariously and killed the senator with a needle to the neck and then threw him back into the pool, dead."

"I didn't have to break in, the door was left ajar and he was drowned."

"I know, I read your report. It's just so unbelievable how news outlets like CNN can misrepresent the facts to suit their own twisted desires."

"What do you think their objective is in doing that?" TJ asked seriously.

"You know as well as I do that they are totally in opposition to President Trump and don't want to see him re-elected in 2020. For heaven's sake, they are having a meltdown with him being elected once let alone twice! When the President wins in 2020, half of them will likely turn to crime and hostilities…openly."

"I heard on Fox that Joe Biden is thinking of running in 2020."

"Well, if you ask me, that pond scum couldn't win a school yard fight let alone a presidential election. Like Hilliary, he would be a flawed candidate from the start. Anyway, President Trump with his successes stacking up would have a field day with him and any others who want to join the pack. The American people are now having a taste of success for our country and it tastes real good to them."

"I wholeheartedly agree with you."

"So what are you up to right now?" his boss asked him.

"Before you came in, I was watching Tucker Carlson and enjoying some popcorn…It's really a great show tonight," TJ stated happily. "He mentioned the unexplainable death of Senator Burris and had an argument with another senator…Senator Sinclair who was an invited guest on his show and who walked out on Tucker because he couldn't take the heat. But don't worry boss, I have the Lidio file right here and I'm just getting started on it…again."

"That's what I came to talk to you about. We need to ice him for right now."

"Take him out now without me finishing my intel?"

"No…of course not; I mean to stick that file on him back in your safe for now as we have another candidate who just stepped forward."

"Let me guess, Senator Sinclair by chance?" TJ questioned.

"Senator Sinclair by chance is correct," his boss confirmed.

"Ok, I'll get right on it before he can cause any more problems for the President or anyone else for that matter. I'll go down and get his file to study."

Just then, there was a knock at the door.

"No need, I called down to have it sent up and that's probably it right now."

Randy took the liberty of telling them to come in and the door opened and in stepped Jessy with the file held securely in her arms. She walked up to TJ's desk and laid it down in front of him.

"Hi TJ, this is the file that Randy asked me to bring up. Will there be anything else?" she asked very professionally.

"No, that's fine Jessy…thanks a lot," TJ answered.

Jessy did a 180 and left the office very smartly. Noticing the clock on the wall, he guessed that she would be going home soon.

"Well I see that you are now on top of things so I'll leave you to your mission. Don't worry TJ, we'll eventually get back around to Lidio. Have a good night, I'm out of here."

TJ said goodnight to Randy and thought about how lucky he was to have such a great boss. Tucker was still on and he turned back on the sound to hear Tucker Carlson speaking to an older gentleman on the show.

From the television came: "Ok, I think that we are finally ready to meet a gentleman who is trying to make a difference for our disabled veterans; at least this story should be better than our last two. So how's he going about changing the world for these selfless patriots you might ask? Let's ask him."

As the camera panned back, viewers were then able to see an older man---older than the host---sitting across from Tucker.

"We have Pat Parker with us today, all the way from Carson City, Nevada, and he's advocating for legislation that will help our disabled veterans in some small way. Welcome to the show Pat."

"Thank you Tucker…it's good to be here."

"So tell us about this legislation that you are advocating for and how will it help our disabled veterans."

"Sure Tucker. On January 12, 2017, Senator Dean Heller of Nevada introduced S. 116 which is a bill to amend title 10 of the United States Code, to establish a space-available transportation priority for veterans of the Armed Forces who have a service-connected, permanent disability rated as total. On February 7, 2017, Representative Gus Bilirakis of Florida introduced H.R. 936 which is a companion bill to S. 116. These two gentlemen have through their actions, shown their compassion and support for our disabled veterans by sponsoring these bills that are cost-neutral and help our selfless patriots with a privilege that they should have been given a long time ago due to their sacrifice of health and quality of life issues."

Tucker was staring at Pat in awe that he could spit all of that information out at one time.

"That's amazing! How do you remember all of that?"

"Well Tucker, I have been advocating for this type of legislation since 2012 and through a lot of research and passion, it helps to know your material. There is no reason Tucker that anyone in Congress would not support this legislation. There is no funding needed to pass this legislation into law and it helps our disabled veterans. It's cost-neutral and a no-brainer Tucker."

"From what I know personally about this issue---which isn't a whole lot---I would tend to agree with you. Why not help our disabled veterans; it seems like we are helping everybody else…including China and the whole world for that matter. Why not do something to assist our disabled vets?"

"We do have some support in Congress with co-sponsors, but what has happened over the years is that the bill will go to the Armed Services Committee and no further. What we need is to get the bill included into the 2019 National Defense Authorization Act or better known as the NDAA. Someone told me just the other day, unfortunately, that you basically have to shame Congress into action and doing what's right for our military."

"I would have to agree with you there. I see that Congress wastes millions if not billions of dollars on stupid stuff that the American people don't care about. So what do you think the holdup is?"

"I was told by a staffer in Senator Heller's office that they believe that it is Senator Melvin holding things up."

"I see…isn't he a veteran as well?" Tucker asked.

"You are correct Mr. Carlson," Pat responded.

"Please just call me Tucker Pat; we are not formal on this show. That's the Hannity Show that you are probably thinking about where they are much more formal."

Pat nodded his acknowledgement and said "ok" so softly that it wasn't picked up by his microphone.

"So tell us Pat," Tucker continued, "how can Senator Melvin hold this legislation up in Congress?"

"As you know Tucker, all bills are assigned to a committee and this legislation was no different and was sent to the Armed Services Committees for both the House and the Senate and Senator Melvin is the Chairman for the Senate Armed Services Committee. On Capitol Hill, the Senate side of Congress is the more dominant one of the two and Senator Melvin seems to think, I was told, that if he was to allow this bill to advance and pass, then others may want to fly Space Available as well."

"Who can fly now under current law Pat?"

"Funny you should ask Tucker. Before going on the air, I gave your producer a chart that contains data from the DoD Instruction 4515.13 Air Transportation Eligibility Manual that would answer that question if he would like to post it for your viewers. I anticipated your question in advance due to the list being so long for me to remember everything."

"Do we have that available?" Tucker asked of his producer. He was always amazed at how fast his staff could respond to his requests and he felt that at Fox, he had the best staff in the business!

The following chart appeared on a split screen with Pat and Tucker for the audience to view:

DoD Instruction 4515.13 Air Transportation Eligibility Manual

    a. Uniformed Services Members

    b. Civilian Employees of DoD Components

c. Command-Sponsored Dependents of Uniformed Services Members
d. Non-Command-Sponsored Dependents
e. Dependents Accompanying DoD Personnel on Official Business
f. Employees and Dependents of Nonappropriated Fund (NAF) Activities
g. Employees and Dependents of Other USG Agencies
h. Nonprofit Services Organizations
i. Invited Travelers
j. Foreign Government and International Organization Travelers
k. Contractor Personnel
l. Educators not affiliated with the DoD Education Activity...
m. Athletes and Entertainers
n. Civil Air Patrol (CAP)
o. Reserve Officer Training Corps (ROTC)
p. Junior Reserve Officers Training Corps (JROTC)
q. International ROTC Programs
r. Naval Sea Cadets
s. National Guard Youth Challenge Program Participants
t. Persons Transported Under the Authority of the Military Extraterritorial...
u. Other Individuals Not Affiliated With the DoD

Tucker Carlson stared at the extensive list inconceivably and responded accordingly.

"Well, I definitely don't see 100% disabled veterans listed anywhere on your chart, but it does appear that everyone else made the list, including people from foreign countries. So the big question now is...who else wants to fly Space A?"

"We are not completely sure about that yet. But in any case, we feel that 100% disabled veterans should be able to fly in the same manner and to the same extent as retirees based on their sacrifice to the country and are more than deserving of this privilege that is so freely given to many others."

"Well, I tend to agree with your statement, so what can our viewers do to help?"

"A group of veterans and I have started an organization called, Project Patriot. This is the platform that we chose to utilize in advocating for this legislation. It seems that Congress doesn't really take you seriously if you are just an individual. They stand up and take notice a little more if you have an organization behind you."

"Is your organization a non-profit and where do I send a donation?"

"No, we are not Tucker, but, you can buy postcard stamps and mail them to us for our Postcard Campaign to Congress and that will help to offset some of our costs."

"What if I just write you a check…would that be alright and you can purchase the stamps on your own and then send me a receipt for my records?"

"That'll work for us Tucker…you'll just have to write the check in my name since we are *not* a non-profit and just a contingent of professional veterans advocating for Space A travel for our disabled veterans. In the memo section of the check, please just write 'Project Patriot' in parentheses and that way everything is kept honest and open."

"Unlike Congress; I have no problem with doing that Pat. After the show I will then donate $4,000.00 to the cause," Tucker announced proudly.

"That's very generous of you Tucker and I really thank you for that. That will support approximately 8,000 postcards to Congress and keep us busy till the end of the year!"

"No problem, I don't mind supporting a good cause especially for our military. Plus, Congress needs to hear more from citizens like you anyway. Now, what can our viewers do to help and how do they get more information?"

"Viewers who want to help can go to our website which is: www.ProjectPatriot.info and then contact their Congressional members and ask them to co-sponsor this meaningful legislation. Let's urge Congress to do their job in helping our previous military at *no* cost to taxpayers. Any help is greatly appreciated…I can assure you Tucker!"

"Amen to that and well stated. Well thank you for what you are doing for our disabled veterans Pat and again for letting our viewers know how they can help. When we return…"

TJ then turned off the T.V. and picked up the file on Evan Sinclair. *Let's find the best way to eliminate this issue once and for all*, he decided as he opened the file.

Republican Support Party Meeting #5

This time the Support Party was meeting at the Rayburn House Office Building and all of the usual guests were present. As the meeting was called to order, the sonorous voice of Representative Curt Click could be heard loud and clear.

"I want to start by thanking everyone for you patronage at these meetings. I know that we all have busy schedules with bills lining up and then there is the trouble with these Liberal Democrats. However, we have one less of these to worry about. In case you didn't hear on the news, Senator Cole Burris was found drowned at the Brothers Swim Center right here in D.C.," Representative Click stated as he stared out over the attendees. Before he had a chance to speak again, laughter burst from the members. While keeping a straight face, he brought his gavel down several times before regaining control of the meeting. Once quiet ensued and everyone looked on seriously at the Support Party Chair, he then started to laugh also and was joined by the others in uproarious laughter. He allowed everyone to get this out of their system before proceeding.

"The Dems are having a difficult time with our President. At every turn he is besting them and they look so foolish and downright stupid."

Representative Home indicated that he wanted to be called on by halfway raising his hand.

"Yes Dwight, what do you have for us?" Representative Click asked.

"Just a question if you will," he started. "Do the Democrats really comprehend how stupid they look to the average American citizen? I don't think that they get it personally."

"I would have to agree with you on that one. They are so out of touch with reality and don't realize they are hurting themselves. They have no real leader and no real message other than to impeach the President and to obstruct what benefits the country as a whole; they are a detriment to society, but their detriment is to our benefit with the American people," Representative Click stated seriously.

The meeting continued on for a short time as they all wanted to get home to watch Judge Jeanine on Fox!

Justice With Judge Jeanine

"Hello and welcome to Justice and thank you for making Justice number one again on Saturday nights. Now for my opening statement…the woman must be dumber than a doornail. It could be that she has nothing else to do. This week my favorite ex-politician, Hilliary Clinton, released the following tweet and I quote… 'I say this as a former Secretary of State and as an American: the Russians are still coming. Our intelligence professionals are imploring Trump to act. Will he continue to ignore and surrender, or protect our country?' Say what Hilliary? The Russians are still coming? You're kidding, right? Hopefully they are coming for you dear. Our intelligence professionals are imploring?

Where do you get that from? You don't even have a security clearance anymore. You should talk. You didn't seem so worried when the Russians came and took 20% of our uranium. Oh that's right. They were such good guys back then because they donated $145 million to your foundation and $500 thousand in your hubby's pocket that you're enjoying now. You surrendered one of our most valuable resources, Moly 99 and it is used in nuclear medicine and used to diagnose and treat cancer in 45 million people a year. And you want to criticize Donald Trump? Unlike you and Bill, Donald Trump cannot be bought. Hilliary, it has got to be tough being you. You used all the money that you illegally took from foreign powers to create a false dossier to use against Donald Trump. You got fed debate questions. You deleted thirty-three thousand emails that were under subpoena. You gave out cell phones and $1,500 dollars in cash to have losers start fights at Donald Trump's rallies and yet you still loss to someone who you said was unfit to be President. You Hilliary, created your own sick environment and now you want to blame everyone else? Deal with it honey. I have an idea for you Hilliary. Just relax at home and keep tweeting about how bad Donald Trump is for our country and how you should have been the president and when the men come with a white jacket, I urge you to go with them peacefully because, you're a mental case Hilliary and they will come for you! Donald Trump is addressing mental health issues now and honey, you're on the top of his list and I predict that they will be coming for you. So I implore you to not ignore them and don't kick and scream and to just surrender peacefully when they do come for you, and that's my opening statement."

Clinton Home

Hilliary had just turned off the television after watching Judge Jeanine's opening statement and fumed. Bill just happened to walk into the room at the wrong time.

"That fucking bitch; you should hear the things that she is saying about me!" Hilliary practically screamed.

"You mean that woman on Fox? Why do you watch or even care what she says for that matter?" Bill asked seriously.

"Shut up and pour me a drink you moron."

Bill walked over to the liquor cabinet and reached for a bottle of scotch. *She apparently needs the strong stuff,* he decided and he poured the dark amber colored liquid onto the ice cube in the glass and then walked over and handed it to Hilliary who had sat down on the divan. She grabbed for the glass and downed it in seconds while still seething. All this time, Bill was thinking that tonight will be another good time on the ole farm; nut farm that is! Ever since she had lost the presidency, she has had many mental breakdowns. *It's good*, he thought, *that reporters don't know this as they're likely to go for the jugular when they smell blood!*

As he now watched his wife pitifully, he thought to himself that at least he's the more normal one at present in the relationship. He still had the decanter in his hand when she held out her glass for another refill. As he watched her shake and drink, he was glad that no one was there to witness this spectacle. *However, it would be quite nice if someone else could baby sit her for a while. Oh well, this is the hand in life that I was dealt and now I have to live with it...and her too!*

He was able to get her to calm down some and more level headed by the time that he helped her into bed in her own bedroom. But, in a couple of hours---which he knew would happen---the scene changed once more for the worse as she was running through the home screaming, "The Russians are coming, the Russians are coming." She was delusional...again. He thought caustically about what *if* Hilliary *had* won the presidency and what *if* she would be running through The White House right now screaming that the Russians are coming. That would not be a pretty picture and was something that he wasn't prepared to handle, and he didn't want to! In his heart he knew that she blew her last chance for power...and she blew it big time; he was suddenly reminded of his favorite waitress Inez, who works at the Codfather Café!

After a while, he was able to catch a hold of his wife and he led her back safely to her bed. He figured that another drink for her was out of the question as she had to be somewhat prepared for her debut before a Congressional panel. She had been subpoenaed to testify about all the crap that she had been involved in from Benghazi to Uranium One to deleting over 30,000 emails. *What a life,* he thought, *and only in America can this shit happen to me!* "Well, if someone was to have her committed, then Inez could move in with me," he voiced out loud.

Then as an afterthought, "I wonder if Obamacare covers mental health issues?" Then as he was shaking his head came: "Obamacare...it's the craziest thing in the world!"

CIA Building

TJ was working late again this night studying the file for Senator Evan Sinclair. While reading through his file, he got the impression that the man was a pussy. He would act tough due to his size and position but apparently did not have a backbone when it was really needed. That analogy made sense with what he saw tonight on Tucker.

It appears that he just recently got married at a courthouse in California...how romantic he thought. His file also revealed that this dirt bag has a Twitter account like most politicians these days. Let's check in on Twitter to see what he has to say.

TJ had a Twitter account anonymously through the CIA, so his real name would not show up anywhere and the account was kept confidentially because it did belong to the CIA.

As he studied the comments made by the junior senator, he learned that he liked horseback riding. *That's interesting,* he thought. *Now where does he do his riding at?*

He couldn't find out on his Twitter account, so like his father always told him: if you want an accurate answer to your question, you go straight to the horse's mouth. *I'll just call the senator's office and talk to an intern!*

TJ located Senator Sinclair's phone number from the Senate directory that he had bookmarked previously on Firefox and dialed the number from a secured line. The senator's phone only rang once before an intern answered it.

"Senator Sinclair's office, my name is Josh, how may I help you today?"

"Hi Josh, my name is Andrew Jackson and I'm with Horseback Rider Magazine. I'm doing an article on Senator Sinclair and his love for horseback riding. Is there someone that I can get some information from?"

"Who are you with again?"

"I'm with Horseback Rider Magazine."

"And what's your name again?"

"My name is Andrew Jackson."

"Let me check and see if someone is available."

While put on hold, TJ waited patiently while listening to some crappy music and he thought about how dumb this intern really was. He'll probably come back with everyone is in a meeting, can I help you instead? After another minute, Josh returned on the line.

"Hi, are you still there?"

"Yes, I'm still here."

"They are all in meetings right now Mr. Rider. Can I be of some assistance?"

"Ok, we can give this a try. How well do you know Senator Sinclair?"

"Well, I have been working for the senator for over a year now."

"Are you aware of his love for horseback riding?"

"Of course, he talks to the staff all the time about his love for horses and for horseback riding."

"How often does the senator like to ride?"

"He told me that he needs to ride at least three times a week…that's what he told me one day."

"I see; where does he like to ride at?"

"Well, he keeps his horse, Nixon, at the stables in Largo and rides on Monday, Wednesday and Fridays between 3:00 and 6:00 p.m."

TJ knew that Largo was in Maryland and not too far from Joint Base Andrews. However, he still liked to call it Andrews Air Force Base. So now he asked the critical question: "What is the name of the stables son?"

"I don't know if I should tell you that since I really don't know you that well."

"Well my name is Rider and I work for the Horse Jones Foundation and when I do the story, I'll make sure that *we* mention your name and you can tell all of your friends that your name is listed in our popular magazine. Our next edition will be coming out next month."

"Ok, I guess it will be alright. But promise me that you won't go there to interview the senator since he doesn't like to give interviews anymore. He had a bad situation on the Tucker Carlson show recently."

"I can promise you that I will not be seeking an interview, Josh."

"Ok, the name of the stable is Jack Ass Stables."

"Thanks Jack Ass," TJ asserted.

"No Mr. Rider, my name is Josh. You got confused with the name of…"

TJ hung up the phone before the intern could finish his sentence. "What a shame," he thought out loud, "what a shame!"

Chapter 12
Ω

"How do you know that the North Korean regime is lying? Because their lips are moving!"

--- John Bolton, Former U.S. Ambassador

President Trump is to meet with Kim Jong Un, the NRA files a lawsuit against the Sunshine State and a U.S. Navy sailor jailed for taking photos of classified areas of a nuclear submarine earns a pardon from President Trump. These were the headlines from the day before that TJ had on his mind while working early at the office.

He was hoping that when President Trump meets with the murderous dictator of North Korea, that he would walk softly and carry a big stick! TJ didn't believe for one minute that the dictator had found religion overnight. He felt that there was some ulterior motive for Kim Jung Un in wanting to meet with the President; maybe a delaying tactic.

Florida's Governor, Rick Scott, signed into law a new package of laws to assist Floridians in what he believes will protect students at schools. However, the NRA doesn't believe that raising the age to buy a gun from 18 to 21 is the right answer. TJ was ok with lifting the age limit but the underlying problem was that we have evil people in our country and evil people that want to kill…and will if they have the opportunity. Plus, there was clearly a break down in the general public. He believes that our changing society was what was causing our country's issues, like taking prayer out of schools along with teachers not being able to spank students anymore, parents not properly parenting their children and leaving it up to the school system, allowing disrespect to our flag and others in general and violent video games being sold to kids. Along with the dishonest media, kids and others were being brain-washed; *wake up America, propaganda does work…just ask North Korea!*

He was glad to hear that President Trump issued a pardon for the sailor that was busted for taking pictures inside a nuclear submarine. He felt that it should have happen sooner than later though. Especially with all the crap and destruction that Hilliary and her cronies caused the country and no one is locked up…yet, unbelievable!

He was locating the Jack Ass Stables on the internet when Judy walked in with a hot and steamy cinnamon roll without the icing but with melted butter on top and a cup of milk.

"Here you go Mr. Law," Judy beamed as she laid the plated cinnamon roll with a fork and cup of milk on his desk.

"Thank you Judy. But where did you get this huge thing at this early hour?"

"Well, I just happened to know that you have the right friends in the cafeteria who think a lot about you. So I was able to get one from Chef Tony. In fact, he had just taken this batch out of the oven while I was there. He even added extra cinnamon on yours. He said that you like it that way."

"Well, he does know my taste and you're awesome Judy! You are one of the reasons that I love coming to work every day," TJ stated seriously while thinking about other good reasons as well!

Judy retreated back to her work area while TJ started to tear apart his snack and savor the flavor of the hot cinnamon while washing it down with milk.

After finishing off his roll, he was back on his computer again. He retrieved the address for the stables and decided to head out early to case the property.

He checked out with Judy and headed down to his CIA provided truck in the secured parking garage and was on his way.

He sped up as he approached the George Washington Memorial Parkway. Traffic was not too bad and the day was nice and sunny. According to his outside temperature gauge, it was 61 degrees out.

He had set the address in his GPS and was following the instructions. In no time he arrived at his destination…the Jack Ass Stables.

After parking, he approached the office and noticed brochures in a rack outside of the office door and took one. Glancing at it, it told him that the property was 2,500 acres, they have 72 horses and you could have a guided tour or a self-guided tour…the self-guided was cheaper; makes sense. Also, he noticed a map of trails and a statement that announced that you could board your own horse there for a hefty fee. However, he only wanted to ride and decided on the 3 hour self-guided tour whether he needn't it or not.

As he walked into the office, he was greeted by a jovial fat man behind the counter smoking a fat cigar that was stuck in between fat fingers of his left hand and who promptly stuck out his right hand and declared that his name was Jack. TJ wondered if his last name was Ass since he had a big one!

At a Starbuck's located near the CIA building, Ching Ching was residing in her car in the parking lot this morning making a phone call. After a few minutes of conversation in Chinese with an unknown person, she finished her call and headed for CIA Headquarters for work and she didn't even buy a cup of coffee!

The Clintons had arrived at the Ronald Reagan Washington National Airport early this morning in preparation for Hilliary's debut before the House's Judicial Committee which was scheduled to take place at 1000. The typical black government issued SUV was waiting for them at the airport and whisked them off to the Rayburn House Office Building. For obvious reasons, Bill noticed that his wife wasn't in the best of moods. He hoped that she would be able to hold it together long enough to make it through the hearing without any more damage being done to their good names.

TJ rented a horse named May and headed off on a self-guided tour with his map in hand. Of course, because of personal liability, he had to initial and sign an 8-page contract that would hold harmless the stables due to his injury or death. He didn't spend all day in reading the contract. He just provided his initials on each page and a signature on the last page and paid his money for a 3-hour ride. He wasn't sure if he needed three hours or not, but decided to pay anyway. Plus, he enjoyed riding horses.

He set off on a trail that went towards a road that eventually paralleled the trail that he was on. It was a nice day out and he was really enjoying his ride. As he swayed with the motion of his horse, he was taking in the scenery, but not for its beauty, but for the purpose of his upcoming mission. TJ was hoping that the senator would not only show up today, but choose this one trail. He could park along the road and jump over the simple barb wire fence and with all of the underbrush, trees and large rocks, he should be able to complete his assigned task in an expedient manner.

After an hour and a half of riding, he decided to head back to the stables and arrived on time with no further charges being incurred. In his pickup, he located the road that he noticed from the trail and parked under a shade tree to wait patiently for the senator.

House Judiciary Committee

"Do you solemnly swear to tell the truth, the whole truth and nothing but the truth, so help you God?" asked the committee's Chair.

Hilliary was standing with her hand raised in the committee chambers and being sworn in to testify before a packed House. News reporters crouched down low in front of a pony wall and pictures were being snapped; cameras were recording the event live for their viewers and microphones were strategically placed on the table in front of Hilliary that would capture her every word.

"Of course I do," Hilliary stated with her right hand raised for the oath and her left hand behind her back with two fingers crossed that no one seemed no notice.

As the questioning got under way, Hilliary became more irritated by the questioning and became increasingly irrational in her answers. So much so, that the Chairman of the House Judiciary Committee had it noted officially.

The hearing lasted only four hours but by that time, Hilliary had had enough already and couldn't depart fast enough. Bill and her took the same black SUV back to the airport and flew back home to their sanctuary away from people and their prying eyes; the cameras.

Once home, Bill felt the need to give Hilliary her usual dose of two Prozac pills and tucked her in to bed as it had been a long day for both of them; especially for Hilliary.

Democratic Resistance Party Meeting #6

The following were all present at this highly anticipated meeting with the exception of Senator Burris and Senator Sinclair:

Representative Jarl Lidio – (D-GA)
Tim Payat – DNC Chairman
Representative Maybel Wileen – (D-CA)
Kadin Elkhart – DNC Deputy Chairman
Senator Maro Wesley – (D-VA)
Senator Burney Sherman – (I-VT)
Representative Abel Stoner – (D-CA) Resistance Party Chair

And via conference call:

Senator Jace Melvin – (R-AZ) Line 1
Senator Bow Crenshaw – (R-TN) Line 2
Senator Jory Flann – (R-AZ) Line 3

"This meeting will now come to order," Chairman Stoner intoned. He knew that everyone wanted to find out what the hell is happening to their members and hence all the chatter. Hell, he wanted to know that as well!

"Has anyone seen Sinclair lately and why is he not at this meeting?"

Everyone was looking at each other when Senator Maro Wesley spoke up.

"I found out from a staffer that he went horseback riding out at Jack Ass Stables."

Before Chairman Stoner had time to respond, another voice hollered out, "He's at the right stables asshole," and then came some laughter as Chairman Stoner banged his gavel several times.

"That's enough. He shouldn't be missing any meetings. Can you pass that along to him Senator Wesley?"

"I will be happy to let him know of our dissatisfaction with his absence."

"Thank you. Now, our big news tonight is that someone possibly killed Senator Burris," Chairman Stoner announced and raised a hand to quiet people down from their grumbling as he made that statement and then went on.

"I know what you're thinking and I agree. There is some controversy about what is happening to our people and I sympathize with you all. Is it the Russians or someone else or just a coincidence?"

"I say we impeach 45 and throw out all of them so called Russian diplomats," Representative Wileen stated matter-of-factly.

No one rebuked her for mentioning "impeach 45" since she only said it once this time and she wasn't yelling it with passion like she usually does.

"Yes, we have already sent some diplomats packing and maybe others will be following them soon enough. So here's what I want everyone to do. I want some ideas as to what may be out there that people are talking about. Keep me informed. Anything of value I want to know about it. In fact Tim, why don't you get a hold of our Russian friends in Fusion GPS and see what you can find out."

Tim acknowledged this request with a nod of his head.

"Now let's talk about DACA. Trump sure screwed us with offering that DACA deal. Now the DACA kids know we don't give a shit about them and that asshole Trump could be costing us votes. So I want everyone to continue on with our campaign: 'we care about the DACA' kids.' In fact, step it up if you can. I want Trump out of office the next time around even if I have to run myself!"

There was some muttering with that statement but everyone felt the same way.

"Also, if anyone else comes up dead or missing from our group then I want to know about it and damn quick!" Chairman Stoner stated with passion. "We have lost too many of our members already and the cops haven't found out shit. If they have, then they are not telling anyone. Sherman, you know some corrupt folks in the FBI, check and see what they know and what they don't want us to know."

"I'm not sure if any of my corrupt friends are still available. Trump seems to be cleaning up not only The White House, but the FBI house as well!" Senator Sherman vehemently responded.

"Well check anyway," Stoner insisted. "And keep a low profile on your actions. I don't want Trump getting word of what we are doing."

"Because he's a vindictive prick," Senator Sherman stated.

"That was so eloquently stated Senator Sherman and you are correct. If he knows what we are doing, then he'll continue to outsmart us and I don't want that. The way he handled the DACA deal was a pure stroke of genius. I might not like the guy, but I have to tell you honestly, he's as sharp as any tack in the barrel…and then some!"

Then from line 1 the voice of Senator Melvin …

"Excuse me people, I would like to say something if you don't mind."

"Go ahead Senator Melvin," Chairman Stoner insisted, "you have our undivided attention."

"Thank you Chairman Stoner. As you all know, I do have some medical issues to deal with and I might not be able to attend the next few meetings. I have an upcoming CAT scan and a prostate operation not to mention the fact that they might start treating me for my brain cancer at any time if we still have any uranium left…since that fucked up bitch of yours allowed 20% of our uranium to go to the Russians for $140 million dollars."

Chairman Stoner interrupted the senator for a moment.

"No name calling please senator. Before you had your medical issues you were ok with her then, so keep in mind that we are all on the same train."

"Yeah, well sorry about that Stoner. I have to tell you honestly though that I don't think I'll be back for another meeting. I have a feeling that this thing that I got will kill me yet and I'm scared as hell. So just in case I'm not back and gone to Hell…I mean Heaven, I wish you all good luck with your conquest. Thanks again everyone and thank you for the get well card that I received as well. Oh wait a minute…that was from my own party! Belay my last then."

Everyone could hear a click and realized that maybe Melvin was right in that he wouldn't be returning any time soon. For some reason Stoner thought, he seemed bitter…maybe because we didn't think about getting him a 'get-well-card' and besides…he's a Republican anyway!

After a while, the talk swung back around to the DACA kids and the border wall with Representative Wileen contributing her thoughts yet again.

"Ok everyone, I know how we can get back at Trump on the DACA deal. We just have to convince him that there are other cheaper ways to protect our border."

"But I thought that we need illegals for their voting power?" questioned Representative Lidio.

"That is true but just hear me out," lamented Representative Wileen. "We just put out the word that we are ok with the DACA deal as long as there is no wall."

"Well I for one can tell you that he will not go along with that, especially since that was a campaign promise of his," Chairman Stoner stated.

"But wait. We agree to a tradeoff. We tell him that instead of a wall, we'll just use the money instead to mow the grass that is along the border!"

"That's crazy," Kane replied. "How will mowing the grass---if there is any---stop illegals from coming over?"

"Exactly," Representative Wileen beamed because she knew in her mind that she came up with a great idea.

"Wait a minute," the Chairman broke in. "We don't refer to them as 'illegals' from this point on. They are simply 'undocumented' minions. Now go on."

Then from line 3 the voice of Senator Flann remarked, "You're a flake you old biddy!"

Before anyone else could comment, Chairman Stoner stepped in.

"Ok, that's enough. I'm getting tired of all this bickering and name calling. We have more pressing issues to discuss than fighting among ourselves."

When it looked like the Chairman had control again, he continued:

"Now then, I have a big announcement for everyone here. I wasn't going to do this now, but I think the timing is appropriate."

Everyone became respectfully quiet and was looking at each other wondering if the news was bad and about them. Stoner did not know how this news would affect his group because of their loyalty for Hilliary, but he figured that it was time to find out their true feelings.

"A decision has been made not to back Hilliary and that Michelle Obama will be our new leader. As you know, they had Hilliary back on the Hill testifying again. I have the feeling that there are bad times ahead of that woman and that we shouldn't be associated with her any longer."

As he looked around the room, the grim faces suddenly turned to smiles and his group started to clap. *Amazing,* he thought. He figured that he might have to argue with some of them. Apparently, they must have been feeling the same way that he did and the need to distance themselves from Hilliary was the new norm if they were to take back power.

Chairman Stoner pounded his gavel and brought back some semblance of order.

"Now then, there is only two questions left, who wants to tell her or should we even tell her?"

★ ★ ★ ★ ★

TJ was able to finish his mission and was on his way back to the office to type up his report. However, he was currently in bumper to bumper traffic and changed his plans. He would go home instead. He could always type up his report tomorrow morning he decided.

Tucker Carlson

"Welcome to Tucker Carlson and of course, I'm Tucker Carlson. We have a good show for you tonight and a meaningful show it will be I predict for our viewers.

"First, let's start with why the Democrats are so against President Trump's DACA deal. I don't know if many people have thought to analyze what is currently happening, but we did and what we discovered will shock you.

"President Trump has offered to give a path to citizenship for nearly 2 million illegals providing that the Democrats will go along with money for a border wall, end chain migration and the visa lottery system. But the Democrats turned that down. That is almost 3 times more than Obama proposed to do. Now why would they do that? I thought that they cared about the 'DACA kids?' Apparently not true.

"Our next guest will explain some of this to us so that we can try to make sense of what's happening to DACA. So let's welcome to the show, Congressman Curt Click."

As the cameras pulled back, Representative Click came into view for the viewers to see and they saw a gentleman who seemed pleased to be on the show by his smile.

"Thank you Tucker, it's great to be here."

"Ok congressman, can you explain to our audience why the Liberal Democrats don't want this DACA deal even though President Trump increased the number of recipients to almost triple? I wonder what their beef is."

"It's real simple Tucker if you think about it."

"I've thought about it a lot and I can't figure it out," Tucker stated.

"That's because you are not thinking like a Liberal Democrat Tucker. You're thinking as a rational Republican and to figure out why the Liberals do certain things, then you need to think like them.

"So here it is in a nutshell Tucker. If the Democrats agree to Trump's DACA deal, that would mean an end to a new stream of voters for them. I have talked to a Democrat friend of mine and he has agreed with my assessment. In order to recover power, the Democrats playbook includes illegals and felons and freaks all voting for their party. The reason for that is clear. Where would their loyalties lie if these groups get to vote? I mean felons and illegals; freaks already have the right to vote. Also, Democrats are all about skirting the rule of law and criminals in general would be in favor of voting for them, especially since the Republicans are for upholding the law and the Constitution. So I ask you again, where would their loyalties lie if they get to vote?"

"I imagine with the Democrats," Tucker ventured.

"And you are correct. So if they agree to the border wall and ending chain migration and the visa lottery program, there goes their plan to recruit millions of new voters, and Tucker, we are talking about millions of voters.

"Democrats are working overtime behind the scenes with pressuring states to issue driver's licenses to illegals so they can then illegally vote. If the illegals don't mind breaking our federal law involving illegal entry into our country, what would stop them from breaking other laws as well?"

"I guess nothing congressman."

"You see Tucker, the Democrats road to power is through felons, freaks and illegals so that they can once again win back the House, the Senate and of course, The White House. Once they get the power then they are not planning on losing it again, I can tell you that. Do you want to know what our country will be like if the Liberal Democrats get control?"

"I can probably guess."

"You don't have to guess Tucker…I'll tell you. Just take a look at California."

"I can see the correlation congressman. So how can the Republicans or the federal government stop these kinds of tactics?"

"Funny you should ask Tucker. The federal government has three lawsuits against the State of California involving sanctuary laws that the state has passed that some California municipalities have opted out from; state laws regarding their cooperation with ICE. Also, Congress is currently working on H.R. 400 which is the Protect America Act."

"Now how will that law help our country if passed, with sanctuary cities and states and illegals voting and receiving driver's licenses?" Tucker questioned.

"The Protect America Act essentially outlaws sanctuary cities and states; it outlaws companies from hiring illegals with stiff penalties if they do, including prison time for certain company officials; it outlaws states that don't want to cooperate with federal law enforcement agencies with elected leaders being held accountable, and, the federal government will take over the responsibility of ensuring accurate and equal voting in the states. Let me just say this, this law has some teeth to it and people will begin going to prison. We can't just sit back Tucker and be witness to our country becoming a third world country, it's too painful to even imagine."

Tucker had that serious look on his face as he stared at Congressman Click who continued:

"This law provides money to build an illegal detention center in Arizona and Texas near the border for illegals that are captured here in the U.S. No more of this 'catch and release' crap where illegals will figure out a way to come back. The law will be that they are incarcerated for a minimum of three years for a first offense and five years for second and third offenses and they will work in prison…it won't be a country club for them as it may have been in the past and violent criminals will get longer sentences. The idea is to punish and to create a *deterrent* and to protect our country. Once they serve their time, then they will be returned to their respective countries."

"Well said congressman. After hearing that, I can tell you that I would not want to come over illegally if I was from Mexico or any other country for that matter."

Kremlin

The Russian President and his Prime Minister were in conference in his office when the phone rang.

Putin answered his phone and indicated to his secretary that he did not want to be disturbed until she told him that it was President Trump calling…so he changed his mind and took the call.

Putin: "Yes, President Trump, what can I do for you?"

Trump: "I just wanted to wish you congratulations on winning the election in your country."

Putin: "Well, that is nice of you and I thank you…also, I want to thank you for not meddling in our election like we did yours."

Trump: "That's ok, but I can't promise that for the next time."

Putin: "I understand. Oh, by the way, do you need a nice donation to your foundation perhaps?"

Trump: "Why? I have never known you Russians to be charitable."

Putin: "We need another 20% of your uranium! Ha ha."

Trump: "You are not dealing with a dumbass this time Vladimir."

Putin: "So what is your answer Donald?"

Putin heard a click and knew that President Trump had dumped him. *The nerve of the American President to hang up on him,* he thought caustically. At least Obama had some class he felt and didn't have the fortitude to hang up on him when *he* was in office. *This Trump is really a PIMA,* he concluded…*a Pain in My Ass!*

He then realized that Dmitry was addressing him.

"Your Excellency, what did the American President want?"

"He just wanted to congratulate me on winning the election. But, they know and I know that they know, that our election is fixed, so I'm somewhat surprised by his phone call. What could it mean Dmitry? I wonder."

"Maybe it was in, what's the English word, oh yes…in earnest?"

"I don't think that is so," Putin countered. "This guy is kind of sneaky."

"Why do you say that, my comrade?" Dmitry casually asked.

"I'll tell you why I say that. Remember when Trump went to visit Obama at The White House in November 2016?"

"Yes, I remember."

"Do you also remember what he said about Obama when the cameras were filming?"

Dmitry shook his head no and took another drink from his glass.

"He pointed to Obama and said 'great man there.' But we really know what he thinks about Obama. He thinks the same thing that we do…Obama's a dumbass!"

Both of the men hooted over that true remark. Dmitry lifted the decanter of Jack Daniels whiskey off of

Putin's desk---that they were sharing this time---and refilled both of their glasses.

"No Dmitry, I think that Trump was being…what's the word that I'm trying to think of?"

"I think that the word is 'sarcastic' that you are thinking of Vladimir?"

"Yes, that is it. Thank you my friend. I think he is now being sarcastic to me also. What do you think Dmitry?"

"I think that you could be right. So what does that mean to us?" Dmitry asked seriously.

"I have a feeling that we can't trust Trump. Especially if he says things that he don't mean. I remember when Obama whispered to me one time before the 2012 election, that he would have more 'flexibility' when he is re-elected. Do you remember when I told you that?"

Dmitry nodded in the affirmative while swallowing some of the amber liquid that resided in his glass. He then realized that his eyes were starting to water.

"Well, he was telling the truth. It was shortly after his re-election that we got our hands on their uranium. No Dmitry, we have to keep our eye on this guy. The American people think he's brainless but I think that they are wrong. He's up to something but I don't know what…yet."

"I wouldn't worry too much my commander," Dmitry rendered a salute to Putin. He knew he was drinking too much again, but what the hell? Life is too short and maybe even shorter with Trump as President! About then he passed out and Putin called for a Federation soldier to take Dmitry to his room that was located in the Russian Palace a couple of floors above Putin's office.

Putin was still contemplating about his phone call from Trump several minutes after Dmitry was taken to his room. "Yes, this is one man that I need to pay close attention to."

OPERATION: Ωmega

The White House

President Trump had just hung up the phone on Putin. *What a dick. I would like to drop a MOAB on his ass!*

The President then picked up his phone and asked his aide to put in a call to John Bolton. John was going to be his new National Security Advisor next month, but he wanted some advice from him now, if possible.

After a few minutes, President Trump heard the voice of his aide coming across the intercom speaker letting him know that John Bolton was now on line one.

"John, how are you?" President Trump asked.

"Just fine Mr. President. What can I do for you?"

"Do you have a few minutes to talk or am I interrupting you in something?"

"I can talk several minutes Mr. President and I was just sitting down to watch Hannity."

"Well in that case, I'll be brief. John, I just wished Putin congratulations on winning the election because I thought that it was the right thing to do. However, he pissed me off and I was wondering what we can do about that."

"Well you know that I'm transitioning into the NSA position Mr. President and working closely with H. R. McMaster and I was informed by him that the United Kingdom is expelling several Russian Diplomats for that nerve agent attack on two of its citizens last week. They will be given their walking papers tomorrow and the UK will be giving them just seven days to get out or they will be placed into custody."

The President was in serious thought and taking notes.

"So my advice to you Mr. President is that we follow suit. Some of these diplomats are plain spies anyway and it will behoove us to expel them."

"Do you have any thoughts on which ones we should expel John?"

"I do Mr. President. H.R. and I came up with the following list...there are 12 in the United Nations that need to go and another 48 in the Seattle Consulate that should go as well. Furthermore, we need to close that consulate down. The reason for this action is that our Trident submarine base is nearby as well as our most valuable contractor...Boeing. I don't think that we need to harbor Russian spies in that neck of the woods. They probably have picked up valuable intel already as that jackass Obama knew about their activities and did absolutely nothing. He was too busy with trying to make friends with them and then again, reset relations between our two countries. He believed in the concept of 'strategic patience' Mr. President."

"Well you know that is not my style John and I agree with you on all your points. Obama *is* a jackass and I think you are right about expelling 60 of these so called 'diplomats.' "

"But I thought that you are fond of Obama sir after that White House meeting where you called him a great man?" John asked half-heartedly.

"Just being factitious John and I think you know that already."

"You are correct Mr. President," he chuckled. "I did know that, but I don't think Obama knew it."

"Too bad and so sad if that dumbass doesn't know any better. Thanks for your help John and I'll get with H.R. on this since you are not officially in until next month."

"Thank you Mr. President and feel free to call me anytime," John insisted.

"I just might hold you to that John," the President remarked.

"You can sir."

President Trump ended his call with John Bolton and then phoned his NSA, H. R. McMaster and told him what he and the former Ambassador talked about and gave H.R. two thumbs up with expelling 60 of these diplomats/spies within one week and that the federal government will reclaim the consulate as well.

When President Trump left the Oval Office for a bathroom break and to grab a snack from The White House kitchen, a cleaning person entered to empty the Official Trash Can. In so doing, he glanced around President Trump's desk and read several items that the President had jotted down, one of which was about his phone call to Putin to congratulate him on winning his election. Then the man scurried away with the trash and dumped it into another trash can that he had on his cart in the hallway and then quickly left the area before the President's reappearance.

President Trump returned a little later and turned on his favorite show…Hannity. As he sat down to watch, Hannity had just informed his viewers of some bad news…or was it good news? Senator Sinclair was found dead while horseback riding.

"Well, that is dangerous riding wild horses," President Trump stated out loud and along with, "I'm sure he'll be missed…by somebody. Maybe now we can get a Republican finally in that seat!"

President Trump went back to work as it would be another long night for him…and anyone else around him as well! He did not ascribe to the "9 to 5" working hours.

Chapter 13
Ω

"Liberals destroy everything they touch."

---Dan Bongino

Russia counters President Trump's move on expelling diplomats and returns the favor by doing the exact same thing…they expelled exactly 60 diplomats and will close the Saint Petersburg Consulate. They also test launched a new ICBM called the "Satan Missile" as if to intimidate not only the U.S., but the whole world since twenty-seven countries around the world, including the United States, participated in the largest expulsion of Russian diplomats since the Cold War.

President Trump learned of a leak in The White House of his congratulatory phone call that he made to Putin and is having an internal investigation conducted.

Are you a citizen? The President decided to add this question back into the 2020 Census Questionnaire that has the Left in such a twitter. Speaking of Twitter, the President tweeted about how the Governor of California, Jason "Sunstruck" Brent, pardoned five criminal illegal aliens whose crimes included kidnapping and robbery, wife beating and even drug dealing.

These were the headlines and the thoughts that were going through TJ's mind as he relaxed in the hot tub at the CIA building. He found it hard to read his latest Western when these and other detrimental headliners were in the news.

It was early morning and he had decided that he deserved a little downtime in the form of a good soaking in the hot tub. He would type up the file on Senator Sinclair and then afterwards, get back to working on Representative Lidio's file. He knew that he needed to accomplish this task since the need to eliminate Democrats was stacking up pretty fast. *It was almost like they were jockeying for position to be next in line,* he thought. *Well, no hurry people, your number will be called and your ticket will be punched!*

Currently, he was the only visitor in the hot tub area. He picked up his bottle of Black Cherry Sparkling Ice and took a swallow. It tasted really great and had no sugar. He picked up his book deciding at an attempt to read again when the manager of the gym approached him.

"TJ, Randy just called me and said to tell you that he needs to see you right away in his office."

Judy must have informed him of his whereabouts which was ok. *Must be awfully important if he's summoning me up from my hot tub recess,* he resolved.

He left the hot tub reluctantly, showered and dressed and headed straight for his boss's office. Upon arriving at Randy's door, he entered without knocking and took a seat in a comfortable leather chair facing his boss.

"Thanks for coming so quickly TJ. First off, I want to say great job with Senator Sinclair. That was clever putting that empty Russian dressing bottle in his coat pocket."

TJ beamed with pride. It was always nice knowing that Randy appreciated his work and creativity. *But how did his boss know about the Russian dressing bottle?* He hasn't even submitted his report yet.

"How did you know about the Russian dressing bottle? I haven't even submitted my report yet."

"It was on Fox News last night."

"Oh yeah, I forgot how they are always on top of things," TJ commented.

"Yes they are," his boss agreed and then continued. "I need to ask you something TJ. Do you know anything about the death of Senator Melvin?"

"No, should I?"

"He was found with his throat slit in his home and he was clutching a Russian coin in his hand."

This was a shock to TJ. *A Russian clue left behind…what was going on?*

"I had nothing to do with it…I give you my word."

"I believe you, but I had to ask; so that means that someone is copying us, except, they disposed of a Republican that acts like a Democrat; very interesting indeed."

"Well, at least it was someone that gives the President a hard time and offers no value to our country whatsoever," TJ announced.

"That's true. But damn it, he was a POW veteran."

"Boss, listen to me. He may have been a POW and a veteran, but he turned bad and went rogue when he used his status as former military to become a senator. I don't feel sorry for him and the President didn't care for him as well…and you shouldn't either. Plus, he had medical problems and he was old and now maybe he's at peace…if he went on the escalator ride to Heaven that is."

"Well, you are right about all of that. But we need to find out who did this unauthorized killing. Next time it may be someone we do like."

"I agree Randy."

"Randy? I thought it was boss?"

"I know, but now I'm in a Randy mood."

"Ok, but just don't start that Mr. Morgan crap."

"I won't," TJ promised.

Randy and TJ sat pondering this newest development when TJ struck an idea.

"So the FBI will be looking into this I suppose?" TJ asked seriously.

"That is correct, especially when it's a sitting senator and the Chairman of the Senate Armed Services Committee."

"I have an idea then. Ask Director Cray to put Special Agent Mingo in charge of the case."

"I take it that you know this agent then?"

"Yes. I met him when you sent me to Camp Mayberry. We became good friends and he's trustworthy."

TJ used the word "trustworthy" instead of "honest" when describing his friend. The distinction being that a person who is honest may comprise an investigation of this nature whereas a person who is trustworthy will protect the integrity of the investigation…and therefore…the FBI and the CIA.

"If you can get Director Cray to put Mingo on the case, I can work with him on the investigation while still doing my job as well. That way, I will know what is happening in the investigation and I can trust Mingo to handle the case the way we would want the case handled, and, we get along just fine; we are both Navy veterans."

"Alright, I'll talk to Director Lannister and see what we can do. In the meantime, I need you to start working on your next mission."

"I know, I have Lidio's file in my safe and I'll get on it right now."

"Wrong hot shot," Randy enunciated.

"What do you mean boss?"

"I mean we currently have a different and more pressing target for you. Of course, as you know, things can change around here pretty fast."

"Let me guess then. Is it Senator Sherman?"

"Wrong again. He's for later. Are you sure I can trust you to work with the FBI on this other deal?"

"You can trust me and I think you know that already."

"You're right. But remember, three wrongs don't make a right."

"Uh ok…so who is this mysterious target?"

"It is none other than…hey, look at that cloud out there," Randy pointed towards the window and the sky.

"Doesn't that cloud look like Barbara Eden?" Randy liked to tease his number one intelligence officer a little to lighten the mood as he understood that TJ's job was very stressful at most times.

"That's doesn't look like Barbara Eden…maybe Barbara Bush."

Randy chuckled at this comment since he realized that TJ was right…it did look more like Barbara Bush instead of Barbara Eden.

"Are you going to tell me or are we to play twenty questions?" TJ repeated his question.

"I'm sorry. I just like giving you a hard time sometimes to break up the monotony of this place. Ok, your next mission is taking out Representative Stoner. He is the confirmed Chairman of the Resistance Party and has vowed that the Democrats will keep on investigating President Trump even though the House Intelligent Committee has shut down their investigation of Russia-Trump collusion which found no evidence of such, and, Fox News has labeled him the biggest liar in Congress and it's not like he kept it a secret anyway. Even school children watching the news can figure out he's a liar…he's been on the news enough lying and talking too much. So, do your usual great job. I can't wait to find out what Russian clue that you are going to use next," Randy chortled.

TJ agreed with his boss…he couldn't wait either to learn what his next clue would be.

As TJ left Randy's office, his direct boss picked up the phone and called Director Lannister to ask him about communicating with Director Cray their plan about arranging Special Agent Mingo to be assigned lead to the case and that the CIA would then assign Central Intelligence Officer, TJ Law to work closely with him. Luckily, Director Cray was open to this suggestion and immediately notified Special Agent Mingo of his new priority assignment.

TJ hurried down to the file vault area and found Jessy just about to leave her cubicle.

"Hey, are you leaving?" TJ asked.

"I was unless you need something TJ."

"I do. I need two files this time. One being Senator Melvin's and the other being that of no other than…Representative Stoner."

"Ok," Jessy responded and quickly added, "Can I bring them to your office later then? It will take a little longer being two files this time."

TJ told Jessy that that would be fine and left for his office. Jessy looked up the location of the files that she would be retrieving and headed for the vault. Meanwhile, Ching Ching was taking mental notes that she was gleaming from this conversation.

Judy heard TJ enter his office and before he had a chance to sit down, she laid a plate of cinnamon twirls and a glass of milk down on his desk.

"Judy, you're a lifesaver," TJ remarked. "I've been so busy that I missed breakfast."

"I know, that's why I do my best to take care of you, boss. You are always working hard…or is it hardly working?" she questioned jokingly.

"Well actually you would be right on both counts." Then TJ explained how he was hardly working at Camp Mayberry, but working hard now. Judy then told him that she missed him during that period of time when he was at Camp Mayberry and turned to leave. He thought that now she's being a little sentimental.

Jessy dropped by as well with the two files that he had previously requested and he immediately secured them in his safe for later viewing.

He typed up his report from the last case and walked it over to his boss's office. He learned from his boss that his friend Bob Mingo was now duly assigned to the Melvin case and that he was officially on it as well representing the CIA.

Randy instructed him to head on over to the property where the senator was found dead. He gave TJ a sheet of paper with the details on it. It seems that Senator Melvin was given a home by the government to use in the DC area by virtue of being the Chairman of the Armed Services Committee and that made it federal property so the DC police department was not involved with the investigation and the property was corded off and under heavy guard.

He decided instead of just showing up at the scene of the crime that he would call his friend first and dialed Mingo's cell phone number. Bob invited him to come over around 1400 and assured him that the scene was not being disturbed. He informed TJ that the crime lab boys---and one girl---were taking fingerprints and pictures. Bob told him that by 1400 it should be a little less hectic.

So TJ alerted Judy of his plans to catch lunch in the cafeteria and then he would be heading to the address that Randy gave him.

Down in the cafeteria he picked out what he felt like eating at the moment: chicken fried steak, extra crispy hash browns smothered in brown gravy, scrambled eggs with diced ham and whole wheat toast.

Sitting down to eat, TJ silently said a prayer thanking God for his food. As he started eating his chicken fried steak he noticed an exquisite flavor and decided to comment to Chef Tony on this delectable treat.

As he continued to eat, he looked up when he recognized a voice asking: "Is this seat taken?"

"Conrad," TJ exclaimed. "It's about time that you show up. Have a seat."

Conrad placed his tray of food on the table and took a seat across from his friend. The two men started to chat and eat.

"So what's new with you TJ?"

"Not too much. I was assigned to work with Bob on a case."

"Is that the case where Senator Melvin was killed?"

Between bites TJ acknowledged, "That's the one. I'm to meet him at 1400 to go over the crime scene with him."

"Do you think it has anything to do with Melvin being a Democrat…I mean a Republican?"

"Don't know, could be any number of things."

Just then Ching Ching approached the table.

"Hi TJ…don't forget to call me you naughty boy. You promise Ching Ching a movie…don't forget sailor," she spoke frankly with a twinkle in her eye and moved on.

"Wow, who was that?" Conrad asked.

"She's an analyst. She actually sits next to the analyst that was assigned to me."

"Who's your analyst?"

"Jessy…don't remember her last name though."

"Don't know her. But with all of the analysts that we have working here, I'm not surprised. My analyst is Nicole."

"Don't know her either. Same thing you said with all of the analysts working here."

"I wouldn't mind Ching Ching for my analyst," Conrad remarked. "Are you taking her out to a movie? You shouldn't ask her if you are not serious."

"I'm not sure if I'll be able to take her out due to my workload. Plus, I didn't ask her out, she asked me!" TJ exclaimed.

"Well, if it was me, I'd find some time. She's absolutely beautiful."

"We'll see how my work goes and I'll keep you posted."

Conrad agreed with TJ updating him on his love life. Both men finished up their chat as well as their food and went their separate ways. Conrad asked him to say hi to Bob for him and TJ said that he would convey the message.

TJ approached the grill and asked another chef with the tall white hat if Chef Tony was around.

"Chef Tony is off today. I'm the chef on duty currently…Chef Rudy. Can I help you with something?"

"My name is TJ and I'm a friend of Chef Tony and I was just going to convey my sentiments for the chicken fried steak. It's very tasty."

"Nice to meet you TJ and thank you for the nice compliment, that's my own recipe that I created myself," Chef Rudy stated and beamed with pleasure that TJ was the first to say something about his newest recipe.

"Well its excellent anyway…great job."

"Thank you for the compliment as they are always appreciated."

TJ headed back to his office to brush his teeth and then on out to his truck. He punched in the address into his GPS and was on his way swiftly. Traffic was usual for this time of day.

When he arrived at the DC address, he noticed several federal vehicles and the yellow, "Do Not Cross" tape surrounding the property. He parked out of the way and then crossed under a section of tape that was closest to him and was accosted by a Federal policeman. TJ quickly flashed his badge and was waved on. He climbed the four steps to the front porch and entered the home. There was still some investigative activity taking place.

As he approached a gentleman in a suit taking pictures, he asked him about Special Agent Mingo and was directed to the kitchen. When he entered the kitchen, he spotted his friend squatting down beside the body of Senator Melvin. He then cleared his throat loudly enough to cause Bob to look around quickly.

"About time you got here," Bob stated.

"You told me 1400," TJ reminded him, "and according to my watch, I'm right on time."

"True enough. I just wished that I had told you 1300 now. This body is getting a little gamey," he stated and as if to emphasize his statement, he nudged the body with his foot.

TJ noticed right away the slit in Senator Melvin's throat where he had bled out. He also examined the Russian coin that the senator was holding.

"Anything else that's special or unusual found here."

"Yes, we found these photos on the counter here," Bob stated and produced seven pictures. "Don't know if they are connected yet or not." He handed them to TJ for his assessment.

TJ flipped through the pictures that didn't seem to have a rhythm or a reason to this case. He decided that he needed to take them with him and study them later.

Since Bob was in charge of the investigation, he allowed TJ to secure the pictures and informed him that he would need them back…eventually, and TJ readily agreed. He felt that the pictures were connected somehow to this case and that they required further scrutiny by his own eyes.

He headed back to the office to study the file on Representative Stoner. Things were starting to heat up now and another relaxing stay at Camp Mayberry would not be forthcoming.

CIA Headquarters

TJ removed the file on Representative Stoner from his safe and carefully placed the pictures inside and closed and secured the door. He would study the pictures later after Stoner was taken care of.

Reviewing Stoner's file revealed some interesting information that he felt he could utilize in the completion of his mission.

TJ noticed that Stoner was reported to be an alcoholic and a gambler to boot and that he liked to patronize the Full House Bar and Grill which served liquor in the front with poker in the rear. This establishment was a Liberal hangout located just outside of DC in the small hamlet of Chevy Chase, Maryland. He felt sorry for the citizens of Chevy Chase with having to deal with a Liberal den of iniquity in their fair city. He even felt bad for Chevy Chase, the actor, for having a small town named after him and with a constant gang of lowlifes residing at a known political bar.

On his computer, he utilized Google Earth Government which was a military version of Google Earth that was used by civilians. The military version had a lot more tools than the plain civilian version. By utilizing GEG, he was able to get an idea of the neighborhood without actually going there and a plan started to form.

He noticed that Stoner lived nearby… *Probably so he could stumble home if necessary.*

He was rewarded with more revealing news against the representative from his Twitter account. It seems that Stoner visits the establishment nightly for drinking and gambling and socializing with other political Liberal junkies. No wonder Stoner looked stoned when TJ saw him last on CNN and he looked stoned…he probably was! *That's what too much of the good life will do to you,* he decided.

TJ didn't care for social media because you had to reveal too much data about yourself and nefarious people could use that information against you; better to be a private person instead he decided a long time ago.

A pet peeve that he had was people driving around with a blue or red disabled placard hanging down from their rear view mirror. Not only was it illegal to drive that way, it was just plain stupid. *You mean these people were too lazy to remove the placard before driving? Dumb, because it blocks your vision and can cause accidents.*

One other pet peeve that TJ harbored was that dumb people should *not* own a smart phone! That was an oxymoron at the highest level!

Oh well, he can't change the world all at once…it will have to be one Liberal Democrat at a time!

He went about other business that he had to take care of first at the CIA before leaving for Chevy Chase, Maryland. He wondered if they really named the town after the retired actor or, if Chevy Chase was named after the town! He didn't really know or care though as he had more important issues to occupy his thoughts.

After completing several tasks and since it looked to be another long night, he decided to treat himself to Golden Corral first and left the CIA Headquarters after 1900. He looked forward to seeing Dave again as well as the tasty food that they served.

After dealing with the usual traffic flow, he arrived at Golden Corral and entered the establishment.

He approached the cashier and paid for his meal and a drink. He wanted two glasses of milk and a cup of coffee and you had to order them from your server. So he seated himself near a window and waited for his server to arrive to take his order as well as initialing his receipt. When his server finally showed up, he ordered his two glasses of milk and a cup of coffee. However, when she showed up again, it was with a cup of coffee and an empty glass with a carton of milk. TJ knew from experience that it took two cartons of milk per glass and that meant he needed four cartons of milk and two empty glasses then. When he asked his server for three more cartons of milk, she informed him that he would have to pay another $2.38 even though he already paid that same amount to the cashier earlier for his drinks.

He figured that he could go about it a different way and looked around for his friend who was the owner of Golden Corral. He couldn't spot Dave and decided on another tactic. On the other side of the restaurant near the rest rooms, he spotted a different server and decided to solicit her assistance before this whole thing turned out to be a milk crisis!

When he told the server that he needed three cartons of milk and another glass, she assured him that it wouldn't be a problem and asked him where he was sitting. So he pointed across the restaurant floor to the other side and stated that he was by the window at a table and would be reading a book.

He then decided to use the *rain locker*---submarine term for bathroom---first and entered the restroom and took care of his business.

By the time that he helped himself to two plates of food from the line and returned to his table, he noticed that his milk had not arrived yet. He hoped that it wouldn't be too much to ask for as he was really thirsty for milk.

He noticed that his server was busy cleaning off another table, two tables away from his when he spotted the other server bringing him only two cartons of milk and a glass.

As she arrived at his table, she explained that this was all the milk that she could give him without charging him and laid the two cartons and glass on his table. Just then, his server looked up and noticed that TJ had gone over her head to get more milk. She pointed her finger and yelled to the other server, "He is not to receive any more milk." So the server that brought him the two cartons of milk took one back and reached for the other one but TJ was too fast for her and had a hand on it at the same time that she grabbed for it and a tug of war ensued.

As they were struggling with the milk, a kindly gentleman approached as if out of nowhere and ordered his waitress to put the milk back down. It was his friend Dave. She did as was instructed and left to return to her duties elsewhere. Dave took a seat across from TJ and apologized for the milk confusion. He explained that certain people were not to have too many cartons of milk as they would take them out of the buffet; especially if they were traveling.

"No problem Dave. But why not get yourself a milk machine like other fine restaurants in the area?" TJ asked seriously.

"Not the Golden Corral way my friend. But not to worry, I will talk to my people again at our next meeting and make sure that we forget trying to regulate our milk. Sounds like something Congress would want to do anyway and I don't want to be like them," Dave stated matter-of-factly and left to go back to work.

TJ finished his meal and tucked his book away in his cargo pocket. He decided that he needed to get back to work and headed out to the parking lot and climbed into his truck.

He entered the address into his GPS and was off to visit Chevy Chase…not the actor…the City of Chevy Chase, Maryland. He wondered what the real Chevy Chase was doing now since he was retired. Oh well…

He arrived at the Full House Bar and Grill and parked across the street in front of an older home that looked to be painted with John Deere Green…his favorite color. From the files on Stoner, he knew that the congressman would be driving a 2018 Ice Blue Range Rover with a license plate that read "STONED" and that the SUV could be valued at around $90,000 dollars by Kelly Blue Book depending on the options and he was pretty sure that this dirtbag would have all the options possible! It seemed to TJ that Congress was being paid way too much. *How can they all be millionaires on their civil servant salaries?* And, *how come they only had to work about six months a year as well?* At least, he really did *earn* his pay…no lobbyist or special interest income for him!

As he sat there thinking, he knew that it would be hard to tell the color of the congressman's car at night, but how many Range Rovers could there be? Just as that thought occurred, a newer Range Rover pulled up in the parking lot but with the wrong license plate name.

Ooops…I guess there could be more. In fact, by the time that Representative Stoner did arrive, there were a total of three Range Rovers in the parking lot. *Now we just have to wait until he finishes his nightly fiesta.* However, he didn't have to wait too long as it was around midnight when the congressman stumbled out into the parking lot and was trying to unlock his vehicle. TJ was aghast that Stoner would try to drive in his present condition…obviously "stoned" by his body language. *What a dumb bastard!*

Luckily, Stoner had parked in the back of the parking lot next to a vacant grass lot where the lighting was not so good. TJ thought that by taking out Stoner that he would be killing two birds with one stone---pardon the pun, because, he would be making the roads a little bit safer for the good citizens of this community and accomplish his mission as well. He figured that the time to act was now.

Stoner didn't know what hit him since he was stoned.

After the mission was completed successfully, TJ headed for home on Joint Base Andrews. He was ready for sleep and whatever dreams that might come his way. He would have to start on the pictures taken from Senator Melvin's home later today when he returned to the office. *Just not enough time in a day anymore,* he observed and he still had Representative Lidio to take care of also.

After rising for the new day, he ate a quick breakfast, brushed his teeth and headed for the office. Judy greeted him warmly as always and had his coffee ready for him but no food this time. *It's almost like she can read my mind,* he considered absently.

He finished typing up his report and sent it by email to his boss. Next, he removed the pictures from the safe and started to study them. The first picture that he decided to study simply showed a sign that read "Bravo" on a small white painted building and in the background were plenty of trees. Green grass was abundant in the area as well. There was an old gas pump standing proudly next to the building with its globe still intact.

He then put that picture aside and picked up the next picture. This picture showed the area of a golf course. Looking at the picture he could see a flag next to a hole. But what hole was it? He couldn't tell but maybe that didn't matter. The grass he noticed again was nice and green and well-trimmed. There were a few trees in the background and not much else of any consequence…he noticed.

The third picture showed a road heading towards the mountains. On the right side of the picture was a sign that read, "Indio City Limits." TJ was pretty sure this was a picture taken in Indio, California. *But what did it mean? What did any of these pictures mean? And why were there two of the same pictures with the word Indio?* These were all good questions that required answers.

He then determined that these were not casual pictures that would be taken as if on a trip or if one was on vacation. He realized that these pictures had a real purpose. *But what was that purpose?* Could only be one thing…to communicate a message. *But what message?* These pictures he noticed were not of anything special unless you considered that antique gas pump and the old building. *What could they mean?*

As he was in deep thought, a knock sounded on his door and Randy walked in and took a seat that was off to the side.

"Good work again with the Stoner mission. The dishonest media should really eat this one up," Randy predicted.

"Thanks boss."

"So what have you got going right now?"

TJ handed over the seven pictures to his boss and studied his reaction closely. Randy seemed as perplexed about the pictures as he was.

"What am I looking at here? Are these pictures from your last vacation? I didn't know you played golf," Randy stated seriously.

"I don't. These are pictures from the crime scene of Senator Melvin's home. My friend who is in charge of the investigation is allowing me to study these pictures to see if they may be somehow connected to the death of the senator. Can't figure anything out yet…any ideas?"

"Nice gas pump. Maybe they don't even pertain to the case itself. I had heard somewhere that the senator was a little exotic. Maybe he liked antiques."

"What about the picture of the golf course and the Indio picture?"

"Maybe he liked to play golf in Indio?" Randy suggested.

"Well, that could be I suppose. But, there are still the other pictures that communicate other options."

"Well, I'm sure that you'll figure it out in time. Don't spend too much effort on these pictures right now and neglect your other duties."

TJ had forgotten all about taking out Representative Lidio. He was so engrossed in figuring out if these pictures held a real meaning or not.

"Sorry Randy, I did forget about Lidio…I'll get right on it."

"Don't worry about him just yet. Our newest candidate now is Representative Bret Stanton, a Liberal Democrat from California. He's just begging to be next. Besides that, Fox News reported today that the biggest liar in Congress right now is Representative Stanton …so do what you do best TJ."

Randy departed after giving TJ his marching orders…or in this case, his "take him out" orders.

TJ secured the pictures in his safe and grabbed up Representative Stoner's file and headed down to see Jessy. She was working at her desk when he arrived. He returned Representative Stoner's file to her and asked for the file on Representative Stanton. Jessy instructed him to take a seat and that she would return shortly. So he sat in one of the two chairs that were located in front of Jessy's desk.

As he waited, he saw no sign of Ching Ching and he didn't want to peek into her cubical for fear that she might actually be there and then when she saw him she would pester him again about the movies. *Better to just let that slide for now,* he decided.

Jessy returned shortly with his file and he worked his way back to his office. Once there, he gave Representative Stanton's CIA's file serious scrutiny.

So, here we are with another loser Liberal from the great state of California. California seemed to be the cradle of hypocrisy and idiocy with a little bit of insanity thrown in for good measure, and with that said...the Liberal Democrat was born!

Chapter 14
Ω

"Here you are, you're a Liberal, probably define peace as the absence of conflict. I define peace as the ability to defend yourself and blow your enemies into smithereens."

---Sean Hannity

Jaron Cowan releases a book, "A Lower Disloyalty," which slams President Trump and the atrocious ways in which the former FBI Director was treated. He is currently on a book signing tour around the nation during a time when most of the country hates him for various reasons... Democrats and Republicans alike. It is repeated in the company of the ruling class, that the book sales will support his future legal defense.

President Trump leads an allied force made up of France, United Kingdom and the United States in launching missiles into Syria in response to the use of chemical weapons used on its own people.

Laura Ingraham announces on her new show, The Ingraham Angle, with support from a medical expert, the negative effects caused by marijuana use, including, but not limited to, that the likely hood of suicide is eight times greater in potheads.

Hannity and The Ingraham Angle

Sean was seen by Fox News viewers holding up a $20 dollar bill on a split screen with Laura as an offer for her legal services which he might need in the future. He was currently under attack by the dishonest media for not disclosing his relationship with the President's former personal attorney, Michael Cohen.

After a raid was conducted by the FBI on Cohen's office, it was revealed that Sean Hannity was named as a client of the disgraced attorney since the agency discovered documents with Hannity's name on them. Cohen was presently under investigation over "hush money" that was allegedly paid to women to keep them quiet about past affairs with Donald Trump.

"Hannity, I'm just gonna say this one time. You're almost like a cousin to me and I'm glad that they are onto you now," Laura told Hannity honestly while chuckling.

On his show, Hannity defended himself righteously, "Michael Cohen has never represented me in any legal matter. I never retained his services. I never received an invoice and I sure as hell never paid him any money. But, he was a great person to ask if I had a legal question on my mind. My questions, almost exclusively, focused on real estate. Michael knows real estate almost as well as Donald Trump."

Hannity flashed a $20 bill and told Laura that he would just mail his retainer to her since she had agreed on national television to be his new attorney!

"Alright Sean, thank you so much for that great introduction and also for the promise of giving me $20 dollars as a retainer for representing you as your future attorney, and I would really like to see at least a dime of that money; just kidding Sean. I know that you're good for it…sooner or later that is.

"Welcome to The Ingraham Angle. Have we got a really great show for you tonight and from every angle. Everything from…I'm just being told that we have a Fox News Alert and that we will be taking you to Chevy Chase, Maryland where the body of Representative Stoner was discovered and a news conference is now taking place."

Fox News viewers are now able to see at night, an area that is well lit by high powered lights and a cordoned area without a body. A Sheriff's deputy was situated in front of the cordoned area with a microphone stand in front of him. Behind him off to one side was the Sheriff of Montgomery County. Cameras could be heard clicking from the news media and the buzz of excitement was in the air when the deputy started to speak.

"We are here today due to the finding of a deceased Representative Stoner. I will now hand over this news event to our Sheriff, the honorable Joe Biggs."

The Sheriff looked uncomfortable with the 'honorable' part but let it pass and stepped up to the platform with the microphone stand.

"I'm Sheriff Joe Biggs and I will be brief in what we know right now. Representative Stoner was found stoned to death with a rock in the vacant lot here next to the Full House Bar and Grill. We are still investigating and have already transported the body to the medical examiner's office. It is known by the elevated blood alcohol level of .24 that the congressman was stoned on alcohol as well as marijuana that was found on his person and in his vehicle. His judgment, reasoning and coordination was all affected by his condition and it's obvious that he was planning on driving home in his present condition, which he most likely has done previously I was told. It appears that Representative Stoner decided to take a leak in this vacant lot before going home. He would have been a danger to the community in his condition had he attempted to drive. But, with that said, no one had a right to take the law into their own hands."

The Sheriff took a pause before adding his last remark.

"A Russian *matryoshka* was found at the scene. Thank you."

With that said, the Sheriff walked away leaving reporters wanting to ask questions…but couldn't.

Coming back to the Fox News studio after a commercial break…

"Welcome back to The Ingraham Angle. That was an interesting tidbit of information. I would hope that other members of Congress would be more responsible…yeah right. In case our viewers don't know what a Russian *matryoshka* is, am I pronouncing that right? My producer is telling me no. How do we pronounce it then? Ok, he's telling me that he doesn't know either, great. Anyway, it is one of them nested dolls that you may have seen on T.V. You open a…I think it's made out of wood. You open this doll up and take out another doll and so forth. It's like five dolls all together and they keep getting smaller. That's how they are all allowed to fit inside one another.

"Moving on now, our next guests are Jon Talcott from a resistance group to the legalization of pot called 'Let's Be Smart America' and Rodman Cyril who is a marijuana attorney in Colorado. Jon, let's start with you."

With a split screen, viewers were able to see Jon on the left and Rodman on the right with Laura in the center of the screen.

"Thank you Laura. We are advocating for not making marijuana legal as its use is already abused. Colorado is already a virtual disaster from state legalization and this is a sure sign of what is in store for our country if it becomes federally legal. In fact, we oppose the state for going against federal law and allowing state legal marijuana sales."

"That is so true Jon. I don't think President Trump's base was voting for him in the hopes that he will make weed legal. President Trump did not talk a lot about this on the campaign trail, but his supporters seem to be about law and order. In fact, studies have shown us that most Conservatives are against legalizing pot. We already have an opioid crisis happening now without adding a schedule one drug to the crisis list. Personally, I believe that this is a gateway drug that will allow our youths to go on to harder drugs such as heroine and meth and will hurt our country drastically. There are a lot of young people that may like making pot legal, but what do they know? I'm telling you that we don't need half or more of our country spaced out. Anyway, these kids are immature and we don't need to make our country any dumber. By making a dumb decision on this issue will cost our country in health issues, money, security and our standing in the world and I hope that President Trump is listening because we need his assistance and his leadership on this real issue that affect all Americans, either directly or indirectly.

"I have a friend in Nevada," Laura continued, "who has shared some facts with me. First off, Nevada just legalized pot last year. Secondly, Nevada is spending $2 million in commercials that tell pregnant women not to smoke pot while pregnant. Duh! Are the people in that state really that stupid? If they are doing pot they are. Thirdly, shortly after Nevada legalized marijuana sales, the illegal-legal drug dealers were running out of the product after a short time. I'm told that there were long lines of people trying to get this crap and the governor even declared a 'state of emergency' due to falling pot supply levels. No kidding...I verified that myself. It's so unbelievable, what is happening to our country!

"Rodman," Laura simply stated to give him his cue to speak on the issue. But he was a bit slow to respond.

"Hello...thanks for having me."

"What is your reaction on this issue Rodman?"

"Thanks...for having me Laura."

"Got that...go ahead and speak your piece Rodman," Laura urged him again.

"My reaction...?"

"Rodman, you seem to be moving a tad slow here. We are talking about pot and you seem very lethargic. Why is that I wonder? Did you smoke something before coming on? If this was a comedy show, you are spot on for making my case against pot."

"Ok, I see what you mean…I just spaced out a little due to my first T.V. appearance. Thousands of people want the stuff Laura and the states benefit from the tax revenue. Thousands have jobs due to America's newest industry."

"I don't think that that's what I want my country to be known for is the weed capital of the world," Laura interjected seriously.

"Political congratulations to President Trump and to the senator from Colorado for making a good deal."

Rodman was talking about a deal that President Trump proposed to a Colorado Republican senator if he would quit rejecting his justice nominees. The deal would involve non-enforcement of federal marijuana laws if the senator would play ball with the President. Laura was aghast and totally against this plan.

"What does that mean…political congratulations? Let me ask you this Rodman…did you toke up earlier? You seem to be coming with this 'off the wall' crap. Even Jon is looking a little perplexed. Jon, let's go back to you then. What are some of the bad effects of pot on people? And please be honest with our viewers."

"Well, it causes schizophrenia in people as well as slurred speech and slower reaction times and leads to poor judgment."

Laura interrupted Jon for the benefit of Rodman, the pothead attorney from Colorado.

"Listen to what he's saying closely Rodman. Go on Jon."

"People are six times more likely to be schizophrenia if they use pot on a regular basis. Studies also show that with regular use, you are eight times more likely to kill yourself."

"So this is like what big tobacco did 100 years ago and big money is pushing this issue?" Laura questioned.

"You are right Laura," confirmed Jon.

"Ok, we are out of time for this segment but I want to thank you both for coming on and also I want you both on my radio show later this week." Laura then realized that Rodman fell asleep on live T.V.! "Well, looks like we'll have to wake up Rodman our Dream Weaver; that's what I'll call him from now on because he's probably having a killer dream right now. In any case, we'll be right back after this commercial break."

After the set was officially off the air for commercials, Rodman had to be carried off by two Fox employees to the guest lounge to finish his drug induced sleep.

After three commercials, Laura was back on again.

"We were just talking to our last guests about the real costs of allowing the states to legalize pot in opposition to federal law. Not only are there health costs to be considered, but the reason that it is allowed by the states that have legalized it boils down to one thing…money. Some states will mismanage your tax dollars and then seek more revenue without raising taxes, which is unpopular by everyone. So the new Liberal thinking is that by legalizing marijuana and taxing it, states can make up for their mismanagement of your tax dollars and the young people are just simply, loving it, I have to tell you. Even to the detriment of the country, the federal government is allowing the states to legalize its use. I don't see how that can happen under our current federal laws. So on this show, I am now calling on President Trump to have the fortitude to call on the Attorney General to start enforcing federal laws on this issue. I love what the President is doing for our country, but I'm sorry, this issue is too critical for our country's health and prosperity and safety to just ignore. My message to everyone is this…pot users are losers!

"Now, I want to introduce our next…wait a minute, I am being told that we have another Fox News Alert. It seems that the former director of the FBI, Jaron Cowan, has committed suicide in his car. Police investigating this incident said that Mr. Cowan was driving from a Barnes and Nobel in Florida on his book signing tour to another Barnes and Nobel in the area and apparently just decided to pull his black 2017 Chevy Suburban off the road where he shot himself with his own 9mm handgun and was discovered by police a short time later. In the vehicle, approximately one pound of marijuana was discovered along with a couple of pipes utilized for smoking it. See what Jon and I were talking about? There's a perfect example of why not to become a pothead…it can cost you your job and your life!"

CIA Headquarters

TJ was watching The Ingraham Angle and really liked and admired Laura and her direct way of speaking. He was a lot like her with her directness; *maybe she's a long lost sister of mine* he thought half seriously. And then there was the Jaron Cowan angle. In a way his suicide was a shock but in another way it wasn't, meaning that he didn't have many friends. Democrats hated him and the Republicans did as well. I guess things have come full circle for Mr. Cowan. He felt no sorrow for the man with all of the corruption that he was involved with and realized that he probably would have been assigned to take him out sooner or later; this way saved him some time! He truly hoped that Director Cray would be a much better and ethical leader for the FBI, especially since his friend Bob worked for him.

Now back to work. TJ had been reading the file on Representative Stanton some and studying the remaining pictures as well.

Representative Stanton he noticed was on the Foreign Affairs Committee and often visited different countries. TJ remembered that it was on the news that the representative would be visiting the Philippines for an animal rights summit, and, since it was Fox News that was reporting it, he knew that he could depend on the accuracy of the story!

But, when would he be leaving? TJ couldn't remember. So he searched the internet for the answer to that question and found a Fox News clip on YouTube that they had filmed on the animal rights conference with the representative. The news clip was actually a press conference that Representative Stanton was holding at the Capitol in the National Statuary Hall with several of the media attending.

TJ clicked on play and Representative Stanton was speaking…"I just wanted to let everyone know that I will be attending the Asian Pacific Animal Rights Conference in Manila, Philippines in three days. Our position is that the Philippine government needs to make and enforce laws that will protect animals from abuse. Of special interest is in the abuse of dogs. Stray dogs are often beaten and eaten and this is perfectly legal under their laws. The Philippine government has pointed out that by allowing this type of activity to continue, poor Filipinos will be fed and the streets are managed by the citizens instead of the government having to fund an animal shelter like we do here in the U.S. I know that the Philippine Islands are a poor country, but if they will adopt some animal rights, I will work on getting them a $1 million dollar grant. Ok, I will now take some questions," and he pointed to a young woman with a CNN logo on her shirt.

"Representative Stanton, don't you have a meeting with President Trump in three days? We heard that he invited you to the Undocumented Worker Conference that he is hosting at The White House."

"Well, I'm not attending…next question."

But the young woman from CNN was persistent and would not be ignored as she had a follow up question and raised her voice accordingly.

"Why are you not attending congressman?"

"Because, I might lose my head and say something that wasn't politically correct to Trump, so I'll just stay away from him," he replied and pointed to a MSNBC News reporter.

"Congressman, how will you be going to the Philippines? With everything in the news about waste, fraud and abuse these days, is that a concern with you?"

"It is as with all of us Democrats, so I will be flying on a C-5 out of Joint Base Andrews that is scheduled to go to Clark Air Base and I will spend the night there at the *Pipi Asno* Hotel which is being offered to me for the night by President Duterte. In the morning, I will then continue on with my trip to *Ninoy Aquino* International Airport on the same C-5 for the animal rights conference; same plan with my return trip."

The congressman pointed to another reporter that just happened to be from a Fox News affiliate.

"Congressman Stanton, why are you so concerned about animal rights in the Philippines; shouldn't human rights be more of a concern to you?" asked the reporter.

This became the last question to be asked by reporters as the congressman turned and walked away.

TJ had heard enough anyway and shut the television off. *But what day is he leaving on?* That is the question. Due to military scheduling, he thought that he could figure that out with the help of a phone call to the passenger terminal at JBA, since there were probably not that many flights to Clark Air Base.

Since the U.S. formally returned the base back to the Philippine government on November 26, 1991, regular flights had stopped and a portion of the base became known as Clark International Airport. However, in June 2012, due to the actions of the Chinese claims on West Philippine Sea, the Philippine government agreed to the return of American military forces to Clark Air Base.

He pressed the speaker button on his phone and dialed the DSN to JBA. DSN stood for the Defense Switched Network which is the DOD worldwide telephone system. DSN telephone numbers can only be dialed from one DSN telephone number to another telephone on the Defense Switched Network which TJ had access to.

After dialing 850, he was able to get a DSN line and then he dialed the DSN telephone number of 858-8102 for the passenger terminal at Joint Base Andrews and found out that the only flight to Clark Air Base within the next seventy-two hours was leaving tomorrow afternoon…and he was going to be on it and added his name to the passenger list.

Now that he had that out of the way, he turned his attention back to the mysterious pictures that were so…mysterious.

The next picture that he picked up showed a calendar for the month of November 2011; that was all. No dates were circled and no information was written on the calendar. Interesting… "So what was the point of the picture then?" he asked himself. He decided to wait on the last two pictures and go home and get some sleep. Tomorrow was another day to solve these mystery pictures.

He arose early the next day, ate a quick breakfast consisting of a banana and a piece of toast with peanut butter on it. It wasn't much to go on especially since the slice of bread that he ate was the heel. But TJ knew that Judy would take care of him with something else that he liked.

After brushing his teeth and rinsing, he was off like a rocket on his way to work. As he walked through the halls of the CIA building, he was noticing that more people were greeting him now days. That was due in large part that he had become a regular fixture at the place now. It was almost like a second home to him…in fact, it was his first home in reality!

He took the elevator up to the sixth floor and entered the door that read "Panama." Several minutes after he had sat down at his desk, Judy popped in with a hot buttered cinnamon roll, with raisins and a cup of hot coffee just the way he liked it.

"Good morning Mr. Law," Judy beamed as she set the items down before TJ.

"Morning Judy," TJ greeted. Good to see you as always. How's your mom?"

"She's doing fine in the nursing home. She would rather be at home with me, except that, she needs the care that the nursing home offers and that I can't give her anymore and thanks for asking, that was sweet of you."

"Judy, I'll be leaving on a flight to the Philippines this afternoon. My C-5 flight leaves at 1500."

"Well ok then, I'll mark it on your personal calendar. Have a safe trip boss. When will you be returning?"

"Within a few days I'm sure."

Judy departed for her work area and TJ departed as well for other tasks that he needed to complete before his flight. Upon returning to his office, he turned on Fox News and learned that the Democrats are so desperate to win elections, that now their playbook consists of not only illegals and convicted felons voting, but now they want children as young as sixteen to be able to vote! They also mentioned that the DNC is suing the Trump Campaign for the Trump-Russia collusion and the man that is leading the charge is none other than the DNC Chair... Tim Payat... *Another piece of crap that needs his day in my court,* TJ decided.

He left the office and headed for Joint Base Andrews. He did not inform Randy of his plans because when Judy updated his calendar, his boss would see that he was on his way out of the country.

He made it to the base in plenty of time and checked in by displaying his CIA badge. He did not have any luggage, other than a hand carry, since he was not planning to stay long; just long enough to complete his mission. Before taking a seat in the passenger terminal, he purchased a sack lunch for $10 dollars. He was allowed to take it on the plane but decided to eat it now since he had missed lunch. However, he did bring a can of honey roasted peanuts with him in his hand carry bag for any "snack attacks" that might crop up on the plane since it was a long flight…even longer on a cargo plane!

After finishing his lunch, he turned to reading his latest book which was a mystery by Alfred Hitchcock. Every so often he would look up from his reading hoping to espy the congressman. He had never met this asshole personally, but would immediately recognize him from seeing his picture in his file. Speaking of which, TJ did not return the congressman's file back to Jessy but locked it in his safe instead. He decided that he would return it after his mission; reason being, he figured that his boss would assign him to another target that wasn't Representative Lidio. That file was still secured in his safe as well.

While sitting there reading his book and waiting for the congressman to show, his phone rang. Not really rang exactly, because he always kept it on vibrate. He removed the phone from the cradle attached to his belt and noticed that it was Randy calling. So before answering it, he arose and walked outside for his phone call with his boss.

"Yeah," he answered.

"Is that how you are supposed to answer the phone?" Randy questioned.

"Well, you didn't like my last way of answering when I would say, 'CIA,'" TJ countered.

"Ok, in that case, yeah is acceptable then. I was just funning with you anyway. Are you sitting down?"

"I am now that you asked me. What's up?"

"Senator Bow Cutler was found dead a while ago. Same as with Senator Melvin…throat slit. Your friend Mingo is on it right now if you have the time to call him."

"I will right now. I still have plenty of time before my flight leaves. Thanks for informing me; you're a good boss!"

Before Randy had a chance to respond, TJ had already hung up on his superior. He felt like teasing his boss at times as well. *Wow… another Republican taken out! At least he was a piece of crap so the American people will suffer no great loss.*

While outside, he dialed his friend's cell phone hoping that he would answer. He wanted to find out about the particulars on this next case.

"Yeah," answered FBI Special Agent Mingo.

"Is that the way you are supposed to answer your phone?" TJ asked.

"Well, you didn't like the way I answered the last time," Mingo stated.

Then a thought occurred to TJ, since he had just told his boss the same thing, it felt a little like déjà vu!

"I just told my boss the same thing not a minute ago…strange. Anyway, I heard about Senator Cutler. I heard he got his neck sliced."

"You got that right."

"Was there a Russian clue left behind?" TJ questioned.

"A Russian coin just like last time," answered Mingo. Where are you right now?"

"I'm at Andrews waiting for a flight to Clark."

"Ok man, we'll take pictures and I'll get a report to you as soon as possible since you are on vacation."

"No vacation…on a mission."

"Yeah, well, be sure to leave them Filipino girls single. I know how they like to marry Americans."

"Don't worry about me as I can handle myself just fine thank you."

"Just trying to help by giving sage advice; in any case be careful."

"I will and thanks for your concern my friend. I'll see you sometime when I return."

TJ then returned to the passenger waiting area and spotted his target at once. How these Liberals can really stand out in a crowd was in his thoughts. He took a seat again and then went back to reading his book while keeping an eye on the congressman.

When he checked in, the agent at the counter informed him that he would be flying on a C-32 to Travis Air Force Base. Then from there, it would be a C-5 to Clark with a stop at Elmendorf Air Force Base in Alaska for refueling. Well, that was good to know. He knew that he would have a more comfortable flight on the C-32, minus the stewardesses that were usually on commercial Patriot Express flights. Patriot Express flights are a government contract flight which provides support to U.S. military members and their families when no DoD aircraft were available. These flights are operated by various commercial airlines and provide service worldwide and they come with stewardesses!

No matter, being an ex-Navy SEAL, he learned to be comfortable in any environment.

He didn't have to be bored with the estimated twenty hour flight as he had his book with him---in fact, 3 of them---as well as the last two pictures to study. Now it was just a waiting game until he managed to get to Clark Air Base and then an opportunity to *visit* his target. It was nice to get away sometimes, but it was also just as nice to get back home again…safely he hoped. That was one thing that he appreciated about flying on military aircraft, he trusted them more than commercial flights due to the rigorous maintenance program that they were subjected to.

At last came the time for everyone to board the aircraft. Everyone who had luggage had had it loaded onto the plane already. TJ followed in line with the passengers and took a window seat. On military aircraft, seats were not assigned; it was first come, first serve.

The flight to Travis was uneventful and he was able to scrutinize the congressman very little.

Upon arriving at Travis, a flight of stairs was brought out to the tarmac and passengers deplaned and boarded a C-5 nearby. While boarding, the luggage was already being transferred to the cargo hold of the huge cargo plane. Luggage was stored against the cargo ramp with a vertical net attached to the deck and the top of the fuselage. He knew that the C-5 Galaxy was the largest cargo plane available to the military and it was made by Lockheed---now known as Lockheed Martin---and was many years old as production on the plane stopped in 1989. The layover was less than an hour. The flight to Elmendorf he knew would be about five hours.

Once in the air, he decided to take a break from his book and study another one of the pictures. The next one that he chose to study was of the Grand Canyon. This was a nice simple picture of the Grand Canyon. However, he noticed right away that it had been doctored---probably in Photoshop---because it showed three sound waves as though it's indicating an echo. *That's it*, he thought. *This picture is practically screaming out an echo! But how was an echo connected to Senator Melvin? Was someone angry with the senator?* Obviously so or he might not be dead right now. But, TJ knew from his line of work, that that was not always the case. It could just be business as usual.

Let's see now...who would want the senator dead, a Democrat maybe? Could be...anything was possible. Senator Melvin was the Chairman for the Senate Armed Services Committee, which is the most powerful committee in D.C. That could have something to do with it. Maybe he stonewalled on a bill and kept it from passing? It was too early in the game to make that conclusion. Then again, why was a Russian clue left behind as if a copycat to his mission? Did someone figure out what he was doing and have it in for Republicans? Too many questions and not enough answers. He raked his brains for another thirty minutes and gave up and went back to his book.

The layover at Elmendorf was exactly one hour. Those who wanted to rest inside the passenger terminal were allowed to do so. He wasn't planning on going in, but when he saw the senator stand up and put his jacket on, he stood up as well and stretched and was acting very nonchalant so as not to bring attention to himself from the senator.

He followed the senator into the terminal and was planning on using the head until the senator had the same idea and entered the restroom. TJ did not want to be too close to the senator and decided to wait until he returned.

Afterwards, he took a seat near the gate where he could surveil the senator and watch what was happening on the runway. Then he noticed something unusual. There was a chicken running around out on the blacktop and a military man was chasing it. *That's weird…* but not the weirdest thing that he had seen in his lifetime!

Once the plane was refueled, everyone was led back out to the C-5 Galaxy and was boarded. Basically, it looked to TJ that everyone resumed their same seats with the exception of some new fliers.

The flight to Clark Air Base was long and boring so he slept some, read his book some and studied the congressman some. He did not observe anything unusual however.

The plane touched down at Clark Air Base at 2200. He knew that the congressman would probably want to get to his hotel directly which was outside the airport in Angeles City, Pampanga. TJ did not have any reservation for a hotel, but he knew that a Holiday Inn Express was located somewhere in the city. *Thank heaven for that*, he thought. *Hopefully they would have a room for him and then he could start back for home the next day.*

After completing his mission that night, with no issues, he did locate the Holiday Inn Express which was only two blocks away and they did have a room for him. After checking in, he went directly to his room and crashed onto the bed and didn't wake until morning.

In the morning he awoke refreshed. After bathing, he headed down to get his free, included breakfast. After eating, he headed back up to his room where he brushed his teeth and watched the morning news. Nothing yet about Representative Stanton being found; he went back down and grabbed a jeepney to take him to Clark Air Base. A jeepney was the most popular mode of public transportation in the Philippines and dated back to World War II.

Upon arriving at the passenger terminal, he inquired at the ticket counter about a flight home.

"Hi, may I help you?" asked the nice looking Filipino woman.

"Yes, I will need a flight to Andrews please, for today if possible," and TJ showed his credentials before the woman had the opportunity to ask.

"I see. Let me check," the woman responded and started to work on her computer. After a minute the woman informed TJ of the bad news and the good news.

"I have a flight leaving in three hours," she stated.

"So, what's the bad news?" TJ asked.

"You'll have to take the long way back sir."

"What's the long way exactly."

"In three hours, we have a C-5 leaving for Andersen Air Force Base in Guam and from there your next flight would be on a C-130 that would take you to Aviano Air Base in Italy and from there we have a C-17 that would take you to Kadena Air Base in Okinawa, Japan and from there a KC-10 would take you to Elmendorf Air Force Base and after refueling, the same plane will go to Travis Air Force Base and refuel and then on to Andrews."

TJ thought, *Wow…that really is taking the long way home!* However, at this point he didn't care and signed up for the flight. He didn't fully realize that it would be two whole days before he was home again!

As he was waiting in the passenger terminal, he noticed a very familiar face…it was none other than Central Intelligent Agent Jerney!

Chapter 15
Ω

"If you don't trust police or government, but you think they should be the only ones to have guns…you might be a Liberal."

– Jeff Foxworthy

Obstructionist Democrats feel the need to file a multimillion dollar federal lawsuit against Russia, WikiLeaks and the Trump Campaign alleging election conspiracy and fraud to disrupt the 2016 election. This indicates a new low for the Democrats as the conspiracy theories against President Trump and Russian collusion evaporate as quickly as the failing DNC's fundraising! In FEC filings for closing out the 2017 year, the party had $6.1 million dollars in debt with just $6.5 million dollars in the bank; that leaves the DNC with only $400,000 dollars to their name!

In order to gain voters, some of the Liberal Democrats are concentrating their efforts on allowing illegals, felons and children as young as 16 to vote.

Fox News is reporting that Americans are fleeing tax-heavy Liberal "blue" states (California, Illinois & New York) at a record pace to Conservative "red" states (Arizona, Florida & Texas). Arizona, Florida and Texas offered better opportunities and lower taxes while California, Illinois and New York are raising taxes, have higher unemployment and are letting their infrastructure crumble. Additionally, in these states with higher taxes, under the Trump tax reform, you can no longer deduct your state and local (SALT) taxes.

Why should the rest of the country subsidize a handful of states that have higher than average taxes due to poor management of tax dollars? More than 450,000 Americans have fled these three deep blue states last year alone!

Bill Cosby was found guilty on all three charges in his sexual assault trial!

This was just some of the news that TV Patrol---which is a popular Filipino news broadcast station---was reporting on that TJ had watched in the morning before departing for Clark Air Base from his Holiday Inn Express.

On his flights back to the states, he had a chance to catch up on things with Jerney. He filled him in on the fact that he is working with FBI Special Agent Mingo in connection to the killing of Senator Melvin. He showed his friend the last picture that he was trying to figure out.

The picture showed a very lovely girl with long black hair wearing a long, red colored dress that almost touched the ground. The dress had some designs on it and looked to be from the 17th century.

"I've seen that girl somewhere before," remarked Jerney.

"Really?" TJ asked incredulously.

"Yup...now where did I see her? Let' see...hold on a minute."

TJ waited patiently while his friend struggled with his memory.

"Maybe you're getting old," TJ suggested.

"And yet I'm still younger than you," Jerney pointed out. And then, all at once it came to him. "I saw her on television one time...that's Juliet."

"Juliet who?" TJ questioned.

"You know, as in Romero and Juliet."

As TJ studied on that idea, it did seem plausible.

"Ok, so let's say it's Juliet, what's so significant about that?" But his friend didn't seem to have any more ideas.

Joint Base Andrews

His plane touched down early evening and TJ caught the base shuttle for a ride home. Once at home, he then turned on his television in order to catch any news that he might have missed. Since a commercial was on, he unpacked his bag and took a shower. After his shower, he trekked to the living room where The Ingraham Angle was already on and he heard Laura say: "So these migrants are country shopping just like the Democrats like to judge shop. I get it. They are getting their lessons from the Democrats."

Then the voice of Laura's guest with: "That's right Laura. The Democrats don't care about safety and security; they just want new voters for their party. The word has already gone out to these future illegals that the Democrats are your friends and that they want to help you. In fact, they hear this from U.S. immigration attorneys from California that travel down to parts of Mexico for seminars with the message that California is your friend and that that is the place to go when crossing. These attorneys coach these simple minded people on what to say in order to be successful in getting a political asylum hearing schedule in the future."

"Unbelievable. I hope more Americans will wake up and smell the coffee."

Laura was about to close out the segment when her guest requested to make one more comment.

"Go ahead, you got about 30 seconds and then we are at a hard break."

"Sure, thank you Laura. I just wanted to say that you cannot communicate reason with unreasonable people, or in this case, deranged and demented Liberals. In fact, every time the Democrats point the finger at President Trump and accuse him of doing something nefarious, we then find out that the truth is that *they* are the ones involved in vicious and corrupt behavior. They have big, loud mouths with no substance."

"You are so right my friend and I want to thank you for coming on."

Then the show was interrupted by a producer telling Laura about a Fox News Alert with the Fox News Alert sound bite and visual coming across the screen.

"It looks like we have a Fox News Alert. I'm told that Congressman Stanton has been found dead in his hotel room while in the Philippines for an animal rights conference. Listen to this…how can I say this properly? He was found with his head severed from his body. A bloody machete is the apparent weapon of choice that was discovered in the room. Also, a Russian beer bottle was found in his room. The Philippine government is reporting that it appears that the congressman was knocked in the head unconscious and then his head was severed and that's all we know so far. However, I'm told that we have a clip to play before the congressman left for the Philippines and here it is."

At this time, regular viewers of Fox News were reminded of, and remembered, the congressman talking about missing a meeting with President Trump in this Fox News clip…

"I just wanted to let everyone know that I will be attending the Animal Rights Conference in the Philippines in three days. Our position is that the Philippine government needs to make and enforce laws that will protect animals from abuse. Of special interest is in the abuse of dogs. Stray dogs are often beaten and eaten and this is perfectly legal under their laws. The Philippine government has pointed out that by allowing this type of activity to continue, poor Filipinos will be fed and the streets are managed by the citizens instead of the government having to fund an animal shelter like we do here in the U.S. I know that the Philippine Islands are a poor country, but if they will adopt some animal rights, I will work on getting them a $1 million dollar grant. Ok, I will now take some questions."

Representative Stanton pointed to a young woman with a CNN logo on her shirt.

"Representative Stanton, don't you have a meeting with President Trump in three days? We heard that he invited you to the Undocumented Worker Conference that he is hosting at The White House."

"Well, I'm not attending…next question."

But the young woman from CNN was persistent and would not be ignored as she had a follow up question and raised her voice accordingly.

"Why are you not attending congressman?"

"Because, I might lose my head and say something that wasn't politically correct to Trump, so I'll just stay away from him," he replied and pointed to a MSNBC News reporter.

The clip ended and Laura interjected her thoughts now for the viewers…

"Well, he lost his head alright and he wasn't even at a meeting with President Trump…guess he should have gone to the meeting with Trump and took his chances with the President!

"So what happened? Was this an Isis attack? Was it the Russians and they forgot a bottle of beer by chance? All good questions; stay with Fox News and we will keep you updated as more information comes in.

"Now I'm being told that ABS-CBN, a Fox News affiliate, is covering the incident and we'll take you there live."

From Angeles City, Pampanga, Philippines, the heavily accented voice of a male reporter addressed the host of The Ingraham Angle…

"*Magadang buhay* Laura," he greeted. "For your American viewers who may not know me, I'm RG Cruz, a news reporter with ABS-CBN News here in the Philippines. Today we are covering the mysterious death of an American Congressman Bret Stanton, who was attending the Asian Pacific Animal Rights Conference. Mr. Stanton was discovered deceased by housekeeping here at the *Pipi Asno* Hotel, loosely translated means, Dumb Ass Hotel. Don't ask me Laura why the owners named it that because we are still wondering the same thing ourselves here in the Philippines. If you look behind me right now, they are removing the body, which for obvious reasons is contained in a body bag and in that smaller bag that the other emergency worker is carrying, is the head of the congressman. The remains are to be taken to Clark for transport back to the United States aboard a military aircraft."

Fox News and ABS-CBN viewers saw two men in white jackets carrying what appeared to be a body in a body bag, presumably, that of Congressman Stanton, along with another man carrying a bowling ball bag which probably contained the head of the congressman.

TJ, feeling like God's Right-hand man, shut the television off and went to bed for some much needed rest; *back to work tomorrow!*

CIA Headquarters

He was in his office early the next morning, even before his personal assistant. He had his report already typed up by the time that Judy arrived and sent a copy of it over to his boss. Then he laid out all seven of the pictures on his desk and studied them. There was the picture of the golf course; two of the city sign of Indio; the bravo sign; the November calendar; Juliet and the Grand Canyon. It seemed that all of the pictures had to have a common denominator, *but what was it?* he questioned himself.

As he was in deep study on the pictures, Judy entered and announced, "Mr. Morgan would like to see you Mr. Law."

So TJ walked over to Randy's office, knocked on his door and then entered without waiting for a reply and took a seat.

"Great job on your last mission…it was very successful."

"Thanks boss."

"What are you working on now?" Randy questioned.

"I'm studying those pictures to see if I can get a lead on who killed Melvin. Oh, I forgot about Representative Lidio. I'll get on that as well," he assured his senior.

"Never mind, I have two new items for you this time. Go and meet with your FBI friend and contact and gather all of the information that you can about the death of Senator Cutler and then your next target will be Tim Payat."

"The DNC Chair?" questioned TJ.

"Yes. He is causing a lot of problems for the President as well as the whole country. He is the main reason for the lawsuit against the Trump Campaign. I think it's abundantly clear that he needs to go to the place where all bad Liberals go."

"To that Liberal hangout in Maryland called the Full House Bar and Grill?"

"No, to Hell where he belongs and will feel welcomed by his other friends that are already there waiting for him," Randy corrected his subordinate.

TJ couldn't agree more and immensely liked messing with his boss whenever the opportunity presented itself!

Back at his office, he placed a call to his friend Bob and left a message for him to return his call when he had the time and then he headed to see Jessy once more with a file tucked under his arm.

Upon arriving at Jessy's cubicle, he noticed right away her typing speed. *Much faster than me,* he thought as he sat down in a chair across from her.

"Morning TJ, what can I do for you?" she asked politely.

"Well, I wanted to return Congressman Lidio's file back to you in case someone else needs it, and secondly, I need the file on Tim Payat."

"The DNC Chair?" questioned Jessy.

"That's the one," TJ confirmed.

"Alright, let me look up the location then."

Jessy wrote down the location on a Post It Note and then left telling TJ that she would be right back. She was also going to return Lidio's file as well and had that location written down as well.

As he sat there waiting for her to return with his next target, his phone vibrated so he answered it. It was Mingo.

"Hey Bob, where are you right now?"

"I'm in my office, why? You want to come over and see me about Cutler?"

"My boss is urging me to find out what was discovered at the scene of the crime. He made it clear that that is one of my priorities."

"Sure, what time are you coming over?"

"What about right now?" TJ asked. "I just have to finish getting a file and then I can leave for your place."

"Ok, I'll make sure to hang around until you arrive."

"Thanks, I owe you."

"No problem, just take me out to Golden Corral sometime," Bob suggested.

"You got it buddy…and with pleasure!" and TJ meant it.

After he finished his phone call, Ching Ching just happen to pop in. He had forgotten all about her cubicle right next to Jessy's.

"Hi you naughty boy; why don't you call Ching Ching for movie I wonder? Do you have another Chinese girlfriend that you are not telling me about?"

TJ thought that it sounded like she was referring to them as a couple…odd. But then again, she was Chinese and a little different…but very beautiful!

"Hi Ching Ching, how are you today?"

"I be fine cowboy. When you planning to take Ching Ching to movie…I still waiting."

"I've been very busy lately. But I have your number and I'll let you know when I have some free time."

"What number you have sailor?" Ching Ching inquired.

"I know your work number here and I promise to call you when I have some down time."

"Oh, I see. Ok then and remember no funny stuff hero when we go together."

"I understand," TJ reassured her, thinking that she was indeed a prim and proper woman.

Ching Ching turned around and went back to her desk. He thought about what she said calling him hero. *What did she mean by that? Maybe she really did consider him a hero just because he is working for the CIA, or maybe, she meant that he was her hero; who knows?*

Jessy returned shortly after his meeting with the beautiful and seductive Ching Ching.

"Here you go TJ," and she handed the file to him. "Sorry it took so long and I hoped you weren't too bored."

"Not at all," TJ replied to her concern for him. "I always carry my book with me and I had an interesting time…waiting for you."

"While reading your book?"

"Uh yeah, sure…it's a great book."

"Liar," admonished Jessy. "You are a poor liar my friend. I just bet that you were busy reading something else maybe?"

"What else could I be busy reading?" TJ asked seriously. "You didn't leave any magazines out this time."

"I wonder…" said Jessy, with a quizzical look on her face.

While walking back to his office, he thought about his chat with Ching Ching. Just think, if he accepted her as his girlfriend, and they got engaged, and, they eventually got married, what a lucky guy he would be. She's very beautiful with a good job at the CIA and she liked watching movies.

He wondered what else she liked. Maybe he'll find out sometime…

In his office he locked up the file on Tim Payat and headed down to get his vehicle and then on to the FBI Building in D.C. There were two FBI locations in DC and his friend worked at the headquarters which was 935 Pennsylvania Avenue, which was close to The White House…

FBI Headquarters

Upon entering the building, he showed his credentials and was allowed access after inquiring about where to find Special Agent Mingo. He grabbed an elevator and made his way to the third floor.

While in the elevator, he remembered that the President was recommending that the current FBI building (J. Edgar Hoover Bldg) be torn down and a new modern building to be built. Of course, the FBI was all for a new building…*who wouldn't want a new workplace?* However, the process might take a while.

Once on the third floor, he turned right and walked down the hall until he came to a door that read "330" and entered. There was a lady at a desk that asked if she could help him. He told her that Special Agent Mingo was expecting him. She offered him a seat which he took and waited for his friend to arrive and probably escort him to his work area.

After several minutes of waiting, Special Agent Mingo showed up and welcomed him warmly. After several words of greeting, Bob offered to show him around the department which TJ readily agreed. Bob showed him the crime lab which made up the whole fourth floor; the forensics lab which was the entire fifth floor; most of the sixth floor was dedicated to computer and technology forensics. TJ was impressed with everything that his friend showed him, but, he wouldn't trade his CIA building for the

FBI building for anything; maybe when they get a new building? Probably not he thought, since he felt that he had it made where he was now.

After the tour, they then ended up at his friend's work area and talked over what they both knew or surmised. The productive meeting lasted about an hour and ended with Mingo handing a typed up report to TJ on Cutler. Afterwards, his friend treated him to lunch in the cafeteria. He didn't feel that it was as nice as the CIA's cafeteria; *maybe because they were lacking a Chef Tony!*

When TJ was ready to leave the building, he extended an invitation for his friend to visit him sometime at CIA Headquarters and Bob readily agreed. He just wanted to show off to his friend a little is all!

CIA Headquarters

Late that evening, TJ was back at his desk studying the file on Tim Payat. It was late enough that Judy had already left for home a couple of hours earlier. He was planning on working late that night and was starting to get drowsy. He took another sip of his now cold coffee as his eyelids fluttered. He thought that maybe if he could just rest his eyes for a little while, then he would be revitalized and feel refresh again. So he allowed his eyes to close, relaxed his arms in his lap and leaned back in his leather chair and fell asleep and welcomed another deep dream…

"Welcome to The 2 ½ Show and I'm your host, Roscoe Rivers. This is our first show and for our viewers who don't know why we are here, I'll tell you. Fox found out that the ratings were low for The Five and that the salaries were too high. They decided to cancel the show and wanted to replace it with another show but didn't know what to replace it with. Someone suggested to Fox, namely myself, "The 2 ½ Show" with myself as the lead star with no Liberal Democrats hosting and here we are! With The Five cut in half, Fox will now save money on salaries and, with the help

of our viewers, we will take the show to ultimate ratings. At least higher ratings than CNN and that shouldn't be too hard to beat with the help of my co-hosts."

Next to Roscoe sitting in chairs, were a nice looking blonde woman and beside her was a midget.

"Right next to me we have the very beautiful and seductive, Catalina."

She nodded her head to the cameras in acknowledgement.

"And beside her, someone who is always a little short on change, we have Mr. Mann."

"Hey, is that a pun on me Roscoe?" Mr. Mann questioned.

"No it's not little Mann. I came up with that when you said you couldn't afford to buy me a soda earlier today because you were short on change."

"Well, ok then," Mr. Mann responded.

"I think that we should now share our backgrounds for our viewers," Roscoe suggested.

The other two co-hosts nodded in agreement as Roscoe started to explain his background.

"Before this gig, I worked for several years cleaning up around the Fox Studios and offices and I would shine some of our executive's shoes. I made friends in the right places and suggested my idea to one of the executives, I won't mention any names, but you might say that I was a 'shoe in' for this position."

The live studio audience chuckled at this thought of how Fox promoted people in the company.

Camera 2 swung to the right to cover Catalina. When she saw the red light on top flick on, she knew that it was her turn to speak.

"Well, I was working in the Fox's gift store selling to tourists that would tour the Fox Studios, when I was approached and offered a promotion, so I considered and said yes!"

Camera one that was covering Roscoe came on and as if on cue, Roscoe added to what Catalina had just said.

"That someone was me as I needed a co-host to complement my looks."

That brought another bout of laughter from the audience.

Camera two was already fixed on Mr. Mann when the red light came on.

"I'm a dummy," Mr. Mann simply stated. Some in the audience gave an audible gasp and then Mr. Mann continued:

"I have a business with a partner who is a ventriloquist where I sit on his lap and I pretend that he is making me talk, but I do my own speaking. Fox would hire us on special occasions to entertain executives and special guests. The name of our business is Strange Magic because we do magic tricks as well. I met Roscoe in the cafeteria several years ago and we became fast friends and here I am today."

"Alright, thank you Mr. Mann. The purpose of our show is to discuss the demise of certain Liberal Democrats by the Russians. Let's start with Congressman An Gozol. It appears that the Russians took him out."

Catalina broke in with, "We don't really know that he's dead. All that we've heard so far is that his 'American people paid for yacht' was found floating down in the Gulf of Mexico with the lights on and nobody home."

"But there was a Russian clue found on the boat and I believe that it was a cocktail flag of Russia," Mr. Mann stated.

"It's too easy to blame Russia for everything bad that happens in our country," Roscoe enunciated. "Let's move on to Representative Nadia Paloma. She is a very Liberal Democrat and she killed herself. She was found hung in her foyer. I believe that Conservative pressure got to her. In other words, she lost her mind to TDS."

"What's TDS Roscoe," Catalina asked seriously.

"Trump Derangement Syndrome," Mr. Mann added to the conversation. *"However,"* he continued, *"I believe that a Russian lapel was found near her body."*

"That was a Russian Federation lapel pin," Roscoe interjected.

"Ok, I misspoke. Just like when Hilliary Rotten Clinton insisted that she simply misspoke when she claimed she landed in Bosnia under sniper fire 12 years ago...so sue me!" Mr. Mann screeched.

"So what does that prove finding a Russian lapel pin near Paloma?" Roscoe asked. *"We have to stop jumping to conclusions when we are a little short on evidence,"* and looked right at Mr. Mann when he stated that.

"Hey, is that a pun on me?" Mr. Mann questioned.

"Of course not you little bastard, I was just stating a fact. You need to lose this paranoia that you are always harboring my friend."

What the audience didn't know was that this was all part of the show in order to increase television ratings.

"I'm not paranoid, it just seems that way," Mr. Mann defended.

Catalina was just looking from one to the other as this dialogue took place on each side of her, then she would look toward the live studio audience and smile.

"Ok, let's move on to our next deceased political Liberal hack," Roscoe insisted.

"Wait a second," Mr. Mann requested. *"I have something to impart about myself here."*

"Go ahead," Roscoe invited.

"Speaking of Nadia Paloma killing herself..." Mr. Mann started and then was interrupted by Catalina.

"We don't know for sure if she did that on her own."

"Fair enough, but let's just say for the books that she did and made a lot of Conservatives happy to boot. My point being is that I wanted to kill myself at one time," Mr. Mann confessed.

"Is this a true story Mr. Mann?" Roscoe asked.

266

"Very true," Mr. Mann conceded. "I was low and all alone; short on happiness, almost like depression, when I realized that I was emotionally depressed. So I picked up the phone and called the National Suicide Hotline for compassion and guidance. Instead, what I got was someone that answered the phone line and then put me on hold...with elevator music no less! So I decided that carbon monoxide poisoning is the way to go. I went out to my 1969 VW Bug and started it up with the windows down and the garage door closed. It was a smoker; not me, my bug. Anyway, after several minutes and much smoke, I thought that I was a goner. However, my wife opened the door and stepped into the garage. I felt embarrassed that she found me that way and I started to act as if my garage door opener wasn't working. I almost died that day...but look at me now. I'm a pretty big, little man..."

TJ then awoke with a start and realized that from his dream, he knew exactly how Tim Payat would die…

Joint Base Andrews

TJ felt a sense of urgency as he awoke a little late the next day, at his home from working deep into the night at the office. When he awoke, he was feeling a little remorseful that he was sleeping single in a double bed and then quickly remembered that Tim Payat lived nearby in the town of Clinton, Maryland. *No wonder he's a Clinton supporter, he lives in a town named after her!*

He ate a quick breakfast, brushed his teeth and was off to surveil the home of his next target. As he was driving, he deliberated about what he had read previously in the file of Payat. It seems that Payat lived in a home by himself in Clinton, not married (probably no one would have him) and no children (that's good!). Hopefully, this one would be expedient and simple…which was always a plus.

As he arrived, he noticed that the neighborhood was fairly nice and expensive. This scumbag was living high off the hog with a three car garage! TJ cased the home and learned that there was no alarm system which was to his advantage. There was an Audi parked in the garage with a large stuffed bear in the passenger seat. Since the car had a lite tint to the windows, it appeared that Mr. Payat was using the carpool lane illegally…with a bear as a passenger no less! There was also an aluminum fishing boat in the garage. Ok, that only substantiates that this guy is a fishing-loving dirtbag and carpool cheat! He then headed back to the office with the idea that he would return later that evening.

★ ★ ★ ★ ★

That night, TJ sat in his vehicle monitoring the home of Tim Payat. He was there when Payat arrived at his home at around 2000. Two hours after the kitchen light was turned off, he decided to go in for the kill…literally!

CIA Headquarters

TJ typed up his report and sent it out by email to his boss. He then went back to studying the details on the death of Republican Senator Bow Cutler that Special Agent Mingo had given him as well as studying the pictures from the Senator Melvin case. He was deep in thought when his boss entered and seated himself.

"Another great job TJ," Randy stated matter-of-factly. "Excellent work as always and I can tell you honestly that the President understands what an asset you are to the country."

"Thanks boss, I really appreciate it. I do my best and take my job to heart."

"I know you do," Randy agreed.

"Did you have any questions about the report?" TJ invited.

"I just wanted to clear up a couple of your statements. Not that they aren't clear mind you, but I just wanted to chat a bit with you as well."

"Shoot."

"So, when you found Mr. Payat, you wrote that he was as drunk as a *hillbilly*."

"That is so true. He was stumbling around his home in his underwear singing, 'take me to the river.' They make it so easy for me when they are soused."

"Understandingly so," Randy agreed. "Reports show, unfortunately, that most members of Congress are true alcoholics."

"From what I see in their homes, with all of the alcohol around, that is not a big stretch of the imagination."

"Then you found a large stuffed bear in the passenger seat of Payat's Audi. You think that was to skirt our carpool laws?"

"Yes. Figure the facts. He was a Liberal Democrat and as we know, Liberal Democrats don't like to obey laws; his windows were tinted and he had a large stuffed animal riding around with him. In fact, the bear was even wearing dog tags mind you. You do the math," TJ invited.

"What did the dog tags say?"

"It was, 'B T Jones;' a 'Social Security Number;' blood type as 'A Positive;' 'Liberal Democrat,' and the last line read, 'Congress.' I'm telling you boss, this guy was a total dirtbag and loser and it felt good taking him out."

"It definitely sounds like he was a sick puppy," Randy admitted. "Why do you think that the dog tags had 'Congress' on them?"

"I personally think that's so he can tell people that he rides around with members of Congress on a daily basis; who knows for sure, other than God I mean? Anyway, just from seeing his home, I can tell you that he had the intelligence of your average tree toad. In fact, I feel that way for most of Congress. However, it's just that most of the Republicans are in a higher class is all."

"You are so right my friend," Mr. Morgan conceded.

Randy took a deep breath before informing TJ of his next mission. TJ felt his boss was having a hard time with this and decided to step in and make it easier for Randy.

"I took Lidio's file back since we kept putting him on hold," TJ informed his boss.

"He's the least of our problems right now. The next one that we want you to take out is Senator Maro Wesley. He is causing the latest uproar for the President."

"Well, it does appear that Senate seats are becoming readily available…all of a sudden."

"Yeah well, the President is hoping that more quality Republicans will fill these new available seats which will aid greatly to his MAGA agenda."

"What's MAGA?" TJ asked seriously.

"Make America Great Again," Randy stated incredulously as he truly thought that TJ would recognize the acronym since he was a big fan of the President. *Maybe I'm working him to hard!* In any case, he didn't have much of a choice as it was fundamentally necessary for the health and safety of the country that TJ continue with his death missions.

"Ooops, I should have known that one," TJ acknowledged.

"You are correct. However, you must be tired from the increased work load so I'll let it slide this time and not fault you too much on that one."

"Thanks."

"Sorry for all of the extra work, but the President…I mean we, feel that it's a necessary evil to clean house in America's government."

"No problem. I love my country and if I can help even in a small way, then I'm all for it."

"Don't sell yourself short…you're helping in a big way." Then Randy looked down upon the pictures that were spread out on TJ's desk and reached out and picked them up and asked, "Anything figured out with these pictures yet?" Randy questioned while shuffling through the stack.

TJ told him what he knew so far and Randy responded with, "These pictures remind me of the phonetic alphabet." Then his boss turned and left him standing there with his mouth agape.

Chapter 16
Ω

"Liberalism, if left unchecked will destroy our country and our way of life."

---Lou Travis

A former Trump personal lawyer and U.S. attorney announced that the President will not agree to be interviewed by special counsel Robert Mueller in his Russia collusion probe because it has devolved into a "bad faith" investigation.

House Intelligence Committee Chairman Devin Nunes announced that he will hold Attorney General Jeff Sessions in contempt of Congress for not complying with a subpoena that was issued two weeks earlier requesting documents relating to the FBI's abuse of the Foreign Intelligence Surveillance Act (FISA) in their scrutiny of the Trump campaign. Fox News reported that it is apparent that Sessions is "stonewalling" and it is unclear as to why. Does the Department of Justice or the Mueller team have something on Attorney General Sessions and is using that to hold over his head and is keeping Sessions from doing his job in an ethical, honest and complete manner?

Former mayor Rudy Giuliani calls on Sessions to end the Mueller probe since there are so many unethical, dishonest and conflicts of interest concerns. One of which is that every member of Mueller's team was a Hilliary supporter...no Republicans can be found anywhere on his team.

Trump pulls the United States out of the Iran nuclear deal much to the dismay of the U.S. allies.

TJ was trying to concentrate on the pictures that were on his desk while receiving his latest Fox News fix. His boss was correct in that there seemed to be a phonetic connection. As he looked at each picture in turn, he wrote down a corresponding letter to each phonetic name. There was Indio, times two; Bravo; Golf; Echo; November and Juliet.

I • I • B • G • E • N • J

He believed that he was on to something here as he tried to think of what possible words these letters could spell and possibly having a story to tell. He decided that it would have to wait as he needed to get the file on Senator Wesley.

He headed down to visit his friend Jessy in the file vault to get another file that would be immensely helpful for his next mission. Before going into the file vault area, he bumped into Ching Ching who was coming out.

"Oh hi TJ, I bump into you by accident."

"No, it was my fault Ching Ching and I'm sorry."

"Don't worry about it lover, I don't mind anyway."

Did she call me lover? He continued on his way. Jessy was busy with typing and wore a serious look upon her face. He almost hated to bother her…almost, because his mission was important. His country and the President were counting on him. No matter how busy Jesse was, she always greeted him professionally.

"Hi TJ, what brought you down here today?" Jessy questioned and then held up her hand to him. "Let me guess…you need another file?"

"You know me so well. I guess you could say that we are simpatico," he stated as he took a seat.

"Well, I would say that is so true. I feel like I really know you by now and I can tell that you're a good man that is assigned some difficult cases."

He knew that she knew what he did and only wanted to hint about it. *Who else knew or suspected what his true mission in the CIA was?*

"In fact, I might even accept you as a brother." Jessy added playfully.

"You mean a big brother?" TJ asked.

Jessy picked up a small foam football from her desk and threw it at him, because, she knew that he was referring to a "big brother" meaning that she may need a caring adult role model in her life.

When TJ realized that she was going to throw the small football at him, he raised his arms quickly to protect himself while laughing at her antics.

"Thanks and I know that the CIA got a good deal when they hired you," he stated and meant it. He bent down and retrieved the football and felt safe enough that he laid it back on her desk; he didn't think that she would throw it at him again.

"Who do we need today?" Jessy asked professionally.

"I need the file on Senator Wesley. In fact, if you could get that for me, I'll go use the bathroom and then come back."

"Of course, no problem," Jessy stated and then added with a mischievous smile on her face, "don't forget to wash your hands when you're done."

TJ assured her that he always washed his hands after, "bathroom activities."

He left the file vault area and walked down the hall to the restroom. As he confronted the stand-up urinal, he had a lot on his mind. One item that he was chewing on was an article that he read in a paper earlier that Trump was told *not* to attend the funeral of Senator Melvin and that the senator's family is requesting that former presidents Bush and Obama deliver the eulogies. *Well, good riddance,* he thought, *as he was a piece of shit anyway and a true Liberal Democrat in Republican's clothing.* He was sure that President Trump would not even bat an eye at that request. *Maybe the Russians really did take him out,* TJ considered briefly, but seriously doubted. The narrative just didn't fit the crime, even though a Russian coin was discovered at the crime scene. He felt in his heart that the Russians were being framed by someone or some country.

After finishing, he zipped up his cargo pants and walked over to one of the five sinks and gave his hands a good scrubbing.

As he stepped out into the hallway, he once again bumped into Ching Ching. This time she slipped her arms around him and it felt good to have her hold him close.

"We meet again TJ."

"Sorry Ching Ching, I have stuff on my mind and wasn't paying attention I guess."

"No need to apologize tough guy. You never hear me complain. Don't forget to call me sometime…soon." She let him go and walked on to the file vault and to her own cubical. He waited until she was out of sight and thought that that was one woman he wouldn't mind as having as a lover…maybe.

He then continued on and retrieved the file that Jessy had waiting for him and trekked back to his office.

After studying the file for some time, one thing that caught his attention was that the senator was on the Select Committee on Intelligence. *I wonder what the committee is up to these days.* He decided to make a phone call to the senator's office to gather some "intelligence" of his own.

"Senator Wesley's office, can I help you?" the voice asked.

"Who am I speaking with please?"

"I'm an intern."

"That's nice. Do you have a name other than intern?"

"I am not allowed to give out that information due to security reasons. Who are you may I ask?"

TJ had to think quickly and noticed the Scotch tape dispenser on his desk and confidently stated, "I'm Commander Scotch," with a grin on his face.

"Yes commander, I think that I have heard your name mentioned from the senator and that you are a friend of his. If you are calling for him sir, I have to inform you that he is currently out of the office and is in Congressional session right now."

"That's ok. I'm planning a fishing trip for us and I need to know his schedule, oh let's say, for the next three or four days."

"I can help you with that then since you both are friends. Otherwise, I wouldn't be able to give that information out."

"I appreciate that intern."

"Sorry commander…my name is Seth. Let's see here. Tomorrow he is leaving for Nevada and won't be back till…"

TJ interrupted the intern.

"What's in Nevada?"

"Oh, he's going to speak with a Captain Kirkland on recent UFO sightings at Groom Lake. Do you know Captain Kirkland sir?"

"Yes I do," TJ lied. "When does he come back from there?"

"He's only there for two days sir."

"Would you happen to know where he is staying the one night that he's there?"

"Of course; let's see…here it is. He'll be staying at the Extraterrestrial Hotel in Rachel."

"Alright then, do me a favor Seth."

"Yes sir…if I can."

"Don't tell my friend that I'm planning a fishing trip for us as I want it to be a surprise."

"You got it sir!"

TJ hung up and was amazed at how easy that was. These young interns are so stupid. "Don't we have any real education in this country anymore?" he wondered out loud.

TJ utilized his computer and found out that another name for Groom Lake was Area 51. It was a highly secretive Air Force base located 83 miles north-northwest of Las Vegas, Nevada. The CIA referred to the base as Homey Airport or Groom Lake. It was known to everyone else as Area 51 where many regarded it as an UFO hotspot.

He called the passenger terminal at Joint Base Andrews and learned that there was a C-40 flight leaving for Nellis Air Force Base that night. He added his name to the flight list and also discovered that Senator Wesley was scheduled on that flight as well.

Nellis was located in Las Vegas and was the closest base to the area…other than Homey Airport itself. It would have been an extremely difficult task to fly into that highly classified Air Force Base as he was sure that there were no flights going there anyway.

Now that that was taken care of, he turned his attention back to the pictures and the letters that they represented. After shuffling the letters around, he could only logically come to one conclusion…Beijing!

★ ★ ★ ★ ★

He caught his flight to Nellis Air Force Base and according to the picture that he had of the senator, he made the flight as well. It really didn't matter if he kept an eye on Senator Wesley or not. He knew his destination and had an idea of what to do. He would wait until the senator had his meeting on the Air Force Base and as he was returning, he would strike. More importantly though…he just hoped that the Extraterrestrial Hotel had a hot tub!

At the Nellis passenger terminal, he was able to rent a Tacoma pickup and headed for Rachel, Nevada and his hotel. He imagined that the senator would be doing the same thing.

He arrived at the hotel ahead of the senator and checked in. Good news…they had a hot tub! They even had a dining area that offered a free breakfast between the hours of 0600 and 0900, just like Holiday Inn Express. He would make sure that he was up early enough so he could surveil the senator while he ate breakfast.

As he walked down the hallway of the first floor where his room was located, he took notice of several pictures depicting UFO's and aliens; some were green, some had big heads and one even had antennas on his head! *Who would want to meet up with any of these creatures?* He continued on to his room…115.

He decided that he would rest first and then on his way to the hot tub later, he would stop by the front desk to make a wakeup call for 0500.

He dozed off and never made it to the hot tub and instead drifted off to another adventure in another dream…

He found himself on the Extraterrestrial Highway that went out to Area 51. He was outside the boundary that marked the base by virtue of the signs warning that unauthorized entry any further would be met with deadly force. He waited patiently near his rented truck for the senator to drive up. At last, he saw a car coming towards him and took out his 9mm handgun and was prepared to welcome the senator to Hell.

As the car was approaching, he stepped out from behind a tree (one of the few around) and flagged down the car. The senator stopped thinking that he wanted a ride into town due to engine problems; however, TJ had other plans.

"Do you need a ride?" the senator asked.

TJ pointed his gun at point blank range and answered in the negative.

"What do you want then? I have a few bucks that I can offer to you so that you can get you truck fixed," the senator offered.

"I don't need or want your money you piece of shit. Get out of the car," TJ ordered.

Hesitantly, the senator stepped out of his car and waited for the next command which he knew would come. TJ motioned with his gun for the senator to begin walking towards his truck. Once the senator was next to the truck, he had him lay belly down with his hands behind his back and TJ, using duct tape, bound the senator's arms. As he was helping the senator up, he heard him muttered something.

"What was that senator?"

"I said that's why I'm against handguns."

"You think that by taking people's guns away from them that that will stop crime in this country and that DC dirt bags like you would be safer? Wrong. I have nothing but contempt for you fucking loser Liberals. Now get into the truck."

The senator climbed in and made himself as comfortable as possible under the circumstances. TJ then buckled the senator in...for his safety.

"Where are you taking me?" the senator asked.

"I am sending you to meet your Maker Senator Wesley. Then He will most likely send you to Hell." TJ then secured a piece of duct tape over the senator's mouth so he wouldn't have to hear him speak anymore, but the senator looked at him with pleading eyes. It didn't affect TJ though as he had a job to do. Then as an additional touch, he added a metal band to the senator's head that had two spring antennas which had a miniature glow-in-the-dark alien head on each spring which bobbed around as he moved his head. "There you go senator, now you are ready to disappear with the other aliens that will be leaving soon for their own planet. I hope that you're ready for the ride of your life!"

TJ then parked the senator's car off the side of the road and got back into his truck and drove south towards Las Vegas...

The next morning, TJ just happened to wake up at 0505 and got ready for the day's events. With the dream, he now had a better idea of what to do with the senator. *Is God helping me?*

After his shower, he moved down to the dining area for his included breakfast and filled two plates with food and sat down to eat. Sure enough, after a short time, the senator entered and he knew that the senator wouldn't be able to turn down a free breakfast.

After the senator finished eating, he walked out to the parking lot and entered his car which looked to be a 2017 Volvo…TJ figured. *Damn,* he thought, *I don't get to brush my teeth this morning!* Oh well, his country came first and he followed the car at a safe distance so as not to be spotted.

The senator drove down the Extraterrestrial Highway towards Area 51. Just before arriving at where the warning signs were posted, TJ turned off at what looked to be a small rest area. He noticed that no other cars were on the road and allowed the senator to continue on without him. He decided that he would wait there until the senator returned. While waiting at the small rest area, he viewed himself in his rearview mirror and thought, *just look at me now.* Here he was in the middle of the Nevada desert waiting for a senator that he was required to kill, who was classified as a clear and present danger to the country by the CIA. He could never have dreamed that this would be his life in a million years…*what a country!*

It was almost dark when he observed the senator's car heading his way. Just like in his dream, he flagged down the senator, and just like in his dream, the senator stopped. TJ followed his dream to the letter, including, putting antennas that he bought in the hotel's gift shop on the senator's head and drove off away from the base and the prying eyes of the federal government. From a rise, he stopped and looked back in his rear view mirror and noticed what looked to be runway lights that were as bright as the crack of dawn and then drove on.

The Extraterrestrial Hotel

TJ had dinner in the dining room and then went up to brush his teeth, changed into his swimming trunks, slipped on his flip-flops, grabbed his latest book and a towel and headed for the hot tub to read and relax. His flight for the next day didn't leave until late evening, so he had some time now to unwind. After an hour of reading his book in the hot tub, he returned to his room.

★ ★ ★ ★ ★

The next day found TJ eating his breakfast and then a return to the hot tub and back to his room to watch Fox News until his check out time at 1200; he wasn't in a hurry…not until his boss called him.

"How are things out your way TJ?"

"The eagle has landed."

This statement conveyed a message to Randy that he had accomplished his assigned mission successfully.

"That's good. But, I have a couple of news worthy items for you." Randy then paused for a few seconds before continuing. TJ knew that it had to be serious for his boss to call him during a mission. "Senator Flann was found deceased in his home and he was holding onto a Russian coin…his throat was slashed."

"Sounds like someone is copying my duty except with Republicans," TJ offered.

"That's my thought as well. Did you come across any ideas from them photos that you were working on?"

"I'm afraid we have an internal problem. I'm confident that those pictures spell out one word…Beijing."

"How is that an internal problem?" Randy asked.

"There's an analyst that sits next to Jessy named Ching Ching who is consequently from Beijing. I'm afraid that she must have figured out what my work is and probably has an operative, maybe Chinese, doing the dirty work for her. You might want to assign someone to her and see what you can figure out."

"What a shame…one of our own. Well, this is what happens when you hire a nationality whose country is basically our enemy; I'll put Intelligence Agent Lonzo on it. I believe you are friends with Conrad, is that correct?"

Before TJ had a chance to answer, Randy continued on. "If I remember right, you met him at Camp Mayberry and became fast friends?"

"That's right. Conrad's a good man and he is the right agent for this job. Let him know that I suggested to you about her being a possible traitor to the CIA. I'm not a hundred percent sure boss, but I have a sick feeling in my gut about her, even though she is very beautiful and captivating."

"Knowing you, you probably fell in love with her."

"Once again, you may be correct. I seriously thought about starting a relationship with her. In fact, she kept asking me to take her to a movie, but due to my workload, I wasn't able to take her up on her offer."

"That's how it starts TJ, always with a movie; then buttered popcorn; then a kiss; then sex; then…"

"Ok, I got it boss," TJ interrupted Randy.

"Sorry, I'm a hopeless romantic sometimes. Are you ok with all of this? Especially if we find out that it's all true and she would have to be arrested?" Randy asked compassionately.

"Yeah, I'm ok. I'm just glad that I didn't take her up on her offer. Let's change the subject though. What was the other item that you had for me?"

"We have your next mission which is in California. So we need you to complete it before returning."

"Who's the lucky Liberal?" TJ questioned with a raised eyebrow.

"None other than Governor Jason Brent," Randy stated.

"Old Sunstruck, huh?" TJ called him by his nickname that was given to him by an out-of-town reporter back in 1979 who thought that Jason was a little touched in the head from too much sun and commented about it on the news. "I wondered if we would get to him eventually. I heard about the issues that he is causing for President Trump, California citizens and the country in general."

"That's right, so we now have permission to send old Sunstruck to Hell."

"Well, since that is where he belongs then we'll just have to accommodate him. But I don't have his file."

"That's ok. Did you take your laptop with you?"

"I did," TJ answered knowing where his boss was going with this line of thought.

"I had Jessy put the file on our secured server for your review. You remember how to access it?"

"I do. Ok, at the hotel that I'll stay at tonight I'll do my homework. I'll see if I can get a flight to Naval Air Station North Island."

"If I remember right, that's where you were based out of when you were in the Navy, right?"

"We have a winner," TJ announced having fun with his boss again with no disrespect intended. Randy wasn't offended at all.

"Why there? Why not go to Travis?"

"Because, I'm going to let Sunstruck come to me in San Diego."

"And what makes you think that he will come to you there?"

"It was on Fox News just a little while ago, that tomorrow he would be checking out the National Guard that he sent down to the border and would be giving a, 'Freedom for All' speech."

"Good job paying attention to things like that," his boss complimented and then added, "be careful."

"Thanks boss, and don't worry too much, I'll take care of things as always," TJ assured Randy.

"I know you will. You have my full confidence and blessing."

TJ then decided to head back to Nellis and return his car to the rental office which was located right next to the passenger terminal.

Nellis Air Force Base

At the passenger terminal, TJ lucked out with a C-9 flight to NASNI. However, he had to bump out a Space Available flyer since he had priority. It was a Navy veteran that he bumped who was assured by the passenger terminal that he would be able to fly to his destination on the next day. He waited for a short time for his flight and then boarded.

When his feet hit the ground at North Island, they took him to the car rental office where he rented a compact 2018 Jeep Renegade. He drove along the pier to view which aircraft carriers were in. It looked to be only the USS Ronald Reagan (CVN-76). He remembered when his father was stationed on the ship as well as when he was assigned to the USS Constellation (CV-64). President Reagan declared it America's Flagship and now it was down in Brownsville, Texas waiting to be scraped into razor blades. Too bad they couldn't have kept it for a museum like the USS Midway (CV-41).

He then headed for the Navy Lodge and was able to secure a room. After checking in, he headed straight to his room as he wanted to prepare for old Sunstruck. However, that was not to be. Upon arriving at his room on the first floor, his phone rang and it was his friend Conrad so he answered the call.

"Hey Conrad, what's happening?" he asked as he open the door to his room and entered and sat his bag down on the bed.

"I was assigned to a case that you have some knowledge of," Conrad simply stated.

"My boss told me that Senator Flann was toasted. That's all that I know."

"Well my boss told me to keep you informed of any possible information about the case that I may turn up. Any thoughts?" Conrad asked.

"I told my boss that there is a Chinese girl there at our building that I'm highly suspicious of now. She is very beautiful and her name is Ching Ching; she's an analyst."

"What makes you suspect her?"

So TJ explained to his friend about working with their other friend on the death of Senator Melvin and about the pictures. He went on to tell Conrad how he believes that the pictures are a clue and how they just happen to spell *Beijing*; the same place where Ching Ching just happens to be from. Also her cubicle is right next to Jessy's.

"Why would someone leave a clue like that behind?" Conrad questioned.

"Possibly they just want to mess with us or maybe just me. I don't know if she is a party to these killings, I'm just conveying to you my suspicions; maybe a gut feeling too."

"Ok, I'll check her out; anything else that I should know about?"

"Just be careful buddy."

"Don't worry, I will. By the way, where are you?"

"They have me on a case in San Diego, so right now I'm at NAS North Island."

"Been there myself a time or two; ok, get back to work and I'll let you go."

When he checked in earlier at the lodging office, he had picked up from the counter, the free San Diego Union-Tribune with the headline that read: "Governor Brent Visiting Border Tomorrow." The article went on to say that there would be a press conference and speech for the National Guard at 1500; three miles East of San Ysidro, next to a section of a new border wall that President Trump was able to kick start with a limited amount of funds that was allocated from Congress.

Looking through some material left in his room on information regarding nearby eating establishments, much to his surprise, was a Golden Corral in El Cajon which was only 20 miles from the base.

While he was on I-8 heading for his favorite restaurant, he noticed a caravan of psychedelic buses ahead of him and switched lanes to pass. As he approached the first colorful bus and glanced up, he noticed six freaks riding on a platform that was attached to the roof. He then glanced at the occupants inside briefly and noticed peculiar behavior happening. He saw several freaks dancing to music; some had orange and purple hair; some long, some short; some had earrings and one even had a nose ring. There were some doing drugs, including the driver who was clearly smoking and enjoying a cannabis cigar who waved at TJ with it as he passed by. He could see that the inside of the bus was pretty smoky; the other two buses that he passed were much the same as the first and all had an added platform attached to the back of the bus with several freaks waving and distracting drivers; an accident waiting to happen.

He was reminded of something his uncle used to say to him when he was younger and when his uncle would encounter freaks: "Teddy, don't ever get that way. Our big problem here in California is that we have too many freaks and not enough circuses." TJ then remembered that Barnum and Bailey circus closed down last year after 146 years of entertaining the masses. *Maybe these freaks were out of work from Barnum and Bailey,* he considered seriously. The Democrats did not seem to be doing any favors for California or the rest of the country with their Liberal views. He remembered seeing Senator Karmen Helena of California on the news suggesting that by smoking more weed would improve the quality of life in the state! He thought that she was doing a little too much of that herself! But the California people duly elected her to her U.S. Senate seat. Her underlying concern stems from the possible new tax revenue that would be generated through drug sales. *Yeah, that's all we need is more pot smoking freaks and losers!*

He had a nice dinner that evening and returned to the base for a good night's sleep. The next morning was bright and sunny; the birds were chirping outside of his window and he felt that today would be a good day. After eating breakfast at the officer's club, which he was allowed to eat at due to his status as a CIA Intelligence Officer, he then headed for the commissary. He needed to find something that he could use as a Russian clue once he took out the California governor; he still didn't have an idea on how to do that yet. He would have to think of something on-the-fly though.

At the commissary he found some Russian chips called *Russkart*. The bag came with a warning: "To be opened only if you are prepared to finish the bag." Since he only needed the bag, he would have to sample them.

He then decided to head on down to the border and reconnoiter the area.

He arrived at the border area where the Governor's speech would take place. Looking around, he noticed approximately a dozen porta potties; a raised platform with a podium and several chairs; a backdrop of a blue curtain; several microphones from the press on a stand. There were a couple of roach coaches present as well as a couple of lunch trucks. Since pot was now legal in California, there were several people in line to buy pot joints from the roach coaches and only three visiting the lunch wagons. TJ supposed that these people were State of California employees apparently assigned to set up the area. Several workers were working on a new border wall and there even were what looked like some homeless Mexicans---*probably illegals*. Noticeably, were the dozens of National Guard personnel patrolling the border area.

TJ walked over to a lunch truck and purchased a hot dog and added some ketchup and sat down near a tree to wait while eating his American hot dog and his tasty Russian chips.

Several hours later, more people arrived. It was almost time for the governor and he still didn't have an idea of how to accomplish his mission. If necessary, he was prepared to follow the governor to Hell and back to accomplish his mission. Then, he spied a motorcade coming down the border dirt road. The motorcade was led by CHiPs---California Highway Patrol. This was going to be tough with the: CHiPs, the National Guard and the media! He had to be sure that when the time came to strike, that he could escape unnoticed.

The stage was all set as Governor Brent climbed the steps of the stage followed by several others who sat in the provided chairs. He noticed that the governor did not look to be his correct age which was 81; however, 81 was still just...81.

As Governor Brent arrived on stage, he shook several pairs of hands before approaching the podium. The lt. governor was on stage as well behind Governor Brent. TJ noticed that the National Guard was called over to attend. Now there was no one watching for illegals crossing the border. Oh well, maybe the *anticipating* illegals won't notice. The border wall construction workers and some illegal Mexicans---TJ was sure---streamed over to hear the governor's speech.

"Welcome everyone. I'll get right to the point. It is unprecedented for the federal government to come into our state and force a border wall upon us when it is the belief of my administration that open borders for our Mexican *amigos* is good for everyone versus a border wall that isolates our Mexican friends. It is not the American way to block immigrants from coming to our country. President Trump is a racist and we will continue to fight his administration every step of the way. I would much rather die on the shitter than allow Trump to win this fight and as long as I breathe, I will not give up!"

The governor took a pause and had a drink of water from a plastic water bottle before continuing.

"This is directed to our California National Guard. We will *not* assist President Trump in his efforts to seal the border. But since the feds are paying the tab, this will be good training session in any case. You will not stop or detain any illegals…I mean undocumented travelers of any race, if the federal border patrol wants to deal with them, then they will not have the assistance of the California National Guard. I hope that I'm making myself clear."

TJ just happened to notice several illegals crossing the border with some holding hands while running. *What a piece of work this governor is,* he thought.

Governor Brent finished his speech after another 15 minutes and then leaned over and whispered something to his lt. governor and then headed for the group of porta potties. He selected one and then entered. While the governor was taking care of some on-the-border paperwork, others were meeting with the press and hand shaking was happening all around. However, TJ kept an eye on the portable crapper that the governor was using.

After about 30 minutes without seeing the governor's return, he started thinking that Governor Brent must have a lack of fiber in his diet and obviously needed a little more time than most others when doing his business. But his staff seemed to be worried and one of them walked over and knocked on the outhouse. With no answer forthcoming, the staffer walked over to the lt. governor and said something to him. The next thing that he knew was that the lt. governor had summoned one of the construction workers over and with a pry bar and commenced to opening the plastic door. When the door swung open, TJ notice Governor Brent with his pants down around his ankles and he was slumped over in the apparent deceased mode.

The paramedics and the coroner were called for and Governor Brent was pronounced dead at the scene due to a heart attack. The lt. governor---who was now the governor---

decided to take advantage of the situation and gave his own press conference and speech which basically contained the exact same message that Governor Brent had communicated. Since he was no longer needed, TJ left the area and headed back to the base.

Back at North Island, he called Randy to tell him what happened to the governor and that God did his job for him this time. His boss was satisfied with the results, no matter how it was accomplished. He then conveyed to his favorite intelligence officer, his next mission…he would be staying in California a little longer than he wanted.

Chapter 17
Ω

"But you have a group of investigators, they're all Democrats. In some cases, they went to the Hillary Clinton celebration that turned out to be a funeral."

---President Donald Trump

Three American hostages are returned to the United States from North Korea, prior to President Trump meeting with the dictator in Singapore which will take place in June. The President met the hostages personally at 0300 at Joint Base Andrews and welcomed them back home.

The American Embassy finally opened in Jerusalem amidst much controversy as the United States finally put past words into action.

To celebrate the 25th Anniversary of the popular computer game Myst, Cyan is offering a complete series of all 7 games together for the first time that will run on Windows 10!

TJ discovered that his next mission involved taking out Representative Maybel Wileen. He was silently hoping for a shot at her as she was a clear mental case; all the time chanting, "Impeach 45, Impeach 45, Impeach 45." He was so sick and tired of hearing her Liberal chants that he wouldn't mind taking her out for free! But he knew that his boss and the CIA in general wouldn't go for that, so he'll do his job with pleasure and get paid for it. Some (mostly on the Left) might think that he was an evil person for wanting to kill someone, even if they are evil. That is not how it works in real life. Though, this was what the mainstream, typical

American wanted: good winning over evil. This sector of the population understood that it comes down to good versus evil and that evil don't play fair and that means in order to win, good couldn't afford to play by different rules...or it will lose every time. The majority of Americans wanted to see, good winning over evil, every...single...time, no matter the process to success. Just like what happens in a good, Western book: the "good guy" would always wrap up the story as the winner.

This is the trouble with the Republican Party. They just can't learn to stick together for the bigger win that will take place in the long run. And then there are those Republicans that are really Democrats in ideology. They run as a Republican to get elected and then work against the good of the party and support the Democrat's sick agenda, such as the late Senator Jace Melvin, Senator Bow Cutler and Senator Jory Flann. It seemed to TJ that the Senate harbors the worst of Congress.

He felt that all of this death was a necessary evil to combat evil; like fighting fire with fire. The corruption surrounding the Liberal Democrats like Paloma, Simpson, Payat and many others, calls for nothing less than their complete elimination from the country; the only real solution available to the American people. The degree of corruption that was being uncovered by the Inspector General, Michael Horowitz, investigating the Obama Administration corruption, seems to be on steroids compared to Watergate according to Sean Hannity. Horowitz seems to be a captain sailing through a sea of crap and corruption. From all accounts though, he was diligently investigating all of this corruption fairly and honestly. In essence, TJ was assisting his government along with Horowitz---and some others---taking care of those that needed...taking care of, either by death or imprisonment and they would get their comeuppance!

He studied the CIA files on Representative Wileen. His boss had told him that she was going to Los Angeles to give an anti-Trump speech tomorrow at UCLA. The speech was to take place at 1000. He learned that she had a $4 million dollar home in the Brentwood area and that her former husband died from a gunshot wound---no surprise there; too bad she wasn't shot as well! She hired a cleaning woman who was an illegal alien that would come by once a week to clean and who would let herself in with her own key. The home was located in the same area where O.J. Simpson used to live. *Must be something special in the neighborhood to attract utter crap to that area,* TJ thought. He had been in that neighborhood before and knew that the houses were not located close to each other; that was good to know. He would have to plan for his mission to take place at her home. It worked for O.J. so he shouldn't have a problem as well. He still had his Russian clue to leave behind and he had a desire to use it!

He phoned for a room at the Holiday Inn Express in Brentwood.

"Holiday Inn Express Brentwood, my name is Layla…how may I help you?"

"Hi Layla, I need to make a reservation for tonight."

"Sure, are coming to the area for business or pleasure?"

"Both."

"Great. Are you a Rewards Club member?"

"Yes I am."

"Would you have your Rewards Club number handy?"

TJ dug out his wallet and located his IHG Rewards Club card.

"Here it is. It's 8675309 Layla."

Layla punched up the number on her computer and came up with his name and discovered that he was a Gold Elite member.

"Yes, I have you right here and see that you are a Gold Elite member. I also see that you are a veteran and I want to say thank you for your service Mr. Law."

"No problem," TJ answered. He felt a little embarrassed when people would thank him. He was just doing a job…for his country and didn't require a thank you. But it was still nice to hear once in a while.

"Let's see what I have available. I have a two-room suite or the presidential suite available."

"What's the price difference?"

"The two-room suite tonight goes for $158.00 dollars and the presidential suite is $8,584.00 dollars for tonight."

"I think I better take the two-room suite Layla."

"The Presidential Suite also includes a catered dinner from Lawry's for two."

"You mean Lawry's like the seasoning salt company?" TJ asked inquiringly.

"That's correct Mr. Law."

"I still better take the two-room suite Layla."

He decided not to check out of his room on base just yet because he will probably still need it for the next night and left for Los Angeles.

★ ★ ★ ★ ★

After a three hour drive, he arrived at his hotel and checked in and then left to surveil the home of Representative Wileen. When he returned to his room, he was just in time for Hannity on Fox.

"Alright, thanks Tucker, we have breaking news all over the place tonight starting with the disappearance of Senator Wesley who left on a fact finding mission to Area 51 concerning UFO sightings. He met with the base commander and was never seen again. Our Fox News affiliate in Rachel, Nevada is standing by live out at Area 51."

"Thanks Sean. I'm Roberto Sanchez Jones and right now I'm out on the Extraterrestrial Highway leading to the Air Force Base. As you can see behind me, the senator's rental car from Nellis Air Force Base is being loaded onto a military tow truck from the base where I'm told that a Naval Criminal Investigative Service unit that is stationed at Nellis will be pouring over the vehicle for clues. This is not the first time that this unit has investigated disappearances. Through the years, many have disappeared from this area and one thought is that aliens are to blame. The car was found deserted by renowned Bigfoot hunter, Bill Cassidy. Bill told me earlier that he was on the trail of a baby Bigfoot when he came across the vehicle."

"Are you talking about illegal aliens Roberto?"

"No Sean, not this time; it is believed by many that *galaxical* aliens from another universe are capturing people that are unfortunate to be in this area and are taken back to their own planet for in-depth research. In fact, it is believed that Area 51 is an actual landing zone for alien spacecraft, but the U. S. Government refuses to confirm or deny that theory, which in turns creates more belief to the truthfulness that it is an alien landing zone; back to you Sean."

"Thank you Roberto and keep us posted if anything else turns up."

"You got it Sean."

"We now have a Fox News Alert. California Governor Jason "Sunstruck" Brent was reported to have died at the border today while using a porta potty. I'm told that he had just finished addressing the media and the California National Guard deployed by President Trump and entered into one of a dozen portable toilets and was found dead an half hour later of a heart attack. All of us here at Fox will miss him and our condolences to his family," Sean offered facetiously.

★ ★ ★ ★ ★

The next day, TJ ate breakfast early in the hotel's dining room and left for Representative Wileen's home. He wanted to visibly watch her leave. He did arrive on time and witnessed the Congresswoman leaving in her newer black Mercedes. As she backed out of her driveway and started forward, he noticed the vinyl lettering in her back window that read 'Impeach 45!' *Wow, she really does have a one track mind!* He entered her home discreetly and went directly to her living room and turned on the television. As her speech was going to be carried live on the news, he wanted to watch it. Not so much for her anti-Trump ranting, but for an idea of when she would be returning home.

UCLA Lecture Hall

"Impeach 45...impeach 45...impeach 45," Representative Wileen was leading the chanting of the students in the Lecture Hall and was encouraging them to join her.

Once the chanting calmed down, she noticed that she had a protestor waving a large Trump-Pence sign and signaled security to remove that person promptly, which they did. *There just has to be one in every crowd*, she decided.

"I want your vote young people. You are the destiny of this great state and I want to be there with you," she spoke into the microphones while the news stations filmed her live. Viewers could see their television station names on their respective microphones as all the big names were present; CNN, Fox and MSNBC.

"I will tell you this. With your vote to keep me in power...I mean in office, I will keep working for you, the people of California to impeach Trump. In fact, I would rather be hung upside down than to work for that animal any longer. He only won because the Russians helped him...and we all know it!" she yelled out this last part.

At this point, Representative Wileen waved to the cameras and smiled from ear to ear before continuing.

"Trump is a bully but he can't bully me or you...right?" A cheer went up from the attendees.

"But I need your help. If you see anybody Trump official in a restaurant, in a department store, at a gas station, you get out and you create a crowd, and you push back on them, and you tell them they're not welcome here. I want you to harass as many Trump officials as you can and do whatever it takes in harassing them so that they will get the message…loud and clear. Then these Trump officials will resign and dump Trump like a bad habit. We won't be silent until a Democrat is back in office."

She paused briefly and allowed the cheers to consume others that may not be cheering…yet.

She then resumed speaking with: "I call him Don Juan the Con since he's a conman. Just like that trashy tax bill that he was able to pass and some Americans received a tax break that were just crumbs. If I have my way, we will tear up that bill and raise taxes in order to pay for the programs that you, the American people, need and want and deserve." Not much of a cheer went up that time.

Representative Wileen continued: "He says I have a low IQ and that I'm a mental case. Well, I'll tell you this, he's a name caller and I wake up every morning expecting to hear him calling me a name, just like when he called Senator Simpson, the head clown, or when he called Senator Willow, Pocahontas. Now he wants to call me a low IQ person and a mental case? Well, I have a high IQ you can be assured of that since I graduated right here at UCLA and that dumbass shouldn't be calling good people names. However, I am not intimidated by his name calling or the fact that he graduated from that Wharton school in Pennsylvania that no one has even heard of. Keep in mind, only an animal would call other human beings an animal. He was just on the news the other day calling the gangsters from MS-13 animals. The Bible tells us that we are all His children and that He cares for us all…equally. As a Liberal Democrat woman in Congress, I can tell you that the Democratic Party cares about these youths who may have taken the wrong road in life and we are here to support them."

She then paused for a drink of water from her plastic bottle, that contained a plastic straw and noticed that there were no more cheers and thought to herself that she should change the subject and screw sticking up for the MS-13 gangsters. It was perfectly clear that that group of people wasn't working with her base. *Remember to tell them what they want to hear,* she reminded herself.

"I believe that our youth is our foundation and future and why should they have to pay for college I ask you…why? That's what our government is for…for the people!" This last part she yelled out and pounded on the podium with her Left fist and the cheers resounded back. *It's so easy to manipulate these young fools these days,* she admitted truthfully. *Give them something shiny or free and there onboard with you!*

After another thirty minutes of Trump bashing, she thought that she has them in her corner and wrapped up her speech in a blaze of glory!

On the way home, she decided that she would pick up some Church's fried chicken to celebrate with while watching the Cosby Show. She planned on heading back to DC next week and might as well live it up a bit she thought. Especially since her speech seemed to be a huge success.

She parked her car in the garage and pushed the button on her remote to close the garage door. She was salivating about eating her fried chicken since it smelled sooo good. As she wrapped her arms around her food in anticipation of a nice meal and a good show, she entered her home and discovered a rugged looking man standing in her kitchen who was obviously waiting for her.

"Do I know you?" Representative Wileen croaked out the question but was already sure of the answer. She dropped her food on the floor and was about to use her powerful vocal muscles to scream when a hand covered her mouth and another was placed at the back of her head and she soon expired…

NASNI

Back on base, TJ phoned his boss and let him in on the good news that Representative Wileen will no longer be chanting to the American people to impeach 45. Additionally, he told his boss that he was planning on coming back the next day and asked if he had another target selected yet. His boss told him no and said to just come on back.

He called the passenger terminal and secured a seat on a C-21 morning flight to Andrews. He would be glad to get back home.

CIA Headquarters

He sat at his desk typing up his 3 reports for his boss. Judy had brought him his coffee earlier along with his cinnamon twirls. Just as he had finished typing, his phone rang. Caller ID identified this caller as a CIA agent…Conrad Lonzo.

"Yeah Conrad," he answered the call.

"Hey buddy, about time you return from another vacation!"

"I wish. I was working in case you have a need to know."

"I was just kidding. From watching the news, I knew you were working."

What did Conrad mean from that last remark? Did he truly know what his missions were? TJ just decided to let it slide; after all, Conrad was a friend anyway.

"How's it going with Ching Ching?" he asked.

"That's the reason that I'm calling you. Are you busy with anything right now?"

"Not right at the minute…why do you ask?"

"I need your help on this case. I cleared it with Randy already and he agreed that it was ok as well as being necessary. In fact, Director Lannister has already requested search and surveillance warrants from the judge."

Conrad explained that Ching Ching did meet with a Chinese man who he believed was a Chinese operative. Ching Ching handed a manila envelope to the man. They talked for a few minutes and then separated. Conrad was able to take some surveillance photos which turned out clear enough, that the CIA's database was able to identify the man as none other than, Chen Chang, a Chinese military operative. He was removed from the United States back in 2015 for nefarious actions and now it seemed that he had returned. Since he was forcibly removed, there would have been a signalize note in the CBP database that would have flagged him from being admitted for a ten year period. But since he was here now, TJ figured that he must have come across the U.S.'s porous southern border.

"Sure, what do you need from me?" TJ asked.

So Conrad told his friend what he had in mind and TJ readily agreed. It was nice that he would be working with his friend. Sometimes working alone became stale. So he picked up his phone to make a call to a certain CIA analyst…

"Hello," Ching Ching answered.

"Hi Ching Ching, its TJ."

"Hi, you naughty boy; I don't see you for a while…what happen to you?"

"Work related and I was out of town."

"You have nice trip?" Ching Ching curiously asked and her curiosity wasn't lost on TJ.

"It was alright. Hey, I have a question for you."

"What is it Boy Scout?"

"Do you have a DVD player at your home?"

"Of course I do. Why you want to know for Yankee?"

"I have a movie that I can bring over to your home and we can watch it together with some popcorn instead of going out tonight."

"Why at my home?" Ching Ching asked suspiciously. "Maybe you want to take advantage of Ching Ching?"

"No, I just thought that it would be nicer is all. I don't really like crowds."

"Ok, but no funny stuff CIA man."

"No problem Ching Ching. I'll bring some microwave popcorn…how's that?"

"Yes, Ching Ching has microwave and I like popcorn, but not too much butter. I have to watch my figure you know."

"Trust me, I know," TJ affirmed.

Ching Ching gave TJ her address. She told him that she was renting a small condo in Rose Hill, Virginia. He had agreed to meet her there at 1900 with a movie and with popcorn in hand.

Conrad and TJ met later to go over their plan for that night. Because Ching Ching was a CIA employee, they had to do things a little differently. They would have to take this investigation a little farther than normally required and that meant that TJ would have to do whatever it takes in order to get her to talk about her possible crimes against the United States and he was more than willing to help out…for his country of course!

Conrad insisted that his friend be wired. That was just a term from the old days when listening devises did have wires. Now in modern times, devices could transmit without an actual wire. *Technology was great,* Conrad thought, *especially since he was going to be on the receiving end of the eavesdropping and recording Ching Ching and TJ with an electronic devise in his vehicle!*

He was just a little envious of his friend because Ching Ching really was a beautiful and sexy woman, but she could be deadly as well he reminded himself. What a combination! Ah, if things worked out tonight, then she would be taken into custody with proof of her infidelity to her adopted country. Conrad had already alerted their FBI friend, Bob Mingo, to stay by his phone and to answer it if he received a call from one of them and he gave Bob the address where they would be at that night. Conrad and TJ had both readily agreed that they wanted Bob to get the credit for the arrest if there was going to be one.

Before leaving his office, TJ set his DVR to record The Ingraham Angle. He wanted to see if Laura had any interesting news to report. He then stopped by the CIA's Medical Department located on the first floor. TJ remembered from reading his employee handbook that the agency encouraged and promoted safe sex and offered their employees free condoms as a means of assisting them in making better choices.

As he entered the lobby, he noticed a sliding glass window and walked up to it. A young female nurse slid back the glass and asked: "May I help you?"

TJ cleared his throat before answering with: "Yes, I would like to pick up a package of condoms please."

"Please come through the door and follow me," the nurse requested.

He opened the door and followed her down the hall to a backroom that was apparently a storage area. She reached up and retrieved a cardboard box that was the size of a shoebox and opened the lid. TJ noticed that the box was completely full of smaller packages. The nurse told him to take as many as he needed and that there was 3 condoms per package. So to be funny, he reached out and took the whole box from her hands thinking that she would laugh and ask for the box back. However, that was not her reaction at all. With a mischievous smile on her face, she replaced the lid and wished him a nice day as she walked him back to the lobby! Out in the hallway, he read a label on the box that indicated the contents was 300 hundred condoms! A man that was approaching the medical department gave TJ a sly look as if he knew what he was holding in his hands and TJ responded with: "Stocking up for the holidays!" The man continued on through the door just shaking his head. *Maybe he's worried that I took them all, or maybe he's just jealous!*

He decided to stop by his truck first to drop off his precious cargo before meeting with his friend and co-worker, Conrad. No use in allowing him to see the box of 300 condoms and get the wrong idea! Even a Navy SEAL could not utilize that many condoms in one night…especially a former one!

TJ placed the box on the back seat while slipping out a package of condoms and placed it in his front pocket and went to meet Conrad.

While Ching Ching was working, the two men went to surveil her condom---condo, just to have an idea of the surrounding area and then it was on to Golden Corral where Conrad insisted that TJ buy and he reluctantly agreed.

TJ showed up in time at Ching Ching's condo while Conrad waited in his vehicle in the street. He rang the doorbell and after several seconds, the door opened and Ching Ching was there with her long, black silky hair hanging low and wearing a very sexy satin kimono. After seeing her open the door that way, he thought to himself that maybe she wanted to pop more than just popcorn! He instantly felt a tightening in his pants and realized that this was going to be a hard mission! By the way she talked to him several times before, she somewhat took him by surprise…but not completely.

What he didn't know was that she dreamed of the day when she could make love to this man that she was so attracted to and who worked at the agency. She did know his mission at the CIA and felt that it was a noble cause for the country. Her heart was rapidly beating because she knew that tonight would be the night that she finally fulfills her passionate needs; she knew that she was in control.

To keep him off balance, she pulled him roughly into her home and quickly slammed the door shut behind him. Looking around, he noticed several items from China that adorned the walls as well as on tables. Her condo was neat and orderly which indicated that she was a very clean person. He liked clean girls but didn't have much time to get his bearings when she boldly approached him and pulled TJ against her yielding body and French kissed him right on the mouth! She held him tightly and was obliviously trying to get him aroused. She really didn't need to try too hard he thought! He kissed her back with passion and held her close to his body. After several minutes of passionate kissing, she pulled away from him.

TJ cleared his throat and announced, "I brought a movie and popcorn," and held them up to show her. However, he got the notion that she didn't really want to watch the movie or eat the popcorn when she grabbed them both out of his hands and tossed them behind the sofa. Clutching his hand, she led him into her bedchamber (he tried to resist…a little). He noticed that the perfume that she wore was intoxicating and he felt somewhat out of control with his resolve weakening. She was a beautiful woman with sex appeal and power and she was utilizing her God given arsenal on him at that moment in time; he felt powerless to protest and wasn't sure if he wanted to!

Standing by her bed, the two people held each other close lost in their own thoughts. As TJ was kissing her neck with Ching Ching moaning slightly, he was hoping that he would be able to pump her for information about her involvement in the death of the three Republicans…if she did play a part in their demise.

While standing by her bed, which was very sensual in itself, she slowly and provocatively undressed and then assisted him in undressing as well. He placed his flannel shirt---which held the microphone---on the back of a chair that was placed next to the bed and his pants on the chair's seat while removing his one package of condoms carefully from his front pocket. She quickly noticed that he was hung like a horse and surprise was clearly etched on her face as she thought that he must be from Texas…or South America, with that anaconda! TJ remembered briefly about Conrad. He would be getting an earful in a minute and he felt helpless to stop any of it. He figured that his friend would understand though, how necessary it was for him to fornicate with this beautiful Chinese woman…for information of course, and, in the line of duty. He would suffer naturally, but that was all in a day's work with the CIA!

Next to the bed, Ching Ching was very playful as she nipped at his ear and he nipped back at her ear and then kissed her neck softly again and again. She then pulled him onto the bed with her while inviting him to enter into her den of love. However, he wanted some foreplay first and kissed her full, red inviting lips that automatically parted for him and then he kissed her neck and slowly worked his way south to her two perfectly shaped assets and suckled first one and then the other.

Through her body language, she urged him to take her as she was already hot and moist. He did not want to disappoint this beautiful seductress and slipped on the condom quickly and entered her with abandonment. As he broke through her tight portal, he heard her gasp as she dug her French manicured nails into his back. Like a hydraulic ram, he moved rapidly in and out, in and out, in and out, very efficiently. However, for some odd reason though, he started salivating for a cheeseburger and that had never happened to him before while in this situation!

He was like a tiger with her, demanding more of her body and she was like a tigress to him, yielding to his needs fully and completely, yet there was delicacy that was perfectly balanced and controlled and modulated with a certain amount of passion mixed in for good measure.

Just before he brought himself and his partner to an ultimate climax, he noticed that her eyes seemed to be glowing as she whispered, "I love you," and then he heard himself say, "I love you too," as his eyes rolled back into his head and he felt enraptured with visions of stars and fireworks in his mind as he planted his seed deep into her honey pot (or condom), it was just that good!

But did he really love her or was it a just a natural reaction to repeat what she had just shared with him? He wasn't exactly sure because he was no expert on love. That was a weak point in his life. He was a very cynical type of person and while most people saw the good in others, he was always looking for the bad. He felt safer that way as it tended to guard against people taking advantage of him. But it wasn't an exact science he noted.

He rolled to the side and lay there totally spent with his condom full of semen (he believed in safe sex) next to a beautiful and exotic Chinese woman that he didn't know much about and that she may or may not be a traitor to the country. He had his arm around her and his head nestled in her lightly scented hair. She had her arms wrapped around him as well. After lying there in perfect contentment and harmony for several minutes, he somewhat regained control of himself and remembered that he was there on a mission…maybe his hardest duty yet or maybe not, depending on how you viewed it!

"Ching Ching, I need to ask you some questions," TJ started.

"Yes lover…that was wonderful!" she confessed and gave him a kiss on the cheek.

"It was awesome, but why did it happen? I thought you didn't want me to take advantage of you?"

"I don't feel that you took advantage of Ching Ching because I wanted it and so did you…I can tell that you needed it as much as I did. I love you TJ so I felt that it was acceptable for a man and woman when in love to make love," she stated simply.

"But I'm not sure it's love on my part. You're a beautiful woman and I was really attracted to you. I haven't made love to a woman for a long time so my desire was intense and maybe clouded my judgment."

"It doesn't matter, you will find out in time that you love me too. Sometimes, love just happens. Now that ice is broken, you can come to my home and be with me anytime that you want sweet boy…and spend the night if you like."

He thought that that would be nice but, Ching Ching might have to go to prison if she is found guilty of these murders of Republicans. Even though he took out several Democrats, he was justified in doing his job and had no regrets. With Ching Ching, she was not under any orders though. However, he won't miss any of those Republicans because they were crap anyway and it was for the good of the country.

He didn't know how to ask Ching Ching tactfully about the death of the Republicans, so he just came out with a direct question.

"Do you know anything about Republicans being killed Ching Ching?" he questioned.

She had an incredulous look on her face as she was taken totally by surprise with his question. She gave pause before answering. *Does she dare admit the truth? Will he understand her good intentions? Will love keep them together?* Based on her love for him, she decided to be frank with him.

"Wrong again sailor, I don't do it TJ."

She paused as he waited patiently, while he knew more would be forthcoming.

She explained to him how she figured out what his mission was with the CIA and decided to help him because of falling in love with him, but, she wanted to help with the "bad" Republicans, since he was taking care of the "bad" Democrats. She filled him in on the Chinese operative that she was working with. He was someone that she knew back in China that was working for the Chinese government and she asked him for his help. However, she reassured TJ that the Chinese government had nothing to do with *these* killings.

"You very smart lover. You figure out Ching Ching's clues…right?"

"Yes I did."

"I wanted to test your ability and you pass with flying colors. But, you solve picture puzzle faster than Ching Ching think you can."

TJ decided that it was time to go as she had already confessed to her part in what happened to the "bad" Republicans. Either she knew that he couldn't or wouldn't arrest her, but she doesn't know about his friend Bob from the FBI that can and will.

As he dressed, she put her Kimono back on and followed him to the door. There they both kissed for several minutes. TJ found himself being aroused again and was forced to break away with a parting, "Goodnight."

He didn't want Ching Ching to know about Conrad as she was probably watching out her window, so he drove down the block a ways and Conrad followed. Back in Conrad's car, he then filled TJ in on Bob's arrival in the neighborhood. Bob said that he wouldn't move in until he got the word from Conrad or TJ. TJ gave the nod for Conrad to call Bob and give him the authorization to effect the arrest.

As they watched, Bob pulled up in front of Ching Ching's home and walked up to the door. At the sound of the doorbell, she thought TJ had come back to spend the night with her. However, she then realized that she was sadly mistaken when the man at the front door held up a badge and declared that he was with the FBI with a warrant for her arrest.

The men waited for several minutes until Bob and Ching Ching exited the home with her in handcuffs. They watched as Bob assisted her into his car and they drove off heading for the FBI Headquarters and Conrad followed.

TJ left in his own truck for home to get some much needed rest as it had been a most stressful day for him. He didn't exactly know what would happen to Ching Ching and hoped that she loved him enough to keep his mission a secret, if that indeed was the truth. At the end of the day though, it didn't really matter too much since he was working under orders on a classified program. She didn't have any real proof to offer up to the district attorney anyway. She would be questioned about her role in the death of the trio of Republicans and her contact with her Chinese operative friend. Since she did not actually commit their murders herself, that should work in her favor. He was sure that the FBI would put out an all-points bulletin on the Chinese operative, but, it stood to reason that he would be on the run back to China if he was smart enough.

Chapter 18
Ω

"But Attorney General Sessions is there in name only. He is absolutely worthless; it is a rudderless Department of Justice."

---Jason Chaffetz, Former Congressional Representative

President Trump vows to never forget our fallen heroes with a most powerful Memorial Day speech at Arlington National Cemetery.

Oregon student was suspended for wearing a t-shirt to school that read "Border Wall Construction Co…The Wall Just Got 10 Feet Taller." He is now suing his Liberal Oregon school district for nominal damages as well as the right to wear his shirt to school.

President Trump is now optimistic about the North Korea summit after he had canceled when Kim sent signals that he might not be serious about the meeting. It seems that a delegation from North Korea and the United States were supposed to meet in Singapore and the U.S. was stood up.

Justice With Judge Jeanine

"Welcome to Justice and I'm Jeanine Pirro. Thanks for being with us tonight and thanks again for making us number one on Saturday nights for total viewers. Now for my opening statement: We have come face to face with the harsh reality of the massive amount of corruption uncovered in the Obama administration. For those of you that believe that Obama is innocent and didn't know a thing about any of it…you're full of shit! I suppose you still believe in the Easter Bunny as well! Let me call out the Obama Crime Family. First, you have daddy Obama followed by Biden, Bill and Hilliary, Clapper, Kerry, Rice, Holder, Powers, Brennan, Lynch, Styles and Page, Wasserman Schultz, Abedin, Weiner, Mills, Andrew and Jill McCabe, McAuliffe, Brazile, Steele, Sherman, Mueller, Yates, Rosenstein, Rhee and others, you all need to be in prison…yesterday! I have a prediction to make based on President Trump's administration, you will be soon be going to the lockup. No, I don't have any inside information mind you, but I know the President and I can see all of the shit rising to the top in DC. They say shit rises to the top, you better believe it. Do you corrupt Liberals know why you are going to prison…I mean besides breaking the law? I'll tell you why. You thought that your precious Hilliary was going to be your next president and then you all could take your time in destroying millions of incriminating files and records. Wrong! You're caught so give up peaceably when the marshals come for you and good riddance is what I say. You are the swamp and President Trump is the swamp drainer. As a judge I can tell all of you this: you have the right to remain silent and I would do it. But of course, you losers can't because of TDS. You all are struggling with Trump Derangement Syndrome. That's right, you're all sick with corruption and greed and President Trump upset your apple cart. Now we have some spoiled apples. Poor Liberals, Trump kicked over your hive and now you are all mad and want to destroy him with any means available to you. Well, keep this is mind: President Trump has plenty of friends and I'm one of them.

"On a side note while I'm warmed up, Jeff Sessions is a loss cause and a burden to the Justice Department. Why don't you do your job Jeff? What are you hiding? I have a feeling that you need to be in prison as well. I predict that you supported Trump only for one reason…you wanted to be the attorney general and you knew that President Trump by nature, believes in loyalty. Then once you got your 'dream job,' you then recluse yourself from doing your job. I bet it's this way, your covering up for a few bad actors in our government because you feel that they will spill the beans on some your past activities. I'm calling you out Jeff. If I'm wrong, feel free to call me and I'll give you time to explain your substandard conduct. But I fear that you don't have the balls to come on my show and explain yourself to the American people. Prove me wrong Jeff, I dare you!

"That's my opening statement. Now, let's talk about…I'm just being told by my producer that we have a Fox News Alert. It seems that Senator Wesley was discovered dead in the desert outside Area 51 in Nevada. He was found leaning up against a cactus by an extraterrestrial miner with a donkey that was exploring the immediate area. He was searching for UFO debris…the miner that is and not the ass. The senator was dead at the time of the finding and was wearing what has been identified as a 'Glow-in-the-Dark Alien Headband Boppers.' Basically, my producer is telling me that it's a headband with two springs and two small alien heads that glow-in-the-dark that is connected to the springs that jounce as you move your head. These miniature alien heads were glowing in the dark and that's how the senator was able to be found at night. It appears that the senator's throat had been slit with a Russian *Boker* knife which was discovered next to his body.

"That's all that we know of at this point. But the more important question is this: was it the Russians or aliens? My money is on the aliens, which by the way are not considered illegal. That's probably because we want to talk to them.

"Now let's get back to…what, another Fox News Alert? Ok, it looks like we will be taking you to our Fox affiliate in Los Angeles. Gina, this is Judge Jeanine, can you hear me?"

"Yes Judge I can. We are here at Representative Wileen's home where she was discovered deceased. She was found by her housekeeper hung upside down in her garage with a broken neck."

"Do the police have any clues or suspects?" Judge Jeanine asked seriously.

"No suspects yet per se. However, investigators did retrieve a Russian chips bag that was left behind, which maybe be from the perpetrators. It's just too early to tell Judge."

"Thank you Gina for that great reporting. We'll look forward to more updates from you on this story."

"Of course Judge, we'll keep you posted as we receive more information from the public relations officer here with the LAPD."

"Looks like a busy night here at the Fox News studio. We'll be right back after the break where I'll head outside for Street Justice to find out what New Yorkers think of our great President."

Clinton Home

The family doctor was visiting the Clintons but not as a social call. Hilliary was acting up again screaming about calling a meeting of her cabinet and Bill was forced to call in Dr. Darwin. By the time that the good doctor arrived, Hilliary was beside herself verbally attacking Bill as well as the two Secret Service men stationed at their home. Dr. Darwin was able to administer a 10 mg Valium and 60 mg of Prozac to the anxious Hilliary and working together, the two men were able to get her to bed where she was now resting peacefully. Bill questioned the doctor about her condition.

"She is showing signs of anxiety and is also obviously delusional brought on by TDS," Dr. Darwin stated.

"TDS…what's that?" Bill asked.

"Trump Derangement Syndrome," the doctor announced confidentially.

"Are you sure that's what it is and is it for real?" questioned Bill.

"It's a guarantee. I actually have some other patients with the same thing. It's actually on the rise with Trump's success."

"Can it be cured Dr. Darwin?"

"Only if someone other than a Trump retakes The White House I'm afraid," the doctor confided to Bill who had a perplexed look on his face.

"I can see that you think I'm joking and I wish I were, but the fact is that TDS is strangely real. Kind of like when we had some of our troops come back with Post Traumatic Stress Disorder. No one wanted to believe that PTSD existed and that it was just a misdiagnosed condition. But several studies proved that it was authentic. So let her rest and she should be better tomorrow…hopefully," Dr. Darwin added.

"Doctor Darwin, what if Trump stays in office for another six years, will this condition really stay with my wife for that long?"

"I'm afraid so Bill. Since six years is a long time, we may have to admit her to Bellevue Mental Hospital where they can give her the attention that she really needs. Remember, she took it pretty hard when she lost the election. As you recall, you called me to her room on the night that she lost the election and I was afraid that this would progress to this stage. But for the time being, we'll do what we can and hope for the best. If we do need to admit her, then I will write the order at that time."

Bill shook the doctor's hand and escorted him to the front door. As he was walking back to his study after the doctor departed, he was thinking how great it would be if she was locked up in a mental institution, then he could go back to a lifestyle that he was more comfortable with. He thought about that honey-eyed blonde that was working the day shift at the Codfather Café. He knew that she liked and wanted him by the way she flirted with him. *This could be a good thing.* Plus, if Hilliary was locked up, he wouldn't have to deal with these outbursts that had taken hold of her anymore.

Street Justice With Judge Jeanine

"Welcome to Street Justice and I'm here outside of Trump Tower to find out about what New Yorkers think of our President."

A man with a trench coat and wearing a nice Fedora hat approached and Jeanine was already with her microphone and was loaded with a question.

"Excuse me sir, do you know me?" she asked shyly.

"Yes Judge, I watch your show every weekend. I love you and Fox News by the way."

"Great. I'm out here today for Street Justice and I want to find out what New Yorkers think of how the President is doing."

"I think he's doing great. He has accomplished more in 18 months than Obama did in eight years. You know Judge, I have told people for years that we need a successful businessman to run our country instead of some political hack. So I'm very content with President Trump running things and I even feel safer here in New York City since he has the Feds arresting and hauling off our MS-13 gang problem."

"You're right about that."

As the man walked away with a smile on his face, the Judge noticed a spring in his step. She then looked around for another person to interview and saw an average looking woman approaching.

"Excuse me ma'am," Judge Jeanine addressed the woman.

"Yes?" the woman queried.

"What do you think of our President?"

"I like him," she simply stated.

"How do you think he's doing?"

"I think he is adding real value again to our country that was lacking in the Obama administration."

"What about Hilliary?"

"She's a liar and I'm just thankful to God that she isn't our president…that's for sure!"

"Do you think the President is keeping his promises to the American people?"

"No doubt," she replied. "Like President Trump is always saying at his rallies: 'Promises Made, Promises Kept.' It's so refreshing and different not being lied to by a president anymore."

As the woman walked off, Jeanine noticed a young black man with baggy pants and dreadlocks heading her way and decided to approach him. She thought that he didn't appear to be a Trump supporter, but what the heck, why not find out his thoughts?

"Excuse me sir, do you have a minute to talk to me?"

"Yeah, what you want bitch?"

"How do you think our President is doing running the country these days?" Judge Jeanine asked reluctantly.

"Who cares? He hasn't done anything for me."

"You haven't noticed a difference in New York City lately?"

"Now that you mentioned it, I have. Some of my home boys have been arrested and deported. What's up with that?"

"Maybe they deserved it?" the Judge asked cautiously.

"Wrong. Under Obama, they were never arrested and they are living the same lifestyle as back then." Then out of suspicion, he asked Jeanine, "Who are you anyway woman?"

"I'm Judge Jeanine with Street Justice which is a number one rated show on Fox."

The young man then covered his face with his shirt and walked off mumbling incoherent comments that the

Judge failed to understand. *Maybe he was wanted by law enforcement as well,* she considered.

CIA Headquarters

TJ was doing paperwork when his personal assistant Judy entered and presented him with some breakfast from the cafeteria. When he arrived early that morning, he told her that he was planning on skipping breakfast in favor of catching up on his paperwork. She liked him and felt that she was somewhat responsible for him as part of her job and brought him breakfast this day. She had done the same thing for Randy, her other boss as well.

"Thanks Judy, but it wasn't necessary," he stated. But she could tell that he was pleased that she thought enough of him to do so.

He noticed that she had all of his favorites on the plate. However, that could be that Chef Tony had prepared the plate for him. In any case, the most important thing that was residing on his plate at the moment was the hot and buttery cinnamon roll that he was so fond of eating.

He had just finished eating his breakfast when Randy his boss walked in.

"Hey, you're back!" Randy stated with enthusiasm.

"What gave you the first clue?" TJ growled.

"Judy alerted me when you arrived."

"Great," he responded and looked up at his boss and smiled. He was a little tired from all of his missions lately, but he admired and respected Randy immensely.

"Well, I'm sure you are not here for your health, what's up?"

"You seem out of sorts…"

"It's just unbelievable all the fucking crap that we have serving in our government these days, that's all. Sorry for my language."

"You don't have to apologize for telling the truth…just remember that. Also, we are cleaning up our government by draining the swamp. Unfortunately, most people will never know that an idea that you had would be utilized to help the President in keeping his campaign promise of draining the swamp. I also think that most people who voted for President Trump was under the impression that he was talking about firing many of the 'swamp rats' as possible. But I'm sure that many Americans if they knew the facts as we know them would support your mission, just like they did when you served in the Navy."

Randy paused for a brief moment and then continued: "It's like this TJ. Our country would be better served without the massive amount of corruption that is infesting our government like a cancer. We have allowed this corruption in government service to grow and foster without check. Now we are to the point where it is a cancer on our society and it will kill us if we ignore it. Everybody knows you fight cancer with chemo treatments, right?" When TJ nodded his head, Randy then added, "You my friend are our chemo treatment. You are just what our country needs at this point in time and President Trump is well aware of it."

"I know you're right, it's just that I hate to see my country allowing all of this corruption to take place."

"I agree with you wholeheartedly and that's why we are taking care of that problem. Anyway, I'll let you in on a secret. I talked with President Trump yesterday and he has communicated to me that he's very proud of you for doing what must be a hard job for you. He's a very intelligent man and is starting to see a light at the end of the tunnel for our country due to your successful efforts."

TJ felt better for the words from his boss and the President and believed that what he was doing for the country was the right thing. He had to believe in these missions or he wouldn't be able to do his job. Sometimes it took "tough love" to do the right thing in life. Good thing he was tough!

"Thanks boss."

"No problem. Now, let's sweep sentiment aside and get back on course. Unfortunately, we are not done yet."

"Who's next?"

"Kadin Elkhart. He's a congressman and the Democratic National Committee Deputy Chair and also a piece of crap. Pardon my French," his boss added politely.

"Why? Don't apologize when you are telling the truth…remember what you told me?"

"You're right. Good thing you're a fast learner. Anyway, he has worn out his welcome in this life and needs to be shown the door…the door to Hell that is!"

"Consider it done boss and I'll get on it right away."

Shortly after Randy left his office, he headed down to see Jessy in the file vault. He felt a need to go personally instead of calling to see if she would mention anything about Ching Ching being absent. Upon arriving at her cubicle she looked up from her work and smiled at him.

"Well, it's about time you finally need me. That's why you're here…right?"

"I need your help, but if I had more time, I would come down just for a visit once in a while."

"I'm just kidding. I know that they keep you pretty busy," Jessy confirmed.

"How do you know that?" he asked.

"Because, no one else that I know of anyway, gets more files from me than you."

"I see. Speaking of files, I did come down to get the file on Kadin Elkhart."

"See, I was right. Just relax and I'll get it for you."

While Jessy took her leave to retrieve the file that TJ requested, he noticed a couple of well-dressed men, either CIA or FBI (he didn't know which) going through Ching Ching's stuff in her cubicle. Upon returning, Jessy quietly remarked to him about the investigation surrounding Ching Ching's work area.

"I don't know what happened to Ching Ching. She hasn't shown up for work and now they are investigating what happened to her. Maybe she's dead," Jessy stated.

"She's not dead; she's just in a little trouble is all. Because it's an ongoing investigation, I can't tell you anything more."

"I told you before that I was suspicious of her. Anyway, here's your file," and she handed it off to TJ.

He thanked her and then headed for his office to review the material.

★ ★ ★ ★ ★

TJ found himself working late again---just like the President---studying the file on Representative Elkhart. He also studied some of the congressman's speeches. One speech that he took notice of immensely took place in Minnesota which was the congressman's home state and was available to watch on YouTube.

In his speech, he talked to his constituents about boycotting the National Football League. This was due to the controversy that started the previous year when some players would kneel when the National Anthem was played. Even though the NFL had rules preventing players from kneeling, the organization---due to their hatred of President Trump--- decided not to enforce that rule at this time. This was due in large part to the NFL holding a Liberal position concerning politics. President Trump was the first to weigh in on this subject and called out the NFL on allowing this practice to continue and divide the country while showing disrespect to the flag and the men and women in the military who fought and sacrifice for the country every single day.

Finally, due to a drop in attendance and in the sales of merchandise, team owners of the NFL voted unanimously on allowing players that don't want to stand for the National Anthem to remain in the locker room. In this way, fans would not have to watch certain players disrespect the country and flag and those that are connected to the military; past and present.

However, this was not acceptable to dumbass Representative Elkhart. In his speech, he was ranting and raving about how everyone should boycott the NFL. For TJ, he thought that the decision made by the NFL was more than fair and President Trump seemed to approve as well. Congressman Elkhart also spoke about beating Trump with a pen instead of the sword; he was referencing the stale call of impeachment.

★ ★ ★ ★ ★

The next day, TJ decided that it was time for another phone call to a Congressional office. He looked up the number and then dialed remembering all the time that the CIA's phone numbers are blocked and wouldn't show up in caller ID.

"Congressman Elkhart's office, can I help you?" the voice on the other end asked.

"Who am I talking with please?" TJ asked very professionally.

"Who am I talking with?" the voice countered.

"My name is Lieutenant Evans and I'm with the Capitol Police," TJ lied.

"Sorry commander, we just have to be careful these days. My name is Oleander."

TJ did not miss the incorrect title and thought to himself, *it is what it is* and considered what it would be like to have Oleander for a name. *His family named him after a small tree? Where did Congress dig up these young schmucks from?*

"That's alright. I just need to know the congressman's schedule for the next three days."

Oleander went through the Representative Elkhart's schedule and TJ immediately came up with a plan and thanked the young intern for his help.

Two days later, Congressman Elkhart was discovered at his DC home stabbed to death by a Russian Federation pen through the Left eye. The autopsy showed that the pen penetrated the Left eyeball and entered the brain and he was killed instantly. Fox News reported how ironic it was that Representative Elkhart had talked about taking down President Trump with the "pen of impeachment" and instead, he was taken down by the "pen of the Russian Federation!" However, other than the pen, no other clues were discovered and the investigation was not conclusive as to who actually killed the congressman. It could have been one Russian, it could be two Russians or it could be something else entirely. In any case, TJ knew that Representative Elkhart wouldn't be bothering President Trump or the American people any time soon. He hoped that the congressman would be able to see his way clear to Hell with only one good eye!

Chapter 19
Ω

"We now have the Liberal playbook and we know what they are doing, and we are using it against them. Unlike the Democrats though, we aren't out to destroy our society, we are out to save it."

---Mark R. Levin

President Trump has finally lost his patience and confidence in Attorney General, Jeff Sessions. Senator Lindsay Graham has even sent his support to the President if he decides to fire him. Senator Graham told Fox News that the President has a right to have an attorney general that he can work with and have trust in.

While working in the Oval Office, President Trump was working on a way to make the American tax cuts permanent when Chief of Staff, John Kelly entered and informed him that the inspector general needed to see him right away.

The President agreed and had his Chief of Staff invite Michael Horowitz to enter and to have a seat. What the inspector general had to report was no less than shocking.

The inspector general told President Trump that he had uncovered a plot involving members of the deep state for the Department of Justice and the Federal Bureau of Investigation who blackmailed Attorney General, Jeff Sessions into joining the Trump Campaign in order to protect them and their way of life in case Hilliary did lose the election.

President Trump asked how Sessions could accomplish that. Horowitz continued into careful detail about the plan. It seemed that as a senator, Sessions was involved in a racketeering scheme along with other members of the Secret Society---or better known as the "deep state" from Fox News reports---for financial gain. The Secret Society with corrupt members from Congress, DOJ & the FBI, encouraged Sessions to come out in support of Trump and to be the first senator to do so to win his devotion and trust. The Secret Society identified Trump's weakness for loyalty and wanted Sessions to exploit that by becoming a member of the Trump Team. If Trump was to win, Sessions would ask to be attorney general of the United States and Trump was sure to give it to him for his support…*quid pro quo*. After Sessions was sworn in, he would then announce his recusal from the Russian-Trump investigation citing a, "conflict of interest." That would allow the Deputy Attorney General, Rod Rosenstein to head the investigation and to assist in covering up a massive amount of corruption that he was a part of. Rosenstein feared that Jaron Cowan wouldn't be able to stand up to the scrutiny of several investigations and submitted a letter to the President recommending that Cowan be fired and in which case he was. The IG then speculated that Cowan quickly went out and wrote a book to assist in covering his ass and the corruption that he was involved with by deflecting to other issues about the President in his book.

Horowitz took a deep breath and told the President that there was still more and continued on with his report.

The IG allowed that he uncovered another plot by the Secret Society to kill Cowan to shut him up. However, Horowitz believed that Cowan discovered the plot to kill him as well and decided to take his own life.

He then talked to the President about his findings of the Clinton Foundation; Hilliary's deleted emails; the destruction of government property and subpoenaed laptops, phones and servers; the $6 billion that came up missing while Hilliary was the Secretary of State under Obama; the illegal selling of 20% of the United States uranium to Russia and much, much more.

Horowitz confessed to the President that he had uncovered enough substantiated criminal evidence to send the Obama Crime Family to prison for years. However, he communicated to the President that he did not have the authority to do so on his own and that that authority would have to come from President Trump, who is the Chief Law Enforcer of the United States, under Article II, Annotation 16 of the Constitution. He explained that the Constitution does not say that the President shall execute the laws, but that "he shall take care that the laws be faithfully executed." Simply stated, with the evidence that Horowitz secured from his investigation, arrest warrants issued from a federal judge, would give the President the authority to call on the U.S. Marshall's Service to apprehend the accused felons for crimes against the United States.

All of this information swirled around in President Trump's head like sweet music to his ears. It seemed that the corruption was more massive and deeper than he first thought. With what the CIA had accomplished so far and the arrests that Horowitz was speaking about, this would clearly eliminate the criminal Liberal threat to the country for some time to come.

Horowitz interrupted the President's thoughts by asking, "What would you like me to do with this information, sir?"

President Trump looked deadpan at the Inspector General and enunciated his next two words: "Use it."

U.S. Marshals Service Headquarters

The U.S. Marshal Service is the oldest federal law enforcement agency in the United States and is currently an agency of the U.S. Department of Justice. It was established by the U.S. Government on September 24, 1789. U.S.

Marshals who are presidentially appointed are assigned to each of the country's 94 federal judicial districts and oversee deputy marshals that work in the field.

Marshal Thomas Lee was not assigned to any specific district as he was responsible for *all* marshals and deputy marshals across the United States and worked out of the U.S. Marshals Service Headquarters in Virginia.

Today he received several warrants for criminal arrests for some of the most prominent citizens of the country and he realized that this would be the largest gathering of felons ever made by the Marshals Service since its inception. For this operation which was classified as "Eagle Claw," he had assembled 60 U.S. deputy marshals to serve the warrants and make arrests. He figured two deputy marshals for every arrest would be justifiably required. Due to the nature of the operation, he figured to participate as well. He wanted to be involved in two particular arrests.

Clinton Home

Today, William Jefferson Clinton was a little restless. His book had just come out---*The Woman is Missing*---and it was not selling as well as he had hoped.

Hilliary was in her study franticly trying to find words for her next book. She was having a hard time in concentrating on her work though and was not in the best of moods…again. Fox News had started up again about her husband's infidelity. It was almost like they had nothing else to report. *Maybe they just want to torture me,* she thought to herself.

Bill entered her study and addressed her.

"I'm going down to the diner Hun. Are you going to be ok?"

"Why? Are you going to see that trump…I mean, tramp waitress again? I bet she'll put out for you if you ask," Hilliary stated with venom.

"Now stop it Hun. You know that I don't have that problem anymore. That last one happened because she threw herself at me. She was drunk and I just had to give her a ride home for safety's sake. Then I laid her on the bed to sleep it off."

"I know, you *laid* her on the bed alright and then you just happened to pass out on top of her with your dick inside her."

"I didn't know she was faking being drunk," he defended.

Hilliary picked up a book and threw it at Bill and added, "Get the fuck out of my sight, asshole!"

Good thing she took her medicine this morning, Bill thought to himself while taking the hint and communicated to Carl that they would be going to the Codfather Café for breakfast. Carl would be close by but he never interfered with Bill's business and he was well aware that the ex-president was a philanderer. Bill couldn't wait to see his favorite waitress, Inez, that honey-eyed blond who always welcomed him with open arms. *Get rid of Hilliary and then Inez will rock my world!* And he departed out the front door of the Clinton home with a smile on his face and Carl by his side.

Obama Home

Barack came down from the second floor of their rented home and found his lovely wife in the kitchen making *hors d'oeuvres* for their guests that would be arriving later that evening.

He came close to his wife and kissed her on the cheek and thought to himself that he was the luckiest man in the world---he was the first black president in history; beautiful wife running for president; two lovely children and money in the bank! He thought about how the country's founding fathers would turn over in their graves if they knew that a black man, with ancestors who were slaves, became the 44th President of the United States! He, Barack Obama, who wasn't even born in this country; it was too much! Life was good to him.

"Are you going out Barack?" his wife asked and broke into his thoughts.

"Well, it is a nice day out and I hear the birds singing sweetly and I did tell Joe that we can get in a round of golf before our guests arrive."

"Ok, but don't get tied up and miss our dinner party tonight," Michelle admonished.

"Don't worry dear. What can go wrong with Joe and me on top of things?" Barack teased her. "I'll get my clubs out of the garage and take the Jag along with Kane."

Kane was the secret service agent that was assigned to Barack and he was housed in the mother-in-law home in the backyard.

Michelle turned up her radio that she had on and sang to her favorite song and singer, Stevie Wonder who was currently singing, Ebony and Ivory. She had to keep it low when Barack was around because he didn't appreciate her music. The song was perfect timing as Barack and Joe would be playing golf together again as Ebony and Ivory in perfect harmony.

Obama stepped into his four-car garage and closed the door behind him and located his golf clubs next to the garage fridge that was set against the back wall. He reached up and pushed the button to open the garage door for the Jag and was taken by surprise as three U.S. Marshals stormed in.

"What the fuck is this?" Barack asked in total disbelief. This was the kind of thing that was supposed to happen to people like Trump and not to him.

United States Marshal Thomas Lee held up his badge and stated loudly, "Barack Obama, I have the horror of informing you that you are officially under arrest for crimes against the United States. You have the right to remain silent and anything you say can and will be used against you in a court of law."

With a nod to the other two deputies, they seized Obama and handcuffed him with his arms behind his back and were leading him out to their waiting SUV when Barack decided to speak his mind.

"Do you realize who I am damn it? You don't arrest former presidents you freaking idiots. That was always my policy when I was the president; former presidents don't get arrested!" Obama stated with contempt.

"New president…sir," responded Marshal Lee with heat.

As they helped Obama into the back seat of their black SUV and buckled him in, he asked if he could notify his wife first.

"We'll notify her for you," Marshal Lee stated.

"When will you notify her?" Obama asked mildly.

"When she calls our office looking for you," countered Lee.

As Barack looked up from his position in the SUV, he noticed that the birds were still singing in his trees and mumbled, "Fuck you all!"

As they drove away, Michelle had just finished singing with Stevie Wonder.

Clinton Home

Two teams of marshals in separate vehicles arrived at the Clinton Home and were in time to witness Bill Clinton and Carl leaving the property with Carl driving; one of the marshal's SUV followed, but not too closely.

The team that stayed behind to make the arrest on Hilliary came prepared. It was no secret to most people that Hilliary was having some mental challenges since her loss to Donald Trump in the 2016 election; they brought a straitjacket.

The two deputy marshals approached the gate and pushed the doorbell. After a short while, Oscar came out to the gate and inquired what they wanted. Deputy Marshal

Brice showed his badge and requested entry. When the secret service agent started to turn away, Marshal Brice held up the warrant and announced that he wasn't in the mood to play games and that he would go to prison for obstruction of justice. Upon hearing that, Oscar realized that Hilliary wasn't worth it and turned back and allowed the marshals to enter. He told them that she could be found in her study working on her book. He then ventured back to his living quarters.

As Hilliary looked up and from her typing, she discovered two strange men in her home and office; her personal sanctuary and stood up. The marshals quickly discovered that she was in a foul mood.

"Get the fuck out of my home now before I call the Secret Service," Hilliary hollered and pointed to the front door. Marshal Brice held up his badge and identified himself and his partner as U.S. Marshals. That didn't seem to matter to Hilliary who started to reach for something in her desk drawer. Marshal Brice's partner acted quickly and pulled out a Taser X26 and fired it into her ass as she was bent over. The two needle-like probes entered her buttocks at the same time that the deputy marshal pulled the trigger sending 50,000 volts into her body; she dropped like a rock and started twitching!

As she was now incapacitated, the two marshals helped her into the straight jacket that they brought with them and secured it. Marshal Brice then ventured into the kitchen and fetched Hilliary a glass of water while his partner was left with removing the two barbed electrodes; she was visibly shaken.

After a few minutes, she recovered enough and the two men assisted her up and led her to the front door; it was then that she launched into a string of epithets. She claimed that she was the president and that they had no right to do what they were doing. She screamed out that under the Constitution the president was protected; meaning her. She even threatened to tell her husband about their abusive treatment with her, concerning the taser in the ass and the degrading straitjacket.

After they had her buckled in the backseat of their SUV and climbed into the front of their vehicle she asked, "Where are you taking me?"

"Mrs. Clinton, we are taking you to the white house where you may rest more comfortably with the assistance of some medications and orderlies."

"Now we're getting somewhere. How about getting this fucking straitjacket off me before we get there and allow me to enter *my* White House with some dignity?"

The two marshals in the front just looked at each other before Marshal Brice answered and he picked his words carefully; "Wrong White House Mrs. Clinton. The *white house* that you're being admitted to by order of a federal judge is a white house in Rochester named, National University Treatment, or better known as NUT."

Hilliary then tried to spit at the marshals from her position in the back seat; she did not succeed. However, the marshals felt that a spit sock hood was necessary for the safety of everyone and placed one over her head that was held in place comfortably with an elastic band.

Codfather Café

Bill and Carl arrived at the Codfather Café trailed by the U.S. Marshals. They decided to wait until the two men finished their lunch and returned outside before arresting Bill. Inside, Bill and Carl was studying the menu without a cause for concern.

"What are you planning on having Carl?" Bill questioned as he was looking around for Inez.

"I don't know…are you paying sir?"

"Yeah, I'll pick up the tab for you since I'm in a good mood," Bill happily replied.

"Then in that case, I think that I will have the steak and eggs with whole wheat toast and extra crispy hash browns with a glass of milk and a cup of coffee," he declared as he closed his menu and then quickly added, "and one of those giant cinnamon rolls that I enjoy so much."

"That's it? Are you sure you didn't forget anything?" Bill asked jokingly.

"Just be glad that I wasn't hungry!" Carl joked back.

A nice looking younger woman than the two men approached the table with a pad of paper in hand and a ready smile on her face for the former president.

"Hi boys, what's the occasion today?" Inez asked.

"Believe it or not Inez, I just had to see your pretty face one more time," Bill smiled mischievously.

"Is that all you wanted to see honey?" she asked as she showed him her nicely contoured rump.

"Well, now that you mention it, I kinda miss seeing that too, if you know what I mean," Bill stated while winking at her.

Carl cleared his throat and interrupted the two love birds with, "Bill's new book is out Inez."

"How exciting; am I in it darling?" she asked shyly.

"Only if you want to be honey," Bill replied while patting her on the ass which she didn't seem to mind a bit. Carl interrupted the two by clearing his throat and placed his breakfast order followed by Bill's request.

While they waited for their food and talked, Bill confided in Carl about his wife.

"Carl, I need to let you in on something. Hilliary might be leaving us in the near future. I'm sure that you understand that she has some mental issues and I'm afraid that I will have to admit her to a mental hospital for a nice, long, rest soon. If so, then we'll lose Oscar as he will be reassigned."

Carl took all of this information in before he replied, "Does that mean that we'll be seeing more of Inez?" he questioned as he bumped Bill with an elbow.

"Do you know me or what? But what's this 'we' stuff? I believe that Inez is my girl and not yours…remember? Plus, you told me that you have that blow up doll that you and Oscar share. What did you call her? Oh yeah, Greek Girl and that your mother mailed her to you."

That was all true and Carl suddenly felt embarrassed about this information that he shared with Bill and didn't feel a response was required.

Their food came and the men talked and ate for an hour before leaving. Bill made sure to leave a very generous tip since Inez might be moving in soon. As they walked outside they were confronted by the two U.S. Marshals.

"Bill Clinton," Deputy Marshal Mansfield started while displaying his badge, "you are under arrest for crimes against the United States."

Thinking it was a joke from Obama, since Obama liked to pull stunts like this and had done so in the past, he asked, "You mean for patting Inez on the ass? She likes it fellows when I do it to her." When Bill noticed that Mansfield wasn't smiling he added, "Just go on in and tell Inez that you're friends of mine and to put it on my tab." As he started to move on with Carl by his side, the marshals blocked their way.

"Now listen young man, I think you are both nice enough guys and you can go back and tell Barack that the joke didn't land, but we need to get on with our business, so if you will excuse us please," Bill finished and waited to see if the *fake* marshals had anything else to add.

"This is not a joke," stated Marshal Mansfield as he held up a signed federal arrest warrant. "This is an official warrant for your immediate arrest and we can do it the easy way or the hard way, it's up to you," he stated matter-of-factly as he handed the warrant to Carl to view which was mostly to keep the secret service man out of the possible fray that might happen.

As Carl was reading the warrant, Bill decided to walk on and realized after the fact how wrong that decision was as Marshal Mansfield went ahead and wrestled him to the ground and with his Left hand holding Bill's face into the cemented sidewalk, he handcuffed the former president's arms behind his back and then helped him to stand. Carl continued reading the warrant!

"You can't do this shit to me. I'm a former president damn it. When Barack and Hilliary hear about this, I can assure you that heads will roll!"

Marshal Mansfield looked Bill directly in the eyes and replied, "I imagine that they already know."

Carl returned the warrant to the other marshal as he assured Bill that it was all legal. Carl was shocked and stunned at the turn of events today as the men led his boss away in handcuffs. But he knew that Bill will fight this to the core, they just couldn't get away with this. While thinking these thoughts, he heard Bill ask:

"Will I be allowed conjugal visits?"

"Mr. Clinton," Marshal Mansfield started, "your wife has already been arrested and taken into custody by now."

"Who said anything about my wife?" Bill asked innocently as he was shoved into the back of the SUV and secured with a seat belt.

CIA Headquarters

TJ was relaxing comfortably in the hot tub and reading his latest book when Hannity came on the television…

"I'm Sean Hannity and we have one hell of a show for you tonight with breaking news all over the place. Let's jump in and get started.

"My opening monologue tonight has to do with jogging all of my viewer's memories. If you think back and remember that more than a year ago, I made some drastic predictions. Of course, the Liberals claimed that I was crazy. I told you all that a boomerang was coming for the Democrats and it has now arrived.

"I told you that President Trump will be successful and good for our country and that has proven correct in more ways than one."

Hannity then showed the viewers the following scrolling chart that listed all of President Trump's accomplishments to date on a split screen:

- ★ Neil Gorsuch on the Supreme Court
- ★ Stock Market reached an all-time high
- ★ Consumer confidence at 17-year high
- ★ More than 2 million jobs created
- ★ Mortgage applications for new homes rise to a 7-year high
- ★ Unemployment rate at 17-year low
- ★ Signed the Promoting Women in Entrepreneurship Act
- ★ Gutted Obama-era regulations
- ★ Ended war on coal
- ★ Weakened Dodd-Frank regulations
- ★ Promoted buying and hiring American
- ★ Investment from major businesses
- ★ Reduced illegal immigration
- ★ Border wall underway
- ★ Fighting back against sanctuary cities
- ★ Created Victims of Immigration Crime Engagement Office
- ★ Changed rules of engagement against ISIS
- ★ Drafted plans to defeat ISIS
- ★ Worked to reduce F-35 cost
- ★ 5-year lobbying ban

…and the list went on and on! Sean worked his way through about half of the list before he gave up and continued with the show.

"I mentioned to you before about how the Obama Crime Family should be nervous and that they have the right to remain silent.

"I told you, the viewers, that I would not stop until justice is served.

"I also reminded you that these corrupt government officials will go to prison.

"Now with that said, the big news tonight is that the President has authorized the U.S. Marshals Service to serve arrest warrants and apprehend several felons including, Obama, Biden, Bill and Hilliary Clinton, Clapper, Lynch, Kerry, Holder and many others. In fact, Hannity was given exclusive access to film the arrest of Attorney General, Jeff Sessions at the DOJ and we have it all on tape for you to view tonight, take a look," Sean invited and motioned with a wave of his arm to the back screen in the studio.

The clip started by showing five U. S. Marshals, wearing light jackets that identified them as such on the back and arriving at the DOJ Headquarters and they entered the front doors of the building with a march down the hallway to the elevators and on up to the third floor. They arrived at a door marked "Attorney General, Jeff Sessions."

Two of the marshals broke away and continued down the hallway to make their arrest on Rod Rosenstein.

Upon entering Jeff Sessions's office lobby, they were accosted by an older woman who asked if she could help them, but the three marshals pushed by and continued on to Sessions office where he was seated behind his desk and looked up as they entered.

"What is it?" he croaked.

"Jeff Sessions," Marshal Lee started, "you are under arrest for crimes against the United States…"

He was interrupted by Sessions.

"I am not guilty of anything and you have no right to be here. I'm the head law enforcer for the United States and I did not give you any orders to arrest me. You son of a bitches better not lay a hand on me either. Furthermore, heads will roll if you don't leave right now," his voice querulous. "I repeat…I am not guilty of any crimes that you know about," he then corrected himself by adding, "I mean that I know about."

"Wrong Mr. Sessions on both counts; President Trump is the head law enforcer of the United States and we have a valid, federal warrant with your name on it, for your arrest with the President's blessing," Marshal Lee stated. "Also, like William Shakespeare says in Hamlet, 'I think you protest too much.' " At that moment, three security officers showed up responding from a phone call that the woman in the lobby had made to building security.

"What's going on here?" one security guard asked who asserted himself as the leader and was handed the federal arrest warrant for the Attorney General. As he scanned the document, he asked: "Is this really necessary gentlemen?"

"You saw the order," Marshal Lee stated and took the document from the surprised guard. "It's all legal and if you get in our way, we'll arrest you too," and signaled for another marshal to handcuff Sessions.

The Fox News camera filmed Sessions being handcuffed and marched through the offices and out into the hallway complaining and whining the whole time.

"Now stop it! I'm very serious. If you men value your careers or even your freedom, you'll turn me loose right now." Seeing himself being escorted by U.S. Marshals with employees watching, did not set well with Attorney General Sessions. In fact, it was downright humiliating.

As they entered the hallway, the two marshals that went to arrest Rod Rosenstein appeared from around the corner and stopped in front of Marshal Lee's team and his prisoner.

"Rod, do something," Sessions pleaded.

"Shut up you dumb fuck and I mean you better keep your mouth shut," Rosenstein stated matter-of-factly and then added, "or else."

Sessions got the message that Rosenstein was sending him and experienced inarticulate fear.

"Ok you two love birds, that'll be enough out of you. Don't forget your rights…you have the right to remain silent and anything you say can and will be used against you in a court of law. Now get them out of my sight," Marshall Lee told his men and the two accused criminals were marched on down the hallway while Lee turned toward the cameraman.

"Ok, this is it, we'll handle it from here," Marshal Lee told the Fox News cameraman and viewers found themselves back in the studio with Sean.

"Alright, you saw for yourself that President Trump isn't messing around with members of the swamp, even if its people that he appointed to his cabinet. I want the Liberal Democrats to remember this: no one is above the law and if you keep committing crimes against the United States, your number will be called."

TJ climbed out of the hot tub with a smile on his face and an earnest feeling in his heart. Like Sean stated, the boomerang was not only coming back for these Liberal fucks, it had finally arrived! He headed for the locker room to change and to head back to his office to watch more of Fox on these latest developing events.

Later that night in the Oval Office, President Trump made the decision to talk directly to the American people the next day about the latest Fox News events…arrests of prominent Liberal Democrats and promises made with promises kept.

It was curious to some viewers that the dishonest media failed to report on these earth shaking events.

Chapter 20
Ω

"The Liberal Democrats are the gift that keeps on giving!"

---Jim Miller

On August 13, 2018 at Ft. Drum, located in upstate New York, President Trump signed the 2019 National Defense Authorization Act into law…including a little known gem for 100% disabled veterans that allow them to fly Space Available on military aircraft.

The Oval Office

President Trump is kept busy with meetings, tweetings and endorsing Republican candidates for the 2018 midterm elections, which means that he is working late into the night…again. Currently, he is studying a Pentagon report on plans for starting a new branch of the military which will be called, United States Space Force. The Pentagon has identified an area next to Fort Hood in Texas as a likely location for the newest and sixth branch of the military; the suggested name for the base was, Orion Space Force Base. Orion was a good name for the base, but the President had other thoughts and quickly picked up his pen and scratched out the name Orion and replaced it with, Hannity. The reason for the change is that President Trump believes that Sean Hannity is a true American hero for reporting and highlighting the atrocities of the Liberal Democrats and that it's nice to recognize someone *before* they die; plus the

Democrats won't like it that a military base will be named after a Conservative talk show host!

The President knew that the Democratic Party is now made up of true anarchists and social pariahs---basically Liberals who wanted no laws and everything for free. The country could not sustain such a position and still be successful in the world market, especially with China wanting to oust the United States as a global power; economically and militarily.

He briefly thought about TJ Law and realized that he loved that name as well as the man. His mission wasn't easy, but he was needed for the health of the country. The needs of the majority outweigh the needs of the few, someone had once told him…or did he pick that up from a television show? He didn't know or care but understood that the philosophy was sound. He didn't care for the freaks, Liberals or losers. They were a cancer on society.

He heard the door close and looked up from his thoughts; it was his son Barron and he took a seat across from his father who he greatly admired. At a young age no less, he understood two things quite clearly: his father's love of country and that his dad was using his business intellect and common sense to save the nation. His knowledge of living in a divided country did not escape his thoughts and, he loved and respected his father immensely and was extremely proud of him.

"Son, shouldn't you be in bed?" President Trump asked.

"I can't sleep dad."

The President lowered his pen and gave his full attention to Barron and asked, "What's the trouble?"

Barron looked at his father and announced seriously, "What if the Liberals should take over our country in the midterms?"

"I wouldn't worry about that too much because I wouldn't stand for it and I would *trump* their efforts. That's why I'm going to rallies and endorsing our great Republican candidates for office. It would be bad if the Democrats take over the House and the Senate, but I just can't believe that the majority of Americans would allow that to happen, especially with the economy booming. Keep in mind that your uncle Sean is doing his part to help our country with messaging the American people on his show. He's a big help to us in saving our country from going down the drain."

President Trump had told Barron many years ago that Sean was his uncle. Now that his son was older, he wasn't sure if he knew the truth; Uncle Sean was used in name only and Barron had never yet questioned that relationship.

The door to the Oval Office opened and closed once again as Melania entered and walked up to Barron and put her arm around him.

"Shouldn't you be in bed young man?" she asked motherly.

"Ah mom, I'm talking to dad," Barron dejectedly announced.

"Listen to your mom sport, we'll talk again tomorrow. Now get on to bed," President Trump urged.

"I'm going…goodnight dad, love you."

"Goodnight son, love you too."

With Barron by her side, Melania and her son quietly left the Oval Office and allowed the President to resume his work. He thought about how lucky he was to have a loving family. He knew that a lot of families in America didn't have the kind of love, support and family bond that was found with his family. Through the years, the family unit had really disintegrated in society. President Trump thought he knew why this happened. It was due largely in part to parents not parenting their children; allowing the schools to raise their children, without discipline; allowing their children to play violent video games; the lack of teaching children manners and having respect for others and so on.

OPERATION: Ωmega

As the President was relaxing in his chair with these thoughts, he fell asleep and entered into a dream that he rarely had these days due to work requirements...

Chief of Staff, John Kelly entered the Oval Office and announced: "Mr. President, you're wanted in the trophy room, sir."

President Trump relieved a sigh of stress and impatience and rose from his chair and followed John Kelly down to the basement where the President had a trophy room constructed several months ago.

As he neared the room, a sign above the double doors read, "Liberals and Losers Trophy Room," and several voices could be heard talking all at once and President Trump wondered what they wanted with him now. Before entering the room, John Kelly informed him that some of them now believe that confession is good for the soul and that they would like to repent as well. When President Trump asked his Chief of Staff why, he was informed that they believe that if they did the right thing now, then the next stop for them would be Heaven instead of Hell.

As he entered the room and held up his hands for quiet, the prominent Liberal mounted heads on all four walls of the trophy room that he had nabbed stopped talking. He noticed that his collection of trophies were around sixty and each one came with a solid brass name plate that identified who they were, such as, Bill and Hilliary Clinton, Obama, Biden, Clapper, Sessions, Rosenstein, former California Governor Brent, Pocahontas, Head Clown and many more!

With the President now holding a baseball bat in his hands, he asked, "Now what do you losers want to confess about? One at a time because I carry a big stick and walk softly and I don't want to have to club you...or maybe I do, we'll just have to see!"

Respectfully, the heads were quiet as Hilliary was the first to speak.

"Donald, I did steal $6 billion from the State Department when I was in charge. That money, what's left of

it anyway, is in a Swiss bank account overseas and I'm sorry for swindling the American people and..."

The head next to hers rudely interrupted Hilliary with, "Hey, I thought we agreed not to say anything about that since that money is Chelsea's now," Bill screamed out and received a knock on the head from the President for rude behavior...he felt no apathy for his action towards Bill.

"Go ahead with your confession Hilliary," the President urged.

"He's right, we did agree not to say anything since Chelsea's name in on the bank account also, but I changed my mind. Chelsea will just have to learn to stand on her own two feet now," Hilliary stated seriously.

President Trump now turned his attention to Bill who appeared to be a little dazed from the blow to his head.

"I did have sex with those women," Bill trumpeted and received another blow from the President's bat just for good measure!

The next one in line to confess his sins was Obama.

"I knew that I couldn't be a good president to the country, but I wanted to be the first black president and I was a terrific speaker and fooled the American people into thinking that I was something special when in fact, I wasn't. It's true that my administration was filled with corruption, deceit and lies, on purpose, for self-gain and self-satisfaction. I might as well also tell you President Trump that you were right years ago when you challenged my American birthright; I was born in Kenya, Mombasa, Africa, under the name of, Bello Ulan Faba Fanta. For short, my nickname was Buff and that's because of my initials and because my mother always said that I had the hair of a buffalo. Then when my family moved to Hawaii while I was at a tender age, my mother wanted great things for me and felt that my real birth name was not the proper name to utilize in our new, adopted country so we had it changed along with a doctored up birth certificate that we were able to acquire when we moved to California. I realize that I've

made some errors in life and for that I'm sorry. I don't want to go to Hell."

When Obama stopped speaking, President Trump just nodded wearily and looked over to his former Attorney General, Jeff Sessions and moved to stand in front of him.

"Alright, I tricked you, but only because I was being blackmailed by..."

"Shut up you ignorant imbecile," Rod Rosenstein yelled out and received a blow to the head. The President then indicated for Sessions to continue.

"It was Rosenstein, but I was involved in corruption prior to becoming the AG and I regret it very much. There is a real swamp in DC concerning government service."

"Thank you Jeff. I really used to admire you before I learned about your criminal activity and weak nature."

"Mr. President," Sessions started, "I took advantage of your loyalty and for that I'm truly sorry. Let me just finish up by saying that you're a great man and it has been my honor to serve you this short time."

President Trump didn't reply but moved on down the line of trophy heads waiting for someone else to speak out---maybe the bat that he was carrying kept some of them quiet! He now stood in front of Obama's former CIA Director, John Brennan.

"John, do you have anything to say?"

"I want my security clearance back you bastard," Brennan spat out with such venom that the President almost swung his bat, but restrained himself.

"Why John, are you going to need it where you're headed?" President Trump asked casually.

"Go to Hell you son of a bitch!"

"You first you piece of shit," and swung the bat with all of his might which connected solidly and sent Brennan to his next home...Hell!

Next on the list was, Smokey Joe Bandit Biden, so named by President Trump due to his ownership of a 1981 Trans Am which he used to park in The White House's driveway when he was the vice president under Obama. The car was one that was used quite extensively in the movie, Smokey and the Bandit 3, but was kept in excellent condition as another car was utilized for the actual stunts. Joe was able to purchase the car from Universal Pictures at a good price; Bandit was his legal occupation in connection with the American people.

Smokey Joe---for obvious reasons which will be disclosed shortly---did not learn from the past mistakes of Bill Clinton, Rod Rosenstein and John Brennan when he remarked, "I wish that I had the opportunity to kick your dumbass in the school yard years ago. Well, it looks like I'll have to wait in Hell for you, you son of a bitch! Someone needs to clean your clock and I'm just the man to do it," Biden stated positively.

"Joe, I have a confession also. You couldn't fight your way out of a wet paper sack let alone even begin to take me," President Trump announced and then quickly added, "and to show you that there are no hard feelings..." the President swung his 'big stick' and caught Smokey Joe behind the Left ear which tore under the impact and was hanging precariously; Biden went silent and President Trump saw a tear glistened in his Left eye.

The President then stepped in front of Crazy Burney Sherman and gave him an opportunity to speak, which he did.

"We need socialism. Congress is getting rich from the American people and the American people need a receipt for all of their donations to Congress and that receipt is in the form of social justice," Sherman sounded off.

"I'll take it under advisement. Any confessions you want to make now you old fool?" President Trump asked.

"I've been having an affair with Senator Willow," Sherman confessed. "I'm sorry that I did, she's a freak!"

The President thought that maybe Pocahontas would reply, but he guessed wrong. Obviously, she had nothing to add. That figures, she's playing the part of the silent Indian and if she had arms, he was sure that she would be crossing them right now, like one of them wooden cigar Indians that he used to see at drug stores when he was young.

President Trump was looking around the room to see if anyone else wanted to speak and his gaze landed on the Head Clown, Senator Cyrus Simpson.

"Ok, I'll admit it, I was wrong and also a liar. I changed my views on illegal immigration from several years ago because the Democratic Party's plan now is to capture the votes from illegals. What can I say, it's a power play. I'm sorry to see it end this way and that we are on opposing sides President Trump, but I'm fully ready to atone for my sins."

The last one that he decided on giving an opportunity to speak before leaving was a woman from Nevada and he asked her: "Anything you want to say?"

"You're a Right-wing pig and shouldn't be in office," she stated quite frankly.

"Anything else?" President Trump asked.

"Got a cigarette?" the woman asked smugly.

"Smoking is bad for your health," and the President reached up and gave her a smart whack on the head. While looking at someone else, John Kelly missed the verbal exchange but clearly heard the bat striking solidly and asked: "What happened Mr. President?"

President Trump looked his chief of staff in the eye and replied: "Wacky Jacky wanted some tobacky and I told her that it was bad for her health and whacked her one."

"Maybe she wanted some wacky tobacky sir!" John Kelly suggested as both men laughed boisterously. Then he quickly added: "Hey, I'm a poet and didn't even know it."

Finally, the President had heard enough confessions for one day---after all, he wasn't a priest---and turned to leave the room all the while feeling some satisfaction in punishing the swamp. Just as he stepped through the threshold, he caught the squeak of a voice calling out, "Impeach 45, impeach 45 impeach 45...Just wait until they get a hold of that bitch in her next life, he thought, they are going to have a good time with her in Hell!

John Kelly was walking down the hallway to the elevator beside the President when President Trump spoke to him.

"John, I want to change the name of the Trophy Room."

"Yes sir, I'll have that taken care of right away. What name did you want to change it to sir?"

"I want to change the sign to read, 'Liberals and Losers Game Room.'"

"May I ask why Mr. President?"

"Well, it's like this John. When I clubbed those five losers, it reminded me when I was younger and how I liked to play that Whack-A-Mole game. You know, where the moles would pop up and you use a mallet to club them back down? I loved that game and it felt a little like it this time. Just think John, I have my own Whack-A-Liberal game right here in my basement! Whenever I feel some stress, I'll just come down here and whack away!"

"Yes Mr. President. I agree with your sentiments and I wish you would whack that bitch that keeps crying out, 'impeach 45' sir. I remember when that game first arrived on base; a fun time was had by all," John remarked as he reminisced about the good old days. "I made a mental note to change the sign sir and consider it done."

"Thank you John and don't worry, I'll whack that bitch the next time that I come down here...just for you."

"I would like to see that Mr. President."

President Trump drifted to another thought that was on his mind and addressed his chief of staff.

"John, I know that you indicated to me your desire to resign after the midterms. However, I would like to see you stay until I have fulfilled my two terms. I know that I lean on you a lot John, but that's how I am able to accomplish great things...with your assistance."

The men arrived at the elevator just as the doors opened automatically and stepped in. Apparently, there was a sensor that detected when someone was approaching it, thought President Trump. As the doors closed, the President continued his conversation with his favorite chief of staff.

"John, I'm hoping that there is some way that we can negotiate a deal to keep you on," the President solemnly remarked.

"I don't see a possible route to that destination Mr. President," Kelly stated seriously.

"Let's negotiate a little Mr. Kelly," the President started, "I'll allow you to utilize the Liberals and Losers Game Room whenever you are feeling stress. How about that? Will you stay for that benefit alone John?"

"Can I whack any Liberal that I desire, sir?" John questioned the President.

President Trump pondered that request before supplying his answer.

"That's fine, as long as you don't send any to Hell; I want that satisfaction reserved for me since, after all, I am the President of the United States."

As the elevator arrived at their destination, Chief of Staff, John Kelly, gave his answer in these three simple words, "It's a deal," and held out his hand to President Trump as if to shake on the agreement.

The President took Kelly's hand into his own and added, "I'll have to get that in writing John," and chuckled as they walked down the hallway together.

President Trump awoke from his very surreal dream and noticed that the time was 3:46 a.m. and decided that he needed to send out a tweet to his followers before going to bed:

Donald J. Trump
It was just revealed to me the whereabouts of that $6 billion that came up missing (STOLEN) when Crooked Hilliary was in charge of the State Department & we *will*

recover it for the American people. Chief of Staff, John Kelly has decided to continue his employment here at The White House…thanks John, we really need you!

The next day at The White House, John Kelly was in the Oval Office with the President. President Trump confided to his chief of staff the details concerning his dream. Kelly chuckled at the thought of a Whack-A-Liberal game room in the basement of The White House…and that he would get to play as well if he would just agree to stay until the President finished his two terms. *That was an interesting thought.*

John Kelly had been considering a change of heart concerning leaving The White House, and upon hearing about President Trump's dream and tweet, he decided to stay, even if there really was *no* Whack-A-Liberal game room!

Justice With Judge Jeanine

"Good evening and welcome to Justice and I'm Judge Jeanine. As you probably already know, President Trump took the bull by the horns and has struck back at the corrupt Liberal Democrats. U.S. Marshals were sent out by the President to round up corrupt Liberals---all legal I might add---with arrest warrants. They will all have their day in court as our Constitution allows; now for my opening monologue.

"Let's start with Hilliary. Honey, I told you to be prepared for the men that would come for you. They came and they took…took you into custody that is. Now we find out that you are resting peacefully at the National University Treatment center in upstate New York. Good for you. Maybe now, you'll get the help that you finally need.

"As far as your husband goes---we'll call him Billy Appleseed, since he likes to spread his seed around---I hear that he's already was allowed a conjugal visit but not with you Hilliary. He's seeing some waitress from some greasy hamburger joint; another good decision staying with him. You both are a couple of losers!

"Then there is Obama. Now that he's in prison, we finally learn the truth…he was not born in the United States! Are you kidding me? We have allowed someone with no birth right to become president? Unbelievable! This is stuff that you are expected to find in a banana republic! If we keep going in this direction then I have to ask…what's next?

"I hear that Jeff Sessions is squealing like a stuck pig in prison. He's singing to the tunes of corruption and the rest of you better watch out. Sessions will be the last nail in your coffin. In fact, I'm told that Rosenstein had to be put in solitary confinement for attacking Sessions while both men were in the prison yard on recess. Hang in there Jeff, your testimony in court is really needed and the American people want to hear what you have to say about all this deep state corruption and anything else that you're willing to tell us. Maybe you'll get a lesser sentence Jeff for cooperating with federal prosecutors. And Rosenstein, leave Jeff alone you piece of shit! I hope you like solitary confinement you bastard!

"What about you, Brennan, the Liberal goon that you are? I don't suppose that you will need that security clearance now, so don't worry about it John. Just forget it you freaking dirtbag. But just the same, I hope that you will enjoy your stay at the San Quentin Men's Club since that's where you're headed, you lowlife! My advice to you Brennan is this: pick out the biggest and toughest felon to be your boyfriend and if you need cigarettes for your special friend, let me know and I will send you some…maybe!

"Now, for any Liberals that may be left in Congress that are not deceased or in prison, I want to reiterate some of my past comments concerning you corrupt Liberals or Never Trumpers. The 2016 election is over and done. Donald J. Trump won the election under our system of laws. Get over it and move on with life and your work in Congress that should be for the American people, you stinking leakers, sore losers and Liberal snowflakes! Newsflash: Democrats are now the official party of Liberals, losers and lowlifes! Don't forget, losers are always a part of the problem while winners are always a part of the solution. Get with the program you sanctimonious dirtbags!

"As for Brett Kavanaugh, let's get him confirmed to the Supreme Court as he is a highly qualified and strong supporter of our Constitution. Stop the delaying tactics such as obstruction and resistance and let's get back some semblance of normalcy in Congress.

"Alright, now I'm being told by my producer that we will be going to the Oval Office for the President's address on these past criminal arrests…"

As the Oval Office was brought into full view, President Trump was seen by millions worldwide, sitting behind his desk with a solemn but satisfied look upon his face.

"I come to you tonight as your President to address what you have probably already heard in the news. If you are watching Fox News, then I'm sure that you are getting the real news. For those of you that are programmed to the Left's propaganda and fake news, you may not want to hear what I'm about to say.

"On the campaign trail when I was running for the presidency, you, the American people, extended to me your trust and support. In the 2016 Election running against Hilliary Clinton, you continued to give me your trust and support and voted for me. When I told you at my rallies that we would, 'drain the swamp,' you believed in me. Also at my rallies, many of you chanted, 'lock her up,' and I supported that idea. During the second debate with Hilliary, I told her straight forward that I would appoint a special counsel to look into her activities, which you could tell that she didn't like that too much by the evil look that she gave me; if looks could kill…

"The other day, I was informed by the Inspector General, Michael Horowitz---who's a great man by the way and has done a lot of hard work in the face of massive corruption---that he uncovered the evidence needed to lock up many in the deep state, specifically an element in the deep state known as the Secret Society. Members of this Secret Society are prominent figures in government that you know or have heard about in the news that have been taking advantage of our country through, lies, deceit, fraud, corruption and other criminal activity.

"For too long, the Secret Society has reaped the rewards of government while the American people have borne the cost. The Secret Society has protected themselves but not the citizens of our country. Lives have been changed and lost due to the Secret Society's unchecked rein of abusive power.

"Such prominent members of this Secret Society include, former President Barrack Obama, Bill and Hilliary Clinton, Attorney General Jeff Sessions, former Attorney Generals Loretta Lynch and Eric Holder and many, many others. These people have abused the trust that was entrusted to them through government service.

"As your President, I accepted my position of trust and responsibility from you, the American people and I mean to do everything in my power to retain that trust and put America first by draining the swamp.

"The following action that I have taken is unprecedented by any past president. Based on the information that the Inspector General has uncovered, I gave my blessing for him to take this evidence to a federal judge to issue warrants for arrests and to send out the U.S. Marshals.

"U.S. Marshals have already completed this task by arresting and taking into custody, several members of the Obama Crime Family under the code name, Operation: Eagle Claw.

"Our country is now safer and justice is being served. Promises Made, Promises Kept. As I'm at the helm, we will continue to be vigilant and Make America Great Again. Thank you for your trust and respect. Together, we will Make America Safe Again; we will Make America Strong Again; we will make America Great Again and God bless the U.S.A.!"

Epilogue
Ω

"You can't fix stupid."

---Ron White

The White House

The next day, President Trump asked his Chief of Staff, John Kelly, for a report on all of the latest issues to be delivered to him before bedtime…which meant that he had until late that night.

The President was working in the Oval Office deep into the evening when John Kelly entered unannounced and sat across from President Trump.

"Mr. President, I have the report that you asked for," Kelly stated.

The President lowered his pen and leaned back in his chair and asked his chief of staff to just read off the major elements of the report.

John Kelly started off with TJ Law since he knew that the President was really concerned with the young man. He told President Trump that TJ was reassigned to conducting regular CIA operations and that the Omega Agency was suspended until further notice.

"How is TJ taking his reassignment?" the President asked.

"Like a fish to water; no problem there sir."

"Good, I'm happy to hear that."

President Trump was then told that Hilliary would be spending the rest of her life at NUT in Rochester, New York and that she was always medicated and still remains bitter, but she was finally getting the help that she really needed.

"I'm glad. Who would have guessed that she was that far off her rocker?" the President asked.

"Well, to be fair sir, all the things that happened to her played a large role in her mental health. For example, she felt a lot of pressure from Conservatives and Fox News on how she mishandled the Benghazi affair; her husband always cheating on her; two losses of running for president---including a loss to you Mr. President. She came to the conclusion that she had a sure win against you and that was probably her last straw that broke the camel's back, sort of speaking, and she ended up where she is today with Trump Derangement Syndrome."

"Well John, she set her sights too high and reached for the stars and fell hard…quite hard, I'm afraid."

"Yes sir. It is expected that she will recover from TDS after you are out of office. But her disease has left her scarred for life I'm told."

"What about Bill?"

"Bill is now enjoying life at the Federal Correctional Institution in Otisville, New York."

"What do you mean enjoying life?"

"Being a former president, he's allowed conjugal visits sir."

"You mean that they're allowing Hilliary flights down there to see her husband?!" President Trump asked incredulously.

"Ah, no sir; it seems that Mr. Clinton had a squeeze on the side and that she is interested in seeing him even though he's in prison."

"Sounds like that she's interested in more than just seeing him," the President chuckled. "Well good for him.

Bill really wasn't such a bad fellow, just a little misguided. I actually feel sorry for him that he married that bitch though."

President Trump smiled suddenly as he asked John Kelly about his next thought: "How about Barack 'Insane' Obama? Is he adjusting to his new environment?"

"Yes sir he is. He gets conjugal visits as well, except his are with his wife. Mr. Obama has adjusted quite well actually. He is giving speeches to the other felons on how they deserve the right to vote and how he is the reason for the current economic success of the country, and then of course, he's still bad mouthing you. I call it character assassination."

"I'm not surprised," the President remarked. "He was always the 'black sheep' of the Liberal family."

"It seems that you bruised his fragile Liberal ego by unraveling most of his 'so called' legacy."

"I like to bruise more than that. What's the latest with Michelle?"

"With her husband now residing at the United States Penitentiary in Marion, Illinois, she has opted out as the front runner for the Democrats in 2020 and she has moved back to be closer to her husband."

The President listened attentively as Kelly acquainted him with the status of Jeff Sessions and Rod Rosenstein. It seems that Sessions had made a deal with federal prosecutors to testify against Rosenstein and the whole Obama Crime Family. In fact, Rosenstein who was put into solitary confinement for fighting with Jeff Sessions had then attempted to commit suicide; he was now being monitored twenty four hours a day.

Chief of Staff, John Kelly, then informed President Trump about Ching Ching. She was still being held in federal prison awaiting trial and is requesting a presidential pardon. The look on the President's face told John Kelly that this was a deep thought for President Trump and that there was a lot to be considered in her case.

When the President didn't respond, Kelly continued: "Judge Jeanine Pirro is requesting an interview with you sir, concerning some of these issues."

"Make sure she gets it John. Check my calendar and schedule her when it works for both of us. In fact, I'll do an interview with Hannity, Tucker and Laura if they want one as well. They have all been great in their honest reporting for our country. Thank God for Fox News John!"

"Yes sir," Kelly affirmed and then asked, "May I make a suggestion?"

"Of course John, you know that you can speak frankly to me as I respect your thoughts."

"Why not award the four of them with a Presidential Citation sir?"

"You know John, that's an excellent idea. Let's go ahead and set that up. That'll drive the Democrats and the dishonest media absolutely mad," President Trump smiled at the thought and then added, "Only Fox News will be allowed to cover the ceremony John."

"Yes sir, but CNN and MSNBC won't like to be left out in the cold, and missing this award ceremony might even lower their ratings."

"Well, I don't give a rat's ass for the fake news or what they think anyway. In fact, how much lower can their ratings go without them going out of business? I think that they are about done for anyway John and that it's only a matter of time until they are finally washed up for good. The American people have really discovered who is on their side and who is not. Their eyes are quite clear now on a lot of stuff that has been revealed to them."

As President Trump waited for John to continue, Kelly had saved the news about Brett Kavanaugh for last.

"Mr. President, Brett Kavanaugh was just confirmed by the Senate, 50-48."

President Trump then concluded that that was a good thing for the country. Now, he could concentrate on the midterms and then he was looking forward to some more election fights in 2020. He hoped that the Democrats would put up a fine candidate such as Joe Biden, as he liked a good fight!

The End

Appendix

A Transcript of Trump's First Speech as President on January 20, 2017

★ ★ ★ ★ ★ ★ ★ ★ ★ ★ ★ ★ ★ ★ ★ ★ ★ ★ ★ ★ ★ ★ ★ ★ ★

"Chief Justice Roberts, President Carter, President Clinton, President Bush, President Obama, fellow Americans and people of the world, thank you.

We, the citizens of America, are now joined in a great national effort to rebuild our country and restore its promise for all of our people.

Together, we will determine the course of America and the world for many, many years to come. We will face challenges. We will confront hardships. But we will get the job done.

Every four years we gather on these steps to carry out the orderly and peaceful transfer of power.

And we are grateful to President Obama and first lady Michelle Obama for their gracious aid throughout this transition.

They have been magnificent.

Thank you.

Today's ceremony, however, has a special meaning because today we are not merely transferring power from one administration to another or from one party to another, but we are transferring power from Washington, D.C. and giving it back to you, the people.

For too long, a small group in our nation's capital has reaped the rewards of government while the people have borne the cost. Washington flourished, but the people did not share in its wealth. Politicians prospered but the jobs left and the factories closed.

The establishment protected itself, but not the citizens of our country. Their victories have not been your victories. Their triumphs have not been your triumphs. And while they celebrated in our nation's capital, there was little to celebrate for struggling families all across our land.

That all changes starting right here and right now, because this moment is your moment.

It belongs to you.

It belongs to everyone gathered here today and everyone watching all across America.

This is your day.

This is your celebration.

And this, the United States of America, is your country.

What truly matters is not which party controls our government, but whether our government is controlled by the people.

January 20th, 2017, will be remembered as the day the people became the rulers of this nation again.

The forgotten men and women of our country will be forgotten no longer. Everyone is listening to you now. You came by the tens of millions to become part of a historic movement, the likes of which the world has never seen before.

At the center of this movement is a crucial conviction that a nation exists to serve its citizens. Americans want great schools for their children, safe neighborhoods for their families and good jobs for themselves.

These are just and reasonable demands of righteous people and a righteous public.

But for too many of our citizens, a different reality exists.

Mothers and children trapped in poverty in our inner cities, rusted out factories scattered like tombstones across the landscape of our nation.

An education system flush with cash but which leaves our young and beautiful students deprived of all knowledge.

And the crime and the gangs and the drugs that have stolen too many lives and robbed our country of so much unrealized potential. This American carnage stops right here and stops right now.

We are one nation and their pain is our pain.
Their dreams are our dreams and their success will be our success. We share one heart, one home and one glorious destiny.

The oath of office I take today is an oath of allegiance to all Americans.

For many decades we've enriched foreign industry at the expense of American industry, subsidized the armies of other countries while allowing for the very sad depletion of our military.

We've defended other nations' borders while refusing to defend our own. And we've spent trillions and trillions of dollars overseas while America's infrastructure has fallen into disrepair and decay.

We've made other countries rich while the wealth, strength and confidence of our country has dissipated over the horizon.

One by one, the factories shuttered and left our shores with not even a thought about the millions and millions of American workers that were left behind.

The wealth of our middle class has been ripped from their homes and the redistributed all across the world. But that is the past and now we are looking only to the future.

We assembled here today and are issuing a new decree to be heard in every city, in every foreign capital and in every hall of power. From this day forward, a new vision will govern our land.
From this day forward, it's going to be only America first. Every decision on trade, on taxes, on immigration, on foreign affairs will be made to benefit American workers and American families. We must protect our borders from the ravages of other countries making our product, stealing our companies and destroying our jobs.

Protection will lead to great prosperity and strength. I will fight for you with every breath in my body and I will never ever let you down.

America will start winning again, winning like never before.

We will bring back our jobs.

We will bring back our borders.

We will bring back our wealth and we will bring back our dreams.

We will build new roads and highways and bridges and airports and tunnels and railways all across our wonderful nation.

We will get our people off of welfare and back to work, rebuilding our country with American hands and American labor.

We will follow two simple rules: Buy American and hire American.

We will seek friendship and goodwill with the nations of the world, but we do so with the understanding that it is the right of all nations to put their own interests first.

We do not seek to impose our way of life on anyone, but rather to let it shine as an example.

We will shine for everyone to follow.

We will re-enforce old alliances and form new ones and unite the civilized world against radical Islamic terrorism, which we will eradicate completely from the face of the earth.

At the bedrock of our politics will be a total allegiance to the United States of America and through our loyalty to our country we will rediscover our loyalty to each other.

When you open your heart to patriotism, there is no room for prejudice.

The Bible tells us how good and pleasant it is when God's people live together in unity. We must speak our minds openly, debate our disagreements honestly, but always pursue solidarity. When America is united, America is totally unstoppable. There should be no fear. We are protected and we will always be protected. We will be protected by the great men and women of our military and law enforcement and most importantly, we will be protected by God.

Finally, we must think big and dream even bigger. In America, we understand that a nation is only living as long as it is striving. We will no longer accept politicians who are all talk and no action, constantly complaining but never doing anything about it.

The time for empty talk is over. Now arrives the hour of action.

Do not allow anyone to tell you that it cannot be done. No challenge can match the heart and fight and spirit of America. We will not fail. Our country will thrive and prosper again.

We stand at the birth of a new millennium, ready to unlock the mysteries of space, to free the earth from the miseries of disease and to harness the energies, industries and technologies of tomorrow.

A new national pride will stir ourselves, lift our sights and heal our divisions. It's time to remember that old wisdom our soldiers will never forget, that whether we are black or brown or white, we all bleed the same red blood of patriots.

We all enjoy the same glorious freedoms and we will all salute the same great American flag.

And whether a child is born in the urban sprawl of Detroit or the windswept plains of Nebraska, they look up at the same night sky, they fill their heart with the same dreams and they are infused with the breath of life by the same almighty creator.

So to all Americans in every city near and far, small and large, from mountain to mountain, from ocean to ocean, hear these words: You will never be ignored again. Your voice, your hopes and your dreams will define our American destiny and your courage and goodness and love will forever guide us along the way.

Together we will make America strong again, we will make American wealthy again, we will make America proud again, we will make America safe again.

And yes, together we will make America great again.

Thank you.

God bless you and God bless America."

President Donald J. Trump's Partial List of Accomplishments:

<u>Government</u>

US Embassy moved to Jerusalem by President Donald J. Trump
Trump secures release of American prisoners from North Korea
Trump negotiates peace between North and South Korea
Trump signs order calling for work requirements for welfare programs
Trump nominates first woman for head of CIA
Feds collect record taxes in first month under Trump's tax cuts; runs surplus in January
Trump signs sweeping two-year budget deal…MILITARY FUNDED
Trump proposes biggest civil service change in 40 years – 'Hire the best and fire the worst'
Trump signs bipartisan bill to combat synthetic opioids
President Trump set a record for lifetime appointed judges in 2017
Trump signed 96 laws in 2017
Trump Administration set to roll back $900 million in Obama-Era offshore drilling regulations
Individual mandate of Obamacare REPEALED
Climate change REMOVED from 'Threat List'
Trump Administration eliminated regulations 22:1
Trump signs $700 billion defense bill, gives troops largest pay raise in 7 years
Trump declares Jerusalem the capital of Israel
Senate passes sweeping tax reform – 20% corporate rate – largest in 31 years
Trump shuts down CIA funding of Syrian rebels
President Trump declassifies and releases JFK Files
Iran Deal: DECERTIFIED
Trump has written 46 Executive Orders
Fired corrupt and incompetent FBI Director James Comey
Appointed conservative Neil Gorsuch to the Supreme Court
UN Security Council unanimously imposed new sanctions on North Korea
Trump orders a Voter Fraud Commission to investigate 2016 election

Department of Justice

Trump DOJ sues California for interference with immigration enforcement

Four charged with leaks from Trump Administration

Jeff Sessions announces new crackdown on 'so-called' sanctuary cities

The Department of Justice stands by Texas's Voter ID Law

DOJ halts Obama's Operation Chokepoint, which targeted firearm dealers

Veterans Administration

Trump signs VA Accountability Act into law

Trump signs the Space Available Travel Act into law

Trump Administration streamlines veteran medical records

White House to launch veterans' complaint hotline

Enhancing Veteran Care Act

Economy

Black and Hispanic unemployment rates hit record low

Business investments up 39% due to tax cuts

Food Stamps usage drops half a million in single month

Highest ever manufacturing optimism over 94%

Unemployment claims have fallen to a 45-year low

U.S. consumer confidence is at 17-year high

U.S. homebuilding permits soar to highest level since 2007

U.S. jobless claims drop to near 45-year low

Wages jump to highest level since 2009 – up 2.9%

U.S. oil production tops 10 million barrels a day, first time since 1970

Apple to invest $350 billion in U.S. citing Trump Tax Plan

Over 100 companies giving 'Trump Bonuses' after tax victory

Nikki Haley negotiated $285 million cut to UN budget

Surging stock market powers U.S. wealth to $96.2 trillion

National unemployment rate under 4% - lowest in over 16 years

OPERATION: Ωmega

State Department

Trump Administration announces 'Extreme Vetting' plans
UN Security Council unanimously steps up sanctions against North Korea
North Korea designated as 'State Sponsor of Terrorism'
United States announces a new strategy on Iran

Homeland Security

DHS is planning on denying green cards to legal immigrants if they receive federal or state aid
Trump takes 'shackles' off ICE which is slapping them on immigrants who thought they were safe
ICE raid hits 77 businesses in Northern California
DHS announces new procedures for refuge admissions
Ending 'catch and release' immigration policy
Construction on border wall started

Department of Defense

Mosul liberated from ISIS
Top 5 ISIS leaders captured
Trump signs order to keep Guantanamo Bay prison open
Trump signs the 2019 National Defense Authorization Act into law
ISIS has lost 98% of its territory – due to Trump Administration
Trump calls for increased military: Senate passes $700 billion bill
U.S. kills 150 ISIS terrorists in Syria airstrike during U.S. Government shutdown

Trade Deals

Trump orders probe of China's intellectual property practices
Renegotiating NAFTA with Canada and Mexico in order to make better trade deals
Signed an arms deal worth more than $350 billion with Saudi Arabia
Trans Pacific Partnership (TPP) TERMINATED
Trump blocks Chinese purchase of Qualcomm due to national security
Coal exports up 60%
Source: www.magapill.com

Hilliary Clinton's Excuse Tour

* ★ Uneducated women were told by their boyfriends and husbands to vote for Trump
* ★ I'm a woman
* ★ Bill cheated on me several times
* ★ The Russians
* ★ Vladimir Putin
* ★ Anti-American forces
* ★ The FBI
* ★ James Comey
* ★ Low information voters
* ★ Everyone around her assumed that she would win
* ★ Bad polling numbers
* ★ Obama for winning two terms
* ★ People wanting change
* ★ Misogyny/Sexism
* ★ Suburban women
* ★ New York Times
* ★ Television executives
* ★ Media/Cable news
* ★ Netflix
* ★ Democrats not making the right documentaries
* ★ Facebook
* ★ Twitter
* ★ Wikileaks

OPERATION: Ωmega

★ Fake news

★ Bernie Sanders

★ Content farms in Macedonia

★ The Republican Party

★ The Democratic Party

Obama Crime Family Web of Corruption:

⇨ Clinton's illegal private email server

⇨ Destroying 13 cell phones with a hammer

⇨ Uranium One

⇨ Spygate

⇨ IRSgate

⇨ Losers given a cell phone and $1,500 dollars to start fights at Trump rallies

⇨ Deceptive Christopher Steele Dossier

⇨ Unauthorized use of private servers

⇨ Clinton and Lynch 40 minute tarmac meeting

⇨ Democratic primary rigged against Bernie Sanders

⇨ $6 billion missing from the State Department when Hilliary was in charge

⇨ Corrupt DOJ and FBI agencies

⇨ DNC's refusal to turn over Russian hacked servers to the FBI

⇨ More than $150 billion transfer to Iran

⇨ Mishandling of classified material

⇨ Deleting of over 30,000 official emails by Hilliary utilizing 'bleach bit'

⇨ Illegally obtaining FISA court warrants

⇨ Democratic I.T. scandal involving Debbie Wasserman Schultz

⇨ Benghazi corruption and deceit

Possible Crimes Committed by the Clintons

1. **18 USC** § 201---Bribery
2. **18 USC** § 208---Acts Affecting a Personal Financial Interest
3. **18 USC** § 371---Conspiracy
4. **18 USC** § 1001---False Statements
5. **18 USC** § 1341---Fraud and Swindles
6. **18 USC** § 1343---Fraud by Wire
7. **18 USC** § 1349---Attempt and Conspiracy
8. **18 USC** § 1505---Obstruction of Justice
9. **18 USC** § 1519---Destruction of Records in Federal Investigations
10. **18 USC** § 1621---Perjury
11. **18 USC** § 1905---Disclosure of Confidential Information
12. **18 USC** § 1924---Unauthorized Removal and Retention of Classified Documents or Material
13. **18 USC** § 2071---Concealment of Government Records
14. **18 USC** § 7201---Attempt to Evade or Defeat a Tax
15. **18 USC** § 7212---Attempts to Interfere With Administration of Internal Revenue Laws

NATO Members

At present, NATO has 29 members…in 1949, there were 12 founding Alliance members:

- ★ Belgium
- ★ Canada
- ★ Denmark
- ★ France
- ★ Iceland
- ★ Italy
- ★ Luxembourg
- ★ Netherlands
- ★ Norway
- ★ Portugal
- ★ United Kingdom
- ★ United States

NOTE: The NATO Alliance was established to subvert Russian aggression.

DoD Instruction 4515.13 Air Transportation Eligibility Manual

a. Uniformed Services Members

b. Civilian Employees of DoD Components

c. Command-Sponsored Dependents of Uniformed Services Members

d. Non-Command-Sponsored Dependents

e. Dependents Accompanying DoD Personnel on Official Business

f. Employees and Dependents of Nonappropriated Fund (NAF) Activities

g. Employees and Dependents of Other USG Agencies

h. Nonprofit Services Organizations

i. Invited Travelers

j. Foreign Government and International Organization Travelers

k. Contractor Personnel

l. Educators not affiliated with the DoD Education Activity…

m. Athletes and Entertainers

n. Civil Air Patrol (CAP)

o. Reserve Officer Training Corps (ROTC)

p. Junior Reserve Officers Training Corps (JROTC)

q. International ROTC Programs

r. Naval Sea Cadets

s. National Guard Youth Challenge Program Participants

t. Persons Transported Under the Authority of the Military Extraterritorial…

u. Other Individuals Not Affiliated With the DoD

The Following States Have Legalized Marijuana in Opposition to Federal Law:

1. Alaska – 2015
2. California – 2018
3. Colorado – 2012
4. Massachusetts – 2018
5. Nevada – 2017
6. Oregon – 2015
7. Washington – 2012
8. DC - 2015

States That Allow Illegals to Obtain State Driver's Licenses

1. Washington   July 25, 1993
2. New Mexico   March 18, 2003
3. Utah   March 8, 2005
4. Illinois   November 28, 2013
5. Vermont   January 1, 2014
6. Nevada January 1, 2014
7. Maryland   January 1, 2014
8. DC   May 1, 2014
9. Colorado   August 1, 2014
10. Connecticut   January 1, 2015
11. California   January 1, 2015
12. Delaware   December 27, 2015
13. Hawaii   January 1, 2016